BRIDGET WALSH was born in London to Irish immigrant parents. She studied English literature and was an English teacher for twenty-three years, before leaving the profession to pursue her writing. Bridget lives in Norwich with her husband, Micky, and her two dogs. *The Tumbling Girl* is her first novel.

PRAISE FOR *THE TUMBLING GIRL*

'A narrative that neatly weds historical detail and quiet wit' **Sunday Times**

'Walsh does a splendid job depicting Minnie's flea-bitten yet appealing theatrical world and Albert's monied yet treacherous milieu' **Wall Street Journal**

'Walsh's diligent research pays off in spades here, and her rich and nuanced portrayal of the period will leave readers feeling like they're on the soggy streets of London. Imogen Robertson readers will be eager for a sequel to this un-put-downable mystery' **Publishers Weekly (starred review)**

'A sparkling novel and a complete delight to read. The characters and world are wild, vivid and enchanting. A wry, warm and proper rib-tickling slice of dirty Victorian gothic . . . I can't wait to see what Minnie and Albert are up to next' **Julia Crouch, author of *The Daughters***

'Beautifully evocative, deftly plotted and with engaging characters, it was a page-turner from beginning to end' **Sheila O'Flanagan, author of *What Eden Did Next***

'Brilliant . . . Beautifully written . . . keeps you guessing till the end' **A. J. West, author of *The Spirit Engineer***

'Minnie Ward is a woman you want to follow through all the wicked twists and turns of Victorian London. It had me on the edge of my seat until the final page' **SJ Bennett, author of *Murder Most Royal***

'A brilliantly written page-turner. A bravura performance tumbling us into a compelling mystery in a vivid, richly imagined world. You can smell the greasepaint and hear the roar of the crowd on every page' **Imogen Robertson, author of *The Paris Winter***

The TUMBLING GIRL

A Variety Palace Mystery

The TUMBLING GIRL

A Variety Palace Mystery

BRIDGET WALSH

Gallic Books
London

A Gallic Book

Copyright © Bridget Walsh, 2023
Bridget Walsh has asserted her moral right to be identified
as the author of the work.

First published in Great Britain in 2023 by
Gallic Books, 12 Eccleston Street, London SW1W 9LT

This paperback edition published 2024

A CIP record for this book is available from the British Library

Typeset in Baskerville URW by Gallic Books

ISBN 978-1-913547-63-9

Printed in the UK by CPI (CR0 4YY)
2 4 6 8 10 9 7 5 3 1

For Mum and Dad

It was like meeting again a dearest friend whom one has loved for long years, and missed in silence

Stella Gibbons
Cold Comfort Farm

ONE

Minnie Ward wrapped the towel more securely round her hand and took a firm hold of the knife. With one deft movement, she inserted the blade into the hinge of the oyster, twisted it and, with a satisfying pop, prised open the shell. Oysters and beer. Perfect.

A tall young woman in a gentleman's evening suit, complete with bow tie and top hat, leaned over Minnie's shoulder, scrutinising her face in the dressing-room mirror. 'Do you have to do that in here, Min?' she asked, tucking a few strands of dark hair under her hat. 'When I'm getting ready, and all? The smell don't half hang around.'

'Last one, Cora, I promise,' Minnie said, sliding the blade around the edge of the oyster to disconnect the muscle. Then she tipped the meat and liquor into her mouth and drained her beer glass, before smiling broadly at Cora. 'It's like picking a lock, ain't it? That lovely little jiggle and you know you've got it.'

'How do you know about picking locks? Or shouldn't I ask?' Cora said.

'Three months as a magician's assistant,' Minnie said. 'Long time ago. I weren't bad, neither. But me and the doves didn't exactly hit it off. It got messy.'

Further down the corridor of the Variety Palace Music

Hall, bursts of laughter and conversation flared out as other dressing-room doors opened and then slammed shut. An operatic soprano struggled her way up and down a scale, occasionally finding one of the notes.

Minnie winced.

'Pick a key, Selina,' she murmured, 'any key.'

'Wouldn't make no difference,' Cora said. 'She'd still sound like a cat pissing in a tin.'

Pushing the door closed with her foot, she nudged Minnie onto another seat and positioned herself in front of the mirrors. She finished applying her make-up, her tongue peeping out from between her lips with concentration. When she was done, she pushed a copy of the *Illustrated London News* over to Minnie, past the pots of greasepaint, other stage make-up and dirty rags littering the table.

'Here,' Cora said, 'what d'you reckon?'

Minnie glanced at the newspaper headline speculating on the identity of the Hairpin Killer, a murderer who had been plucking victims from the streets around Covent Garden and Soho for the past ten years.

'No, not that,' Cora said impatiently, tapping her finger on an article further down the page. 'This fella. Wouldn't mind him investigating me.'

Minnie glanced at the pencil sketch. A man of about thirty, she reckoned, wearing an evening suit and monocle. The headline blazoned 'Albert Easterbrook: Champion of the Labouring Classes'. She scanned the article. A gentleman detective whose mission was to 'help those who cannot help themselves' had tracked down a pickpocket targeting the elderly and infirm in Bermondsey. The pickpocket was also sketched for the reader, a grisly-looking individual closer to a bear than a man.

Minnie snorted. In her experience, the 'labouring classes' were well able to take care of themselves without the help of any toff.

'Not your type?' Cora asked, wincing at herself in the mirrors and adding a touch more rouge to her cheeks. 'They never are, are they, Min? Pickiness won't win any prizes, my girl.'

'I ain't after any prizes, thank you very much. Although I do wonder what he does with the monocle when … you know,' Minnie said.

Cora lifted one quizzical eyebrow. 'You, Miss Ward, are a very saucy girl, and not the kind of young lady a "Champion of the Labouring Classes" would want to be courting. Me, on the other hand—'

Minnie pushed the paper to one side and eyed the ha'penny bun on the table in front of her. Cora followed her gaze and smiled. Every Saturday Minnie bought herself a cake, a treat for when she got home. Most Saturdays the cake had been demolished long before she left the Palace.

'Here, Miss Monroe,' Minnie said, adopting an aristocratic tone and mournfully handing over the cake, 'remove this delicious confection from my sight.'

Cora placed the cake in a drawer and locked it, throwing the key in amongst the pots and bottles littering the table in front of her.

'Hardly seems worth it, Min,' she said. 'You'll be out of here in a few minutes, won't you?'

'Should be.'

Then, as if her anticipation of leaving the music hall had put the kibosh on the whole idea, she heard her name being called. The voice drew closer, loud enough now that it set the jars on the table rattling. Without even the briefest of knocks, the dressing-room door burst open. A diminutive man – no one dared call him short, not to his face at least – sporting a brown velvet suit and an elaborate set of whiskers stood in the doorway. Mr Edward Tansford, owner of the Variety Palace. Known to everyone as Tansie.

'Where is she?' Tansie bellowed. 'I'm running a music hall not a bloody free and easy. She's late and I've got no one to fill her slot.'

'If you're looking for a mind reader you've come to the wrong door,' Minnie said. 'Who are we talking about?'

'Rose. She's on the missing list.' Tansie turned to Cora and shouted, 'You seen her?'

Cora shook her head and made a show of completing her already finished make-up.

Minnie frowned. 'That's not like Rose.'

Rose Watkins was a regular performer at the Variety Palace. A tightrope walker and acrobat, billed as the Angel of the Air.

'Well, it's like her tonight,' Tansie said.

'Have you asked Billy?'

'Can't find him neither. He's meant to be on the doors in thirty minutes, and he's nowhere.'

'Checked the bar?' Minnie asked.

'No, I haven't checked the bar. I'm the bleedin' proprietor of this establishment, Minnie, not some backstage runner.'

'I could have a look?' Minnie offered.

'Yes, you could, couldn't you? Quick smart.'

Minnie bridled. 'I think the phrase you're looking for is, "Thank you so much for offering to help me, Minnie, when I know you were due out of here ten minutes ago."'

'Just find her, Min,' Tansie growled.

Minnie left the dressing room, navigating her way through the poky backstage corridors. Cigar smoke caught in her throat, its dusty odour always reminding her of burnt coffee. Mingled with the smell of greasepaint and cheap perfume, it felt familiar and safe.

Passing one of the dressing rooms, she heard breaking crockery, followed by quiet sobbing. She glanced at the cards pinned on the door, one of which said 'Betty Gilbert, Plate Spinner'. Minnie didn't know her. Must be her first night and, clearly, rehearsals weren't going to plan. Minnie made a mental note to check on her after she'd spoken to Billy and wondered if she'd ever get home in time for supper.

She came out onto the stage. A tall plant stand, topped with a large aspidistra desperately in need of a drink, was positioned to one side. It was Tansie's idea of a sophisticated accompaniment to Madame Selina, the unfortunate soprano. Facing the row of unlit footlights, Minnie was reminded for a moment of her days as a performer, the hungry eyes trained on her, eager to be entertained. Her stomach turned, and she dashed off the stage.

The lamplighters were at work. Hundreds of gas burners around the auditorium were being coaxed into life. The candles in the chandeliers were already lit and offered enough light for Minnie to see her way. She weaved through the groups of tables towards the promenade at the front of the auditorium. There were four doors tucked behind the mahogany bar that stretched along the front wall. Minnie tried the first two with no luck, before opening the third to find Billy Walker lolling on a gilt-wood couch upholstered in a vivid shade of pink.

Billy leapt up as the door opened, almost dropping his pipe. Seeing Minnie, he relaxed back onto the sofa. He was tall, well-built, as a chucker-out needed to be. Tansie made a lot of noise about keeping a respectable house, and men like Billy dealt with the more unsavoury characters. Leaning back, pipe in hand, he made an impressive sight, with his dark hooded eyes and biceps the size of a man's thigh. But Minnie knew Billy Walker's type all too well, and was unimpressed by his charms. She had tried warning Rose when he'd first started sniffing around.

'But he's so lovely to look at, Min,' Rose had said. 'Those eyes! And his arms!'

Yes, and those fists, Minnie had thought.

'Well, ain't you quite the don,' Minnie said, pushing Billy's feet off and perching on the end of the couch. 'Wait until Tansie catches you in here, Billy. You'll be for it.'

Billy shrugged, tamped down the tobacco and carried on smoking.

'I mean it, Bill. Tansie spent a small fortune doing up these snuggeries.'

'Yeah, and for what?' Billy asked. 'For gentlemen to entertain their lady friends? Toffs and their dollymops, more like. Having a quiet smoke in here's nothing compared to what'll go on later tonight.'

'Look, I ain't here to have a go. Rose is on the missing list. You seen her?'

Billy shook his head. 'Not since this morning. I went round her house just before midday, but she was on her way out. Wouldn't say where.'

Minnie thought for a moment. 'What was she wearing?'

'What's that got to do with anything?'

'Might give us a clue where she was going.'

'I dunno.' Billy shrugged. 'Clothes. She was wearing them shoes.'

'The new ones?'

'Yeah, the new ones. She must think me a proper muff. She got a right collar on, telling me it was none of my business what she did with her time. Let's just say we had an exchange of language, and I ain't seen her since.'

Rose and Billy had been courting for six months, and arguing for half a year. Everyone at the Palace had grown used to hearing them row, but their most recent one had been the worst. Billy had found an expensive pair of cream silk shoes, embroidered with tiny red roses, in the dressing room Rose shared with two other girls. They would have cost several weeks' wages, and Rose wouldn't reveal how she'd come by the money. Billy had jumped to the obvious conclusion, and Minnie couldn't say she blamed him.

'And you've got no idea where she might be?' Minnie asked. 'Don't sell me a dog, Billy. If you know where she is, you'd best say now.'

'Don't know. Don't care. She can sling her hook as far as I'm bothered.' He stood and stretched lazily. The room suddenly seemed a lot smaller. 'If you see her before me, tell her to stay out of my way. I've got a liking to make it a little warm for Miss Rose Watkins.' He clenched his fists reflexively. 'Now, if you don't mind, Min, I've got punters to let in, and troublemakers to keep out. This is a *respectable* establishment, remember?'

He knocked out his pipe on the snuggery floor and strode out of the room, slamming the door behind him.

Minnie retrieved the remains of the tobacco from the

floor. She had no great fondness for Billy but, if he lost his job, Rose might be the one to suffer. Before she left the room, she took a moment to glance up at a poster adorning one wall of the snuggery. Edie Bennett, the Richmond Rocket. The most famous music hall performer of her age, Edie was the reason Minnie had first gone on the stage. She raised her hand, saluted the image and left the snuggery.

As she made her way back to the dressing rooms, the auditorium was slowly coming to life. The gilt-framed mirrors lining the walls reflected back the dozen waiters in dark suits and clean white aprons who were checking the tables were clean and the tablecloths all hanging at the same length. Tansie was a stickler for detail. The walls were adorned with paintings of exotic landscapes and what Tansie assured her were European cities – Paris, Rome, Geneva. Minnie had her doubts. The paintings were supposed to give an illusion of sophistication, but Tansie's fondness for pink and gold undermined the effect. He had heard somewhere that pink made people drink more and had applied the colour with a liberal hand throughout the Palace.

She followed the sound of his hollering until she found him backstage.

'Well?' he said. 'Did you find her?'

Minnie shook her head. 'Billy ain't seen her since this morning.'

Tansie swore. 'Are you on the square? If you're lying—'

'I ain't. I could nip round to her house?' Minnie offered. 'She only lives on Wych Street. There and back in twenty minutes.'

'No. I need you here. You're my right hand, Min. I'm gonna have to change the running order, and that'll set them all off.'

'I'm a writer, Tanse, remember?' Minnie said. 'Songs and sketches, that's me. If you want me here every night to keep things calm you're gonna have to pay me for my time. I was due out of here twenty minutes ago.'

Tansie and Minnie had this discussion at least once a week. Invariably, it ended with Minnie agreeing to stay, although vowing it would be the last time.

'I'm in trouble here, Min,' Tansie said. 'The girls don't listen to me the way they do you.'

'Well, at least send a lad round to her house. It's Rose, Tansie. She's worked here for years, and she's never once been late. Send a lad.'

Tansie frowned, then nodded. He fished in his pockets and extracted a ha'penny. 'Give him a flatch,' he said, handing Minnie the single coin, 'but only once he's back, mind.'

Minnie walked to the stage door, where a group of young lads were loitering as they did every night, hoping for some scrap of work. She picked Bobby, the smallest of the boys, who looked no more than five or six, but was probably twice that age.

'Here,' she said, '14 Wych Street. Ask for Ida Watkins and find out when she last saw Rose. Come straight back with the answer, you hear me? There's something in it for you, mind. But only if you're quick.'

At the suggestion of reward, Bobby sped off. Minnie turned back into the music hall and was accosted almost immediately by Tansie. He eyed her speculatively.

'What?' Minnie asked. 'You're looking at me like I'm the canary and you're the cat that ain't been fed for a week.'

'I couldn't persuade you, I suppose?' he asked her. 'Your old act? The punters loved you, remember?'

Minnie felt the old panic flood her body as memories resurfaced. The paralysis of waiting in the wings, knowing all her words had failed her. She took a deep breath. 'We've had this conversation many times, Tanse. Nothing will make me get up in front of those lights again.'

'But you were a natural, Min. A face made for comedy, that's what I always said.'

'Thanks, Tanse. Just what a girl wants to hear.'

'You know what I mean. Your face moves around a lot.'

'Seriously, Tanse. This much sweet talk could kill me.'

'Oh,' he growled, 'what's the word I'm searching for? Come on, Min, you're the one with the words – expressive!' he shouted triumphantly. 'You have an expressive face. You were a natural mimic, Minnie. You could have wrung laughter out of a stone. It broke my heart when you decided to jack it all in.'

'Enough of the codding, Tanse. I had my reasons. I ain't talking about them. I'm done with all that and much happier for it.'

'Well, I'm delighted for your happiness, but it still leaves me with a twenty-minute turn to fill.'

'Can't you ask anyone to stretch it out a bit?'

'Already tried. If the dog and monkey act are on stage any longer than twenty minutes Kippy says the dog'll eat the monkey. Or is it the monkey who'll eat the dog? Either way, bloodshed. The Mexican Boneless Wonder is already as drunk as a boiled owl, and it'll be a miracle if he makes it to the stage, let alone the end of his act. And the one-legged dancer muttered something unmentionable when I asked her.'

Minnie arched an eyebrow. 'Selina's always keen.'

Tansie gave Minnie what her mother used to call an old-fashioned look.

'I must have been off me chump the day I hired her,' he said, a look of genuine sadness on his face. 'Just hearing her practise gives me the morbs. But if there's no one else we'll have to make the best of a bad deal.'

'Problems, dear boy?'

The voice was rich and syrupy, every vowel stretched to its limits. Bernard Reynolds, a veteran of the theatre, had once specialised in recitations of Shakespeare, but the public had grown tired of his extravagant delivery. Now he termed himself a 'utility gentleman', able to turn his hand to anything required, but in truth he was only ever given what were euphemistically termed 'thinking parts'. Bernard's most distinctive feature was the few strands of hair he combed over his bald head and fixed with a pomade of his own making, consisting primarily of goose grease. On a warm evening, you could smell Bernard before you saw him.

'A tiny bird tells me you're short of an act, dear boy,' Bernard continued. 'I humbly offer my services. A little *Lear*, perhaps? A morsel of the Scottish play? Or would you favour comedy? In the words of the Bard, "I am fresh of spirit and resolved to meet all perils very constantly."'

'I appreciate the offer,' Tansie said. 'I'm just not sure the Palace punters are quite ready for such sophistication.'

'One is always ready for Shakespeare,' Bernard said, affronted. 'But if you feel otherwise, "I will go lose myself."'

Faced with a blank look from Minnie, Bernard offered helpfully, '*The Comedy of Errors*, dearest one. Antipholus of Syracuse. A minor part, but one I played with remarkable poignancy according to—'

'I've thought of something,' Minnie interrupted, before Bernard started reciting his reviews, every one of which had been painstakingly committed to memory. 'Leave it with me.'

She ducked down the corridor to the furthest dressing room. Five minutes later she was back.

'Sorted,' she told Tansie. 'Betty Gilbert. You hired her as a plate spinner, but the dog and monkey act would make a better fist of it. She only took the job 'cos she's desperate, and she won't last two minutes before the punters shout her off, but she can do a full turn as a tumbler. That's her trade. She's watched Rose's act more times than she can think of and knows it back to front. You might need to change the running order, give her time to run through it backstage, but she's game.'

Tansie reached up, grabbed Minnie on both sides of her face, and pulled down her head, planting a smacker on her forehead. 'You, my girl, are a bloody lifesaver,' he said, a rare smile illuminating his face and revealing the glint of a gold tooth. He turned swiftly and headed towards the stage, shouting random instructions at anyone he passed.

Minnie made her way back to Cora's dressing room. Just as she turned the door handle, Bobby appeared, panting hard. Minnie glanced at her pocket watch. Impressive.

'She ain't there,' Bobby said, catching his breath. 'Her ma ain't seen her since early today.'

'And she's no idea where Rose might have gone?'

He shook his head.

'Is it bad news, miss?' he asked.

'Oh, I'm sure it's nothing,' Minnie said. But it didn't feel like nothing. A memory flashed through her mind of the very first time she had met Rose, the other girl about nine and

Minnie herself only a few years older. Minnie, broken by grief at the loss of her mother. Rose, a little slip of a thing, but smart enough to figure out that cake was the way to Minnie's heart, stealing penny buns and getting a slap from Ida, her mother, for her troubles.

Minnie turned her attention back to Bobby. He deserved more than the measly ha'penny Tansie had offered. She felt in her pocket and gave him a penny.

'That money is from Mr Tansford,' she said. 'Know who he is?'

'Little fella. Big voice. Fancy suit.'

Minnie smiled. 'Exactly. And next time you see him, remember to say thank you. He likes to feel appreciated, and there might be more work he can send your way.'

'Thanks, miss,' the boy said, turning to leave.

'Here,' she said, moving towards the table and finding the key amongst Cora's make-up. She unlocked the drawer and gave the cake a last mournful pat before handing it to Bobby. 'Take this as well. You look like you need it.'

The boy's eyes widened, and he snatched the cake from her hand. As he turned away he was already cramming it into his mouth with hungry bites. Minnie knew if the other lads saw him with the cake it would be out of his hands in no time, but still she called out after him, 'Not all at once. You'll be sick.'

He muffled his thanks through a mouthful of cake and was gone. Minnie turned back to the mirrors and tried not to think about Rose.

THE FIRST STANHOPE

IN WHICH MR MOORE MAKES A DISCOVERY

While Minnie was searching for Rose, outside the Variety Palace Charlie Moore was also on the hunt.

He wasn't looking for any particular girl – he wasn't that fussy, truth be told – just someone halfway pretty and willing to take his mind off his troubles for a short while. Here on the Strand it shouldn't take long. He walked past the Palace, its garish posters advertising mesmerists, mashers to rival Nelly Power, and various acrobatic delights, and wound his way through the crowds, past a group of newly arrived visitors to the city. Fresh off the train at Charing Cross, most likely. Eyes like saucers as they took in the varied delights of the Strand. A group of jolly dogs – gents who'd clearly spent the entire afternoon in their club – barrelled past him, nearly pushing him under the wheels of a carriage. He swore at them, but they'd already vanished in a cloud of alcohol fumes.

After a few minutes a hand rested gently on his arm and he heard a whispered invitation.

He looked at her. Not bad. He'd had worse.

'How much?' Charlie asked.

'A bob?' she said.

Charlie snorted. 'You must be joking, love.'

He reached into his pocket, drawing out a meagre handful of coins and carefully keeping the rest of his money out of view.

'Look,' he showed her, 'I ain't got no more than fourpence.'

'All right,' she said. 'But we'll have to go down the Arches. I ain't walking halfway across London for a measly fourpence.'

Charlie baulked. The Adelphi Arches were a network of tunnels facing onto the Thames. Before the Embankment Gardens had opened, they had made an impressive sight from the river; huge arches topped by the houses of Adelphi Terrace. Since the opening of the Gardens, they were less visible but still impressive from a distance.

Close up was a different story. Anyone with any sense kept well away from the Arches. Unless they were drunk, or desperate. Charlie was both.

And she was only fourpence.

The woman led Charlie down Villiers Street, then through a maze of ill-lit back lanes, the soot-blackened buildings glowering down at them. Charlie kept his hands firmly in his pockets, holding tight on to his money and gripping the life preserver he carried with him at all times. The area was notorious for sharps, pinch-faced cockney pickpockets preying on any innocent flat they could spy. Charlie had just been paid and wasn't prepared to hand over his hard-earned money for nothing.

They took a final turn, and the Arches opened up in front of them. The smell made Charlie gag. It had been a while since the Thames had flooded, but the stink of raw sewage still lingered. The woman grabbed hold of Charlie's hand and moved forward relentlessly, as if oblivious to the stench. Heading deeper into the darkness, they passed alcoves and passages housing horses, cows and wretched humans. Charlie jumped, as what looked like a pile of rags suddenly moved and cursed him. In the gloom, the floor writhed with the scurrying of rats. One ran over his shoe, and he kicked it into the shadows. He wanted to turn back, but was unsure of the way out, terrified at the thought of getting lost.

And the woman had a surprisingly strong grip.

Occasionally, the dim illumination of someone's candle offered a respite from the gloom, but then the darkness would descend all the more forcefully. Charlie wasn't sure which was worse – the blackness or the horrors revealed in those stuttering flares of light.

'Where are we going?' Charlie whispered.

'Not much further, love,' Fourpence said. 'I've got a little spot just over here. And I've got a candle or two, so we can see what we're about.'

In his pocket, Charlie gripped the life-preserver so hard he could no longer feel his fingers.

Finally, they reached their destination. An archway indistinguishable from all the others, a mound of cloths in the corner that Charlie guessed was the woman's bed.

'Here we are, love,' Fourpence said, giggling. 'Home sweet home.'

Feeling his way in the gloom, Charlie bumped into a large, bulky object hanging from the ceiling. It swung slowly from where he had collided with it. It was heavy. He backed away.

'What the hell is that?' he said. 'Here, light those candles you said you had.'

'Hang on a sec, love,' she murmured. 'I put me scratchers down here somewhere, now where are they—?'

The match flared, the smell of sulphur briefly cutting

through the stink of sewage and decay. Fourpence turned, sheltering the candle with her hand.

'Now, love,' she said, 'what was it you were saying?'

Charlie's eyes lifted to the object slowly swinging from the ceiling.

It was a woman. Her features were distorted. Her tongue, swollen and purple, protruded between her lips. She looked young. It was difficult to make out many details in the half-light.

Fourpence screamed, dropped the candle, screamed again. The last thing Charlie saw before the darkness descended was a pair of shoes swaying in his eyeline. Cream silk, embroidered with tiny red roses.

TWO

Albert Easterbrook stood at his drawing-room window, looking down at the two women standing on the narrow path leading to his front door. One looked to be of middle age, short and a little stout. She was dressed in full mourning, although she had removed her gloves to fiddle with the crape edging on her collar. Even from this distance, he could see the woman's hands were red and raw-looking.

Fiendish stuff, crape. As if the loss of a loved one weren't enough.

The other woman was much younger, a little taller, dark-haired, also in mourning. She hung back a little, brushing the dust from her dress. Yet something about her suggested she was the one in charge.

'They're still there, Mrs Byrne,' he said to his housekeeper as she entered the room with extra coals for the fire. 'Should I go down and speak to them, do you think?'

Mrs Byrne tutted. 'And what kind of impression will that give them,' she said, 'a gentleman opening his own door? Although they might be forgiven for not thinking you're much of a gentleman.'

She gestured towards his right eye where a bruise was slowly turning from dark purple to yellow, then she joined him by the window, leaning forward and parting the net curtains a fraction. Albert saw the older woman approach the front door. She squinted at the brass plaque above the knocker, licked her thumb, wet the brass, and lightly polished it with her sleeve.

'Well, of all the cheek,' Mrs Byrne said. 'As if I didn't have Mary do that only yesterday.'

'Fingermarks, Mrs Byrne. Easily done. Maybe that's why they're here. A domestic position.'

Mrs Byrne shot him a withering glance.

'You know why they're here. It says so, clear as day, on that brass plaque that isn't good enough for madam down there. "Albert Easterbrook: Private Detective". They want your help.'

'Well, I wish they'd hurry up and knock.'

The younger woman glanced up and saw Albert and Mrs Byrne at the window. She nudged her companion in the small of her back, said something and pushed her towards the front door. Within moments there were two sharp raps, a little louder than necessary. Nerves, Albert thought.

'I'd put that away somewhere,' Mrs Byrne said, pointing at his pistol as she bustled out of the room. 'You don't want to go scaring the horses quite this early on.'

Albert slid the gun into the desk drawer, and took up position by the fireplace.

'Mrs Ida Watkins,' Mrs Byrne sniffed as she showed the two women into the room, clearly not yet having forgiven Mrs Watkins for the impromptu brass polishing, 'and Miss Minnie Ward.'

Face to face, Albert could see the elder woman's mourning dress, made of a thin bombazine, was worn shiny at the elbows. Not her first loss. She pushed up the black veil on her bonnet; her features were pinched and fell into hard lines. Albert glanced at her hands and noted the wedding ring cutting into her flesh, the finger grown fat around it. Mrs Ida Watkins. She followed his gaze and buried her hands in the folds of her skirt.

The younger woman, Miss Ward, had an open, expressive face, with a curious kind of asymmetry that just held her back from beauty, the mouth a little full, the eyes small and dark. Her brow was clear, her eyes darting round the room with an air of curiosity. Life had not yet disappointed her. But then, she was young. Twenty, he guessed. Maybe a little more. At her throat, she wore a mourning brooch of jet.

Albert offered the two women the couch, a rather threadbare chesterfield. He positioned himself opposite them on his Aunt Alice's chair. It was exceptionally uncomfortable, a rickety item with the seat so low he felt as if his knees were under his chin. But he'd been particularly fond of Aunt Alice, and he couldn't bring himself to throw it away.

Ida perched on the edge of the chesterfield, as if ready to take flight at any moment, and distractedly scratched at the crape that trimmed her dress.

'How may I help?' Albert asked.

Ida narrowed her eyes, and looked at him sceptically. Albert understood the confused reaction when people first met him. His voice betrayed his public-school education, but he had the build of a pugilist, tall and broad-chested, with a boxer's flattened nose and heavy hands.

'Are you sure you're Mr Easterbrook?' Ida asked. 'You don't look nothing like your picture,' and she turned to Minnie, who withdrew a dog-eared copy of the *Illustrated London News* from her bag, opened to the page with the ridiculous pencil drawing of Albert sporting a top hat and monocle.

He winced. 'The journalist who wrote the piece felt the story would "sell" better if he portrayed me as some kind of ridiculous toff. It's been so long since I wore a top hat I fear the moths may have made it their home. And I certainly don't own a monocle. As for that ridiculous headline—'

'So you ain't a toff?' Minnie asked. ''Cos you certainly sound like one.'

'Accents can be acquired, Miss Ward,' he said. A memory flashed through his mind: his arrival at public school, and the swift realisation he would need to change the way he spoke if he planned on surviving his school years.

'Wouldn't fancy your chances with a monocle at the moment,' Minnie said. 'Quite a shiner you've got there.'

Albert raised his hand to his eye. 'Perils of the job. An elderly lady with a surprisingly impressive right hook.' He pointed at the newspaper. 'I consented to that interview in a moment of folly. But, since you ask, I am indeed Albert Easterbrook. What can I do for you?'

'I need your help,' Ida said.

Albert nodded and waited for her to continue.

She glanced nervously around the room, her eyes lighting on a copy of *The Times* on a side table by Albert's chair. The front page carried a large image of Lionel Winter, a local businessman who was running for Parliament at the next election.

Albert followed her gaze. 'They're making much of the story,' he said. 'A welcome distraction from the Hairpin Killer, I suppose.'

Ida sniffed. 'Not all news gets in the papers, does it? My Rose ain't on the front page.'

'Rose—?' Albert asked.

'My daughter.' She paused, breathing deeply. 'She was found on Saturday night. Hanged under the Adelphi Arches.'

'I am so sorry for your loss,' Albert said, the platitude rising swiftly to his tongue and failing to convey his genuine sympathy.

Minnie shot him a look.

'And Rose was your … sister?' he asked Minnie.

'No, just a friend. A close friend.'

Her voice was pleasant, the pitch low and melodic, the accent a little more refined than he might have expected.

'There's something we need to settle first, Mr Easterbrook,' Ida said. 'Your costs. I don't imagine your services come cheap.'

Her voice was firm, but her fingers compulsively twisted her wedding ring.

Minnie placed a hand over Ida's. 'We've discussed this already. We'll find the money.'

'That we will,' Ida said. 'But money is money, and it's always best to get these matters sorted out fair and square right at the start. So everyone knows where they stand.'

She turned towards Albert. 'Minnie tells me you did a job for next to nothing, or at least that's what it said in the newspaper. I ain't a wealthy woman, Mr Easterbrook. I'm sure that much is obvious,' she said, instinctively placing her hands over the worn elbows of her dress. 'But I don't take charity. Before he died, Rose's father put some money aside for when she got married. She won't be needing it now. I need to know if it's enough.'

'Might I suggest you tell me why you are here,' Albert said. 'Once we've established whether or not I can be of any assistance, we can discuss payment. Any charge will be within your means, Mrs Watkins. You have my word. So,' he continued, 'your daughter. Rose.'

'The police are saying it's suicide,' Ida said, reaching in her pocket for a handkerchief. 'But I know my girl, Mr Easterbrook. She didn't kill herself. And now they won't bury her, you see, in the churchyard. Well, not in the consecrated part. If it weren't suicide, I could have her moved. And that would mean a lot.'

She turned away. Albert waited quietly.

'Could you tell me a little about her?' Albert asked eventually, leaning forward in his chair and immediately regretting it, as the wooden frame groaned ominously under his weight.

'Like what?' Ida asked.

'Anything you please. Her age? Children?'

Ida looked at Minnie. 'She was nineteen. Four years younger than you, weren't she, Min? Not married, although she was seeing a lad. Billy Walker. No children, thank God. Lived at home with me. Worked at the Variety Palace, tightrope walking, acrobatics. Her and Minnie worked together. Like sisters, you were, weren't you? It was Minnie who suggested I come here today,' she continued, her voice growing louder. 'Said she'd read about you in the paper and thought maybe you could help.'

Ida stopped abruptly.

'I'm sorry,' she said, after a moment. 'I'm speaking too much, ain't I? I've been like that since … it happened. Nothing to say, and then too much.'

Albert nodded his understanding.

'Had there been any change in Rose recently?' he asked.

Ida looked at Minnie again.

'We've been thinking about that,' Minnie said. 'She had been a bit quiet lately. But it weren't enough to make her do away with her own life.'

'People can hide things,' Albert said carefully. 'Rose may have been unhappier than you realised.'

Ida shook her head. 'Like I said, I know my girl. She didn't kill herself.'

'What do you believe happened?'

Ida took a deep breath and then spoke in a rush. 'I think she was killed, Mr Easterbrook. Murdered. I mean, you can't accidentally hang yourself under the Adelphi Arches, can you? Someone did that to her, and made it look like she took her own life.'

She looked at him defiantly, as if waiting for him to laugh, or tell her she was mad. She even moved further forward in her seat, ready to leave, or spring at him in defence of her child.

But Albert did not laugh. 'Do you know of anyone who would want to hurt her?' he asked.

Ida shook her head. 'No one. But there were some odd things the police found.'

Again, she looked at Minnie.

'There were marks on her wrists and her ankles,' Minnie said, fingering the mourning brooch at her neck. 'Like she'd been tied with a rope, but really tight. Her skin was broken and she was badly bruised.'

'How did you learn of these marks?' Albert asked. 'Did the police inform you?'

Ida snorted. 'The police ain't told us nothing, Mr Easterbrook. I'm surprised they even bothered to tell us Rose had died. We identified her. Had to go see her body, lying there on a slab, cold as the grave, all her dignity taken from her. That's how we know about the marks.'

She turned away again, burying her face in her handkerchief and reaching out blindly for Minnie with her other hand. Albert waited for a few moments before asking his next question.

'Did the police offer an explanation for the bruising? The broken flesh?'

'They said it was part of her work,' Ida said. 'You know, the acrobatics and that. They said she must have been doing some new turn for the halls that meant she had to be tied up really tight. You know how it is these days, every hall's trying to better the others, come up with some new trick or turn no one else has done before. The police reckon she were working on something like that. But I worked in the halls myself, years ago,' she said, raising her voice and leaning forward. 'I know you wouldn't think it to look at me now, but I was once a tumbling girl, just like Rosie. And I know there ain't nothing you can do in the halls that would leave marks like that. People pay good money to see beautiful girls, not cuts and bruises.'

'Could she have got the marks some other way?' Albert asked. 'You said she had a sweetheart. Might he have hurt her?'

'I think Billy hit her once or twice, but she always denied it,' Ida said. 'When she was found, I went straight round to his rooms for an answer, but he swore up and down it weren't him. Said he never laid a finger on her.'

'Which is a lie,' Minnie said sharply. 'He'd hit her in the past, I'm sure of it. I saw the bruises. Billy's a doorman at the Palace. He's handy with his fists. Can't always distinguish between those who deserve it and those who don't.'

'Could he have done this?'

The two women looked at each other.

'Maybe,' Minnie said. 'But the bruises weren't the only thing.'

She nodded at Ida, who removed a small gold ball from her bag and passed it to Albert.

It was delicate, no more than half an inch in diameter, and heavily engraved. A golden link was inserted, as if for wearing the piece on a watch chain or from a bracelet. Despite its delicacy, Albert felt the weight of the piece as he turned it over in his hand. He looked up at Ida.

'We found it in her belongings,' Ida said. 'Some gimcrack I thought it was when I first saw it. But my neighbour works in Hatton Garden and he reckons it's gold. Now, what would she be doing with a piece of gold like that, with all that fancy work?'

'A present?' Albert asked.

'Who from? Billy couldn't have afforded nothing like that.'

'Might Rose have had another sweetheart? An admirer from the music hall?'

'What are you suggesting?' Ida said, her face flushing. 'My Rose weren't like that.'

Minnie reached across and patted her hand. 'He ain't saying she was, Ida. Lots of girls in the halls have admirers, don't they? It don't mean nothing.' She turned back to Albert. 'There was somebody else,' she said slowly. 'We don't know who. But he had money. Bought her a pair of beautiful shoes that cost more than a month's wages.'

'And she never said who he was?'

Minnie shook her head.

Albert turned the gold ball in his hand, then held it close to his eye, rotating it slowly. He lowered the piece.

'I'm happy to take the case, Mrs Watkins,' he said, reaching for a slip of paper on the table beside him and writing down his terms. Something about Ida had touched him, her determination, her defence of her child, all the more important now the child could no longer defend herself. She reminded him of his Aunt Alice. The figure he wrote down was a tenth of what he would normally charge, but Ida was not to know that.

He folded the paper and passed it to her. She looked at the figure and nodded her agreement before handing it to Minnie. Minnie shot him a penetrating glance but said nothing.

'Mrs Watkins, would you mind very much if I kept this item for a few days?' he said, holding the golden ball in the palm of his hand. 'The markings on it are very distinctive and I may be able to discover more about its origins.'

'Keep it as long as you need.'

'And could you give me a description of Rose?'

'We can do better than that,' Minnie said, burrowing in her bag and retrieving a small portrait photograph which she handed to Albert. 'All the girls have them now, in the halls. For publicity.'

He looked at the image. Rose was gazing off to one side of the camera, her hair up, with a few artfully trained blonde curls brushing her forehead. An earring dangled from her left ear, and a decorative fan was just visible, holding up her hair at the back. The image was carefully contrived, an illusion of sophistication. But it didn't fool Albert.

'She looks young,' he said.

'She was,' Ida replied. 'And now she'll never get any older.'

A silence descended on the room, the only noise the ticking

of the clock on the mantelpiece and the logs stirring in the fire.

'How does this work, then?' Minnie asked briskly after a moment. 'Do you tell Ida when you've found something? Or does she call on you again?'

'I shall keep you updated on my progress, Mrs Watkins. I normally send a weekly written report but, in a case such as this, where you are so intimately involved, perhaps you might prefer it if we met?'

Ida looked at him then, and a glance of understanding passed between them. He had been right in his assumption that she couldn't read, although she knew her numbers. She nodded her head slowly, holding his gaze.

'I could call again next week?' she said.

He agreed and rang for Mrs Byrne to see the two women out of the house. She appeared with surprising speed, and Albert suspected she had been listening at the door again. Her manner towards Ida had changed. Albert noticed her giving the other woman the gentlest pat on her arm as she led her out of the room.

He went to the window and watched the two women disappear from view. Mrs Byrne appeared at his side. 'So,' she asked, 'how much are you charging this time? Or should I say, how little?'

Albert gave her an apologetic look.

'Albert,' she said firmly.

He winced. He always knew he was in trouble when she used his first name in that tone of voice. Not for the first time he wondered if it had been wise, hiring his old nanny as his housekeeper.

'You were a delightful child,' she continued, 'and you have

grown into a most agreeable man. But you have to charge more money. The butcher has started offering me the cheap cuts without my even asking.'

'I will. I promise,' Albert said. 'But there was just something—'

'I know, I know. Something about this one.' She patted his arm resignedly and left the room.

Albert removed the golden trinket from his pocket. A Stanhope, unless he was much mistaken. He traced the markings on the surface, what looked on closer inspection like an entwined G and C. Raising the Stanhope again to his eye, he focused on a tiny hole on the surface, barely bigger than a pinprick and easily missed. Neither of the women had noticed it, he was certain. Inside the hole was a minuscule lens. It magnified a photograph of a man who, for all the world, looked just like the image of Lionel Winter on the front page of *The Times*.

THE SECOND STANHOPE

IN WHICH MR WINTER IS INCONVENIENCED

Lionel Winter took his hat and coat from the doorman of his club and headed out into the crisp October night. He turned westwards on Piccadilly, ignoring the line of waiting cabs. It was only a three-mile walk home, and he needed time to think.

Even at nine o'clock, Piccadilly was busy. Lionel turned up Half Moon Street and onto Curzon Street. It was a little out of his way, but he liked the walk through Hyde Park.

He thought back over the previous evening's events. He had misread the situation; that much was becoming clear. A week ago, the fellow had appeared to listen to his concerns and promised to do something about them. A misunderstanding, he had said, and then he talked of supporting Lionel's campaign for Parliament. Generous support. Two days later, Lionel had visited the Palace to tell Rose there was nothing to worry about. But he had been greeted with ashen, grief-stricken faces when he had asked for her. Hanged herself, they'd said.

She'd been scared when they'd last spoken. Perhaps the fear had got too much for her. But no, that wasn't quite right. She'd been angry as much as scared. Something was amiss.

So, he'd asked to speak to the chap again last night. Made quite a fuss about it, truth be told. But he was met with silence. Not available, they'd said. Away on business. Which Lionel knew was claptrap; he'd seen the fellow's carriage outside his house only this morning.

He crossed over Park Lane, entered Hyde Park, and turned left down the broad walkway towards Rotten Row. It was a different place at night, nothing like the rush and bustle of the daytime. A solitary carriage headed away from him in the distance. As he walked, he glanced to his right over the expanse of the Serpentine.

Sometimes young lads would sneak in and take a pleasure boat out on the lake in the dark of the night, occasionally with young women in tow, squealing with delight and the pretence of fear. Not tonight. The wind murmured in the trees, and little waves lapped against the sides of the boats, as if coaxing them out into the water.

He looked at his watch. He'd left the club early, unsettled by the lack of response to his request. If he went straight home, Maud would still be awake. He would linger for a while, avoid the inevitable confrontations and accusations. But it was too cold to hang around in the open air. He'd find himself a pub and take refuge there for an hour or so.

He heard the brisk clip of a horse and carriage turning onto Rotten Row behind him. Going a little fast, he thought, even if there was hardly anyone around. The carriage was coming towards him and sounded as if it was gaining speed. Some fool in a hurry to get somewhere, or showing off for a girl. He stepped to the edge of the roadway. Best to be out of harm's way.

The carriage was racketing towards him now, a brougham

drawn by a single horse. From this distance, and in the dark, he couldn't see if there were any passengers inside. The driver was cloaked and wearing a large hat. Lionel stepped back further from the roadway and raised his cane in a gesture of rebuke, shouting at the driver to slow down and take care, his voice crushed beneath the thundering hooves.

And then, although he could not have said how, he realised the brougham was heading straight for him. Deliberately. The driver was leaning forward, his gaze fixed on Lionel, wheels rattling over the bricks. The carriage passed under a street light, and Lionel caught a glimpse of the sheen of sweat on the horse's flanks. He raised his cane again, realising as he did so the futility of the gesture.

Without even glancing behind him, he jumped backwards. He missed his footing and landed on his backside with a thud, then scrambled up, turned and ran from the grass into the undergrowth. He was ungainly, he knew. He enjoyed too many meals at the club. His heart was racing.

The horse and carriage had come to a halt on the pathway. Someone jumped down. They were going to find him. He stepped backwards as quietly as he could, turning to get away. His foot went down a hole, his ankle twisting sickeningly and he scratched his face on a branch as he fell. The pain was excruciating, shooting up his leg in great waves, but he managed not to cry out. He could not move.

Heavy footsteps left the pathway and stepped onto the grass.

Lionel lay in the darkness of the undergrowth. He was trapped. He tried to keep absolutely still, but realised he was holding his breath. Slowly, he exhaled and tentatively moved his ankle. He nearly cried out with the sudden pain. Christ, had he broken it? Another wave of pain, and he thought he was going to faint.

The footsteps moved closer to where he lay. He could see the man's silhouette against the night sky. The fellow pulled off his gloves, raised a hand to his brow. Clear in the moonlight, Lionel could see the man only had three fingers on his hand.

Then he heard another noise. A group of male voices, obviously in drink, and the high-pitched giggles of their female companions. They were walking along Rotten Row, in the same direction he had taken. They came to a halt not far from where he was hidden. One of them was trying to extract a kiss from a girl, who was shrieking in mock protest.

Someone swore under their breath. The three-fingered man. Footsteps on the pathway as he retreated. Lionel heard the slap of the reins, and the horse moved on, the carriage wheels receding in the distance.

Slowly, Lionel raised himself into a sitting position, brushing the dirt from his face and clothes. He was not far from home now. He could leave the park, and take a right on Kensington Road. He would be home in less than twenty minutes if he could manage to put any weight on his damned ankle. But he sat there, in the dark of the shrubbery, whimpering quietly.

It had been no accident, he was sure of that.

THREE

The back room of the White Hart in Milford Lane on a Thursday night was no place for ladies. The air was thick with pipe smoke, catching the back of the throat, and the room smelled of sweat and the iron tang of blood. It was fight night at the Strand Boxing Club. Money was surreptitiously changing hands. There were always police around – in the crowd, and in the ring – and they usually turned a blind eye to illegal gambling on a night like this. But, still, you couldn't be too careful.

The first fight wasn't due for a half-hour or so. Albert was tucked away in a corner of the room, sparring with his friend and former police colleague, John Price. John had lost his last two fights and had asked for Albert's help with his technique. They weren't exactly a match, Albert standing four inches taller than John, and carrying a few extra stone. But they were only sparring. They traded hooks, jabs and uppercuts for a few minutes, until Albert held up his hand.

'Your first problem,' he told John, 'is you're using your head to pull your punches. So, you're taking your eye off your opponent and it's knocking you off balance. Besides which, you're using up more energy than you need.'

John considered for a moment and then nodded.

'Drop your chin,' Albert said, 'and relax. Now, try again, and keep your eyes trained on me.'

John did as Albert had said and the blow landed with more force and certainty. They continued for another ten minutes and then broke off for some water.

'What are you working on?' Albert asked, wiping the sweat from his face with an old rag.

'Hairpin,' John said, a frown forming on his brow. 'Some days it feels like I'll be working on Hairpin until they carry me out of there in a box.'

Albert was familiar with the Hairpin Killer. Everyone in London was, the man's reign of terror dominating the news every few months or so. One time, there'd been eighteen months between the killings, and the city had seemed to relax with a collective sense of relief. And then he'd struck again. When Albert had worked on the force he had been, briefly, involved in the investigation. He understood John's frustration.

'How many is it now?' he asked.

'Twelve that we know of. Maybe more.' John shook himself, as if casting off thoughts of the case. 'What about you?'

Albert outlined the details of Rose Watkins's death. At the mention of the woman's name, a flicker of recognition crossed John's face, but he said nothing, turning away to take another swig of water from his bottle.

'She worked at the Variety Palace. An acrobat and tightrope walker,' Albert offered.

John nodded slowly, glancing around him, although all the attention in the room was focused on the main ring, where the fight was due to start very soon.

'Tompkins's case, not mine,' he said. 'Suicide, weren't it?'

'Her mother doesn't think so. She wants me to investigate.'

'She's wasting her money, Albert,' he said, feinting punches in the air as he bounced swiftly from foot to foot. 'The girl hanged herself. I heard she was having some trouble with her fella.'

'What sort of trouble?' Albert asked.

'The fella – Billy something? – reckoned Rose had taken up with some other chap. Huge barney. A few nights later, heartbroken Rose does away with herself.'

In the centre of the room, a bell rang. The fight was about to start.

'Why would she be heartbroken?' Albert asked, as they moved over to watch the action. 'If she had another sweetheart.'

John shrugged and turned his attention to the ring.

Carter, the first of the fighters, was a terrier of a man with only two teeth left in his head. He was short and carried not an ounce of unnecessary weight. A good boxer, but no match for Grice, his opponent. Or so word had it.

Tommy Grice was a powerful man, fists like rocks, with a legendary left hook. The rumour was he'd once killed a man in the ring, though stories like that were common in boxing circles. Nine times out of ten there was no substance to them. Knowing Grice, though, it might be true. He won nearly all his fights. But Albert had been watching him closely in recent weeks. He was too reactive, not giving himself time to weigh up his opponent. And he was lazy on his feet. Tonight, Albert thought he looked sluggish.

The bell rang for the start of the first round. Carter took a step towards Grice, and his opponent immediately went on the attack with a sharp jab which Carter sidestepped with ease, moving back towards his opponent, jabbing high to raise Grice's guard. It worked. Grice raised his arms to block, and Carter hit low to the left-hand side of Grice's ribcage. That would hurt.

Grice was easily angered. He straightened up and lunged at Carter, throwing indiscriminate jabs to the other man's chest. A roar of delight leapt up from the crowd.

'Grice is wasting energy,' Albert remarked.

John nodded distractedly. His mind didn't seem to be on the fight. 'Your girl,' he said, leaning in to make himself heard above the crowd. 'Maybe it all went wrong with this other chap, too, and that's why she offed herself. Or maybe she was a good girl after all, Billy got it wrong, and she couldn't stand to see her name blackened.'

A roar went up from the crowd as a lucky blow to the side of Carter's head found its mark. For a fraction of a second his eyes glazed and he swayed ominously. Then he seemed to steady himself and leaned to his right, aiming for a left hook. Not his strongest shot, Albert knew. Carter was tired, not raising his hands and arms high enough to land the blow with any force. He tilted in too far, dropped his shoulder and left his face exposed and lowered towards his opponent's fist. Grice took immediate advantage, landing a left hook that sent Carter reeling. From the cries of encouragement erupting from the crowd, Albert guessed there had been some heavy betting on Carter losing the match, and people were eager to secure their winnings.

Carter's relief when the bell rang was evident, his shoulders dropping as he stumbled towards his corner, his coach giving him swigs of water and wiping the sweat off his face.

More money changed hands in the crowd, quickly followed by cries for more beer.

'This Billy?' Albert asked. 'Is he a suspect?'

'No suspects, Albert, 'cos there weren't no crime. Apart from the suicide, of course.'

'You seem to know a great deal about it, John. Given it wasn't your case.'

John said nothing.

The bell rang again. Grice was on his feet first, bouncing from side to side with impatience, eager to be finished. The crowd was clearly on his side, with cries of encouragement from all corners. His opponent was taking his time, and Albert knew some thoughtful positioning on Carter's part could mean this fight wouldn't see a third round. But only if the lad was clever.

'What about the marks on her body?' Albert said. 'Rope marks on her wrists and ankles?'

'Like I said, she weren't my case. Tompkins was the one called out. But Rose was an acrobat, weren't she? Bruises and rope marks? No different to any other tumbler.'

'Not according to her mother,' Albert said, one eye still on the fight. 'She was a tumbler herself. Maintains there's no trick in the world that would leave marks like that.'

Carter moved carefully towards Grice and aimed a swift left hook to the body. Grice put down his elbow, and turned slightly away, exposing his right side. Just as Carter intended. He landed a whip punch to Grice's liver. Then another. And another. Grice dropped to his knees, struggling for breath. He curled up into a ball. The referee, an old fellow surprisingly quick on his feet, started to count to a chorus of shouts and the occasional cheer from the crowd. Grice shook himself and tried to stand, but the crowd already knew the result. Betting slips were tossed onto the floor and most people had turned away long before the referee reached ten. A lanky bookie sporting an eye patch and without a hair on his head looked relieved.

John's small dark eyes glanced again about the room as the crowd surged around them. 'Maybe this ain't the place to be discussing this? What say we have a chat in the Crown? It'll be quiet. Easier to talk.'

Albert nodded.

In the ring, Carter loosened the laces of his gloves with his teeth, pulled one off and reached down to take Grice's hand. The other man swore at him and spat at his feet, the spittle flecked with blood.

Albert and John walked briskly through the chill night to the Crown, just a few streets away from the White Hart. After the heat of the boxing club, the outside air felt bitterly cold, and they hurriedly entered the gloomy fug of the pub.

A few old boys were standing at the bar, nursing pints. One of them was reading the newspaper aloud to the others. He was making a decent fist of it, only occasionally stumbling over the longer words. The men lifted their heads when Albert and John entered, stared at them, then carried on drinking and listening to the news of the day. Albert inhaled the familiar smell of stale beer and smoke, and resisted the urge to take a clay pipe from the bar. Mrs Byrne had been nagging him about the smell of pipe smoke, how it clung to the curtains and the upholstery. Life was easier when Mrs Byrne wasn't nagging him.

The barman, a young lad struggling to grow a moustache

and failing, paused in wiping down the bar, and raised an enquiring eyebrow. Albert ordered two pints and motioned to John to grab a table at the quiet rear of the pub.

Further along the bar, two younger men were arguing.

'I've told Bessie she ain't going out after dark,' the first man said, a short, weaselly-looking chap whose eyes were set too close together.

'The Hairpin Killer ain't gonna go after your Bessie,' his companion said dismissively. He looked as if he lived next door to a pie shop and spent most of his life sampling the wares. 'He's got a type, ain't he? Young, for a start-off. Bessie shaves a few years off her age every birthday, but she ain't fooling anyone. And he likes 'em small, skinny. Bessie's a right jumbo,' he said, the irony of his words entirely lost on him.

The weasel placed his half-empty pint on the bar. He blinked rapidly, puffed out his chest and swore loudly at his companion. The barman glanced at Albert, nervously stroking his excuse for a moustache before shaking his head and retreating to the other end of the bar. Albert sighed and flexed his aching muscles, reluctant to intervene. But nobody else was stepping up to the mark. The weasel swung at his companion, overbalanced and clipped the edge of Albert's arm. He turned back to Albert, fists clenched, ready to take another swing. Then he took in Albert's size and his broad fists still reddened from the sparring session, and took a few steps backwards before turning to his companion. 'C'mon,' he said, 'let's go somewhere else. The beer's shit in here,' the last comment directed with lame venom at the barman.

When Albert got to the table, John was smiling. 'Hope none of my beer got spilled.'

'That was my main concern, of course. I don't suppose it crossed your mind to lend a hand?'

'You didn't need me to chalk it out for you, Albert. Anyway, he got his tail down pretty quick. Remind you of anyone, did he?'

Albert shook his head.

'Fella killed someone outside the Dog and Duck on Whitechapel Road. He hangs for it next week. Hargreaves, his name is. Chaps at the station said you knew him.'

Albert's face darkened.

'You did?' John asked.

Albert nodded, looked down at his pint, running his finger round the rim of the glass. He had always envied the ease with which others were able to share those narratives which shaped their lives. He was reticent, he knew, and many found that off-putting. So it had surprised him, the ease with which he and John had slipped into a comfortable comradeship.

Albert glanced up at John, saw the other's bird-like expression inviting his confidence. He took one of the cigarettes John pushed towards him.

'Do you remember Betsy Morrow?' Albert asked.

John frowned. 'Name rings a bell.'

'She was two years old. Found dead on the pavement outside a tenement on Scott Street, near Whitechapel Road. Her mother's fella strangled Betsy, and threw her out of a second-floor window.' Albert inhaled sharply on his cigarette. 'Jim Hargreaves.'

John looked closely at Albert.

'You couldn't get him for it?'

Albert shook his head.

'Betsy's mother was adamant he hadn't been anywhere near the child when she fell. The pair of them said it was all just "a terrible accident".'

'How did you know it was him?'

'The neighbours. They didn't see him do it, but there'd been arguments coming from the Morrow room at all hours. That afternoon, Betsy had been crying, Hargreaves shouting, and then the baby hit the ground. Couldn't get him to admit it. He wouldn't break. Griffiths, my boss at the time, said I should just beat it out of him. And I nearly did.'

Albert recalled the moment with vivid detail. Hargreaves sitting opposite him in the dingy holding cell, passing a penny coin across the back of his knuckles. And as Albert watched him, he noticed something.

'You favour your left hand,' Albert had said. 'Southpaw?'

'Yeah,' Hargreaves had said. 'What of it?'

'Nothing. It's just the evidence we have indicates Betsy was beaten by a left-handed assailant.'

Hargreaves had paused in his handling of the coin. He had looked up at Albert. And smiled.

'I lost control,' Albert said. 'The thought of the violence that had been done to that child … I lunged at Hargreaves across the table and caught him by the throat. He was a big chap, but I'm not exactly small. I took him by surprise, and I swear I could have killed him.'

'Why didn't you?' John asked. 'Sounds like you'd have done the world a favour.'

Albert sighed, reached for his glass and realised it was empty.

'I joined the police believing I could solve crime with my mind, not my fists. Anyone can use violence to extract a confession. I thought I was better than that. With Hargreaves, I saw something dark inside me. Something I didn't like. That's why I left the police.'

John said nothing for a moment, nursing his pint.

'If it's what will get a confession, Albert,' he said slowly, 'it needs to be done.'

'Not by me.'

'Maybe the rest of us don't have a choice. Some of us can't afford the luxury of a conscience.'

They sat in silence for a few minutes, and then John inhaled sharply. 'Your girl,' he said, his words lightening the atmosphere between them as swiftly as it had darkened. 'You ain't got a photograph of her, have you?'

Albert showed him the photograph of Rose Ida had given him.

John took a swig of beer and wiped his moustache. 'Look, Albert,' he said, tapping his finger on the photograph, 'we see it all the time, don't we? A young girl winds up dead. She's poor, or she's landed herself in trouble, or some fella's broken her heart. Nine times out of ten she's expecting. Girls like that—'

'Like what?' Albert asked coldly, but John didn't seem to notice the chill in his tone. Albert hated this division of people into two moral camps, the 'respectable' and the 'undeserving'. It was never that simple.

'You know,' John continued. 'Careless. Easily led. Girls like that fall into trouble every day of the week. Mothers don't want to believe nothing bad about their little girl or that they were unhappy enough to take their own life. So they look for someone to blame or to give them an answer. That's where people like you get involved. But you know what's gone on here. Do the woman a favour. Tell her the truth and don't take her money. Or is this another one you're doing for tuppence ha'penny?'

Albert said nothing, and John laughed.

'You, my son, are a mug. How on earth are you gonna make a living if you don't get paid a decent wage? Not that you need to worry too much about money, but even so.'

Albert ignored the gentle ribbing. His accent, acquired from his years at public school, was an easy way to pigeonhole him, and he allowed others to believe about him what they chose. Indeed, sometimes he used their assumptions to his advantage.

'I think there's more to this one,' Albert said. 'And I think you do, too.'

John looked away.

'Her mother found this in her belongings.'

Albert placed the golden trinket he had received from Ida Watkins on the scarred and worn surface of the pub table.

John glanced at the object and looked up at Albert, raising his eyebrows.

'It's a Stanhope,' Albert said.

'What's that when it's at home?'

'There's a lens inside that magnifies a photograph. You look through a tiny hole, and you can see the image. To the untrained eye it appears like any other piece of jewellery. You need to know the hole is there, even to think to look for it. Here,' and he showed John the point on the surface where the hole could be found.

John held the Stanhope up to his eye. 'Who's the chap?' he asked.

Albert withdrew a copy of the previous day's newspaper, and laid it on the table, pointing to the illustration of Lionel Winter.

'Well,' John said carefully, leaning back in his seat, 'there's your answer. Rose has a bit of how's your father with this here … Lionel Winter,' he said, looking at the newspaper more closely. 'Her fella finds out, or she discovers she's in the family way. Very sad, but we've seen it a hundred times before. And if you're thinking this is murder, Albert, it's much harder to force someone to put their head through a noose than most people think. There'd be signs of violence on her body.'

'Like rope marks and bruises, maybe?'

John drained the last of his pint and lit a cigarette, offering Albert another, which he refused. Inhaling deeply, John slid his fingers over the engraved surface of the Stanhope. He glanced up quickly at Albert and then looked away again.

Albert waited, letting the silence build between them.

John pulled nervously at his moustache. He glanced up at the bar, where more men had now arrived. No one was close enough to hear him and Albert, but he lowered his voice nonetheless.

'It's easy for you,' John said finally. 'It's always been easier for you. No wife, no kids. Fancy background and a house and private income you inherited from your Great-aunt Jemima.'

'I agree,' Albert said. 'The small inheritance my aunt left me does make life much easier. And her name was Alice. Not Jemima.'

'Details, Albert. Details. The point I'm making is that you never really needed the money when we worked together. So you could stand up to things, make a noise if you felt something weren't right. It's different for me. I've got seven kids, Albert. Seven. Little Florrie was meant to be the last shake o' the bag, but every time Mary sees a pram she gets a moist look in her eye, and I know it won't be long before she's sticking her head in the coal bucket again just for a little sniff.'

'So there is something up with Rose Watkins's death?'

John sighed and lowered his voice even further.

'I thought so at the time, but Tompkins wrote his report and that was that. Said the bruises and rope marks could all be explained away by her line of work. No investigation. Didn't even talk to anyone. And she'll be buried by now, so no chance of finding out anything more unless we get her disinterred. Which ain't gonna happen without a police order.'

'And Jeffers signed this off? No questions?'

John nodded. 'I ain't taking on Jeffers,' he said. 'I've got mouths to feed. The line is Rose Watkins offed herself, and that's official.'

'Well, you do what you think is best. But we both know this doesn't smell right. And the girl was just making a living. Like you.'

John looked at his hands for a minute. 'I could have a look,' he said. 'See what I can find. I'm not taking no risks, mind. I ain't losing my job just to help you. Unless, of course,' and he smiled, 'you're on the hunt for an assistant consulting detective who you're willing to reward generously.'

'Not just yet. Obviously, you'll be first on the list if a position should become available. Well, top five at least. In the meantime, don't put yourself at risk. But I'd like to find out how Rose knew this Lionel Winter. And I'll take a stroll down the Arches. Ask a few questions.'

'Probably won't get you anywhere. Most of them down there are drunk or off their mutts on whatever they can get hold of. Not that I blame them.'

'Still, worth a look,' Albert said, upending his glass and placing it firmly on the table. 'Your round, isn't it?'

FOUR

Minnie and Tansie were seated at a small table in the auditorium of the Variety Palace. Rose had not been dead a week, but for most people life had more or less returned to normal. The last time Minnie had heard Rose mentioned was by two of the women washing costumes out in the yard the previous day. She'd killed herself, silly girl. That's what they'd said. And then they'd moved on to talk about a friend of theirs, caught stealing a pound of spuds, daft bugger. Rose was gone, nothing more than a brief sentence in a dull conversation. But not for Minnie.

As always during the day, the Palace was colder than a polar bear's toenails. Minnie regularly suggested she and Tansie conduct their meetings in Brown's tea rooms further down the Strand, but Tansie was convinced the Palace would disintegrate in his absence.

Minnie made an elaborate pantomime of drawing her shawl closer round her shoulders, blowing on her hands and rubbing her palms together.

Tansie looked up, shook his head dismissively and turned his attention back to what he was reading, a sketch Minnie had written before they had heard of Rose's death. Tansie was sporting a suit of navy velvet, with a mustard waistcoat and matching pocket handkerchief. He held a blue pencil in his hand. Minnie wondered if he'd chosen the pencil to match the suit or the other way around.

'I like it,' he said eventually, leaning back, lifting his notes off the day's newspaper as he did so. 'There's a nice part for Violet, and it gives that bleedin' monkey something to do besides piss everywhere.'

Minnie inhaled slowly. 'This is about a young woman waving her sweetheart off to war. It's a dramatic piece. Where exactly does the monkey fit in?'

Tansie leaned forward and gently patted Minnie's cheek.

'You'll find a way, Min. You always do. And,' he said, tapping the paper with his forefinger, 'we need—'

'No. We don't need a song, Tanse. Not every time.'

'There's always room for a song, Min. And if you can find a way of squeezing in the midgets, we're on to a winner.'

Minnie ignored him. Her eyes strayed to his newspaper. 'Dreadful Murder! Hairpin Killer Strikes Again!' the headline screamed.

'He's done another one, then,' she said, gesturing towards the story. 'How are they sure it's the same fella?'

Tansie picked up the paper and read the highlights. '… Knife to the upper thigh … seven hairpins … young woman. Sounds like the same fella to me.'

'Why the hairpins?' Minnie said. 'Why stick a load of hairpins in their hearts after they're dead?'

Tansie shrugged. 'Loons. They're everywhere, Min. The police have been looking for this fella for' – he scanned the paper again – 'ten years, it says here. And they ain't a step closer to catching him than they were at the start. You watch yourself, my girl. He always kills them round Seven Dials, Clare Market.'

'Well, I'm safe for a while, I reckon. If he's just done one.'

'Don't be so sure. It says here "there is no pattern to the frequency or timing of the killings". Mind yourself.'

A draught swept through the auditorium, nearly blowing the pages off the table. Minnie and Tansie looked up at the sound of footsteps. Albert emerged from the darkness. He certainly drew the eye, there was no denying it. Minnie thought back to her first meeting with him, the many kindnesses he had shown her and Ida. The way he had offered them the comfortable couch, choosing to balance himself on a seat that looked as if it might give way under his weight, and where he was forced to take the full glare of the low autumn sun. His delicacy when speaking of Rose's involvement with other men. His fee, which she suspected was ridiculously low. And he had genuinely seemed to care when he heard of Rose's death, even though she was nothing to him.

But she had noticed him flinch when he had held that piece of gold jewellery close to his eye. There was something he wasn't telling them.

Tansie turned back to checking the evening's running order. When Albert came within earshot Tansie spoke, his lack of interest evident in his monotone.

'Edward Tansford,' he said. 'Manager. What you after?'

'Tansie, this is—'

'The man can speak for himself, Min,' Tansie said, shooing her away with his hand. He always felt the need to exert his authority when faced with men who were taller than him. It made for a complicated life.

Tansie stopped what he was doing, and quickly scanned Albert over the top of his glasses.

'If you're here as a strongman, we've already got one. And we don't need no chuckers-out.'

He turned back to his work, writing brief notes in the margin of one of the pages.

'I'm not seeking employment,' Albert said. 'I am here about Rose Watkins.'

Tansie did not look up, but he stopped writing.

'There's nothing here for ink-slingers,' he murmured, a quiet hint of menace in his voice. 'Best be on your way.'

'He ain't a newspaper man, Tanse,' Minnie said. 'This is that detective I told you about. Mr Easterbrook.'

Tansie removed his glasses and rubbed the bridge of his nose, turning towards Albert as he spoke. 'I feel for Ida. Lovely woman. But there ain't nothing to investigate.' He turned back to his papers.

'Why do you think that?' Albert said.

Tansie shrugged. 'Her mother's hysterical. Can't blame her.'

'Mrs Watkins says Rose was quieter of late. Did you notice anything different about her?' Albert's voice was soft, conversational. The kind of voice that might lull you into saying more than you meant to.

Tansie shrugged. 'That's women for you. I love 'em, mind, but they do fry my brain just the teeniest bit. One minute they're singing like a lark, the next they've got a fit of the morbs, sobbing everywhere, it's five minutes to curtain, and they've got to start their make-up all over again.'

'Yeah, and why are they usually crying?' Minnie said. ''Cos of some fella. Treating them like dirt. That's men for you.'

She turned back towards Albert. 'I couldn't really tell you the full story the other day, with Ida there. She blames herself. Feels maybe there was something she could have spotted. But

Rose had definitely changed. It was more than her being a bit quieter. She was … absent.'

Tansie laughed. '*Absent*, was she? Excuse my esteemed colleague, Mr Easterbrook. Our Minnie is a writer, and sometimes the muse descends like a flock of pigeons and she has a fit of poetry.'

Albert ignored Tansie's interjection.

'How do you mean, absent?' he asked.

'You always knew where Rose was 'cos you could hear her singing,' Minnie said. 'Bleedin' atrocious voice she had, but you got used to it, and at least you always knew where to find her. But in the last week or two? No singing.'

'Did you ask her if anything was wrong?'

''Course I did. Couldn't get nothing out of her, though. And that wasn't like her, neither. She was always nattering about something or other. A length of fabric she was going to make into a dress, or an act she'd seen at another hall. Couldn't shut her up, most of the time. But in the last week or so she was closed up tighter than an onion.'

A loud clattering noise in the distance interrupted the quiet, followed by exuberant cheers. Albert looked at Minnie and raised an eyebrow.

'Skittles,' she said. 'There's an alley behind the Palace.'

Albert glanced at his watch.

'They're in there all day,' Minnie said. 'You don't even notice it after a while.'

Albert looked towards the crimson-painted snuggery doors located either side of the bar. 'I understand Rose had an admirer,' he said. 'Could you describe him?'

'Tall. Dark hair. Maybe thirty, thirty-five?' Minnie said. 'Nicely dressed.'

She turned towards Tansie.

'If we're both talking about the same fella,' he said, 'he was just … ordinary. Nothing to mark him out from anybody else. We get over a thousand people in here on a busy night. I can't keep track of every chap who wants to buy one of the girls a glass of fizz. As long as they behave themselves and there's no complaints, I don't really pay them no mind.'

'And this chap,' Albert asked, 'did he behave himself?'

'Rose never said nothing,' Tansie said.

'Her sweetheart, Billy Walker? How did he feel about her going off to the snuggeries?'

'I ain't his keeper. You got questions for Billy, you ask him.' He swept his papers off the desk with a decisive movement. 'I've got work to do. Minnie here will show you out.'

He pushed back the chair and headed towards the stage, the darkness of the auditorium swallowing him up in moments.

Minnie turned her attention back to Albert. 'Billy knew about Rose going in the snuggeries. Everyone knew. You can't keep a secret in the halls.'

'I take it he wasn't happy about it?'

'What do you think? They had a stand-up barney in here not long before she died. Billy telling her what to do. Rose saying it was none of his business.'

'Who won the argument?'

'Rose, I guess. She certainly went with a johnny at least once afterwards. You could always tell when it had happened, 'cos Billy had a face like thunder the next day.'

'Billy's a chucker-out. Handy with his fists, is he?'

'Wouldn't be much of a bouncer otherwise, would he? Does a bit of bare-knuckle work. The fellas here say he's a tidy little boxer. Tansie's won a few bob on him.'

'And you believe he hit Rose?'

Minnie gave Albert a long look. A lot of men had a casual tolerance when it came to hitting a woman. Albert was probably no different; those fists of his could certainly land a floorer. But there had been a gentleness about him when he had spoken to Ida that had impressed her. 'I can't swear to it,' she said eventually. 'But she came in with bruises once or twice.'

Tansie reappeared from the shadows, and retrieved his tobacco pouch from the table where he'd left it. 'You still here?' he said. 'We've got a show to put on tonight, and it's time you were gone.'

Albert made no move to leave. Impressive, Minnie thought. Most people found it difficult to say no to Tansie, despite his diminutive size.

'Rose's act,' Albert said. 'Could it have left bruises and rope marks on her body?'

'Have you seen our show?' Minnie asked.

Albert shook his head.

'Come along tomorrow night if you're free. We've got Betty doing Rose's act. You'll see for yourself there's nothing that could have marked her,' she said.

'You'll be offering him tickets on the house next,' Tansie said over his shoulder, disappearing into the darkness again.

Albert nodded his thanks to Minnie. 'Billy Walker?'

Minnie led Albert through a doorway beside the stage and down a narrow set of stairs. She was familiar with the spaces of the Palace, could have moved through them with her eyes shut, but Albert stumbled over a length of rope lying across the passageway, and had to turn sideways to squeeze between two racks of costumes. Banging echoed through the empty backstage corridors. Minnie turned a corner and there was Billy, a hammer in his hand and half a dozen nails held between his lips. He wore a pair of tattered and patched trousers, a grubby white shirt stretched across his frame. He glanced up at Minnie's approach, saw Albert behind her and slowly pulled himself up to his full height, dropping the nails into his hand. Minnie had imagined Billy's bulk would dwarf Albert, but she was wrong. In a fight, she wasn't sure who she'd put her money on.

'Billy, this is Mr Easterbrook. Hired by Ida to find out what happened to Rose. He'd like to have a word.'

Billy scowled and threw the hammer into a battered tin toolbox, perilously close to Albert's feet. Albert didn't flinch. Minnie followed his gaze to Billy's bruised knuckles, the skin broken in several places. Billy looked down at his hands, slowly cupping one fist inside the other. His hands were trembling, and even from a distance he smelled like the slop tray in a boozer on a Saturday night.

'I won't take too much of your time, Mr Walker,' Albert said. 'I can see you're busy.'

Billy frowned when Albert started speaking, and then it was as if a shutter came down behind his eyes. He spat out a wad of tobacco in Albert's direction.

Albert didn't move a muscle. 'Your hands,' he commented. 'How did you get those cuts?'

'Boxing. You should see the other bloke.'

'When was the fight?'

'Last night. Whitechapel.'

'Who were you fighting?'

Billy narrowed his eyes. 'Jimmy Ryan.'

Albert slowly nodded his head. 'You did well to land

anything on Ryan. Last three times I've seen him fight it didn't get past the first round.'

Billy gave Albert a long look, as if reappraising him.

'I understand you and Rose argued recently,' Albert said. 'Must be difficult to stomach, that. Seeing your girl with another man.'

Billy's hands tightened reflexively. Minnie tensed. Albert didn't know Billy, didn't know how swift he was to take offence, or how he did most of his thinking with his fists. Albert carried on as if oblivious to Billy's mounting anger, but she noticed him change his stance, putting his weight on his back foot.

'Might drive a man to violence,' Albert continued.

Billy held Albert's gaze. 'Some men. Maybe. But if you're looking for Rose's killer, best you look somewhere else.'

He turned away, the conversation clearly at an end. Albert glanced at Minnie, and she jerked her head towards a narrow corridor which led to the rear of the building. She had a feeling there was more he wanted to tell her, and they were better off away from the Palace.

FIVE

Minnie pushed open the stage door and blinked rapidly, her eyes readjusting to the sudden daylight after the dim interior. The lane running behind the music hall was littered with discarded pipes and other rubbish. The clatter of the skittles alley, a noise she rarely noticed, seemed almost deafening now Albert had drawn attention to it.

'There's Brown's just down on the Strand,' Minnie said, pointing to the left. 'I thought maybe it'd be easier to talk somewhere a bit more private.'

Albert nodded. They turned onto Exeter Street, and then right onto the Strand, navigating their way through the crowds. They entered Brown's tea rooms, a clean, if slightly tired-looking establishment that Minnie knew served excellent cake. The waitress looked as if she desperately needed a break. They chose a table near the window and she took their order.

'There's something I need to show you,' Albert said, withdrawing from his pocket the gold piece of jewellery Ida had given him. 'It's a Stanhope. Look through here,' he said, pointing to a tiny dot on the surface of the ball, just above the intertwined G and C, 'and tell me if that's the chap Rose went in the snuggeries with.'

Minnie looked closely. 'That's him,' she said decisively. 'Who is he?'

'Lionel Winter. Prospective Member of Parliament.'

The waitress brought their tea and a generous slice of fruit cake for Minnie.

'Why didn't you show me this back at the Palace?' Minnie asked, while they waited for the tea to brew and she tucked into her cake.

'Your boss didn't seem very bothered about Rose's death. Billy neither. Lack of concern like that tends to make me suspicious.'

'Tansie ain't my boss,' Minnie said, irritated by his assumption. 'He's my customer. I write songs and sketches, he pays for them.'

'I apologise. I just assumed—'

''Course you did. You and everyone else. And your point about Tansie not caring, that's just an act. He's got a big heart. Bigger than he wants to let on. You threw him a bit. Being so tall and all.'

'That must make life difficult.'

'It does. You get used to it.'

'But still … he doesn't want this to be murder,' Albert said.

'It ain't good publicity for the Palace if one of our girls gets killed. Might turn the punters away.'

'Or it might make them more eager to attend. People do have a ghoulish fascination with murder. You've only got to see the way they devour stories about the Hairpin Killer. Your … Mr Tansford might be able to exploit that kind of interest.'

Minnie added four spoons of sugar to her tea. 'What?' she said, registering the look of alarm on Albert's face.

'It's just … that's a lot of sugar,' he ventured.

'Keeps me sweet,' she said. 'You wouldn't like my sour side.' She stirred her tea, then continued. 'Tansie loved Rose like she was his own daughter. He'd never make money out of her death. If you think that of him, you've got him all wrong. Billy, I ain't so sure about.'

Minnie glanced round the tea room. In the corner, a mother was struggling to quieten her infant with a bottle of what looked like Godfrey's Cordial. Near her, a young couple were gazing at each other across the teacups.

'There's something else,' Albert said quietly. 'An ex-colleague of mine asked a few questions about Rose's death.'

'And?'

'The constable who was first on the scene. He said there were scratches on Rose's neck.'

Minnie nodded. 'We saw them when we went to identify … when we saw her. We wondered if she'd got them off Billy.'

'Possibly. But scratches like those … they're not uncommon with victims of hanging.'

Realisation dawned on Minnie, and she inhaled sharply as tears pricked her eyes. 'You mean … she struggled? Tried to remove the rope?'

Albert nodded. 'It doesn't mean it was murder. Suicides do sometimes change their minds.'

'But you don't think it was suicide, do you? You agree with me and Ida? It was murder?'

'Possibly. Certainly, the police were too swift to dismiss all those marks on Rose's body. At the very least, they should have ordered an inquest.'

'So, when are we going to speak to him? This Lionel Winter chap?'

'We?' Albert replied. '*We* are not going to speak to anyone.'

'Why not? I could help you. Ask questions, find things out—'

'It seems like you've already been doing some of that,' Albert interrupted.

Minnie narrowed her eyes. 'Meaning?'

'Meaning I went to the Arches yesterday to see if anyone remembered anything from the night of Rose's death. Turns out a young woman had already been down there asking questions. About your height. Dark hair. Mourning brooch at her throat.'

'So? I ain't gonna sit on my backside waiting for something to happen.' She took a swig of tea, the heat scalding her tongue. 'Not that it was any use. Everyone I spoke to, full as a goat. Breath strong enough to carry coal. Did you have more luck?'

Albert shook his head. 'As I thought, either they can't remember, or they're not willing to say anything. My point is, Mrs Watkins hired *me* to investigate the case. On my own.'

'Why won't you let me help?' she challenged him.

'It would not be acceptable. You're—'

'A woman? Well spotted, Detective Easterbrook.'

'It would not be appropriate for me to involve you in the investigation, Miss Ward.'

'Oh, for God's sake, call me Minnie. Everybody else does. And I'll call you Albert.'

'No.'

'Oh,' she said after a moment's pause. 'Why not?'

'Because, Miss Ward, we barely know one another.'

She tilted her head to one side and gave him a half-smile. 'Me calling you Albert don't mean you've gotta buy a ring and put an announcement in *The Times*. It might mean that in your world, but not in mine. It'll just be a lot easier, don't you think? If we're working together?'

'We will not be working together, Miss Ward. I work—'

'Think about it,' Minnie interrupted. 'My being a woman is precisely the reason I can help you. There's places you can't go that I can. People who'll talk to me who'll button up tighter than a—' She stopped suddenly, unsure of which comparison would be most appropriate.

'An onion?' Albert offered. 'That was the analogy you used earlier.'

'I was going to say tighter than a cat's arse, but then I remembered who I was talking to. So, yes, they'll close up tighter than an onion if you start asking them questions.'

'I can't agree to your helping me. It wouldn't be right.'

She leaned towards him. 'Have you heard what you sound like? From the moment you opened your garret, I knew you weren't gonna get nowhere with Billy. Or Tansie. They only talk to people like you when they have to. Me, though? A nice girl who knows the halls and knew Rose? They'll open up like a' – she hesitated as Albert winced, and then she smiled – 'like a flower in the spring. And besides,' she continued, 'Rose was my friend. I want to find out who did this to her.'

'I understand your sentiments, Miss Ward. Truly I do. But I cannot accept your help.'

She leaned further forward, pushing aside the teapot and sugar bowl.

'There's things you didn't see back there, 'cos you wouldn't know to notice them,' she said, lowering her voice. 'Those cuts on Billy's hands? He never got them boxing, 'cos he ain't been in a fight since a fortnight ago. I heard him telling Kippy yesterday.'

'I know. Ryan wasn't fighting in Whitechapel last night. Besides, Billy's face didn't have a mark on it. And you said he was a bare-knuckle boxer? If he'd been in a fight last night he wouldn't have been able to pick up a hammer this morning, never mind a handful of nails.'

Minnie narrowed her eyes. 'And how would you know that?'

'I like boxing. I indulge in a spot of it myself.'

'That explains the nose, then.'

Albert reached up reflexively to touch his face.

'There's nothing wrong with it,' Minnie added quickly. 'It gives you … character.'

Albert blushed, and busied himself pouring the last of the tea.

Minnie thought for a moment. 'But if you weren't there, I could have asked him about those cuts on his hands. Got the truth out of him.'

'Perhaps. But if Rose Watkins was murdered and we solve the case, there's every chance we'll come face to face with a murderer. And all the local knowledge and smart talk in the world won't keep you safe if that were to happen.'

She leaned back, a broad grin spreading across her face.

'What?' Albert asked.

'You said "we". "If *we* are successful". That's what you said. You're thinking about it, ain't you?'

Albert shook his head vigorously. 'No. I am not thinking about it. My choice of pronoun was a slip of the tongue.'

Laughing, she reached down to extract her money from her bag. Albert held up his hand, insisting he would pay.

'No thanks,' she said briskly, placing a few coins on the table as she rose to leave. 'That covers my half. When you come back, *Mr* Easterbrook, asking for my help, I'd like a very large cake from here by way of apology. One of them Victoria sponges, preferably, although that fruit cake went down a treat. Oh, and I'll leave a note with the box office that you'll be stopping by tomorrow evening. Just tell them your name and mention me. Will you be bringing anyone with you?'

Albert frowned. 'Possibly,' he said.

Minnie paused momentarily, then repositioned her hat. 'Two tickets, then,' she said.

And she was gone.

SIX

As Albert and John turned onto the Strand, the crowds swelled and the noise washed over them in waves. Albert felt his pulse quicken. As a child, he had never come near this part of the city. His parents had been desperate to put their less affluent past behind them, and had painted the area as the closest thing to Sodom and Gomorrah. When he'd joined the force he'd been introduced to the network of passageways and dark corners that made up the slums of Seven Dials and Clare Market, sitting cheek by jowl with the splendour of Trafalgar Square and the seemingly endless entertainment available on the Strand. Initially horrified, he had become intrigued, and eventually fascinated. He stood outside it, though, always an observer. He wondered if anywhere would ever feel like home.

Tonight, the streets rang with the clash of music from street performers with barrel organs and penny whistles vying to make the most noise and secure themselves a few pennies … shillings if they were lucky. The smells of horse dung, cigar smoke, beer, food and perfumes assailed Albert's nose. None of this was anything new, there was just more of it. More of the constant touch of other people: collisions, pushes, some accidental, some deliberate. He kept his hand on his wallet.

Newsboys were revelling in details of the latest Hairpin killing: 'Hairpin Murderer Strikes Again! Police fail to find the monster! No woman is safe!'

John groaned. 'Christ, it's bad enough down the station, never mind being reminded of it every time I set foot outside the door.'

'And they're right? No leads?'

John shook his head. 'Nothing. He kills. He vanishes. We're no closer now than we were ten years ago. And the press aren't helping. "No woman is safe" – Christ almighty, it's all we need.'

'There'll be something new tomorrow or the next day, and everyone will forget about it.'

'Not everyone,' John said.

They passed the toy shops of Lowther Arcade, with children crowded around their windows, and stepped into the road to avoid a group of women who had taken up the entire pavement, gawping at an eight-foot-tall wooden Red Indian chief positioned outside a tobacco shop.

'Bloody day-trippers,' John moaned. 'Stopping with no warning to look at a map, or standing open-mouthed as if Trafalgar Square were the eighth wonder of the world and they'd never seen a pigeon before. Bloody pests.'

'The pigeons or the tourists?'

'Both.'

The two men walked through the crowds to the Variety Palace. At the box office, Albert mentioned Minnie's name and collected two tickets for the stalls and a running order for the evening.

John's eyes widened when he saw where they would be sitting. 'Well, the stalls'll give you a good feel for the place, I suppose,' he said.

Albert had visited music halls in the past, but nothing quite like the Palace. His most recent outing had been to the Empire in Leicester Square where he had enjoyed a night of Tyrolean singers and dancers, a ballet, and a one-hour performance of *Faust*. Actually, 'enjoyed' was an exaggeration. Now that he remembered it, he had slept through much of the ballet and spent most of *Faust* propping up the bar. The posters inside the Variety Palace suggested a different night's entertainment: 'Miranda the Mermaid: The Wonder of the Age! Pedro the Mexican Boneless Wonder! Miss Daisy Mountford: Queen of Mesmerism!' Beside him, John sniggered.

As they moved further into the auditorium Albert was struck by the heat and noise of the crowd. He guessed there were, as Tansie had said, about a thousand people in the room, but the space looked as if it would only comfortably accommodate a quarter of that number. It felt as if everyone was talking, smoking and drinking at once, competing with the noise of the orchestra, which favoured the drum and cymbals over any other instruments.

Nobody seemed to be paying much attention to the act on stage. Albert glanced at the running order and guessed this must be Paul Prentice. He was attempting a comic song and failing badly. They had already missed Madame Selina, Queen of the Opera. The first act was usually the worst, and given the quality of Mr Prentice, Albert was rather glad they'd arrived late.

He glanced round at the audience. No dress coats, no elegant evening wear. But, on closer examination, there was an air of respectability. Little family parties with parents, sometimes a grown-up daughter or a child, all of whom clearly knew each other from the smiles and handshakes they exchanged. Girls with their sweethearts, respectable young couples who probably worked in neighbouring workshops and factories. An elderly matron or two. And on the edges of the audience, from a vantage point where they could survey both the women in the audience and the women on stage, the local bloods with a cigar behind the ear and a glass of beer never far away. The spectacle would have horrified his parents.

He heard his name and turned to see Minnie approaching. She was dressed in a dove-grey dress that set off the colour of her eyes, the mourning brooch still at her neck. She drew nearer, smiling broadly. It took Albert a moment to realise he was pleased to see her.

'Miss Ward,' he said. 'I'm delighted you could join us.'

She smiled ruefully. 'Permanent fixture, me. Should have been home an hour ago. Seeing as I'm still here, I thought I might sit with you, answer any questions you might have. Not that we're working together or nothing,' she added, casting Albert a sidelong glance. Albert chose to ignore her comment.

He introduced her to John, who eyed her appraisingly and gave Albert a nod of approval behind her back. She led them to an empty table near the stage. A waiter appeared immediately and they ordered beef sandwiches and beer.

'Is Billy Walker in tonight?' Albert asked Minnie.

'Not tonight. It's his night off. He's working somewhere else, most likely. Don't know where.'

As Paul Prentice stumbled from the stage to a trickle of applause, Tansie rose from behind a table positioned in front of the orchestra to announce the next act. Minnie leaned across.

'It's Betty Gilbert up next,' she said. 'She's doing Rose's act now.'

Albert focused his attention as a young woman, tall and angular, was lowered onto the stage from a trapeze swing. She was dressed in what looked to Albert like a pair of bloomers and a chemise. Perhaps the evening would be more entertaining than he'd anticipated. For the next twenty minutes she performed a series of acrobatic moves, both on the trapeze and on stage. The applause was decidedly more animated than for Paul Prentice, but Albert wondered if the bloomers and chemise might have played some part in that.

'See anything that could leave rope marks?' Minnie asked as Betty left the stage to more enthusiastic applause and shouts.

Albert shook his head. The act might have caused the odd bruise or two, particularly in rehearsal, but there was no point at which Betty had been tied by the wrists or ankles.

'And now, ladies and gentlemen,' Tansie announced, accompanied by a drum roll from the orchestra, 'second to none in her mysterious and wonderful displays of mesmerism, Miss Daisy Mountford.'

'Can't stand these hypnotists,' John said. 'It's all a fix. Someone they know in the audience pretending to go into a trance. Another?' he asked, gesturing at Albert's empty glass. Albert nodded, and John rose to go to the bar, but Minnie simply raised a hand and a waiter arrived to take their order.

Daisy Mountford stumbled onto the stage to the reedy sound of a clarinet, clearly intended to mimic the accompaniment of a snake charmer. She was young, fair-haired, remarkably pretty. In fact, all the women Albert had seen so far at the Palace were remarkably pretty. He wondered if it was coincidence, or part of Tansie's selection process.

Dressed in what looked like a redundant genie's costume

from a very second-rate performance of *Aladdin*, Daisy's outfit was draped with a number of scarves. She resembled a salesman for a textiles factory with all his wares on display. On her head she wore a fakir's turban that was too big for her, and kept slipping down over her eyes. She was sweating at an alarming rate.

There was a loud thud from the orchestra pit, and the clarinet stopped abruptly. Daisy glanced nervously at the musicians and then shakily announced her desire for a volunteer from the audience to experience her magnificent powers of mesmerism. Several young lads standing at the edges of the seating area pushed their friends forward as volunteers, or shouted out, 'Here, take me, darling!' But Daisy ignored them all, wisely in Albert's opinion. She came down off the stage and walked amongst the audience, cleverly sidestepping the hands reaching out to grab her, lingering at one table or another before shaking her head regretfully and moving on. Close up, Albert could see how young she was, probably Rose's age. The scarves which adorned her outfit were clumsily sewn.

She approached their table and fixed her eyes on Albert. 'You, sir,' she said in a tremulous high-pitched voice, with an accent clearly meant to sound refined but falling well short, 'you have a magnificent aura. It speaks to me of your receptivity.'

John nudged Albert. 'There you go, Albert. You've got one thing going for you, at least. Lovely aura.'

Daisy raised one hand to her brow, closed her eyes and held the other hand out in front of her. 'The spirit of Mesmer seeks a man whose name begins with … an A!' She drew out the vowel with exaggerated emphasis.

'Blimey, Albert, it's you,' John said, trying not to laugh.

Albert shook his head. 'Not me,' he said. 'Choose somebody else.'

'The choosing is not my own, sir. The spirit of Mesmer is working through me. I am merely his vessel.'

Albert looked to Minnie for reinforcement.

'Daisy *is* merely a vessel, Mr Easterbrook,' Minnie said, with a glint in her eye. 'I think you'll find Mesmer cannot be denied.'

The crowd had picked up on Albert's reluctance and were now stamping their feet and calling out their discontent with shouts of 'Get a move on!' and 'I ain't got all night!'

Daisy looked intently at Albert, then again raised a hand to her brow. 'No,' she said firmly, 'Mesmer says not Albert. Not Albert, but it does start with an A. Anthony? Is there an Anthony here?'

A nondescript-looking chap seated nearby leapt up. 'I'm Anthony!' he shouted, and stumbled towards Daisy.

The crowd cheered, Daisy took Anthony's hand and led him onto the stage, where he was seated in a chair that looked in dire need of some new upholstery.

'Between you, me and the bedpost,' Minnie said, leaning towards Albert and dropping her voice, 'Daisy has the mesmeric powers of a dead kipper. She's only been here a couple of weeks, and I doubt she'll last another fortnight. Another of Tansie's lame ducks. Her and Madame Selina. Don't know where he finds them.'

'And Anthony knows Miss Mountford?' Albert said.

Minnie arched her eyebrows. 'However did you guess?'

'Now, Anthony,' Daisy said from the stage, 'I'm going to ask you to relax.' She removed a ladies' watch from her pocket and held it up, turning towards the audience to show it to them. 'Anthony, all I wish you to do is simply look at this watch. Observe the movement,' and here she slowly started to swing the watch from side to side in front of his eyes. 'Simply pay attention to the movement of the watch, and the sound of my voice.' And with that, the pitch of her voice dropped slightly and the pace slowed.

Anthony was well practised, you had to give him that. Every time Daisy said his name he dropped onto all fours and skittered across the stage, barking like a dog. When she rang a bell, he waltzed, flirting coquettishly from behind an imaginary fan. After ten minutes of this, though, the crowd grew restless, particularly when they realised that if they called out Anthony's name it had no effect. Daisy stared pointedly at Tansie, who leapt to his feet and nodded at the conductor. The orchestra struck up a hasty rendition of 'Just by the Angel at Islington', and Anthony returned to his seat.

The next hour passed pleasantly enough, if a trifle confusingly. The Mexican Boneless Wonder looked to Albert more legless than boneless. The one-legged dancer fell off the stage into the orchestra pit. And the dog and monkey act was, quite frankly, bewildering.

Albert was just rising to go to the bar when shouts ran through the audience. All eyes turned away from the stage and towards the promenade. It was a tiny woman, probably no more than four and a half feet. She was trim, with a nervous energy about her, dark eyes glinting in a face that looked as if it fell easily into a smile. The crowd was parting before her as if she was Moses.

'Bloody hell,' Minnie said, turning towards Albert and John with a look of astonishment on her face.

Albert frowned.

'Crikey, Albert,' Minnie said. 'Don't tell me you don't know who it is?'

John leaned in. 'I swear, Albert, if someone told me you'd been raised by wolves and spent most of your life living in a cave, it wouldn't surprise me. Edie Bennett? The Richmond Rocket?'

Albert nodded. Even he had heard of the Richmond Rocket, possibly the most famous female music hall performer of all time. It was said she could move an audience from laughter to tears and back again in just a few bars of a song, although Albert had never seen her act. She had retired from the stage several years ago, having made a very successful marriage.

The woman drew nearer, her gaze fixed on Tansie, her hands outstretched, a smile illuminating her face. She sported diamond rings on almost every finger, and her wrists were wreathed with gold bracelets that sparkled with precious stones. Around her neck was a pendant with a ruby in it the size of a hen's egg.

She sashayed over to Tansie, gave a final swing of her hips and stood with her hands at her waist, her head tilted to one side in a gesture of familiarity. Tansie made an elaborate bow, then grabbed both her hands, giving her a flamboyant kiss on both cheeks before escorting her to a table marked 'Reserved'.

'Good mate of your boss?' John asked.

'First I've heard of it, if she is,' Minnie said. 'I can't believe he's kept that one quiet. And he ain't my boss,' she added, a twinge of irritation in her voice. John had hit the same nerve Albert had stumbled on the day before.

'Now, ladies and gentlemen, and most honoured guest,'

Tansie announced, nodding and smiling in Edie Bennett's direction, 'I give you the highlight of tonight's entertainment. A truly wondrous act that will leave you spellbound and full of wonder. Prepare to be astonished, delighted and moved.'

John nudged Albert. 'I've heard about this. Miranda the Mermaid. Easy on the eye, if nothing else.'

Tansie moved over to take a seat next to Edie, while two stagehands pushed a large glass tank onto the stage. The tank was filled with water, and inside was a buxom young woman, her dark hair moving freely in the water, her dress clinging to her in what Albert had to admit was a very pleasing fashion. Clearly, the audience felt the same. The air was thick with shouts and whistles, and one fellow cried out enthusiastically, 'Marry me, Miranda.'

She was accompanied by a gentleman in evening dress, a skinny fellow wearing an unsuccessful wig.

'Ladies and gentlemen,' he began, 'scientists have proved that, for us human folk, opening the mouth underwater for any longer than a few moments brings with it instant death. But Miranda is no human, ladies and gentlemen. She is a mermaid, from the rocks of the Barbary Coast, captured by intrepid explorers and brought back to our dear old London town. She will now, for your entertainment and delight, open and close her mouth several times in succession while remaining at the bottom of the tank.'

And so she did. The audience applauded enthusiastically. Albert glanced across at Minnie, but she was stifling a yawn. Having successfully opened and closed her mouth, Miranda then gathered shells underwater, sewed the hem on a handkerchief, and wrote her mother a letter.

'And finally,' the gentleman announced, 'Miranda the Mermaid will adopt the position of prayer.'

The young woman sank gracefully to her knees and clasped her hands together while the orchestra played 'The Maiden's Prayer'. The skinny gentleman with the unfortunate wig reverently bent his head. Albert glanced round the audience. An elderly woman in the ugliest bonnet Albert had ever seen was brushing away a tear, while her husband violently blew his nose.

'Are they … *crying*?' Albert asked Minnie.

'We get some every night. They'd cry at anything. It's a load of old pony, but the punters love it.'

Her prayer concluded, Miranda rose, sleek and dripping, to the surface of the tank, hopped out and bowed.

'Any chance of an introduction?' John asked Minnie, nodding in the direction of Edie Bennett, who was now deep in conversation with Tansie. 'My Mary won't believe it if I tell her I got to meet the Rocket.'

'I could ask Tansie, but I don't know her. She probably won't want bothering by the likes of us.'

As if he'd overheard their conversation, Tansie turned towards their table, and gestured for them to join him. Albert was surprised by how flustered Minnie looked, blushing and fiddling with her hair, as they approached Tansie and his guest. He'd imagined nothing could embarrass her, and wondered what it was about Edie Bennett that was so befuddling.

'The famous Minnie Ward!' Edie said, clasping Minnie's hand in both of hers. 'I've heard so much about you, my dear. Tansie here reckons he's the big boss, but we all know it's the women who make things happen, don't we?' She was like a little doll, with a rosebud mouth and large brown eyes. Her voice was surprisingly deep for such a tiny frame, her accent straight from the streets of Whitechapel.

'Miss Bennett,' Minnie stammered, 'I'm honoured to meet you. Truly honoured. I had no idea you and Tansie were friends.'

Edie winked at Tansie. 'We go back a long way, don't we, Tanse?'

She turned to speak to someone who had approached their table. Minnie leaned in towards Tansie and dropped her voice so Edie couldn't hear.

'Old chums, are you? Funny how you ain't never mentioned it before. What are you up to, Tanse?'

Tansie threw out his arms, as if completely bemused by Minnie's words.

Edie turned back to them. 'I saw your act, my dear – years ago it was, but what a talent.'

'One of the best things you've ever seen at the halls,' Tansie prompted; 'that was what you said, weren't it?'

Minnie gave Tansie a hard stare.

Edie took her cue. 'Wonderful you were. Why on earth did you give up?'

Minnie gave a tight smile. 'Oh, you know. Fellas giving you grief. Pestering you. Not taking no for an answer.' This last comment was addressed directly to Tansie.

Edie leaned in closer. 'You and I, my dear, must take tea together one day. I can tell you all the gossip about Tansie. And this gorgeous giant of a man,' she said, turning towards Albert, and running her eye over him with an appreciative gaze, 'I'm very much hoping he's your fella?'

Minnie snorted.

Albert introduced himself and explained that he was most decidedly not Minnie's fella, but had been hired to investigate Rose's death.

'Oh, that poor girl,' Edie said, raising a hand to her chest. 'Tansie told me. What a dreadful end.' Then she turned to John, who was gazing at her like a dog outside a butcher's window.

'John Price,' he stammered. 'My wife, Mary, she just loves you. Saw your final night at the Marylebone. I don't think she's stopped talking about it since.'

Edie nodded, fished in her bag and handed John a signed photograph. 'For Mary,' she said with a wink. She turned back to Albert, holding out another photograph which he was forced to take, although he had no idea what he'd do with it. Perhaps Mrs Byrne would appreciate it.

Edie pulled herself up to her full height, which still placed her well below most people's eyeline, and surveyed the music hall. She seemed oblivious of the fact that most of the audience hadn't moved, despite the evening's entertainment being at an end. Everyone was staring at Edie, craning forward to get a better look. She inhaled deeply. 'Funny,' she said, 'every hall I've ever been in, they all smell the same.' She turned to the group and smiled broadly. 'Well, ladies and gents, some of us have got homes to go to. It's been a pleasure meeting all of you. Minnie, here's my card,' she said, producing a calling card from an elaborately embossed card holder. 'Let me know when you're free and we'll take tea. Somewhere fancy, eh?'

Minnie nodded, her face flushed with pleasure as she gazed at the card. Edie gathered together her belongings, and strutted out of the music hall. As the doors closed behind her, Minnie turned on Tansie. 'That was a low blow, Tanse.'

'What? Introducing you to your idol? The woman you've admired since you were a tot? Don't know why I bothered.'

'You know what I'm talking about. "What a talent,"' she said, dropping her voice to mimic Edie's with astonishing precision. '"Why on earth did you give it up?" Funny how you've been on at me recently to get back on the boards, and all of a sudden Edie Bennett appears out of the blue.'

Tansie shrugged. 'Coincidence, Min. What can I say? But, now you mention it, what about it? Your old act?'

Minnie said something Albert couldn't quite catch, but which he guessed was less than ladylike, and thumped Tansie hard on the arm. An impressive swing for a woman, Albert thought, and made a note not to cross her.

THE THIRD STANHOPE

IN WHICH SERGEANT PRICE
ASKS SOME QUESTIONS

John hated a death call. You never knew what you'd find, and John had found pretty much everything in his ten years on the force. The woman who'd kept her dead mother's corpse propped up in bed for several weeks during the hottest summer on record, until the neighbours complained about the smell. The fella who'd murdered his wife and then laid the table for dinner with one of his wife's fingers on each of the plates. And, of course, the Hairpin Killer, with a single knife wound to the thigh and the seven hairpins inserted into the heart after death.

The house was part of a smart, newish terrace in Kensington. Highly polished door furniture, and the steps had all been swept. At least it was a reasonable hour, nine in the morning. That was another thing John hated: being called out in the middle of the night.

The door was opened by a nervous-looking parlourmaid, her eyes ringed red with tears and a port-wine birthmark on her face flushing angrily against the paleness of her skin.

'Sergeant Price,' John said, longing for the day he could announce himself as Inspector. 'I'm here about the death of Mr Lionel Winter.'

The maid nodded and led John up the stairs to the bedroom on the first floor. John noted the paintings crowding the walls, the way even the doors to the various rooms had been painted with flowers and exotic creatures. Arty types, no doubt. There were lots of them, Kensington way.

The maid hesitated at the entrance to the bedroom, her hand on the doorknob. She looked nervously at John. 'I can take it from here, miss,' he said, and relief flooded her face. 'Was it you who found the body?'

'Not me, sir, no. It were Tom, the horse boy. He always brought Mr Winter his tea first thing in the morning.'

'His horse boy? Why not you?'

She shrugged. 'Mr Winter had his ways, sir.'

'Then perhaps you could ask Tom to join me?'

She nodded and scurried back down the stairs.

John entered the bedroom. It was a modest size, and made him reappraise the household income. The newspapers had said this fella was running for Parliament. Must have money hidden away somewhere 'cos this house didn't say money to John.

The blinds were down – out of respect for the dead, no doubt – and he crossed to the window and opened them to let in a little light. Then he steeled himself and turned towards the body.

Arsenic, the word had been when the message came through to the station. So he was ready for shit, piss, vomit. But there was nothing. The man, a tall fellow, dark-haired, was lying in bed, his head slightly to one side. His right hand was raised to his chest. Beside him, on a small table, an empty teacup and saucer. John lifted the cup and sniffed. Nothing. But there was an odd smell in the room.

John turned his attention back to the body. The man looked peaceful. Arsenic wasn't a peaceful death. He pushed up the man's pyjama sleeves, checking for puncture wounds. Nothing. He opened the pyjama buttons and detected the first flush of what looked like bruising on the man's chest and arms. Could be something.

He heard footsteps tripping up the stairs and a young man entered the room. Sixteen, seventeen maybe. Short fella, but strong-looking. An honest, open kind of face. Not that that meant anything, of course.

'Tom Neville, sir,' the lad said. 'It was me what found Mr Winter, sir.'

'And what time was that?'

'Six o'clock, sir. I brought him a cuppa every morning at six, and one last thing at night.'

John gestured towards the empty cup and saucer sitting by the bed.

'That was his one from last night. That's when he'd take his arsenic.'

John frowned.

'He took a little every night, sir. Said it was for medicinal purposes.'

'What sort of medicinal purposes?'

Tom shrugged and shook his head.

'Any change to his routine last night?'

'He had friends over. Full as a goat he was when he went to bed. Mrs Winter was out for the night, visiting her sister in Knightsbridge.'

'And did he call for you at any point in the night?'

'No, sir. Quiet as the grave, it was.'

John frowned. If Winter took arsenic every day, he'd have

had some immunity to the stuff. How much would he have needed to take – accident or otherwise – to kill himself?

'He didn't call again for more tea? To dissolve the arsenic in?'

'Why would he do that? He'd already taken it. I watched him.'

Arsenic was very difficult to dissolve in cold water, John knew, and nasty stuff to take on its own. He turned again to look at the body. 'Is your master the same fella as nearly got run down a few days ago?'

'That's right, sir. He was in all the papers. Runaway horse and carriage. Brush with death, they called it.'

John remembered the story. He dismissed the lad and crossed to the nightstand. The usual items: watch, watch chain, coins, notes. Then his eye lit on something that made him take a slight inhalation of breath. A small, decorative gold item, heavily engraved.

Behind him, footsteps slowly mounted the stairs, punctuated by the laboured breathing of Jeffers, his senior officer. John slipped the Stanhope into his pocket. The wheezing grew louder. Jeffers was carrying far too much weight these days. Promotion had made him lazy. Greedy, too.

John turned to see Jeffers leaning heavily on the doorknob with one hand, the other holding his chest.

'Oh, it's you, Price,' he said, barely able to keep the disdain out of his voice. 'And this, I take it, is Mr Lionel Winter.' He nodded towards the body on the bed, wiping his brow with a handkerchief that looked as if it badly needed a wash. 'Arsenic, they're telling me.'

'Maybe, sir,' John said. 'But there's no signs of this being death by arsenic.'

'Well, thank Christ for that, Price. Not that I'd be the one clearing it up, mind.'

John showed Jeffers the teacup, and repeated what Tom Neville had told him.

'We should send it for testing,' John said.

'No need for that,' Jeffers said, dismissively waving a plump hand. 'It's pretty clear what happened here. Servants say he took arsenic for so-called "medicinal reasons". Went to bed full up to the knocker last night. Took a second dose by mistake.'

'Well, the autopsy will confirm it, I suppose,' John said.

Jeffers snorted. 'Autopsy? Don't be a fool, man. It's obvious what happened here. Get the undertakers out quick smart. Remove the body before the widow gets home. Can't stand to see the ladies upset.'

John went to protest, but Jeffers had already turned away without waiting for a response, and started his slow descent of the stairs.

John pulled the Stanhope out of his pocket. He took it to the window and held it to his eye. A woman, young and pretty, her clothes rearranged to catch the eye. A face he recognised from the conversation with Albert in the Crown four nights ago.

Rose Watkins.

SEVEN

Albert leaned forward in his seat, resting his elbows on his knees, while John filled him in on Lionel Winter's death, the fact there had been no signs of arsenic poisoning, and his discovery of the Stanhope containing Rose's photograph.

'So, Rose has a Stanhope with Winter's photograph inside, and Winter has one with Rose. And now they're both dead,' Albert said. 'Did anyone wish Winter any harm?'

'Well, he *was* running for Parliament. But no, according to everyone I questioned, he had no enemies. Or at least none who disliked him enough to kill him.'

'Do we know the contents of his will?'

John shook his head. 'Too soon. Rumour has it Winter's business interests weren't thriving. But that don't exactly fit with his plans to enter Parliament which is, by all accounts, a rich man's game. Ever thought of it?'

Albert ignored the jibe. 'His wife? If you believe what you read in the papers, poisoning's a woman's game.'

'She was away the night of his death. Visiting her sister in Knightsbridge. The servants all confirmed she wasn't in the house.'

'Did you speak to her?'

John nodded. 'Jeffers weren't too happy about it. Said we

should "respect the privacy of a grieving widow". But she didn't exactly seem grief-stricken to me. Shocked, yes. But there was a coldness about her. Like her husband's death was an inconvenience.'

Albert reached up to the mantelpiece and retrieved an empty clay pipe, refusing John's offer of a cigarette. 'Helps me think,' he said, rubbing the stem of the pipe between his thumb and index finger. 'Don't know why.'

A few moments passed before Albert spoke again. 'Were there any signs of forced entry? It could have been a burglary gone wrong.'

John shook his head. 'Nothing. The house was locked up tight. Could only be opened from inside. Or outside, if you had a key. Nothing was taken, neither. The Stanhope was just left lying on the nightstand. Must be worth a bob or two.'

'And who had the keys?'

'Winter. The cook used to have a set, but last week Winter took them off her, which she weren't too happy about, and he had all the locks changed. Got very twitchy after his incident with the runaway horse. Hired a bodyguard, apparently.'

'What?'

'I know. Seems a bit much. If the business with the runaway horse was an accident, why would he be bothered about keeping his house locked up tight? But, if it weren't an accident, if it was deliberate, then maybe we're now looking at murder, and either the killer had a key, or someone inside the house let them in.'

'What about the bodyguard?'

'I spoke to him. He didn't sleep in the house, just escorted Winter when he was outside. He's got an alibi for the night of Winter's death.'

Albert was silent a moment longer. 'Does it bother you?' he asked. 'Not telling Jeffers about the Stanhope?'

'A bit. It's evidence, ain't it? Connecting two deaths. But it struck me there weren't much point in mentioning it to Jeffers. I've always been a bit suspicious of his rise through the ranks, as you know. And he was in a mighty hurry to have the whole business tidied away. He'd have come up with some convenient explanation. Besides, if it weren't for you I wouldn't have known what it was anyway.' He paused, drew on the last of his cigarette, threw it into the fire and lit another. 'And you got to me, to be honest. All that talk about Rose being a good girl, just trying to earn a living. Makes me want to help. If I can.'

'Did you check the body for needle marks?'

'Just his arms. Nothing visible. What looked like bruises on his chest, but I didn't have time to look any closer 'cos the minute Jeffers arrived on the scene the body was whipped away faster than you can say Jack Robinson. If that arsenic was injected, or if Winter was given something else to kill him, we'll never know.'

'Thoughts?'

'Well, maybe Maud Winter finds the picture in her husband's Stanhope. Fit of jealousy. Does away with him.'

'Except you said she didn't appear grief-stricken, so why would she be so consumed by jealousy she'd kill her husband? And it doesn't explain Rose. It would take a lot of strength to hang a fully grown woman and I'm assuming Maud Winter isn't built like a navvy.'

'Could just be coincidence, I suppose. Rose and Lionel knew each other, had a bit of a romance. Each of them ends up dead for entirely separate reasons. Maybe it is all just as it appears.'

'You're not buying that, though, are you? If you were, you wouldn't be here.'

John slowly shook his head. 'No,' he said, 'I'm not buying it. But there's only so much I can do about it. It's been made very clear to me that this case is closed. You, however, are no longer a member of the Metropolitan Police Force, bound by its rules. You are a brilliant detective, and it wouldn't be too difficult for you to discover Mr Winter's address and arrange a meeting with his widow, would it? Particularly not if I tell you he lived at 37 Stafford Street. In the meantime, I'm gonna have a chat with a certain undertaker who took away Winter's body. He owes me a favour.'

EIGHT

Albert had expected a polite refusal to his request to meet Maud Winter, but she had replied promptly, suggesting midday as a suitable time. Albert was intrigued that she had agreed so readily.

It was a walk of about three miles from his home, skirting Green Park and Hyde Park. The day had turned unseasonably mild, and the parks were full of people snatching the last of the good weather before winter set in: governesses with their wards, elderly matrons, young couples. Albert envied them their companionship. Ten years ago, he had been on the verge of marrying Miss Clara Wallace, deemed by everyone an excellent match. Their fathers had been business associates. When he announced his intention to join the police, Clara decided her second cousin was a much more attractive prospect than Albert. Some days he wondered what his life would be like now had he followed the path expected of him. Children, he imagined. A friendly face to talk to when he got home. A warm body to curl up with at night.

The Winter residence on Stafford Street was in an unostentatious terrace, just to the north of Kensington High Street. The houses had been built in the last few years, the trees that lined the pavement still only saplings and the houses noticeably narrower than those on neighbouring streets.

Up a short flight of steps, the front door was adorned with black crape tied with white ribbon, and all the windows had their blinds drawn. At Albert's knock, a parlour maid opened the door with quiet efficiency. She was a sharp-faced young woman, with eyes set too close together, thin lips and sallow skin that looked as if she rarely ventured outside. A ruby-coloured birthmark covered the left half of her face. Over her print dress she wore a black armband. As she took Albert's hat and coat, he noticed her hands were rough and reddened, unusual for a parlour maid. She took his name and led him to the morning room at the rear of the house.

The woman who rose to greet him wore deep mourning, her hair hidden beneath a widow's cap. But, unlike Ida Watkins, Maud Winter's mourning was an expensive jet-black silk. No scratching here, Albert thought. She was tall for a woman, slender, and wore her clothes with considerable elegance. As she moved towards him, Albert was struck by her beauty. Her eyes were a very pale blue, almost grey, with heavy eyelids that made her look as if she was on the edge of sleep. She had a long straight nose and a full lower lip. Beautiful, he thought dispassionately, but not a beauty to move him. For the briefest of moments he thought of the asymmetry and expressiveness of Minnie Ward's face, the vivacity of her movements, and then he pushed the thought from his mind. Maud Winter's skin was unnaturally pale against the black of her dress, and there were dark shadows under her eyes.

Also standing was a middle-aged gentleman in an expensive black suit. He wore his hair and whiskers cut short and had a bright intelligence about his eyes. He viewed Albert with close attention.

'Mr Easterbrook,' Maud Winter said, offering him her hand. 'And might I introduce Mr Gillespie, my late husband's close friend and legal representative.'

There was a clipped quality to her voice as she introduced Gillespie which suggested to Albert she did not welcome the other man's presence.

The two men shook hands and waited for Maud to sit. Albert accepted the offer of tea and glanced round the room. It was pleasant. The rear of the room was fitted with tall windows almost running from floor to ceiling, which flooded the space with light. The William Morris wallpaper and a mantelpiece crowded with Japanese boxes and ornaments spoke to a love of the Aesthetic movement. But on closer inspection, the room revealed itself. What had at first seemed to be oil paintings lining the walls were, in fact, prints, some of which appeared to have been cut from newspapers. Albert was reminded of the parlour maid's roughened hands. The Winters were not as wealthy as they wished to appear; and yet Maud Winter had spent a considerable amount on her mourning dress. And Winter had been planning on entering Parliament.

Albert turned his attention back to Maud, who was looking at him closely. 'I knew the name was familiar to me,' she said. 'You are Adelaide Banister's brother, are you not? Adelaide Easterbrook as was?'

Albert nodded, understanding at once why Maud had agreed to see him. The scandal of his decision to join the police had long died down, but he knew he was still an object of curiosity to many people.

'Yes,' Maud said, 'I believe I danced with you once, years ago, at some tedious ball or party. We were children, really.

You have been notable for your absence from such functions in recent years.'

There was an upward tilt to her voice that suggested she was asking him a question, requesting an explanation for his absence. But Albert's estrangement from his parents had been much talked about at the time. There was no possibility Maud Winter had remained ignorant of the falling-out. If she was trying to unsettle him, it wouldn't work.

'My parents disagreed with my choice of career,' Albert said, holding her gaze.

'Ah, yes. You are … a police officer, are you not?' A faint shadow of distaste crossed her face.

Albert was used to the look; it was one his parents had worn ever since he announced his career intentions. It still hurt to remember his father's lip curled in disgust, his mother's brow furrowed with confusion and distress. But he didn't much care what strangers thought of him.

'I was,' Albert said calmly, 'for a number of years.'

'But then you came to your senses,' Gillespie said, smirking and looking at Maud for validation. She gave him a sour half-smile, and angled her body away from his.

'I have worked as a private detective since '74. Which is what has brought me here today. I am investigating a murder,' he said, choosing his words with care to provoke a reaction, 'and have been alerted to certain … similarities … to your husband's demise.'

Gillespie leaned forward. 'Mr Easterbrook, Lionel was not murdered. It was a tragic accident, but not murder.'

'I did not say it was. Mr Winter was an habitual user of arsenic and he accidentally administered an excessive dose. That is the story, is it not?'

'It's no story,' Gillespie said abruptly.

'An unfortunate choice of words,' Albert said. 'My apologies.' The alarm was evident on Gillespie's face; Albert had found his mark. He paused for a moment as the parlour maid entered the room with tea. She placed the tray on a side table near where Maud was sitting and shot Albert an anxious glance, before hurriedly leaving the room.

'As I said, there are some similarities to a case I am investigating. The death of a young woman,' Albert said, looking carefully at Maud and Gillespie. 'A music hall performer by the name of Rose Watkins.'

The mention of Rose's name produced no response.

'She was found hanged under the Adelphi Arches ten days ago,' Albert continued.

'Hanged? Suicide, then,' Gillespie said dismissively.

Albert suppressed the retort that sprang to mind. 'Not according to her mother,' he said, fighting to keep his voice calm and dispassion-ate.

Maud pursed her lips as if tasting something bitter. 'How could Lionel's death be in any way connected to this ... music hall performer?'

'A certain item was found in the belongings of Rose Watkins. A Stanhope.' Albert withdrew the Stanhope from his pocket and passed it to Maud.

'Does it look familiar, Mrs Winter?' Albert asked.

She peered at it, tracing the intertwined initials with a slender finger.

'It's my husband's club. The Godwin. GC, you see?' she said, holding the piece out to Albert and pointing to the initials. Albert was annoyed he hadn't worked out the connection for himself. 'I believe every member of the club is given an item like this to denote membership. A tie pin, a bauble such as this to hang from a watch chain. This was found in the dead girl's belongings, you said?'

Albert nodded.

'A gift, then,' Maud said. 'Music hall girls do invite … admirers … do they not? Maybe somebody gave their Stanhope to this girl.'

'Maybe they did, Mrs Winter,' Albert said. 'Are you aware of how these items work?'

Maud shook her head. Gillespie had barely moved in his seat since the first mention of the Stanhope.

'If you could look closely at the item again,' Albert said, 'you'll see a tiny hole positioned just above the G and C. Hold it up to your eye, and look inside.'

Maud raised the Stanhope and looked. She parted her lips and inhaled sharply. She held the piece to her eye a fraction longer, then lowered it slowly. Without looking at either Albert or Gillespie, she stood abruptly and crossed to the bureau near the windows looking out onto the rear garden.

Opening a drawer in the bureau, Maud rifled through its contents before removing a small gold item. Even from a distance Albert knew it was the Stanhope John had found in Winter's possessions. Maud turned away from the two men and raised the second Stanhope to her eye. A stillness descended on the room, punctuated incongruously by a burst of male laughter which erupted from the servants' quarters down in the basement and was hastily stifled. Maud said nothing, her back and head remained erect, but she placed one hand on the bureau as if to steady herself. From her pocket she withdrew a mourning handkerchief of the finest linen, with a wide black border, and held it to her hairline and her neck.

With a swift movement, she turned back towards the two men.

'Here,' she said, handing Albert the Stanhope she had removed from the bureau, before sitting back down. 'You can keep it. I have no use for such an item, and no desire to be reminded of my husband's particular peccadilloes.'

Gillespie moved to intervene, but Maud swept him aside with a motion of her hand. 'James, I really don't think your presence is required here any longer. I'm sure you have business matters you need to be dealing with.'

For a moment the two held each other's gaze. Surprisingly, Gillespie was the first to look away. Albert had misread the situation: perhaps the power lay with Maud, after all.

'Of course,' Gillespie murmured, removing his pocket watch and glancing at it. 'I do indeed have a meeting I must not be late for.'

He nodded his goodbyes, and left the room.

Albert looked inside the Stanhope Maud had given him, although he knew what he would see.

'This is your husband's?' he asked Maud.

She nodded.

'The woman in that photograph is Rose Watkins,' Albert said. 'The woman whose death I am investigating.'

Maud smiled bitterly. 'So? My husband was carrying around a grubby little photograph of a music hall girl. Whitechapel tourism, isn't that what they call it?'

'Do you know of any connection that your husband had with Rose Watkins?' Albert asked, once again suppressing the retort that sprang to his lips. 'Did he ever make any mention of her? Did he visit the Variety Palace, the music hall where she worked?'

'I have no knowledge of what my husband did in his leisure hours. He told me he was at the Godwin every night, and I believed him.'

Albert nodded. 'Your husband was a regular user of arsenic, I understand?'

'Indeed. I warned him many times that it was a dangerous undertaking. But he entertained the notion that arsenic improved his circulation. Some nonsense he read in a periodical. There was no arguing with him when he was taken with an idea.'

'Forgive me for touching on such a delicate matter, but do you have any reason to believe the overdose of arsenic might have been knowingly self-administered?' Albert asked.

'If you are speaking of suicide, there is no question of it. Lionel would have described himself as a profoundly happy man. He had everything to live for.'

'Had there been any change in him recently, Mrs Winter?'

She frowned. 'I assume you are referring to the accident my husband was involved in last week?'

Albert nodded.

'The newspapers somehow got hold of the story and wrote a great deal of melodramatic nonsense about it,' she said. 'Such an event might happen to anyone who walks through the park late at night. I expected my husband to dismiss it as a lucky escape.'

'But he didn't?'

'He did not. He was visibly shaken by the whole affair. The next morning he hired a bodyguard to accompany him every time he left the house. A bodyguard ... can you imagine? A filthy man, hands like shovels. Then Lionel had all the spare sets of keys returned to him. Said he would lock up every night. A ridiculous inconvenience, but he insisted. I assumed his fear would pass with time, but there was no opportunity for it to do so. On Thursday he demanded the return of the house keys, and on Monday morning he was discovered dead.'

'Was there any other reason for him to be fearful?'

Her hands lay elegantly in her lap but Albert noticed a compulsive movement on her part, the thumb and index finger of her right hand constantly circling each other.

'No,' she said quietly. 'No other reason for him to be fearful.'

'You seem … distracted. Is there anything you're not telling me, Mrs Winter?'

'My husband has just died, Mr Easterbrook. Distraction is understandable in the circumstances, don't you think? Now, if we're quite finished, I have matters to attend to.'

She rose and Albert took his leave.

Turning left out of the house, Albert removed the Stanhope from his pocket and looked closely at Rose's image. The photograph contrasted strongly with the carefully contrived publicity shot he had been given by Ida. Rose's skirt was pulled up to reveal an attractive expanse of thigh, the bodice pulled down to within an inch of total immodesty. But it was her face that drew Albert's eye. There was an energy about her in this photograph, her head tilted to one side, a smile playing about her lips, her blonde curls loose about her shoulders. This was the real Rose, he felt. The photograph almost brought her back to life.

As he'd anticipated, Gillespie was waiting for him on the corner of Phillimore Street. The two men fell into step, as if the meeting had been prearranged.

'Listen, Easterbrook,' Gillespie said, 'I didn't want to say anything in front of Mrs Winter, but Lionel recently increased his dosage of arsenic.'

'How do you know?'

Gillespie shrugged. 'He told me. It was no secret.'

'And was he taking it for circulation problems?' Albert asked.

'No idea. I've heard tell it's a pretty good aphrodisiac, mind. Tried it once myself, but it did nothing.'

'By how much did he increase the dosage?'

'Couldn't tell you. But arsenic accumulates in the body, or so I've heard. You can end up overdosing accidentally.'

Albert said nothing, merely wondering why this man was so intent on having him believe there was nothing suspicious about Lionel Winter's death. As the two men reached Kensington High Street, Gillespie held out his hand. As Albert shook it, he glanced down at a decorative pin in the lapel of the other man's coat. The symbol was one he was becoming all too familiar with: an intertwined G and C for the Godwin Club.

NINE

Minnie narrowed her eyes. 'Far too big,' she said, assessing Cora in the gent's dinner jacket. 'Needs taking in everywhere.' She reached for her pins and started to make the adjustments.

'You're a brick, Min,' Cora said, as Minnie slowly circled her, mouth full of pins. 'I'd never have managed it on my own.'

Up on the stage, Daisy Mountford lay on a table, a sheet carefully positioned over her body. Standing behind her was Paul Prentice, a stethoscope round his neck, a magnifying lens strapped to his head. And a butcher's cleaver in his hand.

Daisy and Paul were trying out a new act on Kippy, the stage manager. Paul was insistent that it be billed as a Thyestean feast. Minnie had asked Bernard what the word meant; after he'd finished explaining, she would have given a lot to remove the images from her head.

'And, lo, the entrails,' Paul announced, as he appeared to pull a string of sausages from Daisy's body while she turned towards the near-empty auditorium with a look of exaggerated alarm on her face. Beside Paul was a makeshift stove. He threw the sausages into a frying pan and rubbed his hands with theatrical glee.

Kippy sighed. 'At what point does this become amusing, Paul?'

'Well, I thought the old bags o' mystery was quite amusing.'

'No. Sausages, in themselves, are not funny. You have to make them funny. Which you are failing to do, quite spectacularly I must say. What else have you got?'

Paul readjusted his stethoscope.

'And, lo, the liver,' he said, a little less confidently this time, holding up a slimy piece of meat which slid out of his hands and landed with a fat plop on the stage. Before he had a chance to retrieve it, a monkey appeared from the wings, ate the meat in one swift gulp and ran off again.

Kippy yelped with laughter. 'Now that,' he said, 'is more like it.' He turned to Minnie and Cora, who nodded their agreement.

Paul looked confused. 'Not part of the act, Kippy.'

'Well, make it part of the act, Paul. And the script – it needs a bit of work, don't you think?'

Paul frowned. 'If you say so, Kippy,' he said thoughtfully. 'But what exactly is the problem with the script?'

Daisy sat up on one elbow. 'It stinks up here,' she said.

From backstage, Tansie hollered, 'That fucking monkey has just chucked up over my new shoes.'

Cora sighed and smiled to herself. She glanced shyly at Minnie. 'He's lovely, ain't he?'

Minnie removed the pins from her mouth. 'Who? The monkey?'

'No,' Cora laughed, punching Minnie playfully on the arm. 'Tansie.'

'Really? "Lovely" ain't the first word that springs to mind when I think of Tanse. "Loud", maybe?'

Cora sighed again. 'Minnie,' she said carefully, taking a quarter-turn to her right as instructed.

'Cora,' Minnie said, mimicking Cora's intonation precisely as she adjusted the sleeve length by a fraction more.

'I was wondering—' Cora tailed off.

'C'mon, girl. Spit it out.'

'Well. I don't want to tread on any toes, so you can just tell me no and I won't make a move. But, I was wondering. You and Tanse. Is there anything I should know?'

'Like what?' Minnie said, standing back to survey her handiwork.

'You know. I mean, he's lovely, ain't he? And you two are such good chums. I wouldn't blame you.'

Understanding slowly dawned on Minnie. Tansie's success with women never failed to surprise her. Short and brash, a gob on him that would make a navvy blush, and a wallet that rarely saw the light of day. And yet he had women falling all over him.

'You think there's something … *romantic* going on between me and Tanse?'

In the distance, Tansie's voice went up several octaves. 'And what the fuck has he been eating?'

'Well, I wouldn't blame you if there was,' Cora said.

'Tansie? Our Tansie?' Minnie said, holding up her hand, palm down, to a height of approximately three feet from the ground. 'Really?'

Cora looked at Minnie's raised hand and blushed. 'He's so lovely and little, ain't he? You could just pop him in your pocket and take him home to your ma.'

From backstage, Tansie's rage had reached stratospheric levels. He was screaming for Paul Prentice's cleaver.

'No,' Minnie said. 'There's nothing going on between me and Tansie. Fill your boots.' She inserted a few more pins along the waistline. 'There. You're done.'

Cora carefully extricated herself from the jacket, taking care not to pierce herself with any of the pins. She turned towards Minnie. 'You don't think it's too soon?' she said hesitantly. 'You know … after Rose?'

Minnie paused, then reached forward and placed her hands on Cora's shoulders. 'As Bernard would say, "nothing 'gainst Time's scythe can make defence, save breed". Although perhaps get him to take you out for supper a few times first.'

'And you're sure there's nothing between you and him?'

'Oh, I'm certain,' Minnie said.

Cora glowed with excitement, snatched up the dinner jacket and scurried backstage.

A door slammed at the front of the auditorium, and the now familiar figure of Albert emerged from the gloom. Minnie found herself smiling.

'Miss Ward,' he said, removing his hat. 'Mrs Watkins said I might find you here.'

On stage, Daisy sat up from under the sheet. 'Ooh, I know you, don't I?' she shouted across the auditorium, waving vigorously. 'From the other night? It's Albert, ain't it?'

Albert limply returned the wave, his hand barely rising above waist height.

'No more mesmerism for me, Albert,' Daisy said. 'New act. Can't get my tongue round the name of it. I just call it comic disembowelling,' and she gestured to another string of sausages lying across the sheet.

'Only not so comic,' Minnie said quietly.

'You all right, Albert?' Daisy shouted.

Albert nodded.

'So, the Queen of Mesmerism's allowed to call you Albert,' Minnie murmured.

Albert winced. 'That appears to be an unfortunate legacy of Saturday night's events. I don't really know how to stop her now.'

'But it's not killing you, is it? You ain't being arrested by the etiquette police?'

Albert ignored her comment. 'I have some news. Nothing conclusive, but something of note. I've informed Mrs Watkins, but I thought you might also be able to help.'

Minnie raised an eyebrow and offered him a seat.

He glanced up at the stage. 'Somewhere quieter?' he suggested.

'Brown's?'

Albert nodded. Minnie grabbed her coat and hat, and the two made their way to the tea room. Once seated, Albert recounted his visit to Stafford Street, and the curious matter of the two Stanhopes with their connection to the Godwin Club. Minnie listened carefully, not saying or asking anything until Albert had finished speaking.

'The Godwin,' she said. 'That's the fancy one, ain't it?'

Albert nodded. 'The most exclusive gentlemen's club in London. Or so they'd have you believe. Unparalleled luxury, fiendishly difficult to become a member, and its ownership is shrouded in secrecy. All part of the mystique.'

Minnie was quiet for a moment. 'Rose was found hanged,' she said eventually. 'This Lionel Winter was poisoned … maybe. If they're both murders, would it be the same person that did it?'

Albert slowly nodded his head. 'That has been a concern of mine. Killers tend to adopt the same method for each murder. But it would have taken some considerable effort to hang Lionel Winter, a fully grown man. Poisoning may have been more expedient.'

'But it does seem like Rose and this Lionel knew each other, at the very least. What did you get out of his servants?'

'Nothing, yet,' Albert said. 'They were decidedly close-lipped. I'll go back again. See what I can find.'

'Or I could go. They'll be more likely to talk to me.'

Albert sighed. 'Not again, Miss Ward.'

Minnie shrugged. 'Just saying.'

Albert paused for a moment. 'There may be something you can help me with. The Stanhope photograph of Rose; I'm wondering if you might look at it, see if there's anything in it you recognise. Although, I have to warn you, Rose is in rather a … compromising state of dress.'

Minnie gave Albert a hard stare. 'Albert – sorry, *Mr Easterbrook* – I've been working in the halls since I was knee-high to a grasshopper. I live round the corner from Holywell Street. There's nothing you can show me I ain't seen before.'

Albert nodded, and handed her Winter's Stanhope.

She held it in her hand for a moment. 'Pretty, ain't it?' she said. 'And you'd never know, to look at it.'

'That's the whole point, I believe.'

She looked closely at the image. 'Nothing,' she said quietly. 'It's funny, though, seeing her like that. Knowing what happened to her—'

Albert passed her his handkerchief. After a few moments she blew her nose loudly and went to hand back the handkerchief before remembering herself.

'I'll get it back to you,' she said, pushing it up the sleeve of her dress. 'Laundered, of course.'

Minnie left Albert outside Brown's and retraced her steps to the Palace. She let herself in by the stage door, the noises of the street falling away as she closed the door behind her.

The backstage corridors were relatively quiet, the only noise the thud and clatter of bowling balls from next door. There was no sound from the stage. Daisy, Paul and Kippy must have finished their run-through and popped out for a bite to eat; Cora had joined them, Minnie guessed. Tansie was most likely immersed in paperwork in his office.

Minnie could hear her footsteps echoing as she tapped along the rough stone floor to what was ambitiously named the wardrobe room but was little better than a cupboard. Most performers at the Palace brought their own costumes, but Tansie had collected a few bits and pieces over the years that came in handy when a turn forgot their outfit, or something split, worn thin from years of use. The room was lined with hooks screwed into the walls, costumes hanging from them. After searching for a few minutes, Minnie found what she was looking for. A dress of garnet silk that had last been used in a panto two years ago. A dress that looked exactly like the one worn by Rose in the Stanhope photograph.

So, Minnie thought, Rose could have borrowed the dress from the wardrobe. But Tansie kept a close eye on everyone as they left the Palace at the end of the night's performances, and a dress was a difficult thing to hide.

Could Rose have worn it under her own clothes?

There was nothing special about the dress. On close examination, it was torn in several places near the hem, and there was a clumsy alteration, presumably to make it fit a girl much smaller than it had been originally made for. But Minnie remembered Rose sighing over it on more than one occasion, lamenting the fact she never got to wear anything so 'fancy' in her act.

Minnie sat on a stool, the dress lying across her lap. She thought back to the Stanhope photograph. It wasn't just the dress, she knew that. Behind Rose, visible but blurred, there had been something on the wall. Albert had not commented on it, and Minnie assumed he had not noticed. Understandable, given the way Rose held the eye. But Minnie had noticed. It was an image she was all too familiar with.

She rose and placed the dress back on the hook. She walked from the wardrobe room, through the corridors and out onto the stage. From there, she moved quietly through the auditorium to the promenade bar running along the front of the building. She went to the third of the snuggery doors, and opened it, half expecting to find Billy there, as she had on the night of Rose's death. But the room was empty.

The snuggery was lavishly appointed: two sofas upholstered in pink velvet, the walls lined with an elaborate brocade wallpaper. A small table had been painted gold and was positioned between the sofas. Tansie had spent money here, although he needn't have bothered. The punters' thoughts weren't on the wallpaper or the upholstery; they were on the women who would sit opposite, or next to them, on those sofas. Who would drink their champagne and offer a kiss, or sit on their laps, or maybe more. Depending on the chap. And the girl.

All of this was as familiar to Minnie as her own home. So much so, she had almost missed the connection when she looked at the Stanhope image. On the wall facing the door was a poster of a young woman in a print dress, long black apron and a paisley shawl, her hair pulled back into a sober bun. She had adopted a submissive stance, her hands crossed in front of her, her head tilted slightly to one side.

It was an image Minnie loved. Edie Bennett: the Richmond Rocket. When Minnie was maybe eight or nine, she'd sneaked out of the house without her ma knowing and slipped into the Gaiety Theatre behind some woman's skirts. Edie had been headlining, a tiny woman who had the entire music hall in the palm of her hand, with her songs of laughter and loss. She had looked just like the women who lived down Minnie's street. And she sang about people like Minnie and her ma. She made Minnie feel that she mattered, even when the whole world was telling her otherwise.

Minnie was fairly sure Edie had never performed at the Palace. But she and Tansie were old chums. It would have been easy enough for him to get hold of one of Edie's posters to decorate the snuggery. For all Minnie knew, this poster could be in hundreds of theatres and music halls; it might even grace the walls of private homes, so famous had Edie been at the time. The fact it was there, in the background of that Stanhope image of Rose, didn't mean the photograph had been taken in this room. And yet Minnie knew, somehow, it had been. And if it had been taken in this room, then someone familiar with the Palace had taken the photo. And Tansie knew everything that went on in the Palace. Tansie, who had seemed unwilling to entertain the idea of Rose's death being anything other than suicide. Tansie, who had been Minnie's friend and benefactor for more years than she cared to remember.

Minnie rose, and left the snuggery, closing the door quietly behind her. She knew she should tell Albert about the poster, and her suspicions about where the photograph might have been taken. But Tansie was her friend. He had looked after her, years ago, when she had needed help the most. And he had never laid a finger on her, or even tried to. She could not bear the idea he might have anything to do with Rose's death.

Besides, she still wasn't sure what she thought about Albert. She had to admit that the days when he appeared at the Palace did seem a little brighter. But she was cautious around men: she'd learned to be. She didn't yet know if she could trust him. So, for now, she'd keep mum about the photograph being taken in the snuggery.

And she'd keep mum about her plan to get inside the Winter household, and see just how close-lipped the servants really were.

TEN

Minnie and Ida sat at the kitchen table in Ida's rooms. Ida was working on an order of artificial flowers, and Minnie was lending a hand.

'So, you reckon she knew him?' Ida asked, winding a strip of green paper round a wire stalk before passing it to Minnie, who was attaching silk leaves to the wire.

'Well, if she didn't it's very strange that they had photographs of each other.'

Ida pushed back her chair and stood carefully, placing her hands on the small of her back and arching backwards with an audible groan. She took the kettle, filled it from the pump in the yard, and put it on the stove. Minnie and Rose had counted once: Ida had drunk twenty-four cups of tea in a day, reusing the leaves until they were spent.

Ida glanced at the clock. 'Ain't it time you were gone?' she said.

Minnie stood, removing the large apron covering her clothes and sweeping off the strands of silk that had found their way onto her dress.

Ida looked at Minnie, narrowing her eyes appraisingly. Minnie had chosen her dress with care; the lavender print was not her newest, but she knew it suited her.

'You look nice,' Ida said.

'Not too nice?' Minnie asked. She wanted to look friendly, approachable. A little bit simple, maybe.

Ida smiled. 'No, not too nice. Just nice enough.' She paused, wiping her hands on a cloth. 'You will be careful, won't you, Min? You don't know what you're walking into.'

'You sound like Albert.'

'Well, he should know.'

'I'll be careful,' Minnie said, placatingly. 'I'm only gonna have a chat with the servants. See if there's anything the great Mr Easterbrook might have missed.'

Ida frowned. 'Don't you like him? Should we have chosen someone else?'

Minnie shrugged. 'He's all right, I suppose. Won't accept that maybe that fancy accent won't get him everywhere he needs to go. But that's where I come in, ain't it?'

'Well, don't you go upsetting him. We need him, remember?'

'Yes, Ida, I remember,' Minnie said, draining the last of her tea and taking her coat and bonnet from a hook behind the door.

Ida held open her arms and pulled Minnie towards her. The older woman had a familiar smell that Minnie had never been able to pinpoint: something to do with flour and wet wool. Whatever it was, Ida smelled of home. Since Rose's death, she had taken to hugging Minnie at every opportunity. Minnie did not complain.

Taking her leave, Minnie turned left out of the house, an old-fashioned, wooden-fronted affair, with a tobacconist's on the ground floor. Nearby was the notorious Holywell Street; it was a neighbourhood that made most respectable folk blanch, but Minnie had lived on these streets all her life. She no longer noticed the contents of some of the more dubious bookshops; besides, most of the really bad stuff was kept out the back, or up some rickety staircase in a private room. Minnie lived nearby on Catherine Street, close to the Palace and, most importantly, with an affordable rent.

She weaved her way through the maze of narrow, dark alleys and lanes onto the Strand and then crossed the bottom of Trafalgar Square. She remembered her mother telling her about the huge bronze lions that were to be installed around Nelson's Column, her childish delight at the idea. By the time the lions were finally unveiled, after long delays and spiralling costs, Minnie's mother was dead, and Minnie had made a lone pilgrimage to see them.

After a short walk she reached the more affluent area around St James's Park. Although the weather had turned colder and the sky was overcast, it was still pleasant to walk these streets, with their larger houses, steps up to the front door and window boxes enjoying a final flourish before winter set in. Leaves swirled around her feet, the wind whipping at her heels. On another day, Minnie would have lingered, imagining a life somewhere like this. But not today.

After walking for about an hour, Minnie turned into Stafford Street. It wasn't difficult to figure out which house belonged to the Winters, with the visible signs of mourning on the door, and the lowered blinds. As she approached number 37 she shook the dust from her skirts, straightened her bonnet, pinched her cheeks and bit her lips to add a little colour. Checking her watch, she saw it was half past ten. The parlour maid would be busy, and Minnie had just seen the cook leaving with a shopping basket and a list in her hand.

But Albert had mentioned something about a young horse boy. With his master dead, he might be at a bit of a loose end. She approached the front of the house and descended the steps to the servants' entrance.

The lad who answered her knock was young, his features still soft and not yet fully formed, but his heavily freckled skin suggested he spent a good deal of time outdoors. He was short but wiry, with a barely contained energy about him. His brown eyes were fringed with the longest lashes Minnie had ever seen. Wasted on a lad. A smile spread rapidly across his face as he took in the trimness of Minnie's waist.

'Tom Neville at your service, miss,' he said. 'How may I help such a fine-looking young lady on such a beautiful morning?'

He looked up at the overcast sky.

'Well,' he said, 'maybe not so lovely, but it's certainly brightened up since you appeared.'

This was going to be easier than she'd thought. She smiled and tilted her head engagingly to one side.

'I was wondering if you had any positions open,' she said. 'I've just come down from Suffolk, moved in with my sister and I'm looking for work.'

Tom winced and shook his head regretfully. 'Nothing at the moment, I'm afraid, Miss—?'

'Ward. Minnie Ward,' she said, cursing herself for not giving a false name. Some detective she was shaping up to be.

'We've just had a bereavement in the house, Miss Ward. Can't think they'll be hiring anytime soon.'

'Oh,' Minnie said mournfully. 'My sister told me this was no way to find a job, that I should sign up with one of them employment agencies. She thinks she's right about everything, and I wanted to prove her wrong. Just once. I've been knocking on doors all morning, my feet are killing me, and I'm parched. Anyway,' she said, turning away, 'thanks for your help, Mr Neville.'

'Wait,' he said, placing a hand on her arm to stop her and glancing behind him. 'Cook's a right bully-rag about visitors, but she's just popped out to the fishmonger's. She's sweet on him, so I reckon we've got at least half an hour before she gets back, and I'm pretty sure I can rustle you up a cuppa.'

Minnie brightened. 'Are you sure? I don't want to get you in no trouble, Mr Neville.'

'No trouble. And it's Tom. You make me think I'm up in front of the beak when you call me Mr Neville.'

'Oh,' Minnie said, wide-eyed. 'Are you often up in front of the beak?'

Tom smiled, threw open the door and ushered her inside the house. Passing through a short flagstone corridor, he led the way into the kitchen at the rear. He lifted the lid of the teapot to glance inside, nodded to himself, and fetched two cups from the dresser.

Minnie remembered she was meant to be an innocent girl newly arrived from Suffolk, so she hung back, hovering just inside the kitchen door. Tom smiled and motioned her to sit at the kitchen table. He passed her a cup of tea and she sipped it carefully, relaxing when she realised he had already added sugar.

'How long you worked here, then, Mr Nev— Tom?' Minnie said, clasping the cup in her hands.

'With the Winters? Three years now. Although I'm not sure if there'll still be a job for me, with Mr Winter gone. I was his horse boy,' he said proudly. He jerked his head towards the rear of the kitchen, and Minnie became aware of the nickering of horses from a mews behind the house.

'Is it him who's died? Your Mr Winter?'

Tom nodded.

'Was he an old chap, then?'

Tom leaned in closer. 'They're saying it was arsenic,' he whispered dramatically, as if the mere mention of the poison might produce a deadly effect.

'Oh, my word,' Minnie said, her eyes narrowing as she too leaned in closer, 'that weren't him who was in the paper, was it?'

Tom nodded. 'That's the chap. And I found him. Terrible shock. Can't get it out of my head.'

Minnie nodded sympathetically. 'Awful way to go. Takes a long time, they say.' She broke off, shaking her head mournfully. 'Makes you wonder why he didn't ring for help,' she said, after a moment's pause.

'I've wondered that myself. But he didn't. Not a squeak out of him. Must have come on dreadful quick.'

Minnie nodded. 'Papers said he took it all the time. The arsenic. Must have taken an awful lot more to end up dead that quickly.'

Tom held her gaze for a moment. Minnie lowered her head and peeped out at him from under her eyelashes before slowly raising the cup to her lips, allowing the steam from the cup to spread a pleasant glow over her cheeks.

'His chum, Mr Gillespie, told the police he'd upped his dose recently,' Tom said. 'Funny that none of us here knew anything about it.'

'That's toffs for you,' Minnie said, 'always thinking they know everything. I'll bet you know ten times more about your Mr Winter than any friend of his. And I'll bet the police didn't pay you no mind.'

Tom nodded enthusiastically. 'Too right. I brought him his tea every night, and I didn't know nothing about any increased dose. And another thing,' he said, gaining momentum as Minnie smiled at him and nodded her encouragement, 'day before he died, Mr Winter ran out of arsenic. He had enough for that night, but no more. Sent me to the chemist to buy some. I put it in his bathroom cabinet.' He stopped, his eyes widening as he waited for the appropriate response from Minnie.

'And?' Minnie obliged, struggling to hide her impatience.

'And, when I checked the morning he died, that arsenic hadn't been opened. So how exactly did he take an overdose?'

'Maybe he kept another packet somewhere else?'

Tom shook his head. 'I know where he kept everything. The arsenic was on a particular shelf in his bathroom cupboard. And it hadn't been opened.'

The kitchen door swung open, and a young woman entered. An ordinary-looking girl, dark-haired, sallow-skinned, apart from a livid-looking birthmark covering half her face. She looked at Minnie then at Tom, and blushed, raising her hand to the birthmark and covering it instinctively. For a fleeting moment, Minnie registered panic on the girl's face, and then it was gone.

'What you doing?' she asked Tom. 'Cook'll murder you if she finds out you've had someone in here.'

Tom tilted his head to one side and smiled at the girl. 'Well, she don't need to find out, does she? Not unless someone tells her.'

'Who's this, then?' the girl asked, a slight tremor in her voice.

'Minnie Ward, meet Annie Belfer, parlour maid. Minnie's looking for work, and I just offered her a cuppa to help her on her way.'

'Cuppa and a load of gossip. What you doing blowing about Mr Winter to a complete stranger?'

'Oh, that's my fault,' Minnie said, 'I asked him. My ma says I'm a right ghoul, and she's not wrong.'

She drained her tea, stood and gathered her things together. 'Thanks for the drink, Tom. Miss Belfer,' and she dropped a half-curtsy to the girl.

Tom exploded with laughter. 'You don't need to go showing her no airs and graces. She's only a bleedin' parlour maid, and not much of a one at that.'

Annie flushed, the birthmark colouring even darker. 'Mash it, Tom,' she said, angrily. She turned towards Minnie. 'Best you be on your way,' she said, not unkindly, 'Cook'll be back in no time. I'll see you out.'

'What you doing Saturday?' Tom asked abruptly, as Minnie buttoned up her coat.

'Nothing,' Minnie said.

'Fancy going to the Cremorne? The Pleasure Gardens? Madame Speltoni's gonna be walking on a tightrope across the Thames from Battersea. They say it'll be quite the thing.'

Minnie was pretty sure Tom had been about to tell her something more before Annie's entrance.

'That'd be lovely,' she said, and they made arrangements to meet.

Annie led Minnie to the front of the house. Just as Minnie was about to leave, Annie touched her tentatively on the arm. 'Tom's not a bad lad, but you don't want to go paying no attention to his foolish ideas. We're all upset by what happened to Mr Winter. But it was an accident. Nothing more.'

Minnie held her gaze, and knew for sure that Annie Belfer was lying.

'So anything you've heard about Winter increasing his arsenic dose is a load of nonsense,' Minnie said, leaning back in her chair.

She was seated in Albert's drawing room, watching him as he toyed with a pipe in front of the fireplace.

'I suspected as much. Gillespie seemed in an awful hurry to convince me. And John managed to extract a favour from the undertaker who took the body. Turns out Winter's blood was a very distinctive bright cherry-red in colour.'

'Meaning?'

'Meaning he was probably poisoned with prussic acid.'

'What's that when it's at home?'

'Very nasty poison. Can kill you in moments. And not the kind of thing you take by accident. John said there were bruises on Winter's chest. I'm guessing he was held down and injected with the poison.'

Albert reached into his pocket for his wallet. 'Well, Miss Ward, you have been most helpful. I trust this will—'

'What are you doing?' Minnie interrupted him.

'I'm paying you. For your time. I'm not happy you inserted yourself into the investigation, but I can't deny the information you gleaned is useful.'

'I don't want payment,' Minnie said, her voice rising. 'I didn't do this for money. I did it to help find Rose's killer. And we ain't found Rose's killer, have we?'

'No,' Albert agreed, 'but you have provided valuable information that will help me pursue other lines of enquiry.'

'I don't think you understand,' Minnie said, leaning forward in her seat. 'What I got from Tom Neville? There's a lot more there than he's letting on. And Annie, the parlour maid? She knows something.'

'I don't disagree with you, Miss Ward. Miss Belfer certainly acted suspiciously when I visited the Winter household. My intention is to speak to both Tom Neville and Annie Belfer again.'

'Or I could speak to them, couldn't I? Tom told me more over a cup of lukewarm tea than he'd have told you in a month of Sundays. And why? 'Cos he's sweet on me, and no offence, Mr Easterbrook, but I don't think you're his type. And Annie? I'd lay you a pound to a pinch of shit – excuse my French – she won't tell you a thing. But me? A hardworking girl just like her?'

'You have a very high opinion of your powers of persuasion, Miss Ward.'

'I have a high opinion of my acting ability, Mr Easterbrook. And with good reason. I worked as a serio-comic and mimic when I first started out in the halls. And a bloody good one I was, too. I've got the cuttings from *The Era* to prove it. By the time I was fifteen I was earning good money. More than I earn now.'

'So why did you stop? If you were successful and you made good money?'

She paused. Everyone knew she didn't speak about her reasons for leaving the stage. But she'd forgotten that she and Albert had only known each other a short while. She hadn't expected his question. 'I had my reasons,' she said eventually. 'Reasons that are none of your business, as it happens. What I'm telling you is, I'm a good actress. I can play any part and convince anyone. I'll find a way to get chatting to Annie, and I'll find a way to get her to open up to me.'

'And then what? I don't know how many times I have to say this, Miss Ward, before you understand me – I don't work with anyone else.'

'Why not?'

This time he was the one who seemed taken aback by the question. 'I just prefer to work alone,' he said after a moment's pause. 'It's one of the reasons I left the police force.'

'Bit lonely, ain't it?'

'It can be,' Albert admitted.

'So what about Sergeant Price? You're happy enough to work with him.'

'I'm not working with him, as such. He's just having a look around, seeing what he can find. And, besides, John is a trained police officer. He understands the dangers of any situation, and he's well able to look after himself.'

'And I'm not?'

'Well … no, you're not. I know you like to see yourself as this invincible creature, Miss Ward, able to take care of yourself in any situation, but believe me, that isn't the case. I saw enough on the force, enough women whose swagger and bravado failed to hide the black eye, the swollen lip, the broken bones. I'm not going to be responsible for placing a woman in harm's way.'

'Well,' Minnie said, thrown by the honesty of his words, 'that's very sweet of you. But I ain't suggesting you add my name to that shiny brass plaque on your front door. Once we find Rose's killer I'm gone. Vamoose, as the Spaniards say. You'll never see me again. But I can help you with Rose. And I think you know that. So, what do you reckon?'

For a brief moment, the two of them held eye contact. Minnie was damned if she'd be the first to look away.

'Very well,' Albert said eventually. 'But there must be rules. You shall not put yourself in the way of any danger. You will only act under my instructions. And you must accept payment from me.'

'I've got some rules too.'

'You are not in a position to set any rules, Miss Ward.'

'Humour me.'

Albert sighed. 'A large cake from Brown's Bakery?'

She smiled. 'Preferably—'

'Victoria sponge,' Albert interrupted.

'And what else?' she said coaxingly.

'I do not feel comfortable calling you Minnie.'

'Call me whatever you like, but I'm calling you Albert.'

'Very well.'

Minnie held out her hand.

'Do you not want to agree terms of payment, before shaking?' Albert asked.

'I trust you,' she said. 'Now shake my hand 'cos I feel like a right fool sitting here.'

They shook hands.

'So,' Minnie said, rising from her seat. 'Today's Thursday. I'm meeting Tom on Saturday. I'll come here on Monday? Midday?'

Albert nodded.

Minnie grinned broadly. 'Miss Minnie Ward. Consulting Detective,' she said. 'Got quite a ring to it, don't it?'

ELEVEN

Minnie caught the 'bus to King's Road, and followed the stream of people heading towards the Cremorne Gardens. The weather had turned warm again, the sky a brilliant blue, and there was a festive air amongst the crowd, as if they were intent on enjoying a last day of fun before winter descended.

Tom was waiting beside a pair of ornate gates marking the entrance to the park. He looked as if he had shrunk since the last time she had seen him, a frown creased his brow, and his flirtatious air had deserted him.

'You all right?' she asked.

'I've been given the boot,' he said.

'No! Whatever happened?'

'Cook found out you'd been in the house. I reckon Annie must have told her, but she swore blind it weren't her. Anyway, next thing I know, Mrs Winter wants to see me, tells me my services are "no longer required" 'cos they'll be getting rid of the horses with Mr Winter gone. That's what she said, but I know it was 'cos I broke the rules. Which is pretty bleedin' rich, given what goes on in that house.'

'Like what?' Minnie asked, trying not to sound too curious.

'Oh … nothing.' He shrugged and shook his head.

'Looks like something to me.'

He shook his head again. 'Really, it's nothing.'

'So, what will you do? About work?' Minnie asked.

He frowned. Behind the bravado of their first meeting, Minnie could see how young he was.

'I'll find something,' he said, forcing a smile. 'Let's forget about it and enjoy our day.'

They made their way down an avenue of elegant elm trees, past elaborate fountains and flower beds, and a lake with paddle boats. Minnie had visited the Cremorne on many occasions, but she remembered this was all supposed to be new to her. So she gasped at the Crystal Grotto, the Fairy Bower, and the Beckwith Frog, a chap with an act not unlike Miranda the Mermaid's, who walked on his hands underwater and offered swimming lessons at Lambeth Pool.

After half an hour of promenading, Minnie and Tom made their way to the banqueting hall for a lemonade.

'Shame it's not champagne,' Tom said, lifting his glass to hers. 'Maybe next time, eh?'

Minnie was touched by his swagger. He'd have difficulty buying beer, never mind champagne, if he didn't get work soon. They took two seats outside by the Pagoda, where a military band was playing selections from popular operas, and couples rotated round a circular dance floor. Waiters weaved between the tables, with plates of lobster and devilled kidneys.

'You should see it here at night,' Tom said. 'Thousands of tiny gaslights they've got, all round the Pagoda and into the trees. Lovely. And there's a fireworks display once a week, and a hot-air balloon.'

'I've heard there's all sorts goes on here at night,' Minnie said.

'You're not wrong. See those?' he said, pointing towards some enclosed private spaces encircling the dancing platform. 'If you was here after ten o'clock at night, you'd be shocked by what goes on in there.' He paused, then added hastily, 'Or so I've been told.'

Minnie knew about the Cremorne at night, peopled with those seeking pleasure of a very different kind to the brass band and lemonade she was enjoying with Tom. After dark, the streetwalkers would appear, the gentlemen seeking a cheap thrill, and Mary-Anns with nowhere else to go. It must be a desperate kind of longing that would send you out into the darkness for a little company. Minnie shivered at the thought of it.

'You all right?' Tom asked her.

'I'm fine.' She smiled at him. 'I just drank my lemonade a bit quick.'

There was a swell in the crowd, and Tom looked at the flyer they'd been given with their tickets.

'The Great Sea Bear is on in the Theatre Magique,' he said, stumbling a little over the last word. 'It's only showing for another ten minutes. Fancy it? We've got half an hour before Madame Speltoni.'

Minnie nodded. They rose and entered the theatre canopy, joining a queue of people trailing past a large tank filled with water. A chap Minnie recognised from his days working the halls was regaling the audience with tales of the creature and its wondrous exploits. 'See, ladies and gentlemen, how the Great Sea Bear – or Walking Fish, as it is known to the natives in its homeland of Alaska – is as comfortable moving underwater as walking on dry land. What other species can that be said of?'

The queue moved forward slowly. Finally, Minnie and Tom were facing the tank. Minnie peered through the murky water, which most definitely needed a clean. Beside her, Tom frowned as he looked at the creature and listened to the showman's patter.

'Ooh,' Minnie said with exaggerated enthusiasm. 'I've never seen the likes of one of these.'

Tom looked at her sceptically. 'You ain't from Suffolk, are you?' he said.

Minnie hesitated long enough to realise she had given the game away.

'I went there once?' she offered.

He took her arm and pulled her out of the theatre and towards a bench in the shade of the elm trees.

'What you after?' he said. 'I knew something was up. I never have this much luck with girls. And no one, not even someone from Suffolk, is stupid enough to believe a seal is a walking fish.'

Minnie guessed that Albert would urge caution, but something about Tom told her he was to be trusted. So she told him about Rose, and the Stanhopes, and how Rose and Lionel Winter had known each other, and how she was working with Albert to uncover the truth. When she had finished, she sat back and studied Tom's face. She hoped she had made the right decision in telling him. He had regained some of his animation from their first meeting; in fact, he looked positively excited. Minnie ventured a question.

'You said something earlier about how it was rich them sacking you for breaking the rules, given what went on in that house. What did you mean?'

Tom winced. 'I'm not sure I should say anything.'

'Why not?' Minnie asked. 'You don't owe them nothing, do you? Not after the way they treated you.'

Tom thought for a moment or two and then slowly nodded his head. 'Mr Winter had a little room out the back, next to the stables,' he said. 'He took photographs of Annie, the parlour maid, out there.'

'Well, there's no harm in that, is there?' Minnie asked.

'Depends on the photographs. These were ones your ma wouldn't be putting on the mantelpiece, if you get my drift.'

Minnie's mind flashed to the image of Rose in the Stanhope.

'Did he take photographs of other women?' she asked. 'Or bring women to the house?'

Tom shook his head. 'Not so far as I know. What I don't understand,' he said, after a pause, 'is why he took those kind of photos of Annie. I mean, she's what you'd call handsome, rather than pretty, ain't she? What we used to call a twixter, when I was growing up.'

'A twixter?'

'A girl who could pass for a lad. Or a lad who could pass for a girl. You know the sort.'

Minnie nodded.

'She's been acting odd, as well,' Tom continued. 'Quiet and huffy like, just before Mr Winter died, and ever since she's been snapping at everyone, jumping at any little noise.'

People were moving with purpose towards the jetty where the pleasure boats moored, and where Madame Speltoni was to complete her journey across the Thames from Battersea.

'Shall we?' Tom said.

Minnie had no interest in watching a tightrope walker. She'd seen enough of them to last a lifetime, but Tom was keen, so she stood and took his arm.

The press of the crowd grew stronger as they approached the jetty. A steep bank leading down to the river provided a good view of the proceedings. On the opposite bank, the tiny figure of a woman could be seen. She had just started her crossing. The crowd was excited, agitated, people standing on tiptoe to get a better look, children being hoisted onto parents' shoulders. All around, people were speculating on Madame Speltoni's progress with cries of 'Ooh, she's wobbled', 'No, she's all right', 'She's wobbled again'. Minnie had seen more drama on a quiet night at the Palace.

Her eyes scanned the throng of people, and she gripped her bag tighter. This was the perfect setting for pickpockets and, sure enough, she spotted a couple at work almost immediately. Two young men, respectably dressed, had positioned themselves either side of a smart-looking gentleman. The gentleman was looking eagerly across the river at Madame Speltoni. The two young men were not. One of them slid his right hand under his left arm. There was the briefest of movements and then he reached behind the gentleman's back and passed a watch to his accomplice.

Tom leaned in towards Minnie. 'Watch yourself,' he said, nodding towards the two young men. 'Divers.'

Minnie nodded, surprised. Clearly Tom had a little more about him than she had thought.

The two men disappeared into the throng but, a few minutes later, Minnie saw them again. This time, they were joined by a third lad. Two of them feigned a quarrel, while the third, knife in hand, cut the trousers of an elderly man to open his pocket and remove his money.

A groan went up from the hordes of people, and Minnie turned back to Madame Speltoni. Things were not going well. The rope had gone slack, and the woman was now hanging by her hands, suspended over the Thames. There was conjecture on all sides, as people wondered whether the famous wire walker might meet a watery end.

'There's boats, ain't there?' Minnie said. 'Out on the river? Can't someone just sail up and get her?'

'The fall would kill her,' one woman said confidently.

'Done a lot of tightrope walking, have you?' Minnie asked, eyeing up the woman's considerable bulk. 'She ain't that high up. Providing there's a boat on hand to pull her out, she'll be fine. Soggy, but fine.'

A loud cheer went up, followed by rapturous applause. The tightrope walker had dropped into the water. A rowing boat with two men in it was heading straight for her and, within a couple of minutes, sure enough they'd fished her out and she was waving to the crowds on the bank.

Minnie and Tom turned away from the spectacle, leaving everyone else rooted to the spot, as if they were expecting Madame Speltoni to sprout wings and fly away as a finale.

Minnie drew her shawl closer round her shoulders. She had grown cold standing out of the sun.

'Let's walk,' Tom said, 'you look freezing.'

They retraced their steps up the elm-lined avenue.

'Your boss,' Minnie said, resuming their earlier conversation. 'It said in the papers he had friends round for dinner the night he died. Might one of them have hurt him?'

'Crikey, you've got an active imagination,' Tom said. 'You should be writing for the *Police News*. Why would any of them do that? They were all his chums from that club of his.'

Minnie said nothing, remembering the two Stanhopes and their link to the Godwin.

'Tell me about Annie Belfer,' she said after a moment or two. 'What does she do with her Saturday half-day?'

'I dunno,' Tom said. 'But she's part of the Temperance Movement, goes every Monday night, regular as clockwork. Divinity Hall on Cornwall Avenue.'

That was Monday night taken care of, then.

'Fancy a cuppa?' Tom asked suddenly. 'Warm you up a bit? There's a tea room up ahead, but there's always a queue. I could go on ahead and have it waiting for you by the time you get there?'

Minnie nodded, and Tom took off, weaving his way swiftly through the crowd. With his absence, Minnie became more aware of the noises, the press of people around her. The spectacle of Madame Speltoni was over, and it felt as if everyone in the Gardens had chosen to walk down this same avenue.

In the distance behind her, she heard her name being called, clear as day. She turned and scanned the multitude of people, wondering if she'd overshot the tea room and Tom was calling for her. But there was nothing. She turned back.

A man stood directly in front of her. He was shorter than Minnie, with a friendly-looking face. He wore a single red rose in his lapel. Unusual for October. She stepped to her right to let him pass, and the man immediately stepped to his left. Minnie smiled at the confusion and stepped to her left. The man tilted his head, and then firmly mirrored her movement. A flare of irritation shot through Minnie. 'I ain't that kind of girl, mister,' she said. 'Let me pass.'

The man did not move. He raised a plump forefinger to his lips in a gesture of silence. He was missing two fingers.

Minnie tried to step back, but the swell of people prevented her movement, even nudging her a little closer to the man.

He took a step forward, close enough now that she could smell a sweet perfume about him that failed to mask the staleness of his breath. He smiled. 'Mind yourself, Miss Ward,' he said, his voice surprisingly rich and ponderous. 'Nasty accidents can happen to young girls. Especially nosy ones. I'd think twice before you sneak off to Brown's with your detective friend.'

Minnie felt a hand on her waist, a tug on her sleeve, all so quick she had no time to respond. Then the man was gone. Remembering the pickpockets she had watched earlier, she reached for her bag, but everything was still there. She turned, looking for the man, but he had disappeared, the crowd swallowing him up.

She heard her name being called again and saw Tom waving from a table outside a tea room.

'Good timing,' he said, as she approached. 'I'd just managed to— Why, Minnie, what on earth have you done?'

She gave him a quizzical look.

'Your dress,' he said.

Minnie looked down. Running from just below her chest to her stomach was a long cut. She placed her hand to it, and felt through the layers of her dress, her camisole and chemise, between the bones of her corset. All cut right through. Her hand touched the flesh of her stomach, and the surprising contact made her flinch. She looked up at Tom, but he was staring at her sleeve. She touched her arm, her fingers slipping through cut fabric a second time. She felt something wet. Slowly she withdrew her hand, her fingertips stained with a red smear of blood.

TWELVE

Albert took the short walk from his house to the Hailsham Gallery in New Bond Street, where he had reluctantly agreed to meet his sister, Adelaide. Albert loved art. He loved his sister even more. He just hated galleries, the press of the crowds and the way every available inch of wall space was crammed indiscriminately with paintings. But Adelaide had insisted in her note to him that the Hailsham was different. Besides, he needed to see her, to ask a favour.

Albert was early, as was his way. He paid his shilling and waited in the vestibule for Adelaide to arrive. She, too, had the habit of punctuality and before long he felt her arm slipping through his. He turned to greet her.

'You're looking well,' he lied. His sister was gaunt and drawn; she had lost weight and it had given her face a hawkish appearance; her aquiline nose now looked beaky and her lips seemed permanently pursed. But Albert had been raised always to compliment a woman, so he swallowed his concern. Her hair, he noted, was as beautiful as ever. Elaborately coiffured, the dark coils massed beneath her hat highlighted the slenderness of her neck.

'Oh, Albert,' Adelaide said, 'it's just you and me. If we can't speak the truth to each other, who can? I look thin and unwell. I had a nasty influenza I fear I'm not yet fully recovered from. If it weren't that I'm desperate to see you, I should not have ventured out today.'

'If you're still unwell, you must take the time you need to recover. I'll still be here, you know.'

She smiled ruefully. 'Monty says I need to do more,' she said. 'Get involved in yet more charity work.'

'Maybe you need to find something a little more meaningful?'

'Like you did?' Adelaide said, smiling at him gently, as they started to mount an impressive flight of stairs up to the main galleries. 'Another police officer in the family would kill Mother and Father. If such a thing were even allowed.'

'Not the police, obviously,' Albert said, 'but something you enjoy. Something that would matter to you.'

'Nothing matters to me, Albert. I spend my days making calls on other women who spend their days doing much the same. I run a household, I attend charity functions where I can't remember what we're raising money for, and, in the evenings, I sit and embroider antimacassars for the backs of chairs to replace the ones we already have, and wait for Monty to come home.' She broke off abruptly and offered him a weak smile. 'Anyway,' she said, 'enough about me. Here we are, and you must tell me what you think.'

They had turned into the East Gallery, and Albert had to acknowledge Adelaide was right: the room was immediately different from any other gallery he had been in. There was space, for a start. Space between the paintings; a couple of feet at least, and everything positioned at eye level. Albert felt as if he could breathe. The parquet floor, covered with richly coloured oriental rugs, was punctuated by large vases of exotic flowers on pedestals. It felt more like someone's private gallery.

'Why didn't you come here with Monty?' he asked Adelaide. 'It's delightful.'

She snorted. 'Monty makes his annual pilgrimage to the Summer Exhibition and declares that's culture done for the year. Besides, he heard a rumour some of the material here is a little … avant-garde, and you know how conservative he is.'

She paused in front of one of the Burne-Jones paintings, and murmured her appreciation.

Albert leaned forward and squinted at the work. 'His women are a little … passive, wouldn't you say? They're all gazing off rather limply into the distance.'

He imagined what a painter would make of Minnie Ward. The way she held your gaze, a smile always playing at the edge of her lips. How the merest flick of the brush might suggest her sardonic raising of an eyebrow. He glanced at his watch. She would be at the Cremorne now, trying to extract information from Tom Neville. Not for the first time, he regretted his decision to involve her in the investigation. She was, he felt, a little wayward. Unpredictable. One of the attractions of working for himself had been the chance to retain control, not to have to bend himself to others' demands or expectations. So why had he let her persuade him so easily?

'How is Mrs Byrne?' Adelaide asked, interrupting his thoughts. 'Still keeping you in check, I trust.'

'A very tight leash, Addy. Some days I think I'm still back in the nursery.'

'Send her my regards,' she said, a shadow crossing her face. Adelaide had always said she wanted Mrs Byrne as her nanny when she had children of her own. Twenty years of marriage to Monty and the couple were still childless.

Adelaide moved forward, pausing in front of another portrait. Her gasp was audible throughout the gallery.

'Good Lord, Albert,' she said, 'it's not – is it?'

Albert leaned forward to examine the card. The portrait was by someone he'd never heard of and the title gave no indication of the sitter, a young woman dressed in black, her hair pulled back simply from her face. In her hands, a length of fabric, possibly cotton, which she held delicately between her fingertips. She was caught in a moment of reverie, her face lifted from her work and turned towards the light. A face Albert had not seen in years, but which still haunted him.

'It couldn't be, could it?' Adelaide asked, and then shook her head as if to dispel the thought. 'No, of course not. This was painted recently. Hetty would be … what? Thirty-five?'

'Forty,' Albert said dully. 'If she were still alive.'

'Was it really that long ago?' Adelaide asked.

'Eighteen fifty-five,' Albert said. 'The thirteenth of June.'

In his mind he returned to that summer, a village in Suffolk, and a memory he kept buried. He was eight years old, Adelaide an unreachably ancient personage of sixteen. The summer had been, in Albert's memory, endless, with every day warm and sunny. Summers weren't like that any more. On the morning of June thirteenth, he woke to the sunlight creeping around the edge of his bedroom curtains and raced downstairs as usual to spend time in the kitchen with Cook and Hetty Paul, the scullery maid. On that morning, though, Hetty was missing, and Cook was swearing under her breath and making loud noises with pots and pans.

It was the dogs who found Hetty later that evening. Albert's father released the two pinchers into the grounds for a run, and they bolted to a space behind the potting shed, before bursting into a volley of barking. Hetty's body was jammed in between the shed and the brick wall surrounding the vegetable garden, the skin of her neck marked by what looked, at first glance, like a scarlet thread. A leather garotte lay nearby.

And then the police came. Their quiet efficiency impressed eight-year-old Albert. He lingered in the corners of rooms, hovered in doorways or halfway up flights of stairs where no one thought to look for him. He saw and heard much more than he should have done. And during the course of the investigation that resulted in no arrests, no suspects even, he learned two things that determined his future course in life.

The first he learned from watching the policemen. They spoke with strong Suffolk accents, their uniforms worn shiny at the elbows and their tall hats perched uncomfortably on top of their heads. They were the kind of people his parents would not even have glanced at had they passed them on the street. But they told Albert's father what to do, and he did as they told him. Albert wondered if they possessed some magic powers, as he had read about in the *Arabian Nights*. Nobody could make his father do anything he didn't want to do, but these two men could.

The second thing he learned was that his parents didn't care very much about Hetty, or what had happened to her. They were unhappy at the inconvenience caused by her death, but she was only a servant and they shed no tears for her. Albert did. Hetty was his closest friend, the kitchen the only place where he felt at home; it was one of the things that had made boarding school so unbearable, the distance from Hetty, Cook and Mrs Byrne.

By the time the investigation was abandoned, Albert knew

he wanted to become a police officer when he grew up. And he knew he would do everything in his power to protect women like Hetty.

'You're not still looking for her killer, are you?' Adelaide said fondly. 'When you were eight you were convinced you could solve the case.'

'Do you know, Addy,' he said, 'when I first joined the force, I truly believed I might be able to. No useful records, though. Nothing to work from.'

'You've made up for it,' Adelaide said, laying her hand gently on his arm. 'There have been other cases, other Hetties.'

Albert thought of Rose Watkins, and his determination to find an answer for her mother.

'I have a favour to ask,' he said, patting Adelaide's hand. 'I'm wondering if Monty could get me an introduction to his club?'

Adelaide frowned. 'You, a clubman? Really? You've never expressed any interest before.'

'Influential people. I wish to expand my business, and it's always about who you know.' Albert hated lying, particularly to Adelaide. But he needed to get inside the Godwin, and Monty was the only person he knew who was a member. Rose and Lionel were linked in some way by that club.

Adelaide grimaced. 'If you want me to, I'll ask Monty, of course. Although, if you're in need of influence—' She tailed off.

Albert said nothing for a moment, and then, more sharply than he intended, 'How are they?'

'Oh, as usual,' she said. 'The cold weather is aggravating Father's rheumatism, and Mother is ... Mother.'

'Still no mention of me?' Albert asked carefully, looking at a canvas without even registering it, and unwilling to acknowledge how much Adelaide's answer mattered.

Adelaide shook her head and smiled regretfully. 'No, my dear. I raise your name every time I see them, but to no avail. Father always says he made his feelings clear at the time, and nothing has changed.'

Albert's stomach churned as he thought of the last time he had seen his parents. His decision to join the police force had been met first with bewilderment, then anger. His father had clawed his way up from the streets of Southwark, eventually amassing a considerable fortune in manufacturing. He had sent Albert to public school with the intention that his son would be elevated into the social rankings that dismissed Easterbrook senior as 'new money'. And then Albert announced his intention to become a police officer and the arguments began. His father hadn't worked so hard, sacrificed so much, for his son to sully the Easterbrook name. Why on earth would a man with his advantages and education choose to become a thief-taker? He was breaking his poor mother's heart. And finally, when the arguments and entreaties were exhausted, the turned back and the silence.

'I can't change who I am, Addy,' Albert said.

'Nor would I want you to,' she said, not entirely convincingly, 'although it would be lovely to see more of you. And Mother, I know, misses you badly. If it hadn't been for Hetty, our lives might be so different now.'

'Not yours, surely,' Albert said.

Adelaide said nothing. Her role in her father's plans had been to make an advantageous marriage, and she had fulfilled his expectations, marrying Montague Banister when she was eighteen. He came from a good family and was not unhandsome. An excellent match, everyone had agreed. But Albert could remember his ten-year-old self first meeting Monty, and even then detecting the steely glint in his eye, and the way his gaze slid over Adelaide as if she were something unappealing on a menu. Albert had often thought to ask her why she had chosen Monty, but the passage of years had made such a question more difficult. Now, though, seeing her so listless and unwell, he summoned up the resolve.

'Why Monty?' he asked. 'There were other choices, as I remember.'

'I thought he was handsome,' Adelaide said, a grim smile playing about her lips. 'I thought he would be kind to me. Mother and Father favoured him. I was eighteen, Albert.'

The brother and sister stood in silent thought for a minute or two, Albert wondering how Adelaide would respond if he told her to come with him now, to leave Monty and her life of respectable unhappiness behind. He stole a glance at her, but her face was impossible to read.

She roused herself and looked at her pocket watch.

'I must be going,' she said, 'Monty and I are out for dinner tonight.'

They left the gallery and descended the staircase. At the bottom, Adelaide turned to Albert.

'Don't leave it so long next time, Albie,' she said, adopting a lightness of tone that failed to hide the serious import of her words. 'I miss you.'

He leaned in to kiss her cheek, holding her close to him and noting again how thin she had become.

'I promise,' he said.

Albert walked home slowly, worrying about Adelaide and wondering what he could do to help. As he approached his house, a cab pulled up abruptly; a young lad in just his shirtsleeves jumped out and then turned to help a young woman out. She had his jacket around her shoulders and he held her by the elbow, as if she was hurt. She looked up as Albert approached, her face pale, one hand holding her blood-soaked arm aloft. His heart caught in his throat.

Minnie.

THIRTEEN

Albert led her into the morning room, closely followed by Tom. She felt the warmth of Albert's arm around her waist, his broad fingers pressed firmly to her side. Mrs Byrne made herself busy banking up the fire, and fetching blankets. Minnie was shaking, had started as soon as she saw Albert outside the house. She felt foolish and yet …she couldn't stop.

Albert guided her towards the chair nearest the fire.

'Let me see to you first,' he said, 'and then you can tell me what happened. Show me, please.'

Minnie was surprised by his lack of preamble. 'It's nothing,' she murmured. 'A scratch.' But a jolt of fear passed through her for the first time, as if the wound might have grown during the cab ride from the Cremorne. She pulled back the material on her sleeve. It had darkened, stained with blood.

Albert peered closer. 'You're lucky,' he said. 'The wound isn't deep, but it does need cleaning. Mrs Byrne?' he said, turning his head towards her slightly, but still keeping his eyes fixed on Minnie.

Mrs Byrne fetched a large marquetry box from the sideboard, and placed it on the table beside Albert.

'I must wash my hands,' Albert said. 'I'll be back in a moment.'

In his absence, the three of them looked uncomfortably at each other.

'You should go,' Minnie said quietly to Tom. 'You've been a brick, but I'll be fine now.'

Tom shook his head. 'I'm staying,' he said, drawing an approving glance from Mrs Byrne.

'There's some fruit cake downstairs,' Mrs Byrne said to him.

'I'm all right,' Tom said dismissively, a sullen shadow crossing his face, reminding Minnie again of how young he was.

'I'm sure you are,' Mrs Byrne said firmly. 'But this young lady is about to have her wound cleaned, and it's not for the likes of you to be gawping at her. Get yourself downstairs. Cups are on the dresser. Teapot's on the table. And don't tell me you're not my servant,' she said, as a peevish look darkened Tom's face, 'because I know you're not. You're a nice young lad who's looked after Miss Ward. And now you're going to carry on being nice and get her a cuppa. The cake's in the tin next to the cups.'

Tom frowned, and then seemed to realise the futility of arguing. He shrugged, and set off for the kitchen.

'Are you in pain?' Albert asked Minnie as he returned to the room, wiping his hands on a towel.

She shook her head.

'Still,' he said, 'you've had a shock. Brandy, I think, Mrs Byrne.'

She nodded, and crossed again to the sideboard where a decanter of brandy and several glasses stood gleaming. She poured a large measure and presented it to Minnie. It was considerably smoother than any Minnie had ever had before, but her first gulp was too big, and she gasped as it burned her throat.

From the marquetry box Albert extracted a bottle of iodine solution and a small piece of cotton.

'You have no objection, I take it?' he asked Minnie.

Minnie glanced at Mrs Byrne, surprised that it was Albert who was to nurse her. 'I'm fine, really,' she said. 'Like I said, it's a scratch. I could see to it myself, only it's my right arm.'

Mrs Byrne patted her hand. 'Mr Easterbrook knows what he's doing. And there's no good asking me. Can't stand the sight of blood. Besides, it's a bit more than a scratch.'

Minnie nodded. Albert parted the torn sleeve, and she flinched at the sight of the wound.

'Am I hurting you?' he asked, looking up and frowning.

'No.'

'Well, stop squirming, then.'

A retort sprang to Minnie's lips, but she decided now was not the time to argue. At least not until he'd finished dressing her wound. She looked down at the top of his head. His hair was thinning, and she wondered if he knew. His hands were warm. She could feel the roughness of his fingertips as he touched her skin. She was surprised by the delicacy and expertise of those boxer's hands, as he moved with swift facility, cleaning the wound and dressing it. Mrs Byrne passed him items without him even asking.

'There,' Albert said, leaning back when the dressing was firmly secured. 'Shouldn't take long to heal, but it may cause you a little pain in the next few days.'

He suddenly looked embarrassed, as if aware for the first time of how he had laid his hands on her skin.

Tom staggered through the door, carrying a tray laden with teacups and fruit cake.

Albert glanced at Mrs Byrne. 'Any more of that brandy left?' he said.

When all four of them had warmed themselves with alcohol, Albert gave Minnie a long look and placed his glass on a side table, before taking a seat opposite her.

'So,' he said. 'Tell me.'

Minnie recounted what she had learned from Tom about Annie, her plan to attend the Temperance meeting on Monday, and their separation while Tom went ahead to the tea room. 'Then I heard my name being called,' she said. 'Just a voice in the crowd.'

Albert frowned. 'You're sure that's what you heard? Your own name?'

'I'm sure. Then this fella was in front of me, blocking my path. He only had three fingers on his left hand, and ... oh, I remember now, his fingernails were manicured. Like a girl's.' She broke off, overwhelmed by something that felt like shame at the memory of the stranger's touch.

'Go on,' Albert murmured. 'I need to know what happened.'

'He was right there. Right in front of me. The crowd was all around me. Bodies pressing in on all sides. And then he ... touched me.' Her voice broke.

Mrs Byrne moved closer and placed a comforting hand on Minnie's shoulder. 'You can tell me, you know,' she said. 'If you're uncomfortable with the men hearing.'

Minnie shook her head, determined to carry on. 'It was nothing, really. He placed his hand on my waist. Grabbed my arm. So quick, I barely had time to notice it. Certainly not enough time to tell him where to get off. And then he was gone.'

'Did he say anything?' Albert asked.

'Yes. He told me to think twice before "sneaking off" to Brown's for a cuppa with you. Then he went, and I didn't even know he'd done anything until Tom pointed it out.'

Albert thought for a moment. 'You and I, we've only ever gone to Brown's—'

'From the Palace,' Minnie interrupted. 'I know.' In the cab on the way to Albert's house she'd been plagued by the thought that someone at the Palace was spying on her.

'And this young man is Tom Neville, I take it,' Albert said, gesturing towards Tom, who stood, looking uncomfortable, near the door, as if ready to take flight.

Minnie nodded. 'He's been a brick.'

Albert reached above the fireplace and took down an empty pipe. He held it between his hands and said nothing for a moment.

'Miss Ward,' he said eventually, 'I'm so sorry for what happened to you today. It goes without saying that, as of now, you'll no longer be involved in the investigation. I was wrong to accept your help, and this has been the unfortunate consequence.'

'We don't know for certain that this,' she said, laying her hand on her arm, 'has anything to do with Rose. It could have just been some fella off his chump who took a dislike to me.'

Albert closed his eyes for a moment, and took a deep breath. 'You can't really believe this is a coincidence, can you?' he said. 'Firstly, someone in that crowd called you by your name. Then this three-fingered man made a specific threat before cutting you. Has such a thing ever happened to you before? To anyone you know? No,' he said, looking up at her face, 'of course not. You were targeted, Miss Ward.'

'But I'm still alive and kicking, ain't I? With a knife sharp enough to cut through a corset, he could easily have killed me.'

'Exactly. An extra half an inch and we wouldn't be sitting here now, discussing the matter. The attack was intended as a warning. And if you don't think this has anything to do with Rose's death, why did you come here, instead of contacting the police or visiting the hospital?'

Minnie had a horrible feeling she knew which way this conversation was turning. And if he thought he could silence her with a few sharp words, he was very wrong.

'And another thing—'

'Go easy on her, Mr Easterbrook,' Mrs Byrne intervened, moving closer to Minnie and placing a hand on each of her shoulders. 'The girl's had a terrible shock.'

'No, Mrs Byrne, I will not go easy on her. My going easy on her is precisely what's led us to this point. I should never have listened to you,' he said, turning to Minnie and raising his voice. 'Not only have you placed yourself in peril, you have involved a total stranger in the proceedings. You have told this young man' – he gestured towards Tom – 'details of the investigation that should not have been shared with anyone else. You know nothing about him. You based your decision to involve him on … what, precisely?'

'She based it on the fact she's a pretty good judge of character,' Tom said, raising his voice to meet Albert's. 'And she was right to trust me, 'cos I know stuff about what went on in that house, stuff I told her you'd never have found out in a month of Sundays.'

Albert barely acknowledged Tom had spoken, focusing instead on Minnie. 'We're not at the Variety Palace, Miss

Ward. This is not a thrilling stage act. You could have been killed today.'

'But I weren't. So, they tried to frighten me. Well, I don't scare easily, Albert. You can tell me until the cows come home that I ain't on the case any longer, but it won't make a blind bit of difference. I'm gonna carry on asking questions until we find out who killed Rose. And you can't stop me.'

'No,' he said, 'I can't stop you. But I have a duty to ensure that no further harm—'

'Well, you ain't the only one who has a sense of duty,' Minnie interrupted. 'I owe it to Rose and Ida to find out what happened. And surely both of us working on the case is gonna be helpful? Two heads are better than one, or so they tell me.'

'Not if one of those heads is in a state of perpetual concern for the other one. From the moment I agreed to let you help, I have regretted my decision. After what has happened today, if we were to continue working together, I should worry about you all the time, Miss Ward. All the time. The peril you might fling yourself into—'

'I don't deny I can be a little—'

'Impetuous?' Albert interrupted. 'Foolhardy?'

'I was thinking more along the lines of "keen",' Minnie said. 'We can go with one of your words if it makes you feel better, but it ain't a reason for you to end our partnership.' She paused for a moment. 'What if I promised to do nothing without your say-so?'

'That would be ideal. But we both know you won't fulfil your side of the bargain. You'll agree not to take a particular course of action and then, when we next meet, you'll say, "Oops, Albert, couldn't 'elp meself."'

'Is that meant to sound like me? Just as well you're a good detective, 'cos you're a bloody awful mimic.'

They eyed each other belligerently for a long moment, and then Minnie, struck by the absurdity of the situation, burst out laughing. To her intense surprise, Albert did the same. Tom sniffed the brandy in his glass and looked at both of them quizzically.

'So,' Minnie said, after the laughter had subsided, 'where do we go from here? Given that I ain't removing myself from the case, and you know that.'

'Ideally,' Albert said, 'I would escort you everywhere. But that is hardly feasible.'

Tom gave a gentle cough. Minnie and Albert looked at him enquiringly.

'I'm out of a job,' Tom said. 'Mrs Winter's told me to sling my hook. So maybe I could help? Walk Minnie to work and suchlike?'

'It would be placing you in peril,' Albert said. 'I can't agree.'

Tom squirmed, and glanced around the room as if searching for the right words. 'I ain't always been what you'd call on the right side of the law,' he said. 'Nothing serious, mind. But I know how to look after myself. I'm tougher than I look. Today I was caught off guard. I won't be again.'

Albert said nothing for a moment, and then glanced over at the tea tray. 'That tea will be cold by now,' he said. 'Tom, could you nip downstairs and make sure the kettle's back on the range?'

Understanding flickered across Tom's face, and he nodded, picking up the teapot as he left the room.

When he was safely out of earshot, Albert turned to Mrs Byrne. 'Well?' he said. 'Is he to be trusted?'

'Straight as they make them, I would say,' Mrs Byrne said. Albert thought for a moment.

'Anyone wanna ask me what I think of him?' Minnie asked.

'You,' Albert said, 'are not entirely to be trusted.' A smile hovered at the corners of his mouth.

'I've had a cut to my arm, Albert,' she replied. 'Not a blow to the head. For what it's worth, I think he's a good 'un.'

As if on cue, the door slowly opened. Minnie had a strong suspicion Tom had been hovering outside the whole time. He was still holding the teapot.

'We're very grateful for your offer, Tom,' Albert said, 'and we'd like to take you up on it. Helping Miss Ward, though, will mean you are unavailable for paid employment. I could pay you something for your time.'

'And perhaps we could feed the lad?' Mrs Byrne suggested. 'If that would help?' she added, turning towards Tom who nodded enthusiastically, glancing across at the tea tray and the untouched plate of fruit cake.

'Very well,' Albert said. 'It will be a temporary arrangement, Tom, and you will continue to look for a more permanent post. In the meantime, it would be most helpful if you could accompany Miss Ward to the Variety Palace on Monday, and I shall attend the Temperance meeting with her on Monday night.'

Minnie gave an exaggerated cough. 'It's downright charming to hear you two gents sorting out my life for me. But I just wondered – have I got any say in it?'

'Of course,' Albert said, smiling gently. 'Does this arrangement meet with your consent, Miss Ward?'

'There's no need for you to come to the meeting, Albert. I'll get a cab there and you can meet me afterwards.' Minnie said. 'And now can we get started on that cake? My stomach thinks it's my throat that's been cut, not my arm.'

FOURTEEN

Minnie finished giving her description of the three-fingered man to John. He did not look hopeful.

'Fellas missing a finger or two and belonging to the criminal fraternity?' he said. 'More common than you'd think. We'll do our best, Minnie. But, to be honest, we've got our hands full at the moment.'

'Hairpin Killer?' Albert asked.

John sighed, nodded and pushed his seat back from the scuffed table. They were sitting in an interview room at Aldwych police station the day after the attack at the Cremorne.

'We're getting nowhere,' he said.

'Fresh pair of eyes?' Albert offered. 'I worked on the case for a while when I was here, remember.'

'Well, nothing's changed. Same method.' John glanced at Minnie and then looked at Albert questioningly.

Minnie bridled. Another fella trying to protect her. 'I do read the papers, Sergeant Price,' she said. 'They don't leave much to the imagination, and I ain't exactly been falling into a fit of the vapours every time I read about him.'

John shook his head. 'The papers don't include everything, Minnie. We've asked them to hold some details back, in case some other loon decides he's going to copy Hairpin. Although, any day now, I'm sure some ink-slinger keen to make a name for himself is gonna let something slip.'

'So, what isn't making it into the papers?' Minnie asked.

'The type of knife he uses. Short, broad blade.'

'Like something you'd skin an animal with,' Albert added.

John nodded. 'And the hairpins. Well, you know.' He gestured to Albert.

'They weren't hairpins at the start,' Albert said, turning to Minnie. 'Just bits of wire. Then, after the third murder, it changed to hairpins. No idea why.'

'Fancy ones at that,' John said. He shifted in his chair, glanced around him as if fearful he was being spied on. Then he leaned in closer to Minnie, conspiratorially dropping his voice. 'Wanna see one? I mean, it's strictly against the rules, but—'

''Course I wanna see one,' Minnie said, barely able to keep the excitement out of her voice.

'Wait here,' John said, and nipped out of the room.

'I must introduce you to John's wife, Mary,' Albert said, while he and Minnie waited for John to return. 'And his seven children.'

'Meaning?'

'Meaning I think Sergeant Price might be a bit sweet on you.'

'Well, don't worry, Albert. My pa ran off with some loose bit o' goods, and Ma had to raise me on her own. It don't matter how blue his eyes are, I'd never entertain a fella who'd do that to his kids. Mrs Price is safe.'

John came back, closing the door softly behind him. He handed Minnie a hairpin, and she moved closer to the gas lamp to get a better look.

'Pretty thing,' she said, holding it so the light refracted off the seven-pointed star at the end. 'Paste?' she asked, pointing to the tiny clear stones encircling a large green gem at the centre.

John nodded. 'Unusual though, ain't it?'

'I've never seen one like it.'

'Which would make you think it'd be easy to find the maker,' John said. 'I've been to every jeweller, every hat shop, every hairdresser in London. Nothing.'

'Maybe Hairpin makes them himself,' Albert suggested.

'We have thought that,' John said.

'But why the hairpins?' Minnie asked. 'And why seven of them?'

John shrugged and shook his head, unable to offer any answer. He took the hairpin back from Minnie, then turned towards Albert. 'Where you off to now? My shift ends in another ten minutes. If you stay put for a bit, I'll walk with you.'

⁂

Twenty minutes later, the three of them made their way back to the Strand, lapsing into a companionable silence after John had recounted the latest antics of his children.

'When are we next sparring?' he asked Albert. 'You ain't been at the White Hart all this week. You'll be getting rusty, my son.'

Albert winced. 'I know, I know. Soon, I promise.'

'Show me some moves, then,' Minnie said, playfully forming her hands into fists and punching the air in front of her, then flinching as the movement awakened the pain in her right arm. She glanced at Albert, but he hadn't noticed. She didn't want to give him any more ammunition to remove her from the investigation.

'Well, for a start, you don't form a fist like that,' John said, taking her left hand and removing her thumb from where she had tucked it inside her other fingers. 'You'll break your thumb if you hit someone like that.'

'Could you kill a man?' Minnie asked. 'With one punch?'

John glanced at Albert and smiled. 'I know he's annoying, Minnie, but there's no reason to off him just yet.'

She laughed. 'No, seriously though. Could you?'

'A rabbit punch'd do it.' John motioned to the back of Albert's neck with his fist. 'Or you could do it with the side of your hand, like this.' He held his hand out flat, the side of his little finger lying against Albert's neck. 'That'd bring him down. Strictly frowned upon, though.'

'Why?'

'Rules of the boxing ring. No blows from behind. It ain't exactly fair.'

Minnie formed a fist again, placing her thumb in the correct place and feinting a rabbit punch to the back of John's neck.

'Nifty,' she said. 'If only I'd known about that when Three-Fingers got handy with his knife, you might have had him in the nick by now.'

Despite her levity, the memory of the attack sent a jolt through her. Her arm would heal, but she wondered when the memory of those few minutes in the Cremorne would fade. She'd felt helpless, vulnerable. Exposed. All the things she'd worked so hard to protect herself against.

She shook off the thought, telling herself she would deal

with her feelings once Rose's killer was found. Besides, she had other things to occupy her mind. She was going to have a snoop in Tansie's office, see if she could find anything. See if he was the one who had been spying on her. But it wasn't going to be easy.

FIFTEEN

Tom appeared punctually at ten o'clock outside Minnie's rooms and they set out for the Palace. Although the knife wound didn't look much, Minnie's arm was hurting more now as it healed, and she found she was lacking some of her usual energy. Without saying anything, Tom shortened his stride to match hers.

They passed a boarded-up shop, the shutters plastered with posters advertising everything from soap to plum puddings.

'That's my favourite,' Tom said, pointing to an advertisement for a hairbrush for the bald.

Minnie nodded. 'It's a corker, I'll give you that. But does it top this one?' She gestured towards an image of a corset impregnated with magnets. 'It cures everything, Tom. Nerves, rheumatism, paralysis. And it guarantees a blissful night's sleep.'

'Not easy if you're wearing a corset, I'd imagine.'

They turned onto the Strand, past the hoardings of other, rival music halls, all of them offering the best night's entertainment in London.

'Fancy that, Minnie?' Tom asked. 'See yourself as the next Richmond Rocket?'

She shook her head. 'No thanks. Wouldn't mind earning

a bob or two more than I do now, but that's as far as my ambitions stretch. Oh, and I'd like a dog one day. What about you?'

'Nowhere near as modest, but if I'm dreaming I might as well dream big. I'd like to own my own stables. Somewhere in the country. Quiet. Peaceful.'

As if to emphasise his point, a carriage driver hurled abuse at a group of children who had run out in the road and nearly caused an accident.

'Would you race them?' Minnie asked. 'The horses?'

He smiled shyly. 'Truthfully? I'd just like to look after them, know they were mine and couldn't be sold just 'cos they'd grown old, or someone had tired of them.'

Minnie was touched by his compassion. She had been right to trust him.

They turned onto Maiden Lane and reached the stage door. Minnie led Tom through to the rear of the building, their footsteps echoing down the flagstone backstage corridors. Tom looked wide-eyed as they passed poky dressing rooms and tiny closets.

'Can we go out the front?' he asked.

Minnie directed him up a short flight of stairs and onto the stage. A deal table and a rickety chair were positioned for what looked like a run-through of Dandy Bob's act. Tom peered into the gloom of the empty auditorium, his face alight with curiosity. Minnie remembered her own first time on the stage, her belief she had entered a realm of magic and wonder. And, later, the blind panic when she had stood in the wings, an audience waiting for her to entertain them, and the knowledge that she had nothing to say. She shuddered at the memory.

'It's so different, ain't it?' Tom said. 'So quiet and dark. You'd hardly think it was the same place.'

'You been here before? For a show?'

He nodded. 'A few times.'

'Who'd you see?'

'Oh, the usual. Dancing dogs and the like. The American Prize Lady – big girl, she was. And your Rose, I think. I'm pretty sure it was her. Fair hair, gentle kind of face? Did lots of acrobatics with a hoop. Bit of wire walking.'

Minnie smiled. 'That's her.' She wondered when she would stop speaking – and thinking – of Rose as if she were still alive.

Tom walked down the few steps from the stage into the auditorium and weaved his way through the tables. Chairs were stacked on top of them, ready for the cleaners who had just arrived, piercing the quiet with the rattle of buckets and mops. Tom ran his fingers along the table edges, as if hoping to absorb some magic. From backstage, Minnie could hear Tansie shouting for Kippy.

'You should go,' she said. 'I've got to speak to Tansie about the new acts we've got starting on Saturday, and I promised Albert I'd take a cab to the Temperance meeting.'

'Mind if I stay put for a bit? Just to look around, like,' he asked. 'I ain't got much else to do.'

'Suit yourself, but I'll be busy, mind.'

An exasperated female cry came from backstage, followed by a loud crash. Moments later Daisy came haring onto the stage, with a face like thunder.

'Min, thank God you're here,' she gasped, clasping her hands to her chest. 'That bleedin' monkey. I can't tell you what I caught him doing with Dandy Bob's ventriloquist dummy. I threw a pot of cold cream at him, and he legged it. You ain't seen him, have you?'

Minnie shook her head.

Daisy collapsed theatrically onto the rickety chair with such dexterity it could have been placed on the stage for just this occasion. A few blonde curls had worked themselves loose from her upswept hair, and the flush of activity had brought an attractive glow to her cheeks. Pretty girl, Minnie thought.

'Can you sing, Daisy?'

She frowned. 'A bit. I'm no Jenny Hill, but I can hold a tune.'

'And how's the comic disembowelling working out for you?'

'It ain't. I go home every night stinking of raw meat. My ma thinks I'm carrying on with a butcher. Why'd you ask?'

'If your voice is up to scratch, maybe I could write you something.'

Daisy's face lit up as she smiled. 'Oh, Min, that'd be splendid.' She turned her head at the scrape of a chair from the auditorium. Tom emerged from the darkness and ascended the steps to the stage, his gaze transfixed on Daisy.

'And who might you be?' Daisy rose from the chair to offer him her hand.

'My cousin,' Minnie said, repeating the story she had worked out with Tom on the way to the Palace. 'His ma's poorly and he's come to town looking for work that pays a bit more.' She glanced between the two of them. It was the monkey and Dandy Bob's dummy all over again. 'You couldn't look after him, could you, Daisy? Just for an hour or so? Show him around backstage? Tanse'll have a fit if I don't see him soon.'

As if their movements were choreographed, Daisy and

Tom fell into step with each other, walking smoothly off the stage and passing Bernard Reynolds on the way. He looked behind him as they passed. 'Loath as I am to misquote the Bard,' he said, 'but one half of him is hers already.' He turned towards Minnie. 'Tansie has been bellowing for you like a bull in springtime, dearest heart.'

'And though he be but little, he is fierce,' Minnie said.

Bernard smiled and doffed an imaginary cap at her.

❦

Minnie headed towards Cora's dressing room, from where Tansie's last tantrum had erupted. He was nowhere in sight. Cora was sitting alone, facing the looking glass, a dreamy look in her eyes and a dippy grin on her face. She twirled one dark curl round her finger.

'Are you fit, Cora?' Minnie asked.

'Oh, I'm all there, Min. All there,' Cora said, beaming.

'Couldn't do me a favour, could you?'

Cora looked at her expectantly.

'The Bluebell have asked me to write something for them, and they've offered to pay twice as much as I get here. Only I left the song in Tansie's office the other day. If he sees me looking for it – well, you know what he's like.'

Cora nodded. 'Like a hawk,' she said, and smiled to herself. 'A lovely, cuddly hawk.'

Minnie was silenced for a moment. 'Yeah,' she said, eventually, 'a lovely, cuddly hawk who'll tear me to shreds if he finds out I'm writing for the Bluebell.'

'You want me to get his keys off him? Can't you just pick the lock?'

Minnie grimaced. 'It's a fancy one. Beyond me, I'm afraid.'
Cora had several brothers, all of whom dwelled firmly on the
wrong side of the law. She'd managed to stay on the straight
and narrow, but they'd taught her a few tricks over the years,
not least the ability to pick a pocket.

'I'll do my best,' Cora said, her eyes glazing over again as
her thoughts clearly drifted to Tansie.

'I take it things are going well?' Minnie said.

'Oh, Min, he's got me chucked all of a heap. Proper little
popsy-wopsy, he is.'

Minnie heard a cough behind her, and turned to see
Tansie, blushing furiously. He nodded at Cora and suppressed
a smile.

'Well, if it ain't the little popsy-wopsy himself,' Minnie said.

'Enough of that,' Tansie growled. 'We've got work to do.
Where've you been all week?'

'Well, in between supping tea with the Queen and
exercising my horses in Hyde Park, there's been the small
matter of Rose's death to investigate. Or had you forgotten
about that?'

'Don't put the shutters up with me, Min. When you said
you was gonna help that Easterbrook fella, I didn't think
you'd be on the missing list for days at a time. Last time I
checked your job title weren't "assistant detective".'

'Last time I checked, my job title was "writer", but that's
never stopped you getting me doing a million and one other
things. And I ain't anyone's assistant.'

Tansie ignored her comment, heading off down the
corridor to his office. Minnie followed him.

'Who's that muff I just seen Daisy with?' Tansie asked,
settling in behind his desk. 'Something to do with you?'

'My cousin,' Minnie said, surprised at the ease with which she was able to lie to him.

He frowned. 'You ain't never mentioned a cousin before.'

'Distant cousin.'

'Well, tell him to leave Daisy alone.'

'Why's that?' Minnie asked belligerently. 'Cora's your girl, ain't she?'

'She is,' Tansie said. 'It's just that, being as he's so distant a cousin you ain't never mentioned him, I'm suspecting he won't be around for long. And I can't deal with any more drama round here.'

Minnie nodded, and the two of them settled to business. They had three new acts starting on Saturday, all of which had the potential for disaster: a stilt walker, a sword swallower and a trio of child clog dancers.

Eventually, Tansie indicated they were done. He removed his hat and coat from behind the door, and the two of them turned back down the corridor towards Cora's dressing room.

Cora was perched on the edge of her chair, like a child waiting for Christmas.

'I'm taking Cora out to lunch,' Tansie said. 'We need to discuss her act.'

'That's what we're calling it, is it? "Discussing her act"?' Minnie glanced behind her. 'No one here but me, Tanse,' she leaned in and whispered theatrically. 'No need to keep it a secret.'

'Ooh, where we going?' Cora said, drawing on her coat and turning back to the mirror to position her hat.

'Thought we might try the Carlton,' Tansie said, referring to a rather expensive restaurant on the Strand. Bit more upmarket than his usual bowl of jellied eels. Romance was definitely in the air.

Cora squealed with delight and hurled herself at Tansie, almost bowling him over. 'You're spoiling me, Mr Tansford,' she purred, leaning down to kiss the top of his head and pressing it close to her chest as she sneaked her hand into his pocket. Tansie's face went an interesting shade of purple, and he developed a coughing fit so violent Cora had to thump him on the back several times. Minnie couldn't remember ever seeing Tansie blush, and now he'd done it twice over the same woman. Cora slipped her hand in his and pulled him towards the dressing-room door.

'See you later, Min,' she said huskily, passing the office keys behind her back and into Minnie's waiting hand.

Minnie listened to their receding footsteps and stepped back out into the corridor. The Palace felt strangely quiet. The cleaners had left. Bernard was nowhere to be seen. Minnie checked the auditorium, and saw Daisy and Tom seated at one of the tables, heads close together, the low murmur of his voice and the tinkle of Daisy's laughter punctuating the silence. Must be something in the water, Minnie thought. Even the bleedin' monkey was sweet on someone, even if it was only a ventriloquist's dummy.

She figured she had at least an hour before Tansie would be back from lunch. Longer if Cora clasped him to her breast a few more times. She fingered the bunch of keys as she stood outside the door of Tansie's office. No one was allowed inside without him being present. Not even Minnie. He kept his keys securely about his person, was never without them. Silently, she thanked Cora for her criminal relations.

Even as she turned the key in the lock, she felt bad. In her heart, she didn't believe Tansie could have had anything to do with Rose's death. But if Rose had been photographed in the Palace snuggeries, it would have taken time and a lot of equipment. It was a noisy job. Tansie must have known. Besides, she was only going to take a look. Convince herself Tansie had nothing to do with it all.

She closed the door softly after her and moved behind Tansie's desk, where the safe sat snugly on the floor. Rifling through the keys, she found the one she needed. As the key turned in the lock the revolving chambers made a loud thunk that echoed in the silence. Minnie froze, certain someone must have heard. She held her breath, listening. But the only sound was Daisy's laughter in the distance. She breathed again.

Minnie pulled the heavy door open with a tug and a grunt and peered inside. Money and, under it, some papers. She withdrew the papers, and rifled through them, all the time keeping an ear out. Near the bottom of the pile she found something that looked like a legal document, the paper thinning at the folds. She scanned it, but the legal wording made no sense. She went back to the start and read again more slowly.

Minnie had always assumed Tansie owned the Palace outright, but this document said otherwise. Seventy per cent was owned by someone called Bernadette Lohan. And Tansie had never said a word about it.

She crouched down to peer further inside, the movement making her wince, and reminding her of the knife wound. Tucked away in a corner of the safe was something small. She reached in and withdrew it. A leather drawstring pouch, about the size of a pack of cards.

Inside, a dozen or so photographs.

They were mainly women, but some men too. All the

women were young, pretty. All of them in varying stages of undress. The men looked older, less comfortable. Hardly surprising, given what they were up to with the girls. Some of the women Minnie recognised as performers at the Palace, others were unfamiliar to her. For the life of her, she couldn't imagine why Tansie would have these photographs.

And, at the bottom of the pile, as if she had known it would be there all along, the photograph of Rose that Lionel Winter had had in his Stanhope.

She traced the outline of Rose's face with her finger, remembering when she had last seen her alive. Rose had tripped and stumbled through rehearsals, her mind elsewhere. Tansie's yelling hadn't masked the concern in his eyes. And when Minnie had asked her if anything was wrong, Rose had just shaken her head and turned away. Minnie had been too busy to probe any further, had just assumed it was something and nothing, and got on with her day.

She rested her hand on the image a little longer, then, with a decisive movement, placed the photographs back in the leather pouch and tucked it back in the corner of the safe. She replaced the other documents and locked the safe, then stood, brushed down her skirts and turned towards the door. Just as she reached it, the door opened.

Tansie.

'What the—?' he said, his eyes darting from Minnie to the safe. She felt the weight of the keys in her hand, and guessed Tansie had noted their absence and come back for them. She took a small step backwards, reached behind her and carefully slid the keys onto the edge of Tansie's desk.

'Don't kick off, Tanse. You left your keys in Cora's room. I knew you wouldn't want anyone else having them, and I'm off out soon, so I was just leaving them on your desk.'

She moved to one side to show him the keys. Tansie eyed her suspiciously.

'Why didn't you come and find me?' he said. 'I was only up the road at the Carlton.'

'Tanse, we have had this conversation many times. I am not your slave. Besides, the way you and Cora were billing and cooing you might have gone and got yourself a room for all I knew.'

'I don't allow no one in here, Minnie, and you know that.'

Minnie's anger was not feigned. What she had found in the safe had unsettled her. Tansie had been keeping secrets from her. And someone had spied on her and Albert, and passed that knowledge on to the three-fingered man.

'Go ahead and check,' she said, flinging her arms out either side of her body. 'I ain't no bunter, Tanse. I did you a favour but I don't know why I bothered. Next time I'll leave them where I found them.'

She gathered her skirts in one hand and swept out of the room before Tansie had a chance to say anything further.

SIXTEEN

Minnie took a leaflet from a pimply-faced young man on the door and entered the Temperance Hall. A shabby space, poorly lit, with the paint peeling from the walls, it smelled of old cheese, stale cigarettes and something else Minnie couldn't quite put her finger on. It was about ten minutes short of eight o'clock, when the meeting was due to start. There was quite a crowd, which was just as well, because it was bitterly cold. She scanned the room. No Annie.

The crowd consisted mainly of women, but a few of the men turned towards Minnie, and she felt their eyes on her. 'Wanna take a photograph, chaps?' she asked. 'It'll last longer.' The men turned away quickly and Minnie took a seat near the rear of the hall, by the doors.

A draught ruffled her skirts and she looked up to see Annie entering the room.

As several pairs of eyes lighted on Annie, she raised her hand to touch the port-wine birthmark on her face, an instinctive gesture Minnie was coming to recognise. One fellow, with bulging eyes and a messy mouth, leered at Annie, making her blush even more. Minnie gave a shy smile and patted the seat next to her.

'It's Miss Belfer, ain't it?' she said. 'You won't remember

me, I'm sure. Minnie Ward. I was at your place of work the other week. That Tom Neville invited me in for a cuppa. I'm so glad to see a friendly face. This is my first meeting, and I'm awful nervous. Sorry – I'm nattering, ain't I?'

Annie eyed her apprehensively but took the seat, brushing the dust off it first. She said nothing, and Minnie tried to look at her without being too obvious. On close examination, Minnie could spot the signs of drink on Annie: a network of veins like a drunken spider's web crisscrossed her nose and cheeks, the whites of her eyes were closer to yellow, and her leaflet shook in her hand.

The noise in the room was constant, but subdued, like a hall of schoolchildren waiting for the headmaster. Eventually, Annie spoke.

'Did you find work?' she asked. 'You were looking, weren't you?'

Minnie rolled her eyes. 'I found some positions, but I ain't taking them.'

'Why ever not?'

'It's the gentlemen of the house. I've had a bit of … trouble in the past. If you know what I mean.'

Before Annie could reply, a tall angular man, red-faced and with even redder hair, rose and stood on a platform at the front of the room. The noise dropped away, as everyone turned towards him.

'Mr Griffiths,' Annie whispered, 'the commander of our group.'

He waited for complete silence. 'Ladies, gentlemen,' he said, scanning the room and smiling beatifically, 'as usual we will begin with a song, the words of which you will find on your sheet.'

Minnie's spirits lifted. More singing, less sermonising. Maybe it wasn't going to be so bad after all.

'A personal favourite of mine,' Mr Griffiths continued, nodding at the pianist positioned to the left of him, a motherly-looking woman who gazed at him adoringly. 'And one which I know is well loved by many of you, particularly the ladies. "The Lips That Touch Liquor Shall Never Touch Mine".'

Minnie's spirits sank as quickly as they had soared. The congregation launched into the first verse and Minnie found herself longing for Madame Selina. At least she occasionally hit the right note.

Annie leaned towards Minnie, raising her sheet to her face. 'You can't turn down every position 'cos you think the gentleman of the house might have wandering hands,' she said, just loud enough for Minnie to hear. 'If you do, it's gonna take a month of Sundays to find a job.'

'But how do you … stop it?' Minnie replied. 'I don't want to get in no trouble. My ma'd kill me.'

The noise from the crowd swelled at the chorus, but fell away with the advent of the second verse:

> *The homes that were happy are ruined and gone*
> *The hearts that were merry are wretched and lone*
> *And lives full of promise of good things to come*
> *Are ruin'd and wreck'd by the Demon of Rum.*

Minnie would have welcomed a visitation from the Demon of Rum at precisely this moment. Even a small snifter would have done the trick. Next to her, a young woman who had been struggling to find the notes gave up the search and began imitating a drowning cat. Behind her an elderly man was maintaining a vigorous monotone for the entire song.

'Ram a chair up against the door handle of your bedroom,' Annie continued, holding up the song sheet again to mask her words. 'Tell 'em you get nightmares if you sleep alone, bad enough to wake the whole house, and ask if you can share a room with another girl. Try never to be alone with the fella.'

A hatchet-faced matron in front of them turned and threw Annie a glowering look that would have curdled milk. Minnie glanced at her song sheet and realised they were on the final verse. The song mercifully came to an end and the group were invited to sit.

Mr Griffiths moved to stand behind a lectern. His nose was bruised and swollen, and what looked like two black eyes were just starting to ripen. 'Some of you may remember the joy we shared last week at the news that Joe McGinley had signed the pledge,' he said. There were murmurs of agreement from the crowd, with one or two encouraging cries of 'Hear, hear'.

'It is with great sadness I have to report I encountered Joe on my way home two nights ago,' Mr Griffiths continued. 'He had succumbed to the perils of drink. Not for nothing is he known locally as "Fighting Joe". When I attempted to remonstrate with him, he grew belligerent and … bit me on the nose.'

Annie looked at Minnie, wide-eyed, and let out a snort of laughter. She tried to swallow the laugh in her handkerchief but was unsuccessful. The disapproving matron turned round again, leaned forward and hit Annie on the arm with her rolled-up song sheet.

Oblivious, Mr Griffiths continued to rail against the dangers of drink for a further twenty minutes. He could have driven a newborn baby to the bottle, and Minnie found herself calculating how long it would take to get to the nearest pub once the meeting was over. Finally, he sat, and a cloth bag was circulated, for people to contribute to a collection.

'A friend of mine worked for this chap who wanted to take photographs of her,' Minnie said, as she and Annie scrambled in their bags for their smallest coins. 'You know. Saucy ones.'

Annie looked at her. She seemed on the verge of saying something, but changed her mind. 'Like I said, never be alone with him,' she said. 'It'll be hard for him to take photos if his missus is sitting there. And besides,' she added, 'there's worse things than photos.'

'Oh, I couldn't,' Minnie said, pulling her shawl tighter around her as if to protect herself from the horrors of photography. 'The thought of – you know – taking your clothes off in front of someone. I couldn't.'

Annie eyed her carefully. 'There's worse things.' She sounded regretful, as if she herself had done much worse.

The pianist struck up a few chords, and the meeting ended with another song, the imaginatively titled 'No Alcohol for Me'.

Minnie and Annie gathered their things together and joined the stream of people leaving. Mr Griffiths was at the door, urging everyone to sign the pledge if they hadn't already done so. Annie gave Minnie an enquiring look.

'Maybe next time,' Minnie said.

The two women left the hall, pulling coats, scarves and shawls tighter around their bodies. It was cold outside, and the wind had picked up. Minnie indicated she was walking in the same direction as Annie, and the two women walked in silence for a few minutes, fighting against the wind. Annie glanced behind her a few times.

'What is it?' Minnie asked.

'Oh, nothing,' Annie murmured. 'It's just you can't be too careful these days, what with that Hairpin fella.'

Minnie looked behind her. There was someone there, a man in the shadows, but he sped up and overtook them. Nothing to worry about.

'What you were saying earlier,' Minnie said, weighing her words carefully. 'About how to avoid trouble, I mean. I don't wish to speak ill of the dead, but your Mr Winter … he didn't—?'

To Minnie's surprise, Annie gave a guffaw of laughter, with more than a hint of bitterness underneath it. 'Him? Not bleedin' likely.' She registered the surprise on Minnie's face, and reined in her amusement. 'He was more of what you'd call a thinker than a doer. Nice fella. I liked him.' She paused, and then added, almost to herself, 'On the whole.'

They were approaching Stafford Street. Not much time left to find out what Annie knew. Minnie took a gamble. 'Tom Neville,' she said, 'he reckons there was something fishy about the night Mr Winter died.'

'Meaning?' Annie said.

It was difficult to tell in the dimly lit streets, but Minnie was fairly sure a glimmer of fear crossed Annie's face.

'Meaning he don't reckon it was an accident.'

This time, the look on Annie's face was unmistakeable. She was afraid. 'You don't wanna go believing everything Tom Neville tells you,' she said, her voice high and hurried. 'The police said it was an accident, and they should know what they're talking about.'

She pulled her shawl closer around her, glancing behind her again. The street was empty. 'This is me,' she said, pointing to the Winter house. She turned and offered her hand. 'I ain't sure I can make next week's meeting,' she said. 'If you're planning on being there, that is.'

'Definitely. Changed my life it did, tonight. Might even sign the pledge next week. It'd be a shame to miss you.'

Minnie leaned in and gave Annie a quick peck on the cheek, deliberately choosing the side of her face with the birthmark. Annie pulled back and looked at her confusedly.

'You shouldn't worry about it,' Minnie said quietly, gesturing towards Annie's face. 'And I hope you can make it next Monday.'

Annie nodded, turned down the steps to the servants' entrance and let herself in.

Minnie glanced up and down the street. Albert had said he would join her after the Temperance meeting but he was nowhere in sight. She started walking, and then became aware, very clearly, of footsteps. She stopped. Nothing. She turned, looked behind her. There could be someone there, in the darkness between the pools of light cast by the gas lamps, but it was impossible to tell. She carried on walking, and this time there was no mistaking it. There was someone else on the near-empty street.

She started to walk more quickly, the memory of the Cremorne attack flashing into her mind, unbidden. Was it him, the three-fingered man, come to warn her a second time? Or – and her insides felt as if they had turned to liquid as the thought entered her head – was it the Hairpin Killer? She was in Kensington, and the newspapers said he always killed around Seven Dials, Soho, Covent Garden. So, no. It couldn't be him. It couldn't be.

She reached the end of Stafford Street, cursing the fact she didn't know the area. If she'd been closer to home, she'd have known all the shortcuts, the cut-throughs, the busy roads and back lanes. Looking to her right, she felt as if the darkness would swallow her up. Left, then. But wasn't that taking her away from Kensington High Street, where there would be life and noise, where she could lose herself in the crowd? Her pulse thundered in her ears. She seemed to have lost all sense of direction. And the footsteps behind her had stopped again. She willed herself to turn round and look. Nothing. No one. But she knew he was there. In the shadows. Watching her.

Suppressing a sob, she forced herself to turn right, into the darkness, and broke into a run. She could hear him behind her. He was running. He would be on her in a moment. The lights of Kensington High Street lay ahead of her. She could see carriages passing, people on the pavements. If she could just get there. But it all seemed very far away.

She was running hard now, her heart straining in her chest, her breath coming in short gasps.

She glanced over her shoulder and, as she turned back, a figure stepped out from the shadows in front of her and she ran straight into him. The collision nearly knocked her off her feet, winded her so she couldn't scream. She backed off, holding one hand out in front of her, pulling a comb from her hair with the other, knowing it would be no defence.

'Minnie?'

It was Albert.

'Minnie?' he said again. 'What's happened?' And his voice was sharp, curt. In control.

She held a hand to her chest as her breathing slowed enough for her to speak. 'A man,' she said, pointing behind her. 'Following me.'

Albert reached into his pocket and handed her a whistle. She nodded.

'Give me one minute,' he said. 'I won't go far. Wait here.'

He took off in the direction she'd come from. Holding the whistle firmly in her hand, she moved out of the shadows into the bustle and noise of the High Street. She leaned against the wall of a grocer's shop, slid to the ground, and waited, not caring how she looked, or the glances she was attracting.

Less than a minute later, Albert came running back. 'Nothing,' he said, shaking his head. 'Whoever it was, he's gone.'

He took her hand and pulled her to her feet, sliding his hand around her waist. He felt safe, solid. She leaned into him. He smelled lovely, like clean sheets. A sob rose in her throat. Albert held her until she stopped crying.

'I'm fine,' she said, pulling away from him, although she wanted to stay right where she was. 'Really. I might have imagined it.'

Albert shook his head. 'I should have been here earlier,' he said. 'I took a cab. Stupid, stupid idea. The cabbie was half-cut. Got lost, would you believe it. I should have been here,' he repeated.

Minnie laid a hand on his arm. 'And I should have waited. It's what we agreed. But it's all right, Albert. I'm fine. Really. Like I said, I might have imagined it. All that talk of the Hairpin Killer's got to me, I reckon. Let's talk about something else, eh?'

The concern still evident on his face, Albert nodded, and the two of them set off towards Catherine Street. Minnie was keen to put all thoughts of three-fingered men and hairpins behind her, so she recounted what she had learned that evening from Annie.

'Something went on between her and Winter,' Minnie

said. 'But I ain't got to the bottom of it yet. And she knows something about the night of his death. One more chat, I reckon.'

'And she'll open like a flower in the spring?' Albert said, smiling.

'Indeed.'

He grabbed her arm suddenly, and wrenched her towards him. Startled, she sprang back from him.

'Careful,' he said, pointing to a steaming pile of horse dung in the road. She remembered the incident in Tansie's office earlier that day, what seemed like a lifetime ago, his unexpected return. Another near miss. There had to be an innocent explanation for those photographs. She wouldn't tell Albert about it until she was sure there was something to tell.

'Is that why you became a copper?' she asked. 'To rescue young women from piles of horse dung?'

He smiled ruefully. 'In a sense, yes.'

'Tell me.'

He turned and eyed her carefully, as if weighing up how much to share with her. Then he carried on walking. 'There was a young woman,' he said quietly. 'A servant of my parents. She was murdered when I was eight. They never caught him.'

'And you ... cared for her?' Minnie said cautiously, afraid to break the spell of intimacy that had sprung up between them.

He nodded. 'She was kind to me.'

Something in the way he said the words told her there had been precious little kindness in his childhood. She lifted her hand, then stopped herself, unsure of how he might respond to her touch.

'I'm sorry,' she said.

He shook his head, as if rejecting her sympathy. 'I've never told anyone else about Hetty,' he said. He sounded surprised. 'My sister, Adelaide, is the only person I can talk to about what happened. She thinks I see myself as Sir Galahad, rushing in to help the defenceless.'

'Is that why you took this case? Me and Ida were two helpless women?'

He stopped and turned towards her. 'Miss Ward, you are many things, but helpless is not one of them. No, there was something about you and Ida—' He turned away and started walking again.

'What?'

'Your love for Rose. It was moving. It made me want to help you. Even if I couldn't bring her back.'

They walked in silence for a few more minutes, Minnie turning over Albert's words. As they neared Catherine Street, she said, 'You should let your guard down a bit, Albert. There's nothing wrong with letting people know you care.'

'I'm often misinterpreted.'

'How?'

'Well,' he raised his hand, gestured at his mouth, 'the way I speak for a start. Which is somewhat ironic.'

'Why?'

'My family are "new money". I suspect I spoke more like you when I was a child. Then I went away to public school and learned that life would be easier if I changed my accent. So I did. But people still judge me for how I talk.'

'What did your parents think of you becoming a copper?'

He smiled grimly. 'We don't talk about my career choice. Or anything else, for that matter.'

'That must be hard,' Minnie said.

He shrugged, but the show of nonchalance didn't fool her. 'You get used to it. It might be one of the reasons I come across as a little … cold? As I recall, you weren't too fond of me when we first met.'

'Well,' Minnie said, surprised to find herself confused and a little embarrassed, 'you've grown on me since then.'

'Like fungus?'

Minnie barked out a laugh.

'Yeah, just like fungus.'

THE FOURTH STANHOPE

IN WHICH MISS BELFER
CONTEMPLATES HER FUTURE

Temperance meetings always left Annie desperate for a drink, and she knew a gin house that would still be open at this time of night. She checked the time. Minnie Ward would be long gone. No chance of running into her again, nosy little madam.

She crept quietly down to the basement and slipped out of the house, leaving the back door on the latch. Just like they'd asked her to that night.

She moved swiftly, ducking in and out of alleyways and side streets, her feet so familiar with the route she could have walked there in her sleep. She reached the gin house, a foul-smelling hut sandwiched between a brothel and the house of a night-soil man. Scraping through her pockets for a few coins, she handed them over with the bottle to the old crone who ran the place, trying desperately not to touch her calloused hands with their ragged, grimy fingernails. She waited impatiently for the bottle to be refilled, then took a long draught, her hands shaking as she slaked her thirst.

Temperance, Annie reminded herself. Not teetotalism. Temper-ance. It wasn't that she couldn't have a drink, just that she needed to drink a little less. And she had been. She'd been doing very well, in fact, until a few weeks ago, when events had sent her hurtling back to the bottle.

And, really, what had she done after all? Left a door open. Gone to bed and pulled the pillow over her head so she wouldn't hear nothing. That fella, the one with the voice like warm treacle, only three fingers on his left hand, he'd told her he just needed to get inside the house. Take something from Mr Winter's room. A joke, he'd said. Just a little joke.

She left herself enough gin for a nip when she got into bed and started to walk back to Stafford Street. Her stomach cramped violently as the gin hit the mark. She leaned against a wall and doubled over for a few minutes, then straightened up with exaggerated slowness and moved on.

Mr Winter had told her she was beautiful. Which was a lie, but it was still nice to hear. He'd made her his parlour maid, of all things. Told her he wanted to show her off to the world. Foolish man. She smiled to herself at the memory.

And then the photographs. He'd asked her to pull up her sleeves, show her muscles. Got her scrubbing the floor in that photographic studio of his. The dirtier she got, the more he seemed to like it. Dressed her in a gent's suit once or twice; well, most of a gent's suit. Never touched her though, except when he'd moved her around for the photographs. Never anything else.

Mrs Winter, she knew what was going on in that studio. Knew what kind of a man she'd married, but she said nothing. Didn't want anyone knowing what kind of fella Mr Winter was. And she was nervous as a cat now, worrying that the truth would come out.

Annie moved less confidently, slipping more than once and only righting herself just in time.

Three-Fingers had turned up with the photographs. Said Mr Winter had shared them with some of the fellas at his club, and they'd 'fallen into the wrong hands', that's what he'd said. She hadn't liked that. Mr Winter had said it was their secret, but it hadn't been, had it? So when Three-Fingers asked for a little favour, she'd wanted to hurt Mr Winter, truth be told. Besides, Three-Fingers didn't leave her no choice. He told her he'd give her the photographs if she kept her side of the bargain, but she had, hadn't she, and she hadn't seen hide nor hair of Three-Fingers since the night Mr Winter died.

He still had those photographs. And now Minnie Ward was sniffing around. She had a way of asking things, wheedling information out of you, that made Annie nervous. She knew herself; she weren't strong, and sooner or later she'd end up telling Minnie stuff she weren't meant to. And Three-Fingers had made it clear what would happen if she said anything.

Annie paused at the corner of Dukes Lane. She drained the bottle of gin, forgetting that she was meant to be saving some for later. She emptied out her pockets. Not much. But enough for a billet somewhere for a night or two. Somewhere far away, where Minnie couldn't find her. Or Three-Fingers.

SEVENTEEN

'So, I bumped into Mrs Durrant, the Winters' cook,' Tom said. 'She told me there's been no sign of Annie since Monday night. Mrs D heard her getting home from the Temperance meeting, but no sign of her the next morning and she ain't been seen since.'

'She was fine when I left her,' Minnie said, frowning. The memory of that night's events, her belief that someone had followed her from the Winter house, flashed through her mind. She shivered, and drew closer to the fire, avoiding Albert's gaze.

'Well, she's scarpered by the looks of it,' Tom said.

'Could you accidentally bump into this Mrs Durrant again, Tom?' Albert asked. 'See if you can find out anything more?'

Tom nodded.

Albert rose uncomfortably from his ridiculous armchair that looked as if it might give way at any moment, and removed a card from the mantelpiece. 'I am invited to the Godwin Club this evening,' he said. 'The invitation arrived yesterday.'

He handed it to Minnie. She traced the velvety surface with her fingertips, raised the card to her nose and sniffed.

'What's it made of?' she asked.

'Vellum,' Albert said.

Minnie raised her eyebrows. 'Fancy.'

The card bore no ornamentation, just the date and time, and something written in Latin. Minnie pointed to the words. 'What's that, when it's at home?'

'My Latin's a little rusty,' Albert said, 'but I think it's something along the lines of: "What indeed is life, unless so far as it is enjoyed". Club motto, I'm assuming.'

'And this invite is so they can see if you're up to scratch?' Minnie asked.

Albert nodded.

'This is the most exclusive club in London, but one word from your brother-in-law and an invitation lands on your doormat?'

'It's not *what* you know, Miss Ward,' he said, with a half-smile.

'Indeed, Mr Easterbrook,' she said, lolling back in her chair and adopting an elevated accent. 'Did I mention I'm going for tea today with Lady Linton, her as was formerly the Richmond Rocket? Her carriage will be picking me up, don't you know, and then we're off to *her* club.'

'I believe you did mention it,' Albert said. 'Once or twice.'

Mrs Byrne bustled in and started clearing away the plates. She gave Tom a sharp look and he leapt up to help her. The two of them left the room and Albert rose, placing the Godwin invitation in a letter rack on the mantelpiece.

'I think Mrs Byrne is feeding that boy far more than she needs to,' he said. 'A lengthy dissection of the butcher's bill is one of her favourite methods of torture. Since Tom appeared, she's been strangely silent on the subject of meat.'

'Surprised we got him here at all today,' Minnie said. 'He's that wrapped up in Daisy he barely comes up for air.'

'And is his devotion reciprocated?'

'Oh, yes. As Cora would say, Daisy is chucked all of a heap.'

Tom returned, wiping his lips. Minnie glanced from him to Mrs Byrne, who was rubbing her hands on her apron. The air was thick with the distinct aroma of ham.

'Well,' Minnie said, 'we're due at the Palace, and you've got a fancy supper party to attend this evening. C'mon, Tom. Ginger up.'

Minnie and Tom had just turned onto the Strand when they spotted a crowd gathered outside the Palace. Parked in front of the music hall was a stylish brougham with the initials 'RR' engraved on its lamps. Just emerging from the carriage was Edie Bennett. She took her driver's hand and jumped down with a flamboyant wave to the assembled crowd.

Tom stopped in his tracks. 'She really is tiny, ain't she?' he said, his voice dropping to a reverential whisper.

'Wanna meet her?' Minnie said, surprising herself by the ease with which she could extend the invitation.

'Not half. But, no,' he said, grabbing Minnie by the arm to stop her moving forward. 'What if I make a fool of myself?'

'You won't.'

By now, Edie had turned and spotted Minnie. She sashayed over to her, pulling her into a warm embrace, before looking enquiringly at Tom. Minnie introduced Tom as her cousin, up from the country.

'You look like a chap who knows his way round livestock to me,' Edie said, eyeing him appraisingly. 'Horses, maybe?'

'Horses – yes.' Tom stumbled over his words.

'If ever you're out of work, you come and see me,' Edie said. 'I'm always looking for a good horse man.'

'I will, Miss Bennett,' Tom said, blushing so violently even his ears turned bright red. 'I definitely will.'

'Excellent. Now, if you don't mind, Tommy, the lovely Minnie and I are going out for tea. And they don't allow no men where we're going. Well, only as staff.'

Tom murmured his goodbyes and turned back towards Trafalgar Square. Edie linked her arm through Minnie's and led her back to the brougham. When the driver opened the door, Minnie gasped. The interior of the carriage was like the Palace snuggeries in miniature. Everything was painted gold, except the seats which were upholstered in a shocking-pink velvet.

'Subtle, ain't it?' Edie said, motioning Minnie into the carriage.

When the two women were seated and the driver had pulled away, Edie leaned forward, taking one of Minnie's hands in her own. 'Lovely,' she said, holding the tapered fingers. 'Pianist's hands. You play, don't you? Or you used to, when you were on the boards.'

Minnie nodded. 'A neighbour of mine and my ma's, he took a shine to me when I was a little girl. Taught me how to play the piano, read music. We used to write little bits and pieces of songs together. That's how I got started.'

Edie held her own hands up for inspection, the fingers short and blunt. 'Spud-picker's claws, my ma used to call 'em. She weren't wrong. Useful though. We made artificial flowers for a living when I was a girl. Little fingers come in useful for the fiddly bits.'

'Same as Ida,' Minnie said. 'Rose's mother. My friend—'
She tailed off, suddenly overcome by the memory of Rose.

Edie's eyes filled with tears. 'I know,' she said, patting
Minnie's hand. 'It never stops hurting, does it? Tansie told
me how close you were to that poor girl. Like sisters, he said.'

Minnie nodded.

'We don't really know each other, Minnie. Not yet at least.
But I thought maybe I could cheer you up.'

'It's very kind of you, Edie,' Minnie said.

'Well, it weren't entirely – what's that fancy word my
husband uses? – altruistic, that's it. Between you, me and the
bedpost, I miss it all. The halls. The excitement. Wouldn't
mind getting back to it, truth be told.'

Before Minnie could reply, the brougham pulled up to a
gentle stop at Edie's club on Dover Street.

'They called it the Concordia after some Roman goddess,'
Edie said, as the two women descended from the carriage.
'Meant to symbolise how we all agree with each other, what
with no men around. Don't always quite work out.'

She swept forward through the heavy swing doors, signed
Minnie in at the desk and then gestured for Minnie to follow
her. 'I'll give you the full tour later. But first, tea. Or would
you prefer something stronger?'

'Tea would be lovely.'

The two women made their way down a long corridor,
their footsteps muffled by the deep pile of an ornately
patterned carpet. At the end of the corridor was a comfortable
lounge, with a string quartet playing something classical and
unfamiliar to Minnie. Footmen with tea trays moved swiftly
from table to table, where groups of fashionably dressed
women were seated, chatting or listening to the music. The
only men in the room were the waiters.

Minnie tried not to gawp as she took her seat, but it was difficult not to. The room was subtly decorated in shades of cream and gold, pale colours that only the rich could afford. Everything spoke of wealth without the need for ostentation. Edie stood out like a sore thumb. Minnie caught the other woman looking at her. 'Surprised they let me in?' Edie said. 'It's amazing what money can do, Min. And Teddy can be very persuasive.'

'Teddy?' Minnie asked.

'My husband. Lord Linton.' Edie closed her eyes for a moment, as if in pain. 'Funny, when he first inherited the title, I used to get such a kick out of saying that. Lord Linton.' She broke off abruptly and made a show of pouring the tea.

'Weren't he always Lord Linton?' Minnie asked, trying to fill the gap left in the conversation.

Edie shook her head. 'His brother had the title. But he was killed.'

'Murdered?'

'Well, the other fella said no. Said it was an accident; he'd been stopping Teddy's brother from beating a dog. But he was tried for murder, just the same. Managed to escape the noose, but he got life. Obviously.' She shook herself. 'Enough of that. I'm supposed to be cheering you up, remember?' She passed Minnie a cup of tea. 'You married? Courting?'

Minnie shook her head vigorously.

'Very wise,' Edie said, with feeling.

Minnie remembered the newspaper coverage of the unlikely but glamorous union between a music hall star and a member of the aristocracy. Her confusion must have been evident on her face.

'Don't believe everything you read,' Edie said. 'It ain't all champagne and roses.'

As if unconscious of her actions, she pulled the sleeves of her dress down over her hands, hiding her bejewelled fingers, and buried her hands in the folds of her skirt. Tiny as she was, she looked even further diminished, as if the mention of her husband had somehow shrunk her.

A silence fell between them. Minnie looked around the room again. One long wall was almost entirely taken up with stained-glass windows, about twice Minnie's height, depicting what looked like Greek goddesses.

'That one in the middle,' Edie said, pointing to an image of a woman holding a shield, 'that's Minerva. That was the name you went by, weren't it? When you were on the boards?'

Minnie smiled, delighted that Edie knew anything about her life as a performer.

'Why *did* you give it up?' Edie asked. 'I know you saw right through Tansie's cunning plan the other night, but it's true, I did see you once at the Palace. You were really good. I weren't lying when I said it.'

'Stage fright. One night it just came over me and I couldn't shake it off.'

Edie leaned forward, patting Minnie's hand, her voice slow and serious. 'You can do anything you set your mind to. Anything. You've just got to want it enough.'

'Well, maybe that was the problem. I didn't want it enough.'

'I did. It was all I wanted for a while. Wouldn't let no one or nothing stand in my way. And then I met Teddy.' She broke off again. 'All I'm saying, Min, is don't give up the life you have now for a man.'

'That's not very likely,' Minnie said.

'Ain't it? That Mr Easterbrook's very easy on the eye, wouldn't you say?'

Minnie was surprised to find herself blushing. 'There's nothing going on between me and Albert. Or any fella.'

The waiter appeared with a refill for their tea, but Edie waved him away. 'Fancy the tour?' she said, rising from her seat.

She led Minnie from the lounge through to the dining room, standing empty but fully laid out with bone china and crystal for the evening's meal. From there, they went to the smoking gallery and, beyond that, the library, with comfortable armchairs and a selection of newspapers and periodicals alongside a collection of books. In this final room, a young woman was skimming through a novel, giggling to herself. She drew a disapproving glance from a studious-looking woman in heavy glasses who was consulting a weighty volume of an encyclopaedia. The two of them looked like a *Punch* illustration for 'Industry and Indolence'.

'I'd have killed for somewhere like that when I was growing up,' Edie whispered as they left the library.

'Whereabouts in Richmond?' Minnie asked, recalling Edie's moniker.

'Oh, no, that was just my stage persona. I was gonna be the Pocket Rocket, but the fella who ran the music hall reckoned Richmond Rocket sounded better. Anyway, Soho, that's where I hail from. You?'

'Seven Dials,' Minnie said. The two women shared a look of understanding.

'You and me,' Edie said, 'we're very alike. Women like us need to look after each other. Now, if it's all the same to you, I reckon it's time for a little glass of fizz.'

EIGHTEEN

Albert left the house and briskly walked the half-mile to Piccadilly. His destination lay at the far end of the street, through an inconspicuous arch, across a tiled, covered walkway ending in a pair of plain wooden doors. A small brass plaque announced this was the Godwin Club, but nothing else about the entrance indicated anything of significance. Albert noticed the high polish on the plaque. Ida Watkins would have no need to lick her finger and smooth over any fingerprints here.

The doorman, immaculately dressed in a suit Albert suspected cost more than his own, politely asked him his business.

'I'm here as a guest of Monty Banister,' Albert said.

'Ah, Mr Easterbrook. Certainly, sir,' the doorman murmured and ushered Albert into the building.

He handed his hat and coat to a footman waiting in the wood-panelled lobby, and was directed down a corridor, the thick carpet muffling both the sound of his footsteps and the street noise. Ahead of him lay a large, brightly lit room from where the murmur of voices and the tinkling of glasses could be heard.

Billy Walker stood by the door, legs placed firmly apart,

arms folded across his body. So this was where he worked on his nights away from the Palace. Billy caught Albert's eye, flushed and turned away.

The room, high-ceilinged, with an enormous chandelier hanging from an elaborate central medallion, housed what looked like a hundred or so men in evening dress. Circulating smoothly amongst them, dispensing drinks in crystal glasses from silver trays, were a number of smartly dressed young men and women. Albert heard his name being called above the hubbub and turned to see his brother-in-law, Monty, navigating his way through the crowd towards him.

Albert struggled to remember when he had last seen Monty, always timing his visits to Adelaide when he knew her husband would be at work. The years had not been kind to him. His bulging eyes, which always put Albert in mind of a frog, had a rheumy cast to them, and his skin was now heavily veined around the nose. He strode towards Albert, holding out his hand and forcing a smile. A waiter appeared almost instantly at their side.

'Another,' Monty said, holding up a glass containing the last dregs of a brandy. 'You?'

'The same. Thank you.'

Monty drained the last of his drink and placed it on a passing tray. Above their heads, the chandelier cast a warm glow and yet Monty's skin looked pallid and pasty.

'Almost didn't make it tonight,' Monty said, scanning the room all the time. 'Henry has recently stood down from several committees. Making the devil of a lot of work for me, but apparently there's no one else who can deal with it all.' Monty's cheeks flushed with pride at his own self-importance. The Henry he had made casual reference to was Henry

Mortimer, Secretary of State for the Colonies. 'Anyway,' he continued, as the waiter appeared with their drinks, 'you look well. How have you been keeping?'

Albert gave a noncommittal reply and asked after Adelaide. Monty barked out a self-conscious laugh. 'Oh, you know Adelaide. Spending all my money. Her dressmaker's bill arrived last week. Five hundred guineas. And yet she tells me she has nothing to wear.'

Albert reminded himself he was here to court Monty's favour, so he silenced the retort that sprang to his lips. 'She wasn't looking her best when I saw her on Saturday,' he said. 'She told me she had been unwell.'

Monty shrugged. 'That's women for you. Always complaining of some malady or other. And as for looking her best – who is? Time's winged chariot, and all that.'

He took a large swig of his drink. 'Look here, old chap,' he said, as if the second drink had fuelled his determination, 'I hope you don't mind my asking, but why the sudden interest in the Godwin?'

'Most exclusive club in London. Who wouldn't want to be part of that? Own my own Stanhope?'

Monty looked blank. 'Sorry? Stanhope?'

Albert tapped the side of his nose. 'Secret's safe with me.'

Monty looked bemused. Albert knew he wasn't intelligent enough to feign ignorance that convincingly.

'Sorry,' Monty said again, a note of irritation creeping into his voice, 'no idea what you're talking about. Must be confusing the Godwin with some other gaff. Anyway, I thought all this kind of thing was rather beneath you, with your impressive principles.'

Albert smiled ruefully. 'Principles don't pay the bills, I'm afraid.'

'Well, there's an easy solution, old chap. Eat a bit of humble pie, tell the parents you were wrong about joining the police and you're sorry for the shame it caused them. Then find yourself a nice girl with a healthy fortune.'

Albert winced theatrically. 'No stomach for humble pie, I'm afraid. And I want to make my own money. Lots of it.'

Monty smiled. 'All that nonsense about wanting to make a differ-ence.' He grabbed the arm of a hostess passing them. 'Champagne. My usual.' He turned back to Albert. 'Perrier-Jouët, old man. Adelaide wouldn't touch it at first. Far too dry, she said. But then she realised it was all the rage and now she'll drink nothing else. I swear if horse piss became de rigueur, she'd be knocking it back by the pint.'

Albert flinched inwardly at Monty's vulgarity, and wondered how many brandies the man had consumed. He glanced round the room and spotted two familiar faces. Jeffers, John's superior officer, who had been so reluctant to investigate Rose and Winter's deaths, deep in conversation with Gillespie, Lionel Winter's close friend.

He felt a hand laid gently on his back, and turned to see a man of delicate, almost girlish features. He was tall, lean, with intelligent birdlike eyes. Most notable about him was the rapid and exaggerated motion of his blinking, as if he were exercising all his facial muscles. The man smiled benignly at Monty, waiting for an introduction.

'Ah, Linton,' Monty said, leaning forward to slap the man on his arm and nearly falling over in the process. 'Albert, this is Lord Linton, the founder of our feast. Owns the Godwin. Linton, Albert Easterbrook, my brother-in-law.'

Albert swallowed his surprise. The owner of the Godwin, the man whose identity was shrouded in secrecy, was Edie Bennett's husband.

'Mr Easterbrook, how pleasant to meet you,' Linton said, his voice measured and low-pitched, in contrast to the nervous motion of his blinking. '"The Champion of the Labouring Classes", isn't it? I understand you're keen to join our little family.'

'I am. Although I understand I need five recommendations.'

Linton waved his hand in a gesture of dismissal. 'A formality. Monty is an excellent fellow and if he'll stand up for you I can't see there being any problem. Has he shown you the gymnasium? The library?'

Albert shook his head. Linton gave the merest glance to one side and a young woman appeared. She was tall, slender, extraordinarily beautiful. 'Eleanor here, one of our hostesses, will be delighted to show you around, won't you, my dear?' He turned back to Albert. 'Or would you prefer one of our young men?'

'No,' Albert said, 'I'm sure Eleanor will do a splendid job.'

<hr/>

Eleanor was, indeed, an excellent hostess. After she had shown Albert the lavishly appointed gymnasium and the library, she took him to the dining room and offered him a delicious selection of canapés.

'Best chef in London, sir,' she said. 'Poached from the San Régis in Paris.'

She leaned towards him and Albert caught the faintest scent of jasmine. She was undeniably lovely, with a swan-like neck and full lips that seemed permanently parted in anticipation. Yet she was … he struggled to find the word. Lifeless, perhaps. She reminded him of Maud Winter. Perfect and dull. Unbidden, the image of Minnie came to him. Never dull.

On their way back to the main reception room, Albert decided to follow his hunch.

'My footman mentioned some girl he knew who worked here,' he said. 'Rose something. Killed herself just recently. Did you know her?'

Eleanor blinked two or three times in rapid succession. Not so lifeless now.

'Oh yes, sir,' she said, 'Rose worked here as a hostess.'

'Friend of yours?'

'I'm not sure we ever even spoke. It was terribly sad, though, what happened to her.'

And then, with an ease that could only have come from practice, she gave him a wide smile, leaned in towards him and said, 'I almost forgot. Lord Linton would never forgive me if I didn't show you the swimming pool.'

On their way back from the swimming pool, which Albert had to admit was impressive, they passed a staircase leading down to the basement of the building. A chain was placed across it, with a 'Private: No Entry' sign.

'We haven't been down there,' he said. 'Can't have you missing out any of the tour.'

A flicker of concern crossed Eleanor's face, and was gone just as quickly as it had appeared. 'Servants' quarters, sir,' she said. 'Nothing of interest.'

Back in the reception room, Monty was officially drunk. Judging by the noise levels he wasn't the only one. Albert declined the offer of any more alcohol, instead asking the waiter where he might find the conveniences. He quietly slipped out, walking back down the carpeted hallway, past the entrance. Further along the corridor was the staircase, the 'No Entry' sign swinging gently from a chain. He glanced behind him, unhooked the chain and re-hooked it behind him.

The marble stairs of the public areas were now replaced with uneven stone, worn in places by repeated footfall. The staircase narrowed the further Albert descended, until he found himself in the gloom of the basement. He moved forward tentatively, down a dark passageway sparsely lit by gas lamps. His footsteps echoed in the emptiness. He fully expected to bump into one of the black-clad waiters, or the charming hostesses, but the space was deserted.

At the end of the corridor, Albert passed through a narrow archway into a circular area with a low domed ceiling. The walls were simple brickwork with what looked like a lime wash, and the floor underneath was poorly matched stone and brick. Facing Albert, within the circular space, were five doors. Working from the left, he tried the first three. Locked. He was surprised when the fourth door opened smoothly.

In the centre of the room stood a large bed, draped with a richly brocaded paisley bedspread. Albert ran his hands over the silk and velvet cushions piled high at the top of the bed. The walls were painted a deep red, and gas lamps of an elaborate Moroccan design shed a warm glow, the punched metal casting fantastic shadows on the walls. The floor was covered with an exquisite rug, Persian possibly, its rich reds, purples and greens augmenting the luxury. Although nothing appeared to be burning other than the gas lamps, the room smelled of incense, overlaid with something sweet, a little sickly. A full-height cupboard stood to the right of the door. Inside was a shelf of leather cords and two short wooden paddles. Albert was leaning in for a closer inspection when he heard a gentle cough behind him. He pocketed an object he held in his hand, straightened up and turned.

Linton stood in the doorway. 'Lost your way, old boy?' he asked gently.

Albert shook his head and smiled lopsidedly. He slurred his speech. 'Looking for the conve—, conev—, the lavs. Got lost. Was just about to lie down. Little nap.' He gestured clumsily towards the bed, swayed and grabbed the brass bedstead for support.

Linton nodded his head sympathetically. Behind him, Albert could make out a figure in the gloomy corridor. Billy Walker, still avoiding eye contact.

'I'm afraid this area is for members only,' Linton said. 'And, although I see no problem with your application being approved, you are not yet a member. So best you be on your way, mmm?'

'What goes on down here, then?' Albert leered as he followed Linton down the corridor back to the staircase, Billy bringing up the rear. 'Something … saucy?' he snorted.

Linton gave a surprising, high-pitched giggle. 'Oh dear, no. These are simply rooms for our members to sleep in. If they get caught in town, and don't relish the anonymity of a hotel. We're not the first club to introduce the idea, by any means.'

'Wasn't on the tour,' Albert mumbled. 'Lovely Eleanor. Funny place to have a bedroom, though. Dingy, don't you think?'

'Our facilities are somewhat limited, and we don't want every member clamouring for an overnight stay. So we keep it quiet. And if, like you, someone should wander down here, they'd think it was just a servants' area. Probably wouldn't bother investigating any further. We're not all detectives, Mr Easterbrook.' And he giggled again.

'Damned civilised idea,' Albert said, deliberately stumbling up the first of the stairs and muttering his apologies to no one in particular. At the top of the stairs, a footman held his coat and hat.

'Monty's already left,' Linton said. 'We had to … well, *pour* him into a cab and send him home. How are you sorted for transport?'

Albert raised his hands dismissively. 'I'm fine,' he said, leaning in perilously close to Linton. 'Spot of fresh air. Do me good.' And he donned his coat and hat and stumbled out of the club, maintaining the illusion of drunkenness until he had turned out of the covered courtyard and onto Piccadilly.

He glanced behind. No one had followed him. From his pocket, he removed the small item he had taken from the cupboard in the downstairs bedroom. Albert knew what it was, but he'd never actually held one. Two nickel rings, one nestled just inside the other, and a screw to tighten them in place. The outer ring was maybe two inches in diameter, with a row of sharp spikes facing inwards. The inner ring housed a series of small holes. A pollution ring. Positioned over the male member, the inner ring would expand should the man become aroused. But at a certain point those spikes would come into play. Albert winced at the very thought of it, as he turned it over in his hand and wondered what on earth a pollution ring was doing in the luxuriously appointed bedroom of the Godwin Club.

NINETEEN

'And a plum cake without much fruit in it, that's a bellowing cake. See?' Daisy said, flashing a smile.

Albert frowned. 'Not precisely, no.'

'Well, the plums are so far apart they has to bellow when they wishes to converse.'

Minnie entered the Palace dressing room and Albert looked up gratefully, relieved that another adult had entered the room. 'Miss Mountford has been teaching me slang,' he said.

'How charming. Has she told you what a village blacksmith is?' Minnie asked, navigating her way through the cramped space to remove her bag from beneath the table.

'She has taught me many new terms,' Albert said, 'but I don't believe that was one of them.'

'It's the term we use in the theatrical world for an act that don't last longer than a week,' Minnie said, rifling through her bag. 'Normally it happens when someone has been spending their time enlightening fellas as to the joys of the English language rather than rehearsing their new song that someone has so kindly written for them, and which they're due to be performing in two days' time.' She lifted her head from her bag and smiled benignly at Daisy.

Daisy leapt up, grabbed a song sheet from the table in front of her, and scurried out of the room.

'Village blacksmith?' Albert asked.

'It's from some poem. Bernard would know. "Week in, week out, from morn till night, you can hear his bellows blow."'

'No,' Albert said, shaking his head. 'Still don't get it.'

'Week in. Week out. An act what lasts a week. See?'

Albert nodded, wishing he hadn't asked.

'I'm surprised she could tear herself away from Tom long enough to talk to you,' Minnie said, abandoning the search in her bag and turning her attention to the desk drawers.

'Do you disapprove?' he asked, trying to sound nonchalant. He had watched Minnie and Tom as they'd left his house the day before. Minnie had leaned in to say something to Tom, and he'd laughed. There'd been a familiarity about the way their bodies inclined towards one another that had niggled at Albert ever since.

'No. It's all a bit fast, but they do make a lovely couple. Found it!' she exclaimed, extracting, somewhat incongruously, a dog's collar and lead from the bottom drawer of the desk.

Albert looked at her.

'For the monkey,' she said. 'His latest trick is to climb up the rigging and piss on anyone who's on the stage. He got Tansie this morning.' She smiled and waved the collar and lead in the air. 'So, before I spend the next hour or so trying to find the little bugger – the monkey, not Tansie – why don't you tell me what happened last night?'

Albert recounted his evening at the Godwin, the surprising news that Billy was working there as a bouncer, and the fact the club was owned by Lord Linton. Minnie started at the mention of the name.

'Lord Linton?' she said. 'That's Edie Bennett's husband.'

Albert nodded. 'Even I knew that. As I remember, it was in all the society pages at the time. Wedding of the century.'

'What did you make of him?'

'Difficult to tell,' Albert said. 'He appears harmless, but I have my doubts. Why do you ask?'

'Edie mentioned him yesterday, when we were having tea. I got the feeling the marriage ain't exactly how it appears to the outside world.'

'Neither's the Godwin Club,' Albert said. Fleetingly, he considered omitting any mention of the pollution ring. But there was little that shocked Minnie, so he withdrew the ring from his pocket and laid it on the table. 'From one of the Godwin bedrooms,' he said. 'Along with other paraphernalia that suggests some interesting activities take place in those basement rooms.'

Minnie picked it up and carried it over to the window. 'They sell these on Holywell Street, if you know who to ask,' she said. 'Meant to be a deterrent, but apparently there's chaps who like it a little more than they should. It don't mean much, though, does it? I mean, it's surprising, where you found it and all, but does it have any connection to Rose's murder?'

'Probably not. I'm wondering, though, if Linton knows I took it. This arrived in the morning's post.'

He handed her an envelope, containing an invitation to Linton's private residence the following night.

'I thought perhaps we should have a chat with Billy,' he said. 'See what he knows about the Godwin?'

Minnie nodded, and led the way down the backstage corridor to a flight of stairs leading to a lower level. Albert was struck again by the swift and purposeful nature of all her movements, as if she knew exactly where she was going and was in a hurry to get there. He, on the other hand, stumbled his way through the cramped corridor, banging his head at a point where the ceiling suddenly lowered. As they descended, it grew colder and damper, an unpleasant aroma filling the air. Albert pressed his handkerchief to his mouth.

Minnie glanced back at him. 'It's the river,' she said. 'Or the sewers. I ain't sure which. It runs under the Palace, and the lower down you go the stronger the whiff.'

One floor below was a large workspace with flats and scenery, some costumes, and props littering the room. Billy was alone, with a pot of glue in one hand and a brush in the other, incongruously fixing paper flowers onto a wooden bower. He saw Albert and pointedly turned away.

'Billy,' Minnie said, 'can we have a word? About the Godwin.'

Billy said nothing, but the motion of his hand slowed.

'I was there last night,' Albert said. 'As were you.'

Billy shrugged with exaggerated nonchalance. 'So? No law against earning money, is there?'

'None at all,' Albert said, reasonably. 'It just strikes me as a little strange you never mentioned Rose worked there too.'

Billy's shoulders tensed. He placed the glue pot and brush on the floor and wiped his hands with an old rag he had in his back pocket.

'Most of us here work lots of different places,' Billy said. 'It don't mean nothing.'

'Except we're starting to think Rose's death might be connected to the Godwin,' Minnie said. 'Anything you can tell us, Bill?'

Billy glanced at her, then turned away.

Minnie went to speak again, but Albert raised his hand slightly to stop her. 'I think we're wasting our time, Miss Ward,' he said, deliberately amplifying the richness of his accent. 'I spent a very pleasant evening at the Godwin, and I cannot entertain the idea those gentlemen had any hand in Rose's death. As I've said all along, it's more likely to be her jealous boyfriend and his handy fists that did the damage.'

With a speed that belied his bulk, Billy threw down the rag, picked up the glue pot and hurled it across the room. It smashed, and the glue slid sluggishly down the far wall. Instinctively, Albert moved sideways to place himself between Billy and Minnie, but the other man's anger seemed to be spent.

'You know nothing,' Billy said quietly.

Minnie took a step forward and laid a hand on his arm. He shrugged her off, but she repeated the gesture. 'So tell us what we need to know, Bill.'

Billy lifted his head and glanced round the room. 'Not here. The Wellington. Half an hour.'

TWENTY

The Wellington was a ferocious-looking pub three streets away from the Palace. Minnie knew its reputation and had never set foot inside the door. Billy had chosen wisely. No one from the Palace was ever likely to come in here to drink.

Billy arrived a few minutes after Minnie and Albert, adopting his customary swagger. Albert had left money behind the bar, and Billy nodded his thanks before joining them at a table in a window alcove. The window glass was smeared with grease, beer and something unidentifiable Minnie didn't want to think about. Every surface was sticky.

Billy pulled his chair back an unnecessary distance from the table and sat, spreading his legs wide. He downed the beer in three swift gulps, wiped his moustache and leaned back, resting one arm across the back of the chair. He eyed Albert carefully. 'For a start-off, I never hit her. Not once.'

'So how come I saw her with bruises?' Minnie asked. 'You argued like cat and dog, Bill. And we all know you're a bit handy.'

'I never touched her,' Billy said, speaking with deliberate slowness and lowering his voice. 'Any bruises on her, she got somewhere else.'

'Like the Godwin?' Albert asked.

Minnie went to speak, but Albert shook his head almost imperceptibly. He nodded at the barman and raised one finger. Moments later, a fresh pint of beer was placed in front of Billy. He stared at it, as if not recognising what it was.

'Billy?' Minnie prompted. 'We know Rose worked at the Godwin. And we've got a pretty good idea of what goes on in those downstairs bedrooms.'

'Hostesses, that's what they call them,' Billy said bitterly. 'Look pretty. Serve drinks. Rose was mad for it. Said the extra money would mean we could get married, start a family. I didn't see the harm in it. So I said yes. And now I can't—' He broke off, rubbing his eyes angrily with the heels of his hands.

Albert glanced at Minnie and she leaned in. 'What happened, Bill?' she asked gently.

'She was popular. Well, you knew her, Min. Everyone loved her, didn't they? Some of the chaps were keen on her doing a bit more than just serving them drinks. In those basement rooms you know so much about. First I knew of it, she'd already gone down there a few times.'

'And then?' Minnie asked.

'Other times. Other men. That's how she got the bruises.' The bravura had left him entirely. He sat with his shoulders slumped, his voice dropped so low it was difficult to hear him above the laughter and shouts of the other drinkers. Minnie and Albert sat in silence and let the man cry. After a few minutes, he sniffed loudly. Albert passed him a handkerchief and he nodded his thanks.

'How'd you and Rose get work there, Billy?' Minnie asked.

'Tansie got us in. Said he'd got connections.'

Minnie's heart sank. 'Did he get other people work at the Godwin?' she asked, thinking of the photographs in Tansie's safe and ignoring Albert's enquiring look.

Billy shrugged. 'Dunno. Never saw anyone else there from the Palace.'

'What about the shoes, Bill?' Minnie asked. 'The ones with the roses?'

'Some fella she met at the Godwin. He came to the Palace a few times, went in the snuggeries with her. She swore blind they weren't getting up to nothing. Just talking, she said. That made it worse, somehow. She never talked much to me.'

Albert reached into his pocket and withdrew the Stanhope with Lionel Winter's image inside it, the one found amongst Rose's belongings. He passed it to Billy, showing him where to look.

Billy peered at the image, then nodded his head. 'That's him.'

'He's dead, Billy,' Albert said. 'Made to look like an accident, but we're thinking murder.'

Billy's head shot up at the word, genuine fear in his eyes.

'Did Rose do something at the Godwin?' Albert asked. 'See something?'

Billy gazed round the pub, as if aware for the first time of where he was. The full pint still sat on the table in front of him. He looked at the clock above the bar. 'Time I was back,' he said, pushing back his chair with a loud scrape that drew glances from the other drinkers.

Minnie went to stop him, but Albert touched her lightly on the arm, and they let Billy leave.

'Why didn't you push it?' Minnie said. 'He obviously knows something more.'

'He does. What I'm curious about is why he told us anything at all, when he's been so tight-lipped up until now. We'll let him mull it over. Try again in a day or so.'

After Albert dropped her off at the Palace, Minnie walked along the backstage corridor onto the stage. She was hoping she would find Daisy rehearsing. But the stage was empty.

She turned to go, and then heard a panicky whispering from the wings. The voice was Tansie's, and it was so unusual to hear him whispering that Minnie slid behind the curtains. From there, she could see into the left wing of the stage.

Tansie had Daisy by the arm, and was pulling her towards him, saying something Minnie could not catch. Daisy reared back and shook her head. 'You've got the wrong girl,' Minnie heard her say. The light was too dim in the wings for Minnie to see Daisy's face clearly, but she sounded frightened. She pulled her arm away from Tansie's grasp and ran off backstage. Tansie stood for a moment, then slowly followed her.

Minnie heard a noise behind her, and turned to see Cora, her gaze following Tansie's departing back, her lips parted, and her face drained of all colour.

An hour later, after Minnie had dried Cora's tears and convinced her that, perhaps, what they'd both seen hadn't been what it appeared, she walked Cora to the stage door and sent her on her way home. Then she doubled back, trotted down the stairs and found Billy ponderously cleaning glue off the wall with a knife and a rag, neither of which were having much effect. He looked pale, with dark rings under his eyes, but he had regained some of his usual swagger.

'No more, Min,' he said. 'I've said enough.'

'I want you to get me into the Godwin,' Minnie said. 'As one of them hostesses.'

Billy stopped what he was doing and turned towards her, his face even paler. 'I ain't doing that.'

'Whatever happened to Rose, it's got something to do with that club. They've rumbled that Albert's on to them. They know about me, too. But I can change how I look. Wigs, make-up. Not even my own mother would recognise me, God rest her soul.'

Billy shook his head. 'I ain't putting anyone in harm's way.'

'You can be there. Keep an eye on me.'

He shook his head again, turned away and resumed his task. 'Find some other mug,' he said.

'You might not have any choice,' Minnie said quietly.

'Meaning?'

'Rose, what she did in those downstairs rooms at the Godwin, and you sharing the proceeds? The police don't take too kindly to that, Bill.'

With exaggerated slowness, he wrapped the knife in the rag and placed it on top of a trunk full of costumes. His actions couldn't hide the shaking of his hands.

'We ain't never been what you'd call friends, have we, Min? I know what you think of me. And even if you were right, even if I had hit her, it ain't as bad as what you're prepared to do. Ratting on one of your own.' He held her gaze, and Minnie was the first to look away. 'I'll get you in there,' he said.

'It's a deal,' she said, holding out her hand. Billy looked at it and turned away, leaving the room. Minnie was left standing, her heart already thumping at the thought of entering the Godwin and retracing Rose's steps.

TWENTY-ONE

Lord Linton's house was set in a large plot, with what looked to Albert like a generous rear garden. The house itself was unprepossessing from the exterior: flat-fronted, a simple red brick with no ornamental flourishes. Albert mounted the steps and was admitted to the house by a footman with a shock of ginger hair.

Inside, it felt as if Albert had entered the *Arabian Nights*. The entrance hall was tiled from floor to ceiling in a vivid aquamarine. The staircase, which rose up two more floors, was painted black with gold finials, and a stuffed peacock sat on top of an intricately carved wooden cabinet.

Lord Linton stepped forward from a room to the left of the hallway, under an archway flanked with marble pillars. He gave Albert a gentle smile. 'So glad you could join me. The other night was delightful, but rather a melee, don't you think?' He followed Albert's eyes around the room and smiled again. 'Pardon the rather extravagant interior. My wife's choice.'

'Will Lady Linton be joining us? Or any other guests?' Albert asked, accepting the glass of champagne the red-headed footman presented to him. The room had a high domed ceiling and was tiled in gold and green. Recessed seating was piled high with cushions and throws. In the centre of the floor was a small, square pond and fountain.

'No,' Linton said. 'Edie is dining with friends tonight. And with prospective new members I always favour a more intimate gathering. If you're ready to dine, we might move through.'

Past another archway lay the dining room, equally extravagant in its decoration, with rich tiling and heavy brocaded fabric draped on every surface. The proportions were perfectly designed for ease of conversation. Albert was seated opposite Linton at a small dining table, heavily inlaid with marquetry, and the first of the courses was brought out. The food was excellent, although the wine tasted a little off. Albert regretted the fact he could not simply enjoy the evening. Linton was an excellent host: charming, intelligent and an attentive listener.

Seven courses later, the meal was rounded off with a delicate lemon sorbet. 'I am fortunate enough to have an ice house at the Godwin,' Linton said. 'So delicacies such as this are always available to me.' He smiled as the footman removed the last of the plates, and invited Albert to move to the smoking room next door.

Albert went to stand, and felt his legs go from beneath him. He gripped the edge of the table a little too firmly, and knocked over a half-empty glass of wine, its contents immediately staining the linen tablecloth.

'Good stuff, that burgundy, isn't it?' Linton said, placing a hand on Albert's upper arm. 'I saw how much you enjoyed it.'

But Albert knew he had taken very little wine. He tried to straighten up, but was overcome by a wave of dizziness and sat back heavily in his chair. 'I think,' he said, his tongue thick in his mouth as he struggled to speak, 'best go home. Not well.'

'But I've laid on an entertainment for you, Albert. It would be a great shame were you to miss it. Just let George here get you a little water, then he can help you through to the other room, and you can take a seat.' He gestured to the footman, who hurried off and returned moments later with a glass of water.

Albert shook his head and swept away the glass, knocking it out of George's hand and onto the rug.

'Oh dear,' Linton said, blinking rapidly, 'I should never have allowed you to take so much wine. Let's move you through to the other room. What I have to show you is bound to revive you.'

George was joined by another servant, a large, muscular fellow, and the pair of them took Albert by the arms. He felt he was barely walking, being dragged instead by the two men. They led him through a doorway, positioned him carefully on a chair and left.

The room he found himself in was small, about half the size of the intimate dining room. Incense was burning, filling the air with its heady scent. The gas lamps were turned down low, so it was difficult to distinguish many details, but Albert was seated in front of a table, about six feet in length. A sheet was placed over it, a shape visible beneath. Linton stood behind the table. He smiled at Albert and, as he spoke, the excitement was evident in his voice.

'Albert,' he said, leaning forward and lowering his voice to an anticipatory whisper, 'I have a rare treat for you.'

Albert shook his head, trying to clear the fog in his brain.

'Might we …' he asked, 'open a window? Turn up the lamps a little?'

'Later, Albert. But first, the entertainment.' He rested his hand on the sheet. 'I've been longing to show you, almost from the first moment we met. Something about you told me you'd find it intriguing.'

Linton turned back the sheet a foot or so.

It was a woman.

Her left arm was raised and bent above her head, her cheek turned and resting on her upper arm. Her right hand cradled a heavy plait of dark hair. The gaslight caught the glimmer of pearls at her neck. Her hands were small, delicate, the fingernails a translucent pink. She was beautiful, but Albert had no interest in what Linton was proposing.

He tried to rise from his chair and leave. But the weakness in his legs told him it was pointless.

'You don't want to go, Albert,' Linton said. 'We've barely started.' A half-smile played on his lips. With one swift, theatrical movement, like a conjurer revealing the reappearance of his glamorous assistant, he pulled back the rest of the sheet.

Albert struggled to comprehend what was before him. He felt the bitter taste of bile at the back of his throat, and instinctively closed his eyes to obliterate the horror.

The woman had been cut open from the top of her breastbone to just below her stomach, the skin peeled back to display her insides.

This was Lord Linton's entertainment.

Linton stood back from the table, his face alight with pleasure. 'A rare delight, is she not, Albert? You really are very privileged. And look.' He gestured towards the woman's dark head of hair. 'Does she not resemble someone of our acquaintance? A certain Miss Ward? How delightful it would be to explore beneath dear Minnie's beautiful exterior. Don't you think? Of course, if you and Miss Ward would stop interfering in affairs that don't concern you, that charming idea need never become a reality.'

Albert tried to stand, but fell forward onto his knees. His mind was a confusion of horror and disbelief, but he had some idea of covering the woman at least. On all fours, he struggled to right himself. A wave of nausea swept over him, and everything went dark.

TWENTY-TWO

He woke, registered the light bleeding gently round the edge of the curtains, and realised he was in his own bed. He turned his head, a sharp pain piercing his skull. A woman was asleep in a chair beside him, her head gently lolling forward. A few dark strands had come loose from her hair.

Minnie.

Her hand was resting on the coverlet near his own. Carefully, he laid his hand on hers. Her skin was warm and dry, her fingers long and slender, with bones almost as delicate as the bird's skeleton he had found once, as a child, carrying it carefully all the way home to keep it safe. Slowly, he moved his finger so it rested on the pulse at her wrist.

Steady. Strong.

The curtains stirred gently in the breeze from the open window. In the distance, he could hear the sound of children's play and the rattle of carriages. Downstairs the front door slammed and Minnie woke, blinking slowly. Reluctantly, Albert let go of her wrist.

She leaned forward to look more closely at him.

'Still with us, then?' she said quietly, the casualness of her words failing to hide the anxiety in her eyes.

Albert nodded, and winced at the pain.

'Shh,' she said. 'Have a cuppa, and then we can talk about it.' She reached forward and rang the bell by his bed. Moments later, Mrs Byrne appeared.

'I told her,' Mrs Byrne said, gesturing towards Minnie. 'I told her, Albert, it wasn't proper for her to be alone with you in your room. But she wouldn't have it. I only just stepped out. To get you those nice lamb chops you like. I wasn't gone more than ten minutes, I swear. The butcher didn't have any lamb so I had to go to the fishmonger's and get you kippers instead. I hope that's all right—' and she stopped abruptly, the flow of words used up, and burst into tears. 'Oh, Albert, we thought you were dying.'

Albert turned towards Minnie. 'How are you here?' he asked her.

'I popped round yesterday evening to tell you Tom spoke again to Mrs Durrant, Lionel Winter's cook. Annie Belfer's still on the missing list. Just as I was leaving, a cab pulled up with you inside it. Driver was kind enough to help us get you upstairs.'

With a jolt, Albert recalled the events of the night before in nightmarish detail. The woman with her arm raised, her dark plait of hair, the pearls at her neck. And then the horror.

'John,' he said, pushing back the covers. 'I need to see John.'

Minnie laid a hand firmly on his chest.

'No, you ain't going nowhere until you've had a decent cuppa and something to eat.'

At these words, Mrs Byrne sprang forward and rushed out of the bedroom. A few minutes later she reappeared with a cup of tea and a plate of buttered bread. 'Just to tide you over.'

Albert was surprised to discover he was famished, and

extremely thirsty. He gulped down the tea, burning his tongue in the process, and devoured the bread. After Mrs Byrne had brought him a second cup of tea, which he drank with more caution than the first, Albert suggested he might be able to eat some kippers, and she left the room.

He turned to face Minnie.

'No stories, now,' she said calmly. 'No fretting over the fact I'm a woman. Tell me what happened.'

So he did. When he got to the mention of the dead woman, and the way Linton had referred to her as an entertainment, Minnie flinched and he paused in his narrative.

'No,' she said, breathing deeply. 'Go on.'

When he had finished his account, Minnie moved to the window. She stood in silence, her face averted, the sunlight picking out copper tones in her hair he had never noticed before.

'Did you recognise her? The woman?' Minnie asked.

Albert shuddered at the memory, the woman's body laid out on the table, the artful way Linton had displayed her. 'It was … difficult,' he said. 'She seemed small, short, although how I know that, I'm not sure. Just an impression. Dark hair. I think she must have been dead a while—' He broke off, fighting the instinct to push the images from his mind.

'Why do you say that?'

'No blood. None around the cuts, or on the table. It hadn't happened recently.'

The thought of Rose lay between them, so palpable Albert felt as if he could reach out his hand and touch her. If Linton had killed Rose, what had stopped him doing to her what he had done to the woman last night?

'Why didn't he kill you?' Minnie asked. 'I mean …

obviously I'm very glad he didn't, but why did he only drug you? He could've killed you.'

Albert shook his head. 'I've no idea. Maybe he only kills women.'

'But why show you the body? He knows you're on to him, why give you even more of a reason to suspect him?'

Albert thought for a moment. 'My guess is that it was some sort of warning,' he said. 'Showing me what he's capable of. What he could do again if he chooses. Although, to be perfectly truthful, he seemed to derive genuine pleasure from showing me the body, as if he thought I'd be as delighted with it as he was. Whatever the reason, I need to contact John. Get him to accompany me to Linton's house.'

'Won't Linton have moved her by now?' Minnie asked, resuming her seat beside the bed.

'Maybe. But there may still be traces. And we can question the servants. Eventually someone will speak out. They always do.' He paused. 'There's something else,' he said reluctantly.

She raised one expectant eyebrow.

'Linton commented on the woman's resemblance to … to you, Minnie. It was a threat, clearly.'

She shrugged. 'You know how I respond to threats, Albert. Although I am worried whatever he gave you last night might have been more of a floorer than we thought.'

He looked at her quizzically.

She leaned in closer, patting his hand. 'You just called me Minnie, Mr Easterbrook.'

❧

Albert, his head still throbbing from the after-effects of whatever he'd been drugged with, waited impatiently as

John knocked on Linton's front door. With them was a young policeman by the name of Grimshaw, a man almost as wide as he was tall, but with a surprisingly gentle face, full lips and soft features. He had bruising on his cheekbone, and Albert wondered what damage he'd done to the other chap.

The door was opened by a fair-haired parlour maid who tried to take their names, but Albert pushed past her. He rushed through the warren of smaller rooms, past the stuffed peacock, the ornate tiling, the small fountain, until he reached the room housing Linton's 'entertainment'. He was aware of a confusion of voices behind him, the parlour maid's protestations and the louder, deeper voices of male servants. He turned the handle of the door. Locked.

John placed a hand on his shoulder. 'Leave this to us,' he said, and then murmured, 'Strictly speaking, you shouldn't even be here.'

Albert turned. Clustered behind him were the maid, the red-headed footman from the night before and other servants he didn't recognise.

'Open this door,' John said sharply, removing his warrant card from his pocket.

The footman stepped forward. 'Only Lord Linton has the key to that room, sir.'

'Then fetch him. Or my PC here will break down the door.'

'That won't be necessary,' a voice said, and the group parted to reveal Linton, framed by the dining-room pillars. The whole thing smacked of a theatricality that Albert found particularly sickening, given what lay behind the locked door.

'Why, Albert!' he said. 'What on earth are you doing here? And with the police?'

'You know why I'm here,' Albert said, his breath coming in gasps. 'There's a dead girl in there, Linton.'

Linton gave the high, nervous giggle that seemed so at odds with the rest of him. 'Oh dear, Albert, how much did you have to drink? Gentlemen,' he said, turning to John and Grimshaw, 'Mr Easterbrook had supper with me last night and imbibed more alcohol than was, strictly speaking, advisable. Passed out. George here had to put him in a cab and send him home insensible. Whatever he thinks he saw, I can assure you there is no dead body in that room.'

'Just open the door, sir,' John said.

'I'd rather not, if it's all the same to you,' Linton said. 'There are … items in that room – special things only a collector or a man of more refined sensibility could appreciate.' He looked at Grimshaw, running his eyes slowly over the constable's frame, and gave an exaggerated shudder.

'We're not here to be refined,' John said sharply. 'Open the door now, sir, or Grimshaw will do it for you.'

'Very well,' Linton said. He looked pointedly at his servants and they dispersed immediately.

Albert's pulse quickened, and his breath came in tight gasps as Linton removed a key from a chain around his neck and unlocked the door. The curtains were drawn back, and daylight flooded the room. Albert could see now it was lined with mahogany cupboards which had not been visible the night before in the gloom of the lowered gas lamps. The chair had been moved nearer the window, but the table still stood in the middle of the room, a sheet hiding the shape beneath.

Now that he was faced with reliving the horror of the night before, Albert found himself hanging back. He grabbed John's arm instinctively.

John turned, placing his hand over Albert's. 'Wait outside,' he murmured, but Albert shook his head.

Linton moved to the table and turned to the three men. The whole thing was a grim mirror of the previous night's proceedings. Linton lifted the corner of the sheet in one hand and pulled it back.

There she lay. The same dark plait, the same pearls, her arm resting gently above her head. But she was different. Her face, for a start. Her head was tilted back, her eyes half closed, lips parted. She looked as if she were in a state of some ecstasy.

Albert's eyes travelled from her face to her body. No cuts. Her skin was intact. And there was something strange about that skin. Something not right.

Linton indicated to the men to move closer. 'See?' he said, gesturing towards the body. And, with a sickening lurch, Albert realised what he was looking at. A wax model, a mannequin. Lifelike and exquisitely made, but a model.

'She is what they call an Anatomical Venus. Sometimes also poetically termed a Dissected Grace. Some call her gruesome,' Linton said wistfully, 'but I find her exquisite. The most remarkable blend of art and science, and such an indispensable tool for enabling us to understand the workings of the female body.'

John drew closer, a look of fascinated horror on his face. Grimshaw hung back, bewildered. Albert sank into the chair, his head throbbing again, a wave of nausea passing through him.

'Come, come, gentlemen,' Linton said, his voice rising with enthusiasm as he gestured to the men to draw even closer. 'Look, she has real eyelashes – remarkable. Her blood vessels and nerves are made of silk dipped in wax. Beautiful work. And you may not have noticed, but see how tiny she is. She stands at about four feet. Even shorter than my lovely wife. Hugely expensive, of course, particularly for one made on such a small scale, and very difficult to acquire, which is why it was such a treat for me to show her to Albert last night. See, each of her organs can be removed.'

He inserted his fingernails either side of her torso. A panel came away from her body, to reveal the organs inside. Linton lifted out the heart, lungs, liver, placing each of them on a side table. 'And the final detail which, regrettably, Albert here missed, as he'd passed out by then.'

Buried beneath everything else, a tiny foetus attached to the body by a red silk thread.

Grimshaw let out an involuntary cry.

'Pull yourself together, man,' John hissed, although he himself looked pale and horrified.

Albert glanced around the room. Within the mahogany and glass cupboards lay hundreds of tiny figures that looked at first glance like dolls on little beds. Linton followed his gaze and gestured to him to draw closer. 'Anatomical mannequins,' he said. 'I've been collecting them for years. I like to think of them as the forerunners of my lovely Venus.'

The mannequins, all female, looked as if they were made of ivory, each about the size of a woman's hand or smaller and reclining on its own tiny bed, with cloth or ivory pillows. Some had the torso removed, others looked intact.

'The organs are removable on all of them,' Linton said, appearing at Albert's side and leaning in close, his breath misting the glass in the cupboard doors. 'But they lack the detail and accuracy of my Venus. I have been accused of being … ghoulish, shall we say? That's why I keep my collection under lock and key and only show it to carefully selected guests. But if wanting to advance our understanding of anatomy makes me a ghoul, the same could be said of Hippocrates, Galen, Vesalius. You struck me as a man of discernment, Albert. I'm so dreadfully sorry if I caused you distress. It was only meant to bring you pleasure.' He held Albert's gaze for a fraction too long. 'Really I should be flattered by your belief that this was a real body. Although it is rather difficult to see how one could be confused with the other. Doesn't say much for your detecting skills, dear boy,' and he laughed, slapping Albert on the arm.

John gave Albert a pointed look, then turned away. 'So sorry to have disturbed you, Lord Linton,' he said. 'PC Grimshaw and I will be on our way now. Albert?'

The three men left the house, walking in silence for a few yards before John ordered Grimshaw back to the station.

'I don't suppose there's any chance Linton is right, and you did mistake that Venus thing for a real body?' John asked, as the two of them watched Grimshaw disappearing into the distance.

'Because that would make your life much easier?' Albert said. 'Sorry to disappoint you, but no. I know what I saw.'

'And how're you feeling now?'

'My head feels like it's ready to split open, but apart from that I'm fine. Why do you ask?'

John sighed, looked down at his feet, then rubbed his right shoe on the back of his left calf.

'I've got a bit of bad news. The body of a young woman was found this morning in the Thames. They reckon she was probably drunk when she fell in, couldn't save herself. Fella who fished her out, he knew her. What are the odds, eh? Anyway, here's the thing. She was Lionel Winter's parlour maid.'

'Annie Belfer?' Albert said, knowing as he said her name that he'd been expecting this news for some time. 'So that's how they did it,' he murmured. 'Poor thing.'

John glanced up and down the road. 'This is bad, Albert. All these connections, bodies, but no solid evidence that we can pin on anyone. I don't like it. And now it looks like the bleedin' aristocracy are involved, so you can probably kiss goodbye to solving this one. Or, at least, seeing anyone brought to justice.'

'Can't you get Linton for anything?' Albert said. 'I know what I saw, John.'

'But there's no body, Albert. And if there was a law against getting excited by weird stuff, half of the House of Lords would be behind bars.'

'He threatened Minnie.'

'Your word against his. Linton's a queer cove, I'll give you that. But there's nothing I can arrest him for.'

'Have you found anything else?' Albert asked. 'About Lionel Winter? Or Rose?'

John shook his head. 'Nothing. I'll keep digging, though. Maybe we'll get lucky. See you at boxing next week? You said you'd try.'

'I'll do my best,' Albert said.

John gave him a half-smile and squeezed him affectionately on the arm. 'See you then,' he said, and turned away.

Albert gazed after him for a few minutes, then started for the Strand. He needed to talk to Minnie again.

TWENTY-THREE

Across town at the Palace, Minnie extracted another handkerchief from her bag and passed it to Cora, removing a sodden one from her grasp. It had been three days since they'd spotted Tansie in a suspicious-looking conversation with Daisy, and it seemed to Minnie that Cora had not stopped crying since. Cora loudly blew her nose and examined her face in the dressing-room mirror, prodding her swollen eyelids.

'Christ, Min,' she said, 'I look like Dandy Bob's dummy.'

'Before or after the monkey's been at it?'

Cora smiled weakly, and Minnie patted her hand. 'A bit of slap'll work wonders,' she said. 'But you've got to pull yourself together. The punters won't appreciate you breaking into sobs halfway through "Champagne Charlie". And you should talk to Tanse. I know it don't look good, the way he was talking to Daisy. But there are other explanations.'

Cora shook her head determinedly. 'Nah, it ain't just that. He's been acting odd lately. Suspicious, like.'

There was a gentle knock, and Albert popped his head round the dressing-room door. He looked enquiringly at Minnie, and Cora sprang to her feet, giving her nose one final blow.

'I'm off out,' she said. 'Get myself a bite to eat. Maybe the fresh air'll help.' She reached across and hugged Minnie, before turning to Albert. 'Men,' she sneered dismissively, and left the room.

'What did I do?' Albert asked.

Minnie shook her head. 'Nothing. It's Tansie. She reckons he's carrying on with Daisy. And I think she might be right. I'd never have thought it of Tanse. He's had his share of girls over the years, but never someone else's. And he seems really smitten with Cora. I was starting to think we might be hearing wedding bells. She's the only woman I've ever known who made him blush.' She bundled together the sodden handkerchiefs and stuffed them into her bag. 'Anyway, we've got much more pressing matters to discuss. What happened at Linton's house?'

Albert described the revelation of the Anatomical Venus, and Linton's suggestion that Albert had been drunk, confusing a real-life body for a wax model.

'But you didn't confuse them, did you?' Minnie said.

Albert shook his head. 'The Venus is convincing from the neck up. Disturbingly so. But her torso just lifts off in one single piece. The woman I saw? Her skin had been cut. I couldn't have mistaken one for the other.' He paused, inhaling as if preparing himself for an ordeal. 'Futile as I know this will probably be, given your usual stubbornness, I do think you should withdraw yourself from the case. No –' he said, holding up a hand to forestall Minnie's objections, 'please just listen to me, Minnie. You were assaulted in the Cremorne, somebody followed you after the Temperance meeting, and Linton's words about you last night were another threat. The man may be a murderer. And he has you in his sights.'

'Well, he's got you in his sights as well, ain't he? Besides, you and Tom are escorting me everywhere.'

'Indeed. But it's more than that.' He broke off.

'Well?' Minnie asked, leaning forward.

Albert hesitated, twisting away from her slightly and looking down at his hands as if the answer might lie there. Eventually, he raised his head and turned back to face her.

'You matter to me,' he said quietly. 'In the past few weeks, as we have come to know each other, you have become – important to me.'

'Oh,' Minnie said. Unable to meet his gaze, she developed an intense interest in a pot of cold cream on the dressing-room table. 'Well, that's a surprise. When we're together you spend most of the time looking like a bulldog licking piss off a nettle.'

'I have genuinely no idea what you mean.'

'I thought I irritated you, Albert. I thought you found me …distasteful.'

'You are … vexing on occasion. But, no, I do not find you distasteful. Quite the reverse.'

'Well,' Minnie said, alarmed to find herself blushing, and standing up to cover her confusion, 'that's nice to hear. But I ain't giving up on looking for Rose's killer.'

Albert nodded, as if he had anticipated this response. 'Very well. Given the distractions of Tom's romance with Miss Mountford, I think it might be best if I escorted you everywhere from now on.' He coughed and looked away, fiddling with the buttons on his waistcoat, which didn't appear to need any correction.

Minnie gave him a hard look. 'Whatever you think is best,' she said. 'Do you reckon we're getting closer? To Rose's murderer, I mean,' she added hurriedly.

'Not close enough. Too many unanswered questions. Rose and Lionel Winter knew each other, presumably through the Godwin, which is hiding some grubby secrets in the basement. Linton has killed someone, or at least we suspect he has. And he's gone to considerable lengths to show me he's in control. I still don't see how it all connects.'

'There's something else, Albert,' Minnie said.

At the end of the corridor outside the dressing room Tansie announced himself with his usual subtlety, yelling for Kippy. The dressing-room door burst open and Daisy stumbled in. She glanced round the room. 'No Cora?' she asked. Minnie shook her head, and before she could advise Daisy to stay out of Cora's way, the girl was gone.

A few seconds later Tansie barged into the room with typical bluster. 'Cora?' he said.

Minnie threw her arms wide, indicating there was no one else in the room besides her and Albert.

Tansie glanced at Albert, turned to leave and then turned back. 'Could you … have a word, Min?' he said, with uncustomary reticence. 'Tell her it ain't what she thinks?'

'I've tried,' Minnie said.

'Try again,' Tansie said quietly, a frown creasing his brow.

Minnie nodded and Tansie left the room. She turned to Albert. 'Let's make ourselves scarce for a while,' she said quietly.

'Brown's?'

◦～◦

Half an hour later, having reduced an enormous piece of fruit sponge to a few crumbs, Minnie finished telling Albert about the contents of Tansie's safe.

'So,' Albert said, 'Tansie's never revealed he's got an investor in the Palace. Why would he?'

'He tells me everything. Or he used to. Cora's right; since Rose died he's been acting odd. And there's the photos.'

Albert nodded slowly. 'I don't suppose there's any possibility I could get a look at them?'

Minnie shook her head. 'No chance. He's got his keys now on a long chain, never detaches it from his belt.' She paused, eyeing him.

'What?' he said.

'I don't know nothing about the fellas, but the girls in the photos, some of them I recognised. They worked at the Palace for a while, and then they left for better money elsewhere. Happens all the time. Thing is, people pop back, y'know? Just for a chat and a catch-up. But one of them, I never saw again. Didn't think anything of it at the time. Thought maybe she'd moved away.'

'But now you're not so sure?'

'No. Agnes Collins, her name was. Nothing special about her. But what you said about that … Venus, was it?'

Albert nodded.

'It got me thinking. Agnes was dark-haired. Really short. About Edie Bennett's stamp, I'd say. And her features – she was like a little doll. Tiny little rosebud mouth, button nose, big eyes.'

'Did she look anything like Rose?' Albert asked.

Minnie shook her head emphatically. 'Nothing like her. Rose was tall. About my height. Agnes was a little dot of a thing.'

'And what did she do at the Palace?'

'A tumbler, like Rose.'

'When did she leave?'

Minnie thought for a moment. 'Maybe two months ago?'

'Friend of Rose's?'

Minnie shrugged. 'Not particularly.'

Albert sighed, reached into his pocket and drew out a handful of change to pay for their tea. 'Why didn't you tell me this before, Minnie? About what you found in Tansie's safe?'

Minnie turned to look out of the window, trying to buy herself some time. A filthy-looking chap with a ferret on the end of a piece of rope was offering to let people hold it for a farthing. A young woman in a fussy bonnet persuaded her sweetheart to pay the money, and then screamed with terror when the ferret was thrust into her arms.

Minnie looked back at Albert, recalling their conversation on the way back from the Temperance meeting. She had told Albert to let down his guard. Maybe it was time for her to do the same. 'Tansie took me in when life weren't so rosy,' she said. 'Gave me work, set me on my feet. He's been good to me. I can't bear to think nothing bad of him. Thought there might be an explanation for what I found in that safe. But if there is one, I can't find it.'

'And Rose?' Albert asked. 'What was she to you? You're very determined to find out what happened to her.'

She looked down at the tablecloth, herded the cake crumbs into a pile with her finger and absent-mindedly swept them onto the floor, drawing a stern look from the waitress who had arrived to clear their table. Minnie waited until she had left, and then said, 'I never talk about it, Albert, so don't ask me. But Rose and Ida saved my life once. I owe them.'

Albert reached across the table and took her hand. She

felt the strongest urge to tell him everything, all that had happened in her past that had led her to this moment. All the reasons why she couldn't allow herself to care for him. But she never talked about what had happened. She wasn't even sure she could find the words, and just the thought of sharing it with someone else felt like a wire walker suddenly finding nothing beneath their feet, tumbling through space.

Slowly, she withdrew her hand, and turned again to look out of the window. The man with the ferret had moved on.

Heading back to the Palace, Minnie smiled to herself and said, 'If we solve this case, maybe they'll stick one of them plaques on the front of Brown's. You know, the ones they put on important buildings? "Albert and Minnie drank tea here, 1876".'

Albert shook his head. '"Minnie and Albert", not "Albert and Minnie". They'll always put you first.' He stopped abruptly and turned towards her.

'Don't,' she said. 'I know what you're thinking, Albert. Don't do it.'

Albert looked bemused. 'Why not?' he asked eventually.

'Because I suspect you would be rather a good kisser. Which would, inevitably, lead to something more.'

'And that would be bad because …?'

'Because at some point the kissing would stop.'

'Why would it stop? I mean, is there any reason we couldn't carry on kissing, and … more than kissing?'

'For a start-off, can you stop saying the word "kissing"? It's distracting. Second of all, you are a lovely chap, Albert.

You might just be the nicest man I've ever met. Which ain't saying a great deal, but still. However, at some point, you are going to stop playing around with me and do what's expected of you.'

'Which is?'

'Marry Lady Toffee-Nose.'

Albert frowned. 'Is that what you think is going to happen?' he asked after a few moments' silence.

'No, Albert. That is what I *know* is going to happen.'

'And why would I marry Lady Toffee-Nose, as you so charmingly put it?'

''Cos that's what chaps like you do. You might have acquired that fancy accent only recently, but it's still fancy, and you still come from money. Fellas like you, they imagine themselves in love with Peggy or Molly or whoever. But they don't stick around, Albert. So. No kissing.'

'I am not like those men, Minnie. I have no intention of leading you on and then deserting you.'

'Very well,' Minnie said, standing back from him and folding her arms. 'Let's say you're different. What exactly are you suggesting? A little love nest in St John's Wood? A generous dress allowance and Christmas Day on my own every year? Take a quick butcher's at my face, would you? Have I got "mug" written all over it? Didn't think so. You need to find yourself some nice young lady who likes opera and ballet and plays the piano quite beautifully.'

'I don't like opera,' Albert said. 'Or ballet, for that matter. It turns out I like Mexican boneless wonders, and truly dreadful sopranos and one-legged dog and monkey acts. I like this, Minnie,' he said, pointing at the stage door of the Palace. 'I like these people. And you.'

She stared at him for a long time, and then finally spoke. 'Whatever Linton gave you last night, I reckon it's turned your brain. So we're going to pretend this conversation never happened, Albert. You and I will carry on our detective work. We'll catch Rose's killer and then we'll go back to our normal lives. And in the meantime,' she added, her hand on the stage-door handle, 'do not let Tansie hear you talking about one-legged dog and monkey acts or he'll be after Kippy to find him one.'

THE FIFTH STANHOPE

IN WHICH MR BANISTER RECEIVES
SOME UNWELCOME GUESTS

Monty Banister climbed the steps to his front door and entered the house. He had enjoyed a magnificent lunch at the Langham, followed by rather too much brandy. He was looking forward to a quiet snooze before dinner.

Adelaide stepped into the hallway, pulling the door closed behind her. She looked worried and held up a hand to stop Monty mounting the stairs to his study.

'There are two men here,' she whispered, jerking her head back at the closed morning-room door. 'They're calling themselves Mr Dombey and Mr Pocket.'

'What?' Monty said, bemused. 'Dombey and Pocket? As in—'

'Dickens, yes,' Adelaide interrupted, tetchily. 'Not their real names, obviously. Although why the ridiculous subterfuge? They say they are friends of yours, Monty. They've been here half an hour already and are showing no signs of leaving.'

'Well, let me see them,' Monty said. 'It's probably a couple of the chaps having a jape.'

As he moved past Adelaide, she grasped his arm. 'Monty, there's something … not right about them. I rather think we should call the police.'

Monty laughed. 'Well, let me see them first, dearest. It seems a little hasty to call the police on the grounds that these men are "not right", as you say.'

He moved past her and opened the morning-room door. Standing either side of the fireplace were two men. One was large and muscular, full-lipped, his mouth hanging open slightly like a dog after a walk. His eyes were rheumy, with a strange vacancy behind them. The other man was much shorter, with an open, benevolent-looking face that fell readily into a smile. He was leaning with one hand on the mantelpiece and Monty saw he had only three fingers on his left hand.

'Monty!' Three-Fingers said. 'Remember us? Pocket,' he said, placing a hand on his chest. 'Dombey,' gesturing to his companion.

'I'm sorry,' Monty said, 'I don't believe we've met.'

Pocket turned to Dombey and thumped him affectionately on the chest. 'See?' he said. 'I told you he wouldn't remember.' He turned back to Monty. 'The Godwin, old chap. One rather raucous night. Not surprised you can't remember,' and he tapped the side of his nose conspiratorially.

Monty was confused. Nights at the Godwin often ended in a bit of a blur. Maybe he did know these men. Regardless, he did not want Adelaide party to their conversation. He turned to her, hovering just behind him.

'Of course,' he said, weakly, 'Dombey and Pocket. From the Godwin. Best we take this to my study,' and he gestured towards the stairs.

He led the two men up to the first floor and into his study at the rear of the house. There were only two chairs in the room and the men immediately sat down, spreading their legs wide and lolling back as if they owned the place. Pocket lifted the lid of a cigar box on Monty's desk and helped himself to two cigars, lighting them both before passing one to Dombey.

'Why are you here?' Monty said, trying to keep the nerves out of his voice.

'A certain detective gentleman of your acquaintance,' Pocket said, smiling, lifting a paper knife from the desk, 'has been poking his nose in where it's not wanted. Sloping off to the Wellington, asking questions of people who should be keeping their mouths shut. You are going to tell him in the politest possible terms to ... sling ... his ... hook.' With each pause between words, he dragged the blunt tip of the knife across the mahogany surface of the desk, gouging deep scratches into the highly polished surface.

Monty began to feel sick but tried to assume an air of nonchalance. 'I am not my brother-in-law's keeper. I cannot govern his actions.'

Pocket looked at Dombey and tilted his head fractionally to one side. With astonishing speed, Dombey leapt from his seat and launched himself at Monty, punching him hard in the face. A sickening crack told Monty his nose had been broken before the pain confirmed it. He felt as if his head had exploded. His eyes flooded, and he doubled over in pain, blood spurting between his fingers as he clutched at his face. Dombey grabbed him by the throat with one hand and pushed him up against the wall. Monty's eyes smarted with tears and he could feel his heart thumping in his ears.

Behind Dombey, Pocket lounged in his chair, quietly puffing on his cigar. Slowly, he lifted his dark eyes to Monty.

'Damn fine-looking wife you have,' he said, the smile never leaving his lips. 'Easterbrook's sister, isn't she? Maybe we need to move a little closer to home. If we want Easterbrook to do as he's told.'

'Leave my wife out of this,' Monty gasped, his throat aching where Dombey's huge hand pressed on his windpipe.

'Oh, I never like to involve the ladies,' Pocket said, shaking his head as if the mere thought distressed him. 'But my friend Dombey here. Well, that's a different matter. He has a fondness for the gentler sex. He sometimes has a little … difficulty, shall we say … , in expressing that fondness with the delicacy it requires.'

Dombey eased his grip on Monty's neck, and Monty leaned forward, coughing and holding his hand to his nose, trying to staunch the flow of blood.

A few minutes passed. Outside, the normality of everyday life could be heard with what now felt like a nightmarish quality: carriages rattling over the cobbles, children playing. Below, a door closed, and Monty could hear the muffled murmurs of Adelaide addressing the parlour maid.

'What do you want?' Monty asked, coughing again as he spoke.

'Well, I thought I made that clear, but perhaps an idiot like you needs to have it spelled out for him,' Pocket said, lifting the paper knife again from the desk and delicately running his finger along the edge of it. 'We want Easterbrook to abandon this case,' he said, raising his voice as if Monty were hard of hearing, enunciating every word with exaggerated emphasis.

'But I can't make him do anything,' Monty said, his voice rising in panic. 'He doesn't even like me.'

Pocket widened his eyes and adopted a singsong tone. 'Then you must try harder,' he said, as if explaining an obvious fact to a small child. He rose from his seat and walked over to

Monty. He raised his hand, and Monty flinched, turning his head away in anticipation of a blow. Pocket smiled, and gently patted Monty on the cheek. 'Next time we shan't be so nice,' he said.

He turned towards Dombey. 'Straighten your tie, dear boy, and here—' He reached up, flicked an errant lock of Dombey's hair back into place and wiped a daub of Monty's blood from his face. 'Can't have you looking dishevelled, can we?' He glanced back at Monty. 'We'll see ourselves out. Tell your delicious wife it was a pleasure meeting her. A true pleasure.'

The door closed behind the two men, and Monty waited until he had heard them descend the stairs and close the front door behind them. He stumbled from the room to the water closet next door and heaved his magnificent lunch into the pan.

TWENTY-FOUR

The parlour maid, a young girl who looked no more than twelve, took Albert's hat and coat and showed him into the morning room. Adelaide was sitting on the edge of a newly upholstered chair; she was exquisitely dressed in navy silk. Monty stood behind her, in a tweed suit so beautifully cut Albert felt a twinge of envy. Monty's left hand rested on the seat back, his fingers just brushing Adelaide's shoulder. They might have been sitting for a portrait embodying marital respectability. Except Adelaide looked even thinner than when Albert had seen her at the Hailsham Gallery. And Monty was sporting two black eyes, his nose purple and swollen.

Before Albert could ask what had happened, Adelaide rose from her seat. 'Albert, you must abandon the case you're working on,' she said, not meeting his gaze.

Albert frowned. 'Why?' he asked.

Adelaide started to pace up and down, picking nervously and compulsively at a ribbon trim on the sleeves of her dress, her silk skirts brushing against the Persian rug that dominated the room. 'Monty has been threatened,' she said, turning her head towards Monty who had yet to say anything. She dropped her voice as if ashamed of what she was telling Albert. 'Two men. They came to our house – into our *home*, Albert – and committed an act of violence against my husband.'

At the mention of violence, Monty's hand went to his nose. He looked shamefaced, as if he would rather be anywhere else but standing in his morning room, facing down the brother-in-law he had no time for.

'Tell me about these men,' Albert said quietly, addressing the question to Monty.

Monty recounted the visit from Pocket and Dombey and the clear instructions he had been given concerning Albert.

'They mentioned the Wellington?' Albert asked.

Monty nodded.

There'd only been Billy and Minnie at the Wellington, Albert thought. Could Billy be working with these men?

'Monty won't say as much, Albert, but he is afraid. He hasn't been out of the house for the past two days since it happened, have you?'

Monty shook his head dismissively. 'That's nothing to do with the attack, Adelaide. I've a great deal of work on my plate since Henry's resignations. Easier to do it at home. And please sit down, my dear. This constant pacing of yours isn't helping my headache.'

Adelaide threw Albert a glance weighty with meaning, before taking a seat and gesturing for him to sit opposite her.

'Describe them again, Monty, would you?' Albert asked.

Monty reported what he could remember of the men. The one calling himself Pocket certainly sounded like the man who had attacked Minnie in the Cremorne Gardens.

'So,' Adelaide said, leaning forward in her seat and grabbing Albert's hand. 'You will do as they say, won't you, Albie? Abandon the case?'

Albert was surprised to find he didn't need to give the matter much consideration. 'No,' he said simply. 'I won't. I can't.'

Adelaide's eyes filled with tears, and she dropped her head. Monty leaned forward and tentatively patted her hair. He managed to look both pompous and uncomfortable, and Albert realised this was one of the rare times he had seen the two of them making any kind of physical contact.

'But you must, Albie,' Adelaide said, removing a handkerchief from her pocket. 'They will hurt you, I'm sure of it. And, there's something else.'

'Yes?' Albert asked.

'The two men, they threatened my safety as well as Monty's.'

'What?' Albert said sharply, turning to Monty. 'You didn't mention any threat to Adelaide. Why didn't you tell me that immediately?'

'I told him not to,' Adelaide said. 'I didn't want to distress you. You know how protective you are of me. After they had broken Monty's nose, they told him—' She stopped speaking, went back to fingering the ribbon trim on her dress, then inhaled and lifted her head, holding Albert's gaze despite the tremor in her voice. 'They implied it would be me next time. It would be me they hurt.'

Albert stood abruptly and went to the window, saying nothing. He turned back to the mantelpiece, found his fingers reaching instinctively for his clay pipe, and then remembered he was not in his own home. He swore under his breath and returned to his seat.

'I can't see what the problem is,' Monty now interjected. 'This girl whose death you're investigating. She was just some music hall chit, wasn't she? I don't know what you're being paid, but if it's the money—' and he reached into his pocket, withdrawing a handful of notes.

'Keep your money,' Albert said coldly.

Adelaide's hand flew nervously to her throat. 'No, obviously it's not the money, Albert. No one would imagine you were that mercenary. But if it's a question of your own family versus a woman you never even knew ...' She tailed off, as if the rest of her point required no explanation. Which, of course, it didn't if you were the likes of Adelaide, Albert thought irritably, and then rebuked himself for thinking so ungenerously of his sister. She was not Monty.

'You're right,' Albert said, fighting to keep the anger out of his voice. 'I never knew Rose Watkins. But I know her mother, Ida. And I know Minnie, the closest thing Rose had to a sister. Good people, Adelaide. Kind, loving people whose lives have been destroyed by Rose's murder. I can't bring her back, but I can at least try to find the killer and bring him to justice. Ida and Minnie deserve nothing less.'

'Look, old chap,' Monty said, 'it's all very sad, and I understand you wanting to help. Truly, I do. But girls like that turn up dead every day of the week—'

'All the more reason why Rose's death should be solved,' Albert snapped, no longer attempting to control his anger. 'My advice to you both is to go away for a while.'

Monty guffawed theatrically. 'And how do you imagine I'm going to do that?' he asked. 'I'm doing important work, Albert. Work no one else can do. With Henry's resignations—'

'You've made it abundantly clear how vital your work is, Monty,' Albert interrupted, barely able to control his impatience. 'In which case, Adelaide, you must leave town on your own. Don't tell anyone where you are going. Ideally, no servants. No communication between the two of you – you can write through me. And you must stay away until I send word that it is safe to return. Do you understand?'

Adelaide nodded slowly, her eyes again filling with tears.

'Last time I checked, old chap,' Monty said, 'Adelaide was married to me, not you. I'm perfectly capable of taking care of my wife.'

'Are you?' Albert said quietly.

'Now, look here—'

'Enough,' Adelaide said, raising both hands. 'Monty dear, I'm a little chilly. Could you fetch my wrap from my bedroom? The paisley one?'

Taking the hint, Monty reluctantly grunted his agreement and left the room.

Adelaide leaned forward in her chair, clasping Albert's hands again. 'I am begging you, dearest. These men are dangerous. They will hurt you if you persist with this case. I appreciate your desire to find Miss Watkins's killer. No one understands that impulse in you better than I. But this … this …' She dropped Albert's hands and raised a palm to her forehead, as if his actions were causing her physical pain. 'This is insanity, Albert. Pass the case over to the police and move on to something else. Accept this is one dead girl you can't help.'

The memory of Hetty and her murder seemed to fill the room. Once more, Albert was an eight-year-old boy, powerless and ineffectual, unable to bring back his beloved friend.

'No,' he said quietly. 'I can't stop now, Addy. I'm getting close, I know it.'

'Then do it for me,' Adelaide said desperately. 'Your sister. I have never asked anything of you, except this one thing. Monty is trying to hide the fact, but he is genuinely afraid, and he's desperate to do as they've asked of him. If you won't do this, he is capable of making life … difficult. For me.'

She turned away, a blush reddening her cheeks and neck.

'What are you saying?' Albert asked. 'Has he done anything to you? Hurt you?'

She shook her head swiftly. 'Never. But there are many ways of hurting people, Albert, without raising a hand to them.'

Albert had long suspected his sister's marriage was not a happy one. But there was no satisfaction in being proved right.

'Leave him, Addy,' Albert said, trying to keep his voice calm and measured as he voiced the thoughts he had harboured for years but never articulated, for fear of distressing her, or breaking some ridiculous unspoken rule of etiquette. 'You can come and live with me. We can ride out the scandal together. I've had some practice, after all.'

She turned to him, a weak smile playing across her lips as she fought back tears. 'We both know that will never happen, Albie. I'm not brave like you. And, besides, I think any more gossip about the family would finish Mother and Father off for good, don't you?'

She reached forward and cupped his face in her two hands, a gesture she had used often when they were children and Albert had woken from a nightmare. It had always calmed him, slowing his breath and sending him back to sleep, usually wrapped in her arms.

'We're two stubborn old things, aren't we?' Adelaide

said, her eyes shining with tears. 'I shall do as you say. Find somewhere to stay for a while. Perhaps I'll be able to persuade Monty to join me. Perhaps not.'

Albert's mouth was set in a hard line and he was struggling to hold back the tears. She pulled him forward, resting his forehead on hers for a moment, and took a deep breath. 'I think it's time you were on your way, Albie,' she said. 'I'm not sure Monty can pretend to be looking for my wrap for much longer.'

Albert rose, leaned down to kiss her goodbye, and left the room. In the hallway, he glanced up the stairs. Monty stood on the landing, the window behind him casting his face in shadow. His expression was impossible to read.

'So how does Linton know we went to the Wellington with Billy?' Minnie asked.

The two of them were taking a turn round St James's Park, the walk calming Albert after his meeting with Adelaide.

'And how does he know we haven't responded to his threat?' Albert said. 'There'd be no need to threaten Monty if we'd already abandoned the case, and yet this attack on Monty took place the day after John and I were shown the Venus. We went to Linton's house, and then I came on to the Palace to speak to you.'

'Linton knows what we're up to,' Minnie said. 'Could he be having us followed?'

She glanced behind her, but the only person in view was an elderly man so crippled with pain he was struggling to place one foot in front of the other.

Albert shook his head. 'Even if he were, we haven't done anything since the Venus incident to suggest we're still investigating. We've only talked about it.'

'In the Palace,' she said slowly.

'Not just the Palace. In Brown's, on the street. Other times we've discussed it in my home. With Tom.'

'Not Tom,' she said firmly. '*We* invited him to help *us*, remember?'

'After you were attacked in the Cremorne. While you were with Tom.'

'I can't believe it's him.'

Albert shook his head. 'No, nor can I.'

'Those other conversations we had, Albert. At Brown's or the Wellington. We always went there from the Palace. I think someone at the Palace has been listening in, watching where we go.'

'Billy? Or Tansie? He's certainly up to something. Those photographs, and the mysterious co-owner of the Palace he's never mentioned to you.' Albert eyed her carefully. 'You're going to need to make a choice, Minnie.'

'Meaning?'

'Where your loyalties lie. Rose or Tansie.'

TWENTY-FIVE

Albert walked Minnie back to the Palace and then carried on past Trafalgar Square onto Pall Mall. A brougham with a distinctive green and black livery pulled up close to him, the driver reining in the horses to a slow walk. The window lowered, and Linton leaned out.

'Albert, old chap,' he said, smiling beneficently, the exaggerated blinking animating his face. 'Fancy a ride? I am entirely at your disposal.'

Albert's pulse quickened. The sight of Linton stirred the memory of his two visits to the man's home, and the horrors they had revealed. 'No thank you,' he said, 'I need the air.'

'Well, then, let me walk with you,' he repiled, and before Albert could say anything Linton had alighted from the carriage, instructed his driver to return home, and fallen into step beside Albert.

'Look,' he said, throwing his arms wide and then theatrically holding open his cuffs. 'Nothing up my sleeves. No secret potions to make you see dead bodies.'

Albert stopped and turned to face Linton. 'I know what I saw,' he said, 'and you know what you showed me. I can't prove anything yet, but I will.'

The smile hardened on Linton's face, although his words

remained good-natured. 'Hunt away, old chap. There's nothing to find. Events of the other night do seem to have cast rather a blight on our friendship, for which I am very sad. Oh, and your membership of the Godwin? Not possible, I'm afraid. We've had a few new members recently, and there's a cap on numbers.'

Albert nodded, unsurprised, and turned to walk away. Linton laid a hand on his arm. 'When you were at the Godwin you mentioned Stanhopes to Monty. Caused some confusion for the old chap. Although, let's be honest, that's not too difficult with Monty. Why the interest?'

'A connection to the case I'm investigating. *Still* investigating.'

'Not everyone at the Godwin has a Stanhope. Only what we rather romantically call the inner circle. Chaps with a fondness for the finer things in life. But since you're so interested in them' – he reached into his waistcoat pocket – 'have a look at mine.'

He handed Albert the now familiar item, with its ornate gold decoration and the intertwined G and C. Albert's stomach dropped as he held the piece in his hand, and once again felt the surprising weight of it in his palm. He looked up at Linton.

'Go on, old chap. Always happy to share.'

Albert raised the Stanhope to his eye, half expecting to see the body of the dead girl from a few nights ago. But he was wrong.

The girl in the image looked young. Maybe twelve, thirteen. It was difficult to tell. Her hair was down and had been artfully arranged to cover some but not all of her nakedness. She was looking downwards, away from the camera, with an uncharacteristic shyness. But the features were still clear.

Minnie.

'She was lovely, wasn't she?' Linton said, leaning in and never taking his eyes from Albert's face. 'She still is, of course, but the bloom has faded a little. Like a peach left a little too long on the tree, wouldn't you say?'

Albert felt a ringing in his ears and Linton's face blurred momentarily. He shook his head, as if to dispel the image of Minnie, but he could not shake off Linton's words, each one of them piercing his defences.

'Dearest Minerva,' Linton said languidly. 'Although she never goes by that name these days, does she? The diminutive she's adopted is a little … mundane, but then she is no longer the exceptional creature she was, I fear. Has she ever told you why she gave up the stage? There were rumours, but I'd love to know the truth. Maybe you could ask her some time. Perhaps in a moment of *post coitum* intimacy?'

Without allowing himself to think, Albert clenched his hand into a fist and gave Linton a sharp jab to the jaw. The blow took Linton by surprise, and he dropped like a stone. He lay there, flat on his back, his palm pressed hard against his cheek as he tentatively moved his jaw from side to side. 'Well, carry me out and bury me decent, Albert,' he said. 'Who would have thought you had it in you.'

A carriage clipped neatly past him. Albert cradled one fist inside the other, ready to strike again. The street was relatively quiet, but two men ran over, offering to help Linton. He waved them away as if the mere idea of assistance were somehow offensive. He raised himself up, leaning on one elbow, and looked up at Albert. A smile spread slowly across his face. 'I rather feel I've found my mark,' he said, a smirk of triumph distorting his features.

Long and hard, Linton's laughter echoed down the street, filling Albert's ears as he turned back towards the Palace.

He found her in the auditorium, watching Daisy on stage rehearsing the closing bars of a song. Tom was seated almost in the wings, his gaze fixed adoringly on Daisy.

'I'm still not sure it was the sensible thing, introducing those two,' Minnie murmured to Albert. 'Tansie had it right the other day. Said Daisy'll suck Tom in and blow him out as bubbles.'

She turned to him, her smile quickly turning to puzzlement as she looked at his face.

'That's enough for now, Daisy,' she said, barely glancing at the other girl. 'We'll pick it up again tomorrow.'

Daisy looked as if she had also read Albert's face and she scurried off the stage without a word, grabbing Tom's hand on the way. Minnie turned to Albert with a questioning look.

'He has a photograph of you,' Albert said abruptly.

Minnie looked confused. 'Who?'

'Linton. He has a photograph of you. In his Stanhope.'

She frowned. 'What sort of photograph?'

'A younger you. Not wearing a great deal.' The brutality of his words surprised him, and he was even more surprised to discover he wanted to hurt her with those words. It made no sense, he knew. She could not be blamed for something she had done years ago, long before she knew him. But he wanted to apportion blame, nonetheless.

Minnie flushed momentarily, then slowly nodded her head and smoothed down the front of her dress. 'I see,' she said. 'And this is getting you riled up because … why, exactly?'

It was a front. He knew her well enough to know she was disturbed by what he had told her. But he also knew that offence was Minnie's first line of defence, like a boxer flying from his corner, fists swinging indiscriminately.

'I think he's a murderer, Minnie.'

Which wasn't, of course, the problem. But he couldn't tell her how much it had hurt him to see that intimate image of her, the feelings of jealousy it had stirred within him, so soon after the exchange they had had only days earlier. She had made it very clear that their relationship would advance no further. He had been made to feel a fool for even thinking about it. And now, there was this photograph that suggested a much greater intimacy, to be shared by anyone who could afford the price of a Stanhope.

'So? Him having a photograph of me don't mean I'm the next victim,' Minnie said. 'I reckon he'd have offed me by now if he wanted to.'

'He knows things about you. He spoke about you as if he knew you.'

'Like what?'

'He called you Minerva.'

She gave a half-smile and looked down at the ground before raising her eyes to him. He could tell she was trying to defuse the situation. But he wasn't willing yet to abandon the moral high ground.

'A nickname,' she said. 'When I was a child, a neighbour of ours called me Minerva. The goddess of music and poetry, as well as a few other things I can't call to mind. It was my stage name when I started out: Minerva the Mimic. Rubbish name, but it stuck somehow. Minerva got shortened to Minnie, and there you have it.'

'What's your real name?'

'Didn't Linton tell you? Given that you reckon he knows so much about me?'

'What is it?'

'None of your business, Albert. I go by Minnie, and that's my name. So, aside from the astonishing knowledge I was once called Minerva, what else did he know about me?'

'He said there were rumours about why you left the stage. Told me I should ask you about it.'

Minnie's face froze. 'Another thing that is none of your business, Albert.'

'Why? Why are you so close-lipped about what happened to you in your past?'

'Because it's my past,' she said, anger flaring suddenly. 'Not anyone else's. You ain't exactly forthcoming about your life, Albert. It's no different.'

'And the photograph?'

'I did some things I ain't exactly proud of. But I ain't ashamed of them, neither,' she said, lifting her chin in her customary gesture of defiance. 'A girl's got to eat.'

'But how did he get your photograph?'

She shrugged. 'Photographs like that – they ain't difficult to get hold of. You only need to know the right fella to ask down Holywell Street, and you can get pretty much anything you want.'

'So you're saying it's just a coincidence?'

'I dunno. But there's a reason why the word "coincidence" exists.'

'I think he knows you, Minnie. And I'm starting to wonder if you know him, too.'

'Meaning?'

'Meaning we've thought for some time there might be an informant in the Palace.'

'And you think it's *me*? Really. I've been helping you, ain't I? Finding stuff out, getting us closer to the killer?'

'Not close enough, though. We've nothing solid, have we? Just smoke and mirrors is the analogy you might use.'

He held Minnie's gaze for a long time, and he saw her face soften from anger to disappointment. He preferred the latter.

'I'm going now,' she said eventually, her voice disturbingly calm. 'Gotta run a few errands. I don't want you here when I get back. And I won't be needing you to escort me anywhere. Think I'm probably better off taking my chances with Linton, don't you?'

She turned and was gone.

Albert gazed after her, his anger dispersing as swiftly as it had surfaced. He upended a chair stacked on one of the tables and sat in the gloom of the empty theatre, wishing he could take back his words. Wishing the photograph hadn't bothered him quite as much as it had. He leaned on the table, rested his head in his hands and tried to make sense of it all. Piece together what he knew, and how it all led back to Rose's body swinging under the Adelphi Arches.

A discreet cough roused him from his thoughts.

'"She will die if he love her not," Mr Easterbrook.'

Albert lifted his head. Bernard Reynolds emerged from the darkness at the front of the auditorium, near the bar.

'I beg your pardon?' Albert said.

'"And she will die ere she make her love known."'

'I'm sorry? Who are we talking about?'

'Well, it is said of Beatrice. *Much Ado*, dear chap.' Bernard righted another chair and sat opposite Albert. 'But we both know who we're talking about, don't we?'

'No,' Albert said, making no attempt to hide his irritation. 'I don't know what you're talking about. To be frank, I don't understand half of what's said in this place. What with the slang and the obscure quotations and the silences whenever I ask a direct question. So could you possibly stop talking in riddles and just say what you mean?'

Bernard shook his head and raised his eyes to heaven. 'And here was me thinking you were a detective.'

He gave Albert a quizzical look and laughed as Albert shook his head and threw up his hands in a gesture of despair. 'Miss Ward, dear boy. "A wench of excellent discourse, pretty and witty; wild, and yet, too, gentle." And that, Albert, is *The Comedy of Errors*, an apt description for your wooing of our lovely Minnie.'

'I haven't been wooing her,' Albert said.

'Precisely, dear boy. Precisely.'

Albert frowned. 'Are you saying Minnie – *cares* for me?'

Bernard widened his eyes and smiled. '"A woman would run through fire and water for such a kind heart."'

'No,' Albert said, shaking his head. 'Whatever Minnie feels for me, it's not affection. I suspect she may never speak to me again.'

'Because you've been rather a chump, from what I overheard. Not that I was listening, of course,' he added hastily, 'but you were being rather … vociferous.'

Albert said nothing.

'We all have a past, Albert. It doesn't always bear close scrutiny. But "Things without all remedy should be without regard: what's done is done." If we were all to be judged on our former actions, where would that leave us? Women, in particular, sometimes have to resort to less savoury acts to keep the wolf from the door.'

'How long have you known Minnie?' Albert said.

'Not long enough to know anything about any photograph. It's Tansie you need to speak to if you wish to know more about Minnie. He's protective of her, mind. Might meet you with one of those silences you find so vexing. But I believe he's in his office.'

Albert knocked on the door and entered without waiting for an answer. Tansie was squinting at a needle and licking the tip of a length of thread. In his lap lay two pieces of white cotton. He peered over the top of his glasses as Albert entered.

'For the monkey,' Tansie said, gesturing to the cotton. 'Modesty bloomers. There's been complaints. Here.' He passed Albert the needle and thread. 'Make yourself useful and thread that, while you tell me why you've upset my second-best girl.'

'Second-best?'

'Well, Cora's my best girl, ain't she? Minnie's a close second, mind, so I hope you've got a good explanation for the language she's just been polluting these corridors with. Language coupled with your name, might I add.'

Albert took a seat and struggled unsuccessfully with the needle and thread while he told Tansie about the photograph Linton had of Minnie. This might have been the time to question Tansie, find out if he was the Palace informant, but Albert needed to sort things with Minnie first, and he needed Tansie's help to do so.

'Has Min told you anything about her past?' Tansie asked.

Albert shook his head.

Tansie nodded. 'She's what you'd call very close, is our Min. There'll be murders if she finds out I've talked to you, so if anyone asks, it was the boy Jones what told you.'

Albert was surprised Tansie was willing to reveal anything about Minnie, given his usual reticence about even the most mundane subjects. His confusion must have shown on his face.

'I like you, Bert. I think Minnie likes you too. And life is much sweeter around here when Minnie's happy.'

He leaned forward and removed the needle and thread from Albert's grasp. 'Not sure how old she was when I first met her,' he said. 'Told me she was fourteen, but I had my doubts. Thin as a willow whip. Hanging round the stage door, looking for work. Even then, quite the mouth on her. Her ma had just died from influenza. Never knew her father, and no other family. There were only two ways her story was likely to end. Coroner's slab or knocking shop.'

He successfully threaded the needle and started sewing the two pieces of cotton together, throwing Albert the occasional glance over the top of his glasses.

'Rose, who was maybe nine or ten at the time, took a liking to Minnie. I hadn't long bought the Palace, and I weren't exactly flush. I put a few bits and pieces of work her way. Running errands and the like. This was before we discovered she was quite the mimic, played the piano, wrote songs. She first went on stage about a year or so after I first met her, so there was a while where she had to earn her keep as she could.' He stopped again, leaning forward as if to get Albert's full attention. 'I couldn't find her enough work, Albert. I weren't running a charity, and everyone had to earn their keep. A young girl like that is always gonna struggle. So she found the money where she could.'

Albert inhaled slowly. His mind raced to all the ways in which a young girl might earn herself a bob or two.

'Don't you go looking down your nose at her,' Tansie said. 'She weren't born with no silver spoon in her mouth like some folks not a million miles from this room. She did what she had to do. And if that meant showing a bit more flesh than maybe she'd have liked, who are you to judge her?'

'I'm not judging—'

'Yes,' Tansie interrupted forcefully, 'you are. Why else have you had a falling-out with her about that photograph?'

'It's not the photograph,' Albert said.

Tansie looked at him pointedly.

'All right, it is the photograph. Or it's who has it. Do you know Lord Linton? The Godwin Club?'

'Everyone knows the Godwin.'

'Linton's a despicable individual, Tansie. He has that image of Minnie to look at whenever he chooses. It's as if—' He broke off.

'As if?'

'As if he owns her,' Albert said slowly, his voice dropping.

'Well, he don't. No one owns her. Some of us are tolerated by her. Some of us might even be lucky enough to be loved by her. But no one owns her. And if that's what you're thinking, perhaps it's best you and her have had a falling-out.'

Albert looked down at his hands, remembering the way he had held Minnie's after that night at Linton's house. The breeze blowing the curtains, Minnie asleep, and his calm realisation of how much she meant to him.

He looked up. 'I've never looked down on her, Tansie. I've misunderstood her, I think. Thought she was rash and reckless, when really she was just brave. Determined.'

'Well,' Tansie said, biting off the end of the cotton, and holding up the modesty bloomers for inspection, 'you can't deny you've had a rod inserted firmly up your arse for most of the time I've known you.'

'You're not the first person to say so. I'm doing my best to remove it, but it's been up there a long time.'

The two men shared a smile of understanding.

'What do I do, Tansie?' Albert asked.

'Oh, just give her time,' Tansie said, the intensity of his gaze belying the casual nature of his words. 'And cake. She responds very well to cake.'

Albert smiled ruefully, wishing it were that simple.

TWENTY-SIX

Cora repositioned the wig on Minnie's head and stood back to survey her handiwork, concentration furrowing her brow. Minnie leaned round her to catch a glimpse in the dressing-room mirror.

'No,' Cora said, shaking her head, 'it ain't working. You still look too much like you.'

She sat back in the chair and narrowed her eyes at Minnie. 'This club,' she said, 'I'm assuming they employ men as well as women?'

Minnie nodded.

'So Billy could get you in there as some kind of waiter, could he? Or a fetch-and-carry lad, maybe?' Cora asked.

Minnie's eyes widened as she took in Cora's meaning. 'Don't see why not.'

'Stay there,' Cora said and left the dressing room, returning a few minutes later with a simple black suit and white shirt she'd last worn when playing the part of a fresh-faced lad new to the city. She held the clothes up to Minnie's body. 'You're tall, which is good. Not much in the chest area, so we might get away without binding you. Pop it on and let's see what we're working with.'

It was a quiet afternoon, but people had a habit of entering a room unannounced at the Palace, so Minnie slipped behind a wooden screen to remove her clothes. She stripped down to just her chemise and donned the shirt and trousers. The collar on the shirt was tight around her neck, and the trousers felt strange, the material bulky between her legs.

She emerged from behind the screen. Cora nodded, took the weight of Minnie's hair, pinned it up in several places, tucked it inside a hair net and positioned a dark, short-haired wig on her head. She stood back and looked at Minnie appraisingly. 'Better,' she said.

'Crikey,' Minnie said, her eyes wide as she took in the transformation in the mirror. 'I might never give it all back. Think of the places I could go dressed like this. And I wouldn't need to worry about the Hairpin Killer, neither.'

'Your freckles need to go,' Cora said, narrowing her eyes. 'Too pretty. A bit of rice powder should bring 'em down. We'll darken and thicken your eyebrows.'

'Moustache? Beard?' Minnie asked.

Cora shook her head dismissively. 'Might do when you're on stage, but close up? Never looks right. No, you're a clean-shaven young lad looking for work. Now, let's get you out front and we'll practise walking. Mind if I have a bit more of that cake?' She nodded at the Victoria sponge delivered that morning from Brown's.

'Help yourself,' Minnie said. 'There'll likely be another tomorrow. It's the third one he's sent since Wednesday.'

Cora cut a slice and ate it, licking the cream and jam from her fingers like a cat. 'You forgiven him yet?' she said, as they left the dressing room and turned towards the stairs leading up to the stage. Everyone at the Palace had got wind of Minnie's argument with Albert.

Minnie shrugged. 'Maybe. I can understand him getting upset, I suppose. Those photographs didn't leave much to the imagination, as I remember them. But he don't own me, Cora. We ain't even courting.'

'And are you likely to be?' Cora asked, giving Minnie a sideways smile. 'He's a lovely chap, Min.'

'He is, indeed, a lovely chap. But not for me.' Minnie shook herself, casting off the very idea of Albert as a prospective sweetheart. 'And I might ask you the same question about Tanse.'

Cora gave a lopsided smile. 'He says there's nothing going on between him and Daisy. The problem is I'm sweet on him, ain't I? So, yeah, he's forgiven. But I'm keeping a close eye, Min. If I see him with Daisy again, I'll kill him.'

'Or her,' Minnie suggested.

Cora smiled. 'Yeah, or her.'

The two women came out onto the stage.

'Now,' Cora said, standing back and placing her hands on her hips. 'Let's see you walk.'

Minnie obeyed, enjoying the freedom of walking without stays, but also feeling strangely encumbered and restrained by the clothes. She thought back to the night of the Temperance meeting, when someone had followed her. It would have been a lot easier to run in this outfit.

'Well,' Cora said, 'it might serve for a matinee with the Blind Society, but it ain't gonna fool anyone else. Here, watch me. Forget I'm a woman.'

She turned and walked across the stage, Minnie paying close attention.

'See?' Cora said. 'I ain't swinging my hips. My legs are further apart. Women walk like they're on a tightrope, men like something's pushing their legs apart.'

Minnie giggled, and Cora raised a disapproving eyebrow but failed to suppress a smile. 'They take longer strides, Min, so they move more from side to side, less bobbing up and down. They lead with their shoulders, not their hips.'

'It's a lot to remember,' Minnie said.

Cora frowned. 'We've barely started. If it's too much, best we abandon the whole idea now. I've already told you I think it's a bit risky. What if you get caught?'

Minnie had played down any danger when she'd told Cora her plan. But, knowing what she did about Linton, her stomach turned at the thought of entering the Godwin. She pushed the idea from her mind.

'No, it's fine,' Minnie said. 'I'm a quick learner.'

'Right, then,' Cora said, 'let's see those famous mimicry skills of yours. Imagine you're a fella – that Tom chum of yours who's sweet on Daisy, more fool him. Talk to me.'

'Hallo, chaps. That Cora Monroe's rather a stunner, ain't she?' Minnie said, dropping her voice.

'Speak slower. Like you're just assuming everyone'll listen to you.'

The two women shared a knowing glance.

Minnie tried again and earned a nod of approval.

A door slammed in the distance and a few minutes later Tansie hurried onto the stage. 'Here you are,' he said to Cora. 'I've got lunch booked for one o'clock, so get lively.' He glanced at Minnie and threw Cora a questioning look.

'Who's this, then?' he asked Cora. 'Another mysterious cousin of Minnie's?'

Cora smiled and nodded almost imperceptibly at Minnie, inviting her to speak.

'You must be Tansie,' Minnie said, adopting her male persona. 'Minnie's assistant.'

Tansie squared up to her. 'It's Mr Tansford to you, lad, and I own this cocking establishment. Now bugger off out of my theatre.'

Minnie laughed. Tansie peered at her. 'Min? Is that you?' He looked at Cora, a smile slowly spreading across his face. 'Please tell me this is what I think it is. A double act, yeah? Two mashers for the price of one?'

Minnie raised her hands to ward off Tansie's enthusiasm. 'Steady on, Tanse. Cora was showing me a few of her tricks. Thought I'd give it a go. For a laugh.'

'It could work, though, Min,' he said. 'You and Cora. A few new songs. We could try it on the dog, knock the corners off. We'd be pulling 'em in within a week.' His eyes lit up with anticipation, and Minnie could see him mentally counting the takings.

Cora moved to Tansie's side and took his arm. 'Don't be so pushy, Tanse. Me and Min was just having a bit of fun.'

Tansie patted her hand affectionately. 'Just saying, girls. It'd be bang-up.'

'Why don't you go and work your steam off somewhere else?' Cora said. 'Me and Min won't be much longer and then you can take me out to that lunch you promised.'

Tansie left the stage reluctantly and the two women practised until Cora was satisfied with Minnie's walk and posture.

'Last few things,' Cora said. 'Everyone forgets about the hands, but they're very important. Show them to me.'

Minnie held out her hands, palms down. Cora flipped them over. 'Don't ask me why, but a fella always shows you the palms of his hands. Now yawn.'

Minnie complied, covering her mouth with a flat hand. Cora yawned too, but with her hand balled into a fist.

'Hands, Minnie,' she said again. 'It's all in the hands. And with that, I think we're done. And even if we ain't I've got a lunch date with a certain Mr Tansford. And, besides …' She nodded over Minnie's shoulder. Minnie turned and saw Albert had entered the auditorium.

'Mr Easterbrook,' Cora said with excessive formality, a smile playing at the corner of her lips.

'Miss Monroe,' Albert replied, mimicking her tone and removing his hat.

'Lovely cake,' Cora said. 'Just so's you know, I'm rather fond of a Chelsea bun myself.'

'Duly noted,' Albert said.

Cora turned and left the stage. Albert took in Minnie's attire and raised an eyebrow. She was disappointed that he'd seen right through her disguise, but he was a detective. She'd fooled Tansie, at least.

'Just a bit of fun, Albert. Wanna get the spike about it? Or is it only when I'm in the altogether that you take offence?' Minnie had not told Albert about her plans to infiltrate the Godwin. He would only try to stop her, remind her of the Cremorne and the man following her after the Temperance meeting. And she knew he'd probably be right to do so. But she hadn't entirely forgotten the argument over the Stanhope photograph. He didn't own her.

'Brown's have said they'll have to get in a special order of butter and flour if you don't forgive me soon,' Albert said.

Minnie's face softened. 'Tell 'em not to worry. Now I'm on first-name terms with Lady Linton, I won't eat nothing unless it's from Fortnum & Mason's. Now go and do something useful for twenty minutes while I get changed. Assuming we're off for a nosebag.'

TWENTY-SEVEN

Lunch over, Minnie went on ahead to the Palace while Albert wandered down the Strand in search of a tobacconist. Approaching the stage door, he knocked out the old tobacco from his pipe and was reaching into his pocket for a pipe cleaner when he heard a scream. Not the usual kind of scream that came from the Palace, not a cry of frustration when rehearsals didn't go as planned, or an overreaction to some monkey-based chaos. This was a scream of fear and despair, the kind he had heard sometimes on the force. A sound to freeze you in your tracks, make you want to turn and run in the opposite direction, even when you knew you had to follow the noise, and all the horrors it might herald.

What was worse, the scream was Minnie's.

As quickly as it had started, it stopped. A gut-wrenching howl and then – nothing.

Albert had his hand on the stage door when a young lad burst out of it. Bobby, one of Tansie's runners. The boy looked petrified, his face a sickly white.

'Sir,' Bobby gasped, tugging on Albert's arm, 'come quick, sir. I think she's dead.'

Albert pushed past the lad and raced down the corridor. He bumped into Daisy running in the opposite direction. He

271

grabbed her arm, went to say something, ask her what was happening, but she turned a terrified face towards him, her eyes wide and fearful, her breath coming in sharp bursts. She slipped from his grasp and was gone. The bang of the stage door echoed down the corridor.

There was another sound, even more unsettling than Minnie's scream. A long low moan, more animal than human. Albert followed it. Cora's dressing room. He nearly slid on something underfoot, and looked down. Blood. Too much blood. Spreading across the floor. The dressing table, littered with make-up and rags. A knife lying near the wastepaper bin.

And blood. So much blood.

He followed the trail to its source. Minnie kneeling, her hands, arms covered in blood, its iron tang polluting the air. Her face and hair smeared with it. She was holding the skirt of her dress in her hands, pressing it down onto something – someone – who lay on the floor beside her, their face hidden from view.

'Minnie,' Albert gasped, lunging towards her, nearly falling again.

She turned and looked at him, her mouth hanging open, her eyes glazed and unseeing.

'Where?' Albert said. 'Where are you hurt?'

Minnie slowly shook her head. 'Not me,' she said blankly, turning back to the body. Albert followed her gaze.

And finally he understood. The low animal moan was coming from Tansie, crouched on the floor, cradling Cora's head in his lap as the life leached out of her.

TWENTY-EIGHT

Signs had been posted on the doors. The Palace would stay dark that night. When the police arrived, Minnie had been relieved to see John leading the way. While he methodically questioned every member of the Palace who had been present when Cora was killed, Tansie had started frantic preparations for a benefit night for Cora, until Minnie had gently taken him by the hand and forced him to sit with her and Tom in the quiet of the empty auditorium. Others had joined them for a while and then drifted away, perhaps unable to bear the sight of Tansie still and silent.

John closed his notebook decisively. 'Well,' he said, 'there's no mystery. It's clear it was Daisy Mountford who stabbed Cora. But whether it was an accident or something more, we have yet to find out.'

'Cora was jealous of Daisy,' Tansie murmured, so quietly John had to crane forward in the dark and quiet auditorium to hear him. 'Not the other way round. It must have been an accident.'

'Was there anything going on, Tanse?' Minnie asked. 'With you and Daisy?'

He shook his head. 'Nothing. I like my girls clever, Min. You know that. Daisy always struck me as a bit of a mop.'

John had questioned everyone, but the story required little investigation. Cora and Tansie had returned to the Palace after lunch, to find Daisy in Cora's dressing room, trying on one of her dresses. Cora had flown at Daisy in a rage and Daisy had retaliated with a flurry of punches. Then, from somewhere – Tansie couldn't say where exactly – Daisy had produced a knife, and with a few sharp movements brought an end to Cora. It all happened so quickly, Tansie hadn't even known Cora was injured until the blood started to pour from the wound in her neck.

'Well,' John said, inserting his notebook in his pocket, 'we just need to find Daisy now. I've sent a lad round to the address she gave Kippy, but they've never heard of her. You know anything, Tom?'

Tom did not respond.

'Tom?' John repeated.

The lad roused himself as if from a deep sleep. He gazed around the auditorium, as if unsure how he'd got there. John repeated his question. Tom shook his head. 'No. I never went to her rooms. Only ever met her at the Palace, and then we'd go somewhere, but I always dropped her off back here. It's what I did today. Maybe if I'd been here—'

'And she never said nothing about where she lived?' John asked. 'Nothing about friends? Family?'

'Nothing,' Tom said blankly, staring into the distance.

'Well,' John said, easing himself carefully out of his seat and wincing as he straightened up. 'She can't hide forever. We'll find her.'

He nodded at each of them, and took his leave.

The doors banged closed behind him, and Tansie roused himself. He went to the bar at the front of the auditorium and brought back a bottle of brandy and four glasses. He filled them and passed them round wordlessly.

'Cora.' Tansie lifted his glass, his voice breaking as he said her name.

They all murmured her name and downed the brandy. Tansie refilled the glasses and sank back in his seat. Tom continued to stare into the middle distance.

'There's things I need to tell you,' Tansie said, after a moment. 'Stuff I ain't saying in front of that copper. Even if he is a mate of yours, Albert.'

'He's a good one,' Albert said. 'You can trust him.'

Tansie grimaced. 'Never trust a copper. Ever. And particularly not where the Godwin's concerned.'

Minnie started. 'What's this gotta do with the Godwin?'

'Well, it's where Daisy came from,' Tansie said.

'What?' Tom said, suddenly roused, his eyes wide as he stared at Tansie.

'Over the years,' Tansie said, 'I've had what you might call an arrangement with the Godwin. I send them girls who are looking to make an extra bob or two. Sometimes they go to work at the Godwin permanent, like. Occasionally, it works the other way, and they send me girls who don't quite cut the mustard at the Godwin.' He nodded at Minnie. 'That's how come we've got Selina. And Daisy, of course.'

'But why the Godwin?' Albert asked.

Tansie sighed, refilled his glass and passed the bottle to the others. 'I don't own the Palace outright,' he said. 'I've only got a thirty per cent stake in it.'

'We know,' Minnie said, no longer caring to hide what she had discovered in Tansie's safe.

Tansie didn't even raise an eyebrow. The day had held

so many surprises, Minnie assumed that one more barely registered. 'So you know who owns the rest of it,' he said.

Minnie shook her head. 'Bernadette Lohan. The name don't mean nothing to me.'

'That's 'cos you know her as Edie Bennett,' Tansie said.

'What?' Minnie said. 'Edie co-owns the Palace?'

Tansie nodded his head slowly. 'Edie's her stage name. She thought Bernadette Lohan sounded a bit too Irish when she was starting out. Not that it would matter too much in the halls – we take all sorts, don't we? – but she insisted she didn't want no one treating her different. So she became Edie Bennett. The Richmond Rocket.'

'How long have you known her?' Minnie asked. 'And why didn't you ever mention her?'

'Oh, we pretty much started out together. Great chums we were from day one. When the Palace came up for sale, she offered to help me buy it, but said she wanted her name kept out of it all. Never asked her why. Not long after, she married Linton. Teddy to his chums. So, Teddy to almost no one. Queer sort of cove, don't you think?'

Albert glanced at Minnie. 'You could say that,' he said.

'I met him a few times when he was hanging round the stage door, sniffing after Edie,' Tansie said. 'Couldn't see what she saw in him, to be honest. But he was rich. Very rich. And even richer now, by all accounts.'

He went to refill their glasses, but Tom placed a hand over his and shook his head.

'Linton opened the Godwin, and Edie asked me if I could send girls to the club who were in need of a bit of extra bunce.'

'So it was Edie's idea?' Tom said, his voice low and dull, his eyes fixed on the empty brandy glass that he turned compulsively in his hand. Anger darkened his face.

Tansie shook his head vehemently. 'No,' he said firmly, leaning forward in his chair. 'She never said as much, but I know it was Linton's idea. If you ask me, she weren't happy about it at all.'

'Edie doesn't strike me as the sort of woman who could be forced into anything,' Albert said.

Tansie gave a bitter laugh. 'You don't know her. She's changed since she married that cove. Oh, she still puts on a good show, but she ain't the same. She does what he tells her, I reckon. Which is what got me worried. About Edie's investment in the Palace.'

''Cos Linton could pull the plug on it anytime he liked,' Minnie said.

Tansie nodded. 'If she hadn't married him, there'd be no problem. But obviously everything of hers was his the moment he put a ring on her finger.'

'The photographs,' Minnie said.

This time Tansie did react. 'Oh, you know about those as well, do you? Wanna take a guess at my inside leg measurement while you're at it?'

'We had a murder to investigate, Tanse,' Minnie said.

A door banged in the distance, and Kippy emerged from the darkness. 'Everyone's gone home, Tanse,' he said. 'Want me to lock up?'

'No,' Tansie said, 'leave it to me. You get yourself home.'

The man nodded and left.

'Those photographs were insurance, Min,' Tansie said. 'Some members of the Godwin, particular friends of Linton, have this little—' He held his forefinger and thumb about an inch apart.

'Stanhope,' Minnie said.

'Yeah, that's it. The idea is, you can have a saucy picture inside it. No one knows. It's a little in-joke for Linton and his friends. Linton had the pictures taken here.'

'In the snuggeries.'

'Yeah. You can't go to an ordinary photography studio, 'cos there's some fancy equipment, glass slides and special cameras. I knew a chap could do it, and we took the photos here. Sometimes just the girls. But the fellas too. More often than you'd think, given how dangerous those photographs could be if they fell into the wrong hands.'

'So how did you come to have the photographs if they were for the Stanhopes?' Albert asked.

'My photographer chum gave Linton the tiny photograph, and the plate. What Linton didn't know was that my friend made me a single print of all the images. Normal size, so you could see what was going on in them without the need of a Stanhope. If Linton ever decided to pull the plug on the Palace, those photographs were my insurance policy.'

With no warning, Tom leapt to his feet and hurled his glass at the bar. He turned to Tansie, his face aflame with anger and loss.

'Your insurance policy?' he shouted, spittle flecking his lips. 'You've known about this all along, about Daisy coming from the Godwin, those grubby photographs, girls going to work there, and you said nothing? *Nothing?* All so you could keep yourself *safe*?'

Tansie had risen to his feet. Minnie was expecting him to respond with his usual bluster, but he said nothing, his arms hanging limply by his sides. 'There ain't nothing you can say, Tom, that I ain't already thinking,' he said. 'You're right to be angry. You should be. Maybe if I'd said something earlier—' He broke off, unable to complete the thought.

Tom took a step towards him. Albert rose from his seat, but there was no need. Tom's face crumpled and he started to sob. Tentatively, Tansie moved forward and pulled the boy into his arms. Minnie fought back tears of her own as she watched the two of them in their clumsy embrace, drawn together by loss.

Slowly, Tom's sobs subsided.

'And that's the only reason you kept the photographs?' Minnie said carefully, nervous of reigniting Tom's anger. 'You didn't have any other suspicions about the Godwin?'

Tansie frowned. 'Like what?'

Minnie glanced at Albert, who nodded. 'There was a girl from here who went to work at the Godwin,' Minnie said. 'Agnes Collins. Did you ever see her again after she left the Palace?'

Tansie thought for a moment and slowly shook his head.

'Me neither,' Minnie said. 'And we're thinking her disappearance is somehow linked to Rose's death. We ain't sure how exactly, but the Godwin is the thing both Agnes and Rose had in common.'

Tansie rose from his seat, walked towards the bar and back again, as if uncertain where to go.

'I knew something was up with Rose,' he said. 'She was acting strange in the couple of weeks before her death, and I had a feeling it had something to do with Linton and that club. But I didn't ask. Didn't want to know.'

He turned towards Minnie, his face contorted with grief. She held out her hand to him, and he came and sat beside her. 'If I'd said something at the time, maybe they'd both still be here. Rose and Cora.' He fell silent, as if speaking Cora's name had somehow reminded him anew of his loss. 'I weren't able to save Rose,' he continued, 'but I thought maybe I could save Daisy. She was talking about going back to the Godwin. I tried to persuade her to stay. Told her she might get involved in all sorts if she went back to the Godwin. She told me she weren't that sort of girl. Told me to sling my hook. So I did. That's what Cora saw. Got the wrong impression.'

'When did Daisy start working here?' Albert asked. 'In relation to Rose's death?'

Tansie paused. 'A week or two before Rose died?' He turned to Minnie for confirmation and she nodded.

'Could Daisy be the informant?' Albert said, turning to Minnie. 'Would that add up?'

Minnie thought for a moment or so. 'She was rehearsing that new act with Paul when you came to talk to me and we went off to Brown's. And when we spoke to Billy, and headed off to the Wellington—' Minnie struggled to remember who had been in the Palace that day. 'She could have been here. I can't remember.'

'That day after the Venus incident, when we talked in Cora's dressing room about not giving up the case—'

'Yes, she was there then,' Minnie said. 'She came bursting into the room, said she was looking for Cora.'

'But she could just have been listening at the door and got interrupted,' Albert said.

And she took up awful quick with Tom, Minnie thought, but did not say, glancing across at the lad who had subsided back into his loss.

'So,' Minnie said, slowly piecing things together even as she spoke, 'Rose is working at the Godwin. She sees or hears something she's not supposed to. Daisy, pretty girl, charming, just the sort I imagine they'd like at the Godwin, is sent to the Palace to see what Rose is saying, and who to. A week or so later, Rose turns up dead. Made to look like suicide, so no one will bother investigating.'

'It works as a theory,' Albert said, 'but what about Lionel Winter? I still don't see the connection.'

Minnie shook her head. 'Me neither. We need to talk to Billy again.'

'Be careful,' Tansie said. 'The Godwin's got a varied clientele, including some very senior police officers.'

Albert nodded. 'Jeffers,' he said to Minnie. 'John's boss.'

Tansie stood slowly, as if in pain. 'If we're done here,' he said, 'I need to see Cora's parents.'

'I'll come with you,' Minnie said.

Tansie waved away her offer, but she remained firm in her resolve. 'You're not doing that alone, Tanse,' she said. 'You're my friend, and so was Cora. I'm going with you.'

❧

By the time Tansie and Minnie arrived at the house in Southwark, the police had already delivered the news of Cora's death. Her parents barely responded to Tansie's words, simply nodding their heads dumbly and then firmly closing the door. Tansie went to knock again, but Minnie stayed his hand, took him by the arm and led him away from the quiet terraced house with its immaculately cleaned windows, behind which now dwelled an unspeakable grief.

They found a cab, and rode back to the Palace in silence. She had thought that losing Rose was more than she could bear, but now Cora too. With every mile that passed, as she struggled to deal with a loss that she thought might break her,

Minnie's resolve grew stronger. She would find the people who had done this – all of this – and she would bring them to justice.

But, first, she needed to get inside the Godwin.

TWENTY-NINE

Minnie's heart felt like a stone in her chest, and she fought back tears as she finished applying the rice powder to her face. She stood back from the fragment of mirror. Cora had been right. With her freckles covered, her brows and lashes darkened, and her hair hidden under the wig, she made a convincing young man.

'What do you reckon?' Minnie said, turning to Ida for her approval. She had come to Ida's rooms to get ready. At the Palace there were too many people ready to ask difficult questions. Ida's place had its own problems, the biggest being that she only possessed a small piece of mirror, barely large enough to see her whole face. But Minnie needed the companionship. These days, she didn't much like being on her own.

The Palace was open again, but some of the performers had left, saying they thought the place was cursed. First Rose, and now Cora. Those who'd stayed were lacking their usual gusto. There had been complaints, and Minnie couldn't say she was surprised. Tansie had abandoned his plans for a benefit night in Cora's name. Minnie had caught him on his own a few times, gazing into space, a look of quiet despair on his face.

'It's convincing, Min,' Ida said. 'But I still ain't happy. You should tell Mr Easterbrook.'

'If Albert knew I was even thinking about going inside the Godwin, he'd have a fit. This way, I can have a snoop around. Maybe spot something he missed. And I'll have Billy there,' she offered, by way of quieting Ida's concerns. Although she wasn't sure how useful Billy would be in a tight corner, given he was barely speaking to her since she'd threatened to go to the police about him living off Rose's illegal earnings.

She turned back to Ida's mirror, tucking the last few errant strands of hair under the wig.

'Any news?' Ida said carefully, looking closely at Minnie as she spoke. 'About Daisy?'

Minnie shook her head. 'The police have had no luck. She gave a false address to Kippy.'

'And Tom? Her fella?'

'Nothing. He's convinced she's gonna get in contact with him, but there ain't been a squeak out of her. She's disappeared.'

Tom's distress was almost as heartbreaking as Tansie's. He'd taken to walking the streets day and night, just hoping for a glimpse of Daisy, a word as to her whereabouts. He was adamant it had all been a terrible accident, that Daisy was no more a murderer than he was, but Minnie was plagued by the knowledge that Daisy had stabbed Cora in the neck, right at the point where she would bleed to death very quickly. If it was an impulsive act it seemed remarkable that Daisy had landed on that precise spot.

Ida coughed quietly, and Minnie roused herself from her thoughts. She smiled weakly. The other woman did not return the smile, instead taking Minnie's hands in her own.

'Promise me,' Ida said, 'promise me you'll be careful. If anything happened to you as well—' She broke off, and Minnie pulled her close.

'I promise,' she whispered, burying her face in Ida's hair. 'I'll be in and out of there in no time.' But she did not feel one ounce of the bravery she was projecting.

'Now, last thing,' Minnie said, taking a small box of cigars out of her bag and slipping it into her pocket.

Ida looked quizzical.

'Cora's idea. In case I get stopped,' Minnie said, patting her pocket. 'Gives me an excuse for being anywhere. Just bringing one of the gentlemen some cigars.'

She took one last look in the mirror. She was going to do Cora proud.

❦

Minnie hurried along the Strand, crossing Trafalgar Square and continuing up to Piccadilly. She saw Billy in the distance. As she walked towards him, his eyes swept over her, as if she was something of no interest in a shop window. She drew closer, and still he did not react. It was only when she spoke his name that he turned with a start, surveyed her more slowly, presumably in an effort to hide his surprise, and shrugged. He turned his back, assuming she would follow him down Piccadilly and through a maze of alleyways to the rear entrance to the Godwin.

'Wait here,' he said on the corner of Stratton Street. 'Gimme five minutes, and then show yourself at the back entrance. A couple of runners walked out last night. No reason. So the management are looking for someone to step in. Tell 'em you're desperate for work, so you'll do the night for whatever they're offering. See how you fetch up. If you get caught, it was all your idea. Mention me and you're dead.'

Billy left, and Minnie waited in the grubby alleyway, trying not to draw attention to herself. A mangy ginger cat was sitting on top of a wall, washing itself. A group of young lads drew closer, kicking a ball of wound rags tied with string between the tall buildings lining the alley. Minnie lowered her head and bent down to tie a shoelace until they had passed.

After five minutes Minnie approached the rear of the Godwin, an unprepossessing space suggesting nothing of the luxury the club was famous for. She presented herself at the door and recounted her story of needing work. A tall chap with a receding chin looked her over. 'Not much of you, is there?' he said.

'Makes me fast,' Minnie said, remembering her instructions from Cora to lower and slow her voice.

'Mmm,' the man said. 'Well, we'll try you out. You'll just be fetching and carrying for the waiting staff. Do everything you're asked, and only go where you're told.'

Minnie nodded and slipped past the man, entering a warren of corridors and rooms. It reminded her of backstage at the Palace, the frantic movements, urgent instructions, people rushing, weaving past each other. All so that everything out front looked smooth and effortless. It was all just show, she realised. Only nobody ended up dead after a night at the Palace. Except poor Cora, of course.

Minnie pushed the thought to the back of her mind. There would be time later to grieve.

A stout, squat man who reminded her fleetingly of Tansie grabbed her by the arm.

'Oi,' she said, before he could speak, 'get your hands off me.'

The man stopped and stared at her. Too late she realised that, in her anger, she had raised the pitch of her voice. He eyed her carefully, opening his mouth to say something when another man shouted from the doorway of a small anteroom, 'C'mon, all hands on deck. They're coming through.'

Minnie shrugged herself free of the short man and darted into the anteroom. She could hear the hubbub of voices from the dining room next door as the members wandered through for their first course, the scraping of chairs, clink of glasses and bursts of laughter. She imagined Albert's voice amongst them, wondered what he would say if he knew where she was and what she had planned. He belonged to that world of privilege. She would always be on the other side of the door.

Waiters and hostesses flew in and out of the anteroom, asking for more champagne, handkerchiefs, brandy, cigars. Minnie was kept busy, scurrying back and forth to the kitchens and pantries, in and out of storerooms, down to the wine cellars. She had no time to worry about maintaining her disguise, and nobody was paying any attention to her anyway. She was just another pair of hands.

As the fourth course drew to a close, there was a massive crash from the dining room. One of the waiters came flying through to the anteroom, a tall chap with a broad face, and eyes just a little too far apart. He scanned the room and then pointed at Minnie and one or two other lads. 'You lot,' he said, 'come with me. One of the fish tureens got knocked over and there's the most almighty mess.' He handed them piles of rags from a nearby cupboard and paused before admitting them to the dining room. 'Say nothing,' he said. 'No eye contact. Just clean up the muck and get out of there. Understand?'

They all nodded, and the waiter pushed open the door.

Minnie was used to spectacle, but nothing quite prepared her for the Godwin. Some nights at the Palace, when the chandeliers and all the lamps were lit, when the faces of the punters were turned to the stage, glowing with pleasure and anticipation, and a tumbling girl was weaving her magic, or a singer was wringing tears out of the audience with songs of love and longing – those nights, Minnie thought, there was nothing more beautiful than the Palace.

But the Godwin dining room was like nothing she had ever seen. The entire room was candlelit, from chandeliers and candelabra, with candles in wall sconces and clustered on tables and sideboards. Every one of the diners was lit up by the warm glow, the light bouncing off crystal glasses, watch chains and even the shiny buttons on their jackets and waistcoats. Their cheeks were ruddy with the flush of good wine and brandy; each one of them seemed to be smiling with the benevolence of a man well fed. She imagined their Stanhopes, boldly dangling from watch chains, or discreetly tucked away in waistcoat pockets. All those little secrets.

A sharp elbow in the ribs dragged her out of her reverie, and the waiter hissed in her ear, 'Get moving. Over there.' He pointed to a space near the head of the table where the other lads were on their hands and knees, rags in their hands, frantically mopping up the creamy mess of fish in a yellow sauce that was splattered across the parquet floor.

Minnie stumbled over to join them. Head down, she worked swiftly, mopping up the last traces of the spilled food.

'You've missed a bit.' The voice spoke languorously from one of the dining chairs.

Minnie looked up. A remarkable-looking man, his skin the

colour of cinnamon, with eyes like a cat's and the fullest lips she'd ever seen, was gazing at her as if he wanted to eat her alive. He leaned down and placed one slender finger under her chin, tilting her head towards him. 'My,' he purred, 'aren't you a pretty boy.' And then he tilted his head to one side in an exaggerated gesture of curiosity, his eyes widening in surprise. 'Or *are* you?' he said. His fingers traced lightly from her chin down her neck, lingering over where she knew her Adam's apple should be. His hand slid lower, towards her chest. Foolishly, she hadn't bound herself. The man was moments away from discovering her secret.

She felt a firm hand on her shoulder. The waiter with the wide-spaced eyes yanked her backwards and hissed in her ear, 'I told you. No eye contact. No talking.' He pulled her to her feet and pushed her towards the door leading into the anteroom. Minnie glanced behind her. Cat's Eyes had turned his attention to one of the other waiters, a doe-eyed boy who seemed to be enjoying the attention. Minnie breathed a sigh of relief.

After another hour or so, activity slowly died down as the final courses were served. Minnie's fellow workers stood listless and loitering, propping up the walls and chatting quietly. She was just looking for the opportunity to slip away unnoticed and navigate her way to the basement rooms Albert had described, when a flustered-looking waitress, a shimmer of sweat at her hairline, emerged from the dining room and accosted her.

'Lord Ravenscroft wants a lemon sorbet,' the waitress said.

'*Now* he wants it, an hour after we've finished serving. Nip out to the ice house. You'll see a bucket on your left, with a handle on the lid. Bring it to the kitchens and I'll meet you there.'

Minnie looked blank. 'Ice house?'

'Out the back, across the lane. The head chef'll have a key – fella with a dicky eye, makes a lot of noise. Oh, and you'll need a lamp. Black as pitch it'll be.'

Minnie darted off down to the kitchens, retrieved the keys from the head chef, grabbed a lamp and slipped out of the rear door. The alley was deserted now, the ginger cat long gone, the game of football at an end. Facing her across the lane was a single-storey brick building with a domed roof. Minnie's feet were aching and she wished she were at home in bed. But there was work still to be done and the sooner she found this stupid bucket, the sooner she could go snooping.

She turned the big brass key in the lock, grunting as she used her shoulder to push open the heavy door. She gasped at the sudden drop in temperature. A flight of stairs lay directly in front of her, leading down to a level below ground. She held the lamp carefully aloft and slowly descended. Straight ahead were eight, maybe ten huge blocks of ice, taller than Albert and twice as wide. They were packed with straw. Either side of the ice blocks were compartments containing all manner of items: bottles of wine and champagne, joints of meat and various fowl awaiting the cook's knife, large pats of butter, bowls of cream.

Minnie's breath frosted the air as she stepped carefully across the cobbled floor. In the compartments on the left she found half a dozen wooden buckets with handles. They were labelled 'ice cream' or 'sorbet' and then a flavour. Orange, blackcurrant. No lemon. She set the lamp down, rubbed her hands together and peered into the rear of the ice house. The compartments further back looked empty and not worth investigation. But she anticipated the waitress's irritation if she returned empty-handed, the command to look again, all of which might scupper her chances of nosing in those basement rooms. So she picked up the lamp and moved forward. The building extended back a long way, maybe thirty, forty feet; it was difficult to estimate distances in the gloom. She scanned each shelf carefully, but there was nothing there. This part of the ice house looked unused. She was about to give up the search, return to some vestige of warmth and face the ire of the sweaty waitress, when something glinted in the lamplight. The escutcheon around a lock. She was facing a door.

She tried the handle but it was locked. A locked door was irresistible to Minnie. She wouldn't have lasted five minutes with Bluebeard. She pushed against the door. The wood creaked but didn't shift. She reached up, slipped a finger under her wig and withdrew one of the hairpins holding her hair in place. Praying that the Godwin didn't buy their locks from the same place as Tansie, she slid the hairpin into the mechanism. Resting her cheek against the wooden door, she turned the hairpin carefully until, with a satisfying pop, the lock turned and she opened the door.

This room was much smaller, maybe twelve or fifteen feet long, but even colder than the rest of the ice house. There were still the huge blocks of ice, still the shelves either side with narrow walkways. Minnie moved forward tentatively, shining her lamp onto each of the empty shelves. By the end wall, something was lying on one of the shelves. It looked like rags or clothing. She raised the lamp higher, and held it in front of her, gently lifting the cloth with her other hand. When she realised what she was seeing, it felt as if all the air had left her lungs.

It was a woman.

She was dead, her skin cold and hard. Bile rose in the back of Minnie's throat, and she bent over, resting her hands on her thighs, forcing herself to breathe. When her light-headedness passed, she straightened up. Overwhelmingly, she wished she were anywhere but here. Or, at least, that Albert was with her. But she was alone, and there was a job to be done.

Steeling herself, Minnie carefully peeled back the sheet. The woman was naked. A long cut extended from her neck to just below her stomach, the skin peeled back, the organs exposed. Minnie cried out at the horror, her voice echoing off the vaulted ceiling. She gently repositioned the sheet over the woman's body. It was only then that she had the courage to look closely at her face.

The features were distorted by death, her unseeing eyes wide but dull. How long had she lain here? Alone in the cold and dark. Her hair was dark, secured in a thick plait. A rosebud mouth, button nose. Agnes Collins. The woman who had left the Palace to work at the Godwin.

She had been here all along.

Minnie's legs went from under her, and she slumped onto the cobbled floor. She looked down at her hand still holding the lamp, and noticed she was shaking. But it was as if it were happening to somebody else. Her thoughts were muddled and sluggish, and she wondered if it was the shock of what she had discovered or the cold of the ice house.

After only a few moments the chill seeped into her flesh. She placed a hand on the floor and realised it was wet with melted ice. Slowly, she forced herself to stand, and turned back towards the stairs.

She was not alone.

Lord Linton stood in the doorway, blocking her exit. He held a pistol casually in one hand, a lantern in the other. He blinked vigorously and smiled at her.

'Why, Minerva,' he said. 'How delightful to see you again. Although I believe it's Minnie you go by these days, is it not? Might I say, you make a most fetching young man.'

'How did you—?'

'—know you'd be here? I know everything, Minnie. Haven't you figured that out yet? My people were told to keep an eye out for a young lad seeking work, someone we'd never seen before. And then, as if by magic, you appear.'

'But no one knew I was dressing up as a man except—'

'—the unfortunate Cora, yes. Oh, and ...' He stepped neatly to one side and there stood Billy, glowering in the shadows.

Minnie inhaled sharply. Tears pricked her eyes as she exhaled, her breath tracing patterns in the air. Billy held her gaze, a sneer curling his lip.

'Surprised? You shouldn't be. I own young Billy, don't you know?' Linton took a step closer to her and she caught a whiff of brandy on his breath. 'I was an enormous fan of yours, my dear. I went to see you three times in one week, I remember. And each time you were fresh and new and simply entrancing.' He lifted his lamp so the light fell on her face. 'The bloom has faded somewhat. Still, it will be a shame.'

The man was a black cloak and a top hat away from playing the villain in a melodrama, Minnie thought, and she almost laughed out loud. How ridiculous it all was. And yet, what a foolish way to die. Her heart sank with the sadness that she would never again see Albert. She thought of Rose and Cora, and something hardened within her. If this was where she would end her days, she would not give Linton the satisfaction of seeing her beg for mercy.

'You always struck me as a clever sort of girl,' Linton continued, 'so I'm sure you know what's going to happen next. Tragic accident. Young woman locks herself inside an ice house. Albert will be upset, I imagine. But no doubt he'll find someone to distract him soon enough. Billy,' he said, not turning but simply raising a hand. 'Do what is necessary to incapacitate Miss Ward, and then pull the door closed behind you.'

Linton turned away. With her lamp still in her hand, Minnie raised it high and swung it with all her might at his head. Her arm shuddered as the heavy brass thudded against Linton's skull. The glass shattered, and he gave a yelp of pain, but Minnie knew it was not enough. He turned back to her, his exaggerated blinking contorting his face. She launched herself at him, but he slapped her hard and she fell to the floor.

'Now look what you made me do,' Linton said, rubbing the back of his head, and leaning in towards her. 'And this was all going so nicely.'

He gave her a half-smile, then turned away.

Minnie scrambled to her feet, the darkness descending on her as Linton moved off, the lantern in his hand. He was almost at the stairs now.

'Don't!' Minnie screamed, all her resolve abandoned. She ran towards Linton, but Billy was there, like an impassable wall. He placed a hand on her chest and pushed her back further into the ice house.

Then he turned to Linton, took two short steps, raised one huge fist and punched him on the back of the neck, just below his right ear. Linton crumpled onto the stairs, slid down a step or two and lay there, not moving.

Minnie drew closer to Billy. The two of them stood in silence, staring down at Linton.

'You've killed him,' Minnie said, surprised to find she did not care.

Billy reached down, placed two fingers on Linton's neck, and shook his head. 'No. Still ticking.' He turned back to Minnie and held out his hand. 'Come on,' he said urgently. 'He might not be out for long.'

'But … Agnes,' Minnie said, gesturing back to the darkness behind her.

'Forget about it, Min. When Linton wakes up we need to be long gone.'

'We can't leave her, Billy.'

'Yes,' he said, 'we can.'

With one swift movement he grabbed her round the waist and tipped her over his shoulder. He stepped over Linton's body, ascended the stairs and was out of the ice house, leaving the door open behind him, as he and Minnie escaped into the night.

THIRTY

Albert sat in his drawing room, enjoying a rare quiet pipe before retiring to bed. Mrs Byrne had expressed her disapproval, but Albert felt recent events warranted the transgression.

A loud hammering on the front door roused him. He glanced at the clock on the mantelpiece. Half past ten. A strange hour to call. Mrs Byrne scurried down the hallway, voicing her disgruntlement all the way. And then he heard Minnie's voice, high and hysterical. Albert sprang to his feet, and met her in the hallway. She was dressed in a man's suit, the one he had last seen her wearing at the Palace, larking around with Cora. Standing behind her was Billy Walker.

'Albert, I'm so sorry, but we didn't know where else to go,' Minnie said, her voice fast and nervous. 'Make sure you lock and bolt the front and back doors. Do it now.'

Albert nodded at Mrs Byrne who turned swiftly and carried out Minnie's instructions. He ushered Minnie over to the fireplace and seated her beside it, grabbing a blanket to put over her shoulders. She was shaking so violently he wondered if she was ill. He placed a hand on her forehead; her skin was cool and clammy.

'Billy,' she said, gesturing towards the door, where the

other man stood, as if reluctant to enter the room. He too looked shaken, diminished somehow. Albert offered him another chair by the fire, and Billy sat down, dropping his head into his hands in a gesture of despair.

Mrs Byrne returned with four glasses of brandy.

Fortified by the alcohol, Minnie eventually stopped shaking. She recounted her night at the Godwin, what she had found in the ice house and how Billy had saved her.

'I don't know what I'd have done if he hadn't shown up,' she said, reaching across and taking Billy's hand, which swallowed up her own. 'And before you say anything, Albert, I know I should have told you what I was up to.'

'I'd never have let you go,' Albert said.

'Which is why I didn't tell you.'

Billy jumped as a carriage drove past outside. He glanced nervously round the room.

Mrs Byrne drew closer, and laid a hand on his shoulder. He seemed to draw comfort from the older woman's touch, his shoulders dropping. He glanced up at Albert. 'There's things I need to tell you. Things I should have said before but … I was afraid. It don't matter now, though. They'll be coming for me soon, whatever I do or say. And keeping quiet ain't got me very far. So you might as well know it all.'

The others waited patiently for him to speak further, the ponderous ticking of the clock the only sound to disturb the silence.

'I killed a man,' he said eventually. 'A dog fight. Fella started beating the hell out of his dog when it didn't win. I stepped in and the fella turned on me with a whip. I lumped him one, and he went down like a lead weight. Died instantly. And that might have been the end of it, only he was a wealthy chap, so I got charged with murder. Only just managed to escape the noose. Life imprisonment.'

He shuddered and drew closer to the fire. Mrs Byrne darted out of the room and returned with another blanket which she draped around his shoulders. He gave her a grateful look, and continued.

'I don't like to talk about it, and you don't need to know about it anyways, but prison was hell. I knew if I stayed in there, I probably wouldn't last more than a couple of years. So I escaped. Don't matter how, that ain't important now. What matters is that I got out. Started working at the Palace. Tansie weren't too bothered about where I'd come from as long as I worked the door, chucked out the trouble. Which I did. Kept my head down. And that's where I met Rose.' A gentle smile spread across his face, as if she had entered the room. He looked across at Minnie. 'It was never what you thought, Min. I loved every bone in her body. I'd never have laid a finger on her.'

Minnie nodded, her eyes filling with tears.

'Things were going well,' Billy continued. 'we were saving up for a place of our own. Planning on getting married. Babies. I needed a bit more money, so I asked Tanse if he knew of anywhere, and he suggested the Godwin. Said he reckoned it'd be an easy billet. All you had to do was occasionally pour a toff into a cab and that was it. And it was. For a while.'

He paused, then absent-mindedly took the poker and stirred the fire with it, as if he were in his own home.

'Lord Linton, he owns the gaff, but he don't do none of the hiring or firing so I'd never met him. I'd been there a month or so. Then, one night, he was there. And I knew him. He knew me too. 'Cos the fella I'd killed at that dog fight was his brother.'

'That was you?' Minnie gasped. 'Edie told me about it. I had no idea it was you, Bill.'

'Why would you? It ain't something I make a noise about. Linton knew I should be inside, not working at the Godwin. I thought my number was up for sure. Except Linton treated me like a long-lost pal. Said he wouldn't say nothing. Told me I'd done him a favour, 'cos he never would've inherited without me. Said if I did a few jobs for him he'd keep quiet. It would be our secret.'

'What sort of jobs?' Minnie asked.

'Visiting people what had crossed him. Using my size the way I've always done. That's all it was at first. Just threatening, like. A little slap every now and then. But he owned me, and he let me know it. I couldn't get away or turn him down. So, the jobs turned a bit nastier. He had me rough up one or two of his … business associates, he called 'em.'

'Did Rose know about this? About your past? And Linton's manipulation of you?' Albert asked.

'I didn't tell her at first, but I couldn't keep nothing secret from her and she guessed something was up. Thought I was seeing another girl and threatened to break it off with me. So I told her. Everything. She was clever, Rose. Came up with a plan. The money we'd been saving to get married and move to a nice set of rooms, she said we could get to America with just a little bit more. Said Linton would never find us there, and we'd both be free. We needed the money quick, 'cos Linton was miring me further and further in his mess. So that's when Rose said she could make a lot more money by going to those downstairs rooms at the Godwin.'

He broke off abruptly, rose from his seat and started to pace the room. Albert noticed Mrs Byrne glancing nervously at two tall china vases positioned perilously close to the edge of the sideboard. Billy went to the window, parted the curtains a fraction and peered out. Mrs Byrne rose and carefully pushed the vases closer to the wall before resuming her seat.

'I didn't like it,' Billy said, turning back from the window and continuing to pace. 'Some days it just tore me up inside, thinking of her down in those basement rooms, doing God knows what. That's when we'd argue. I didn't feel like a real man letting her do that stuff. The thought of it destroys me even now she's gone. I took it out on a brick wall once or twice.'

He glanced down at his hands, and Albert remembered the broken skin and bruises on his fists when they'd first met.

'But she said it was only for a little while,' Billy continued, 'that she could make enough money to get us both to America. Linton was always dropping hints about his friends in the police force, and how interested they'd be to hear about me. He liked that. Teasing. Torturing. I knew I couldn't stand it much longer, so I agreed to Rose's plan. And we were nearly there. We were a few weeks away from getting on that ship, I reckon. We just needed a few more sovs. And then it all went wrong.'

He stopped and gazed about him as if unsure of how he'd got there. Mrs Byrne patted the seat next to her and he took it, giving her a gentle smile.

'It was a couple of weeks before she died,' he continued. 'Rose was downstairs in the Godwin. I weren't working there that night. She'd fallen asleep after … y'know …, and when she woke up she realised she'd left something in one of the other rooms, so she nipped in to get it. And she found Agnes Collins, one of her pals, lying there. Dead. She tried to bring her round but it was too late. Rose raised merry hell, and they all came running. Linton too. He told Rose that Agnes had been taking chloroform with a chap earlier that night, and she must have taken too much.'

'Chloroform?' Mrs Byrne asked.

Billy blushed violently, even his ears turning red. He glanced at Albert, who avoided his gaze and said nothing.

'Oh, for God's sake,' Minnie said impatiently. 'And they say women are the delicate sex. Chloroform apparently makes things a bit more interesting, Mrs Byrne. In the bedroom.'

Mrs Byrne paused, then slowly nodded her head. 'Well, that's a new one on me. Carry on, Billy.'

'Linton acted like this chloroform story answered everyone's questions. Then, as she was leaving, Rose overheard him telling two of the lads to stick the body in the ice house. No one will know, he said. Leave it a day or two, and we'll let the river have her. Rose couldn't bear the thought of that poor girl's parents never knowing what happened to her. Her never having a proper burial. She was mad with it, came round my drum, woke me up, raving about what had happened, and how it weren't right. Said they was gonna chuck the girl away, like she was so much rubbish. I told her to keep her mouth shut. We were so close to getting on that ship. But she wouldn't let it go. Told me something had to be done. That's what she kept saying. *Something has got to be done, Billy.*'

He gazed at Minnie helplessly. 'You knew her, Min. There was no stopping her once she got an idea in her head. She was gonna say something, and the game would be up. She kept saying we'd find a way round it so the police wouldn't get me. But I knew I was gonna swing. And I was worried what Linton would do if she opened her trap. But I didn't know how to stop her. So I told her to have a word with Lionel Winter.'

'Why Winter?' Albert asked.

'He was one of her regulars at the Godwin. And he was chums with Linton. It's all about who you know, ain't it? We thought Winter could convince Linton to at least leave Agnes's body where it could be found. For her parents.'

'Bit risky, weren't it?' Minnie said. 'Speaking to someone who was chums with Linton?'

Billy nodded. 'We did think that. But Rose said Winter was a nice chap. He never hurt her. Never even touched her, she said. He liked a particular type of girl, a bit manly, so Rose didn't do much for him in that department. But he liked to talk to her, and he gave her one of them … whatchamacallits – them little things with a photograph inside.' He glanced at Albert for verification.

'A Stanhope,' Albert said.

'That's it. She thought it was the cleverest thing, how you couldn't tell anything from looking at the outside, and then that tiny little photograph hidden away. So he gave her one. With his photograph inside. We were gonna sell it when we got to America, give us a few extra quid to get started with. Winter asked her if she'd pose for a Stanhope photograph for him. And she did. I didn't like that much. The thought of him carrying around a picture of her.'

Albert shifted in his seat, uncomfortable at the memory of his argument with Minnie over the same thing.

'I reckon he was sweet on her, even though he never … y'know,' Billy continued. 'I wondered if she didn't feel the same. But she said it weren't like that. Said Winter was just kind, and if he liked to buy her things, where was the harm?'

He fell silent again, and Minnie prompted him. 'So, you told Rose to speak to Lionel Winter?'

Billy nodded. 'I think she'd already had the idea herself, to be honest. Winter said he'd pretend he'd heard some other way about Agnes dying. Keep Rose's name out of it. Whether he did or not, I dunno. A few days later, Rose turned up dead, and Winter died not long after.'

'Why go to all that trouble?' Albert asked. 'If Agnes's death was an accident, why not just come forward about it?'

'Scandal?' Minnie speculated. 'It wouldn't do the Godwin's reputation much good, would it?'

Billy shook his head. 'I don't reckon it was an accident. Linton didn't throw her in the Thames and he didn't leave her body to be found somewhere. Whatever happened in that bedroom with the chloroform, it was deliberate, so that Linton could keep Agnes in the ice house. He used to go out there and – visit her.'

Minnie shuddered.

'That's who you found tonight, Min. Agnes. She's been out there for weeks.'

'How did you know she was there?' Minnie asked. 'Her body was locked away right at the back.'

'Linton took me out there the day after Rose was found in the Arches. Told me if I said anything he'd convince his police chums it was me who killed Agnes. Said he had half the police force in his pocket, with what went on in those basement rooms, and he could make black white if he wanted to. Said I'd hang for sure.'

'What about Rose?' Minnie asked. 'Do you know how she died?'

Billy dropped his head. 'The day it happened, she got a

message from Winter, asking her to meet him. That's where she was going that morning when we argued. Wearing those fancy shoes. Only now I don't reckon the message was from Winter. I reckon Linton tricked her into going somewhere, and they killed her. Then strung her up in the Arches so it looked like suicide.'

'Why didn't Linton keep her in the ice house? Like Agnes?' Albert asked.

Billy inhaled slowly. 'Rose weren't his type. He liked 'em small, he said. Dainty. He had Rose's body hung under the Arches as a message to me. Showing what he could do. That he could get away with murder.'

'And Lionel Winter?'

Billy shrugged. 'He knew too much, I s'pose.'

Mrs Byrne rose and left the room.

Albert, Minnie and Billy sat in silence for a few minutes, then Billy turned to Minnie. 'I want you to know, Min, it weren't me who told Linton you were gonna get inside the Godwin. I'd never do that.'

'Daisy?' Albert said, looking at Minnie.

'She was in the Palace when Cora was coaching me. She could have overheard. Don't suppose you know where she might be hiding out, do you, Bill?'

Billy shook his head.

Mrs Byrne returned. 'The second bedroom's all made up for you, Minnie. Billy, it'll have to be the couch.'

Albert shook his head and turned to Billy. 'You need to make yourself scarce. That money you and Rose saved for America. Have you got it on you?'

'I ain't that much of a mug. It's somewhere safe, mind. I can get to it easily enough.'

'I'll make up the few pounds you're short of. If I remember correctly,' Albert said, crossing over to the side table and picking up the newspaper, 'there's a ship leaving Liverpool tomorrow morning for New York.' He scanned the paper, then glanced at his watch. 'The overnight train to Liverpool goes from Euston in just over an hour. Best we find you a cab.'

THIRTY-ONE

Albert had barely slept. He had lain awake, painfully aware of Minnie sleeping in the bedroom above his, registering every creak of the floorboards as she turned in bed. Even the thought of her in one of Mrs Byrne's nightdresses didn't stop his mind wandering. It had been a very long night.

At breakfast Minnie appeared in the gent's suit from the previous night.

'Couldn't Mrs Byrne find you something?' Albert asked.

'She tried, but we ain't exactly the same size. I looked like an oversized orphan.'

Over breakfast they discussed their next steps.

'We'll speak to John first,' Albert said. 'You need to tell him what you found in the ice house. And we have Billy's evidence, too.'

He withdrew a sheet of paper from his pocket, a hurriedly written account of Billy's statement from the night before that he had marked with an X before heading off into the night for Euston station.

'Linton will have moved her by now, though, won't he?' Minnie said. 'And then it's gonna be the Anatomical Venus all over again, with you looking like a chump and John staring at his shoes.'

'We've still got to tell him, Minnie.'

She nodded, took another slice of bread and liberally applied butter and jam. 'And then what?' she asked. 'Linton's gonna be after us, ain't he?'

'Maybe. Maybe not.' Albert shrugged. 'He might want to stay hidden for a while. We need to get you a change of clothes, at the very least. Although I have to say, you make a rather fetching young man.'

The duty officer informed them that Sergeant Price was out on a call, so they left a note for John filling him in on everything they knew, and headed down the Strand. A crowd had gathered around the entrance to the Palace. Parked in front of the music hall was Edie's stylish brougham with the initials 'RR' engraved on its lamps. Edie was just emerging from the carriage, but she looked different. Even smaller; somehow reduced. Half-heartedly, she waved at the crowd, then turned towards Albert and Minnie.

'Something's wrong,' Minnie said, and the two of them hurried forward.

'Oh, thank God you're both here,' Edie said, holding out her hands to them. 'Is there somewhere quiet we can talk?'

Minnie nodded. 'Tansie's office.'

But, as they walked through the darkened auditorium, Edie stopped.

'Here?' she suggested.

Minnie shrugged. 'If you want. It's not the most private.'

Edie shuddered. 'It's just … backstage – that's where it happened, weren't it? Tansie's girl? I don't reckon I can go back there.'

Minnie nodded, and they sat at a small table.

'That's why I'm here,' Edie said, raising a bejewelled hand to her chest. 'Tansie's girl. Cora, weren't it?'

Minnie's face clouded at the mention of Cora's name.

'Yes. That's her,' Albert said.

'I understand,' Edie said, 'you're looking for someone calling herself Daisy Mountford?'

Albert nodded.

'She's at our house.'

Albert glanced at Minnie. She looked as confused as he felt, his mind racing to make sense of Edie's words.

'I don't get it,' Minnie said after a moment's pause. 'Why on earth is she at yours?'

Edie said nothing for a moment, gazing round the auditorium as if the four walls might provide her with the inspiration to carry on.

'My husband ...' she said slowly, her fingers tracing patterns on the worn surface of the table. She inhaled deeply and started again. 'Daisy worked at the Godwin. Sweet little thing, but rootless. Couldn't really settle to nothing and we all know how that can end up. Teddy and I thought maybe a life in the halls would suit her. She's pretty and she can hold a tune, which is more than can be said for a lot of them. Teddy was really insistent, said it could be the making of her so I asked Tansie if he could find something for her here, which he did.' She paused, nervously twisting her diamond rings and slipping them on and off her fingers. 'I ain't got no proof of this, mind,' she continued, 'but I think Teddy used her to spy on you pair. See what you're up to. Only now she's killed Tansie's girl.'

'Why?' Minnie asked, leaning forward in her seat. 'Why'd she do it? What on earth did she have against Cora?'

Edie looked at her blankly for a moment. 'It weren't deliberate, Minnie. At least, not the way Daisy tells it. She'd taken to carrying a knife 'cos of the Hairpin Killer. Teddy told her if she was ever attacked she should go for the neck. The carotid artery, he said. Easy to reach. When Cora went for her, Daisy lashed out without thinking. Found her mark, more's the pity.'

'And you believe her? That it was just a terrible accident?' Albert asked.

'I do. Daisy ain't the sharpest tool in the box. If she was lying I'd see right through her. She's made a dreadful mistake, and Teddy's convinced she can hide out at our house until the storm passes, but I don't agree. Tansie's my friend. For a long time he was my only friend.' She threw Minnie an affectionate glance, and carried on. 'This has got to stop somewhere. I've stayed quiet for too long.'

'Meaning?' Albert said sharply. He'd had enough of people keeping secrets.

Edie's eyes darted round the auditorium. She rose from the chair, but something seemed to shift inside her. She sat back down and removed a small jewelled hip flask from her bag. Her hands were shaking. 'You don't mind, do you?' she asked, raising the hip flask to her lips and drinking before offering it to Albert and Minnie. They both refused.

Edie nodded. 'It is a bit early, I suppose,' she said, and took another large swig, before she continued speaking. 'My husband is … not the man I thought he was when I married him. It started slowly at first. Little things. Correcting me. Suggesting what I should wear. Letting me know he didn't approve of my friends. He said I "needed telling". That was his favourite phrase. Said I was born from nothing, but now

I'd married up and I needed him to tell me how to behave. I didn't mind too much at first. Thought I could handle him.'

'But you couldn't?' Minnie asked.

Edie shook her head. 'Before I even realised what was happening, I was quite alone in the world. I'd grown used to him telling me what to do. Pointing out how wrong I was about most things. So when he hit me the first time, it just seemed all of a piece.'

Minnie flinched, as if she felt the blow herself. 'Couldn't you have asked for help?' she said.

Edie fiddled again with her rings, not raising her eyes. She reached for the hip flask and then stopped herself. 'I was too ashamed,' she said quietly. 'I blamed myself. Thought I must be doing something to provoke him. And when I married Teddy it was the talk of the town. I left the halls with barely a backward glance. I couldn't go back to those old friends, tell them I'd made the most awful mess of it all. Besides, even if I'd had the gumption to do it, I didn't have the money. The minute I married Teddy, everything I owned was his. And I'm a terrible one for spending. Presents. Nonsense. Extravagance.' She held out her hands to show Albert her rings. 'All paste. I've got nothing of my own.'

She paused, took another swig from the hip flask.

'You said earlier you'd stayed quiet for too long,' Albert said. 'Quiet about what?'

Edie sighed heavily and glanced up at Minnie, who reached forward to take her hand.

'Something happened towards the back end of September. I'd gone to bed. Teddy got back at about three o'clock in the morning. Came into my room in a frightful state, sweating, talking nonsense, pacing the room. He told me this girl had been found dead at the club. Some terrible accident with chloroform.'

'We know,' Minnie said. 'Her name was Agnes Collins. She worked here for a while, then got a job at the Godwin.'

Edie's face drained of all colour. 'I never knew her name. And she worked here, you say? Christ, it could've been me, back in the day. Or you, for that matter.' She looked at Minnie. 'Teddy calmed down eventually, told me he'd take care of it and I weren't to worry. I did, of course. Worried myself sick. Checked the papers every day to see if the body of a young girl had been found, but there was nothing. So I reckoned whatever they'd done, it had worked.'

'You didn't think to go to the police?' Albert asked.

She gave him a long look. 'I didn't have no proof, did I? No body to show anyone. Who'd have believed me? Teddy told me often enough he'd have me locked up in a lunatic asylum if I tried to leave him, or told anyone about his cruel ways. If I went to the police spouting stories about dead girls and secret bedrooms in the Godwin basement, I'm pretty sure I'd have found myself in the Bethlem before I could draw breath. Besides, there weren't much point in going to the police.'

'Why not?' Albert asked.

'You don't get it, do you? A lot of the chaps what go to the Godwin, especially to those basement rooms, they wear a uniform, Albert. A police uniform. Teddy always boasts about how he can do as he pleases, 'cos he's chums with Chief Superintendent This and Chief Constable That. Anyways, I told myself whatever had happened to that poor girl, I couldn't do nothing about it. But Teddy's been acting strange ever since. And it weren't long after the girl's death that he asked me to find work for Daisy at the Palace.'

Albert looked pointedly at Minnie, and she recounted to Edie all they had learned of Agnes's death, and Rose's knowledge of it. At the mention of Lionel Winter's name, Edie recoiled.

'He came to the house one day,' she said, 'maybe a week after the girl – Agnes – died. Him and Teddy were holed up in the drawing room together for an hour. There were raised voices and, after Winter left, Teddy had a face like thunder.'

'Did you hear anything of the conversation between Winter and your husband?' Minnie asked.

She shook her head. 'Nothing. But whatever Winter said, Teddy weren't happy. Do you think he had Winter killed? And your friend Rose?'

'We think it's more than likely, yes.'

Silence descended on the room. In the distance, Kippy could be heard shouting orders, followed by some enthusiastic hammering.

After a few minutes, Minnie stirred in her seat. 'There's something else, Edie. It ain't pleasant, but you need to know. Your husband has this room … in your house?'

Edie shuddered, drawing her fur stole closer around her neck. 'That ghastly thing, the Venus. And those other mannequins. Like tiny dead babies.'

'Your husband showed me something in that room that he maintained was an Anatomical Venus,' Albert said. 'But I'm convinced it was Agnes Collins. We know he's kept her body in the ice house at the Godwin for weeks. For what purpose, I dread to think.'

Edie raised a hand to her mouth and her body convulsed. Minnie leapt up, took Edie's arm and hurried her swiftly to the nearest fire bucket. While they were gone, Albert went backstage and found Edie a glass of water.

When they returned, Edie's face was drained of all colour. She patted her lips with a handkerchief and dabbed the sweat from her brow. She took the water from Albert with a grateful look, and the three of them sat again.

'I'll never forgive myself,' Edie said, so quietly Minnie and Albert had to lean forward to hear her. 'I've known for years that something weren't right. But I told myself I was being fanciful. That it weren't possible he was doing – what I thought.' She broke off again and swallowed deeply. 'When we were first married, when things were good between us, he used to trace on my skin where my heart was. He'd lay his head on my stomach and say he could hear all the veins and organs working away. Said he longed to explore what lay beneath. Find out how it all fit together. This girl. Agnes. Are you saying her death was no accident? Teddy *murdered* her?'

'We think so, yes,' Albert said. 'We think he killed her, moved her to the ice house and he's been … exploring ever since.'

Minnie looked away.

Edie was broken, her eyes resting on some distant point, all the life gone from her. She seemed to have aged a decade in the last ten minutes.

Albert glanced at Minnie. 'I'm going to find Linton and Daisy. Minnie, take Lady Linton back to my house and wait for me there.'

Edie turned her head sharply, as if his words had reanimated her. She shook her head decisively and stood. 'I'm going with you,' she said, with grim determination.

'That's a very bad idea,' Albert said. 'We've no idea what he might do to you.'

'Can't be worse than what he's already done,' Edie said.

'And I can't let him get away with this. He's a very convincing liar, Albert. He'll tell you black is white if he thinks it'll save his own skin. He may find it a little harder to lie if I'm there.' She cast an appraising eye over him. 'My carriage is far too small to accommodate all three of us. We'll need a cab.'

THIRTY-TWO

The cab pulled up outside the house on Holland Park Road, Albert getting out almost before it had come to a complete stop. He hurriedly paid the driver, and helped Edie and Minnie out. As the cab pulled away, the front door was opened by a stocky young man with a shock of red hair.

'George,' Edie said, 'is my husband in?'

'Lord Linton is in his private room, my lady.'

Edie turned and looked at Minnie and Albert. 'The Venus room,' she murmured, and led them quickly through the entrance hall to the rooms beyond.

Minnie glanced around her, noting the exotic touches: the stuffed peacock in the hallway, the small fountain in the middle of one room, the elaborate mosaic tiling in another. But the thing she noticed most was the quiet. Her rooms in Catherine Street were never quiet, the rattle of carriages, the brisk clip of horses' hooves and the cries of street sellers a constant backdrop to her life. The house seemed unnaturally still; even the dust motes caught in beams of sunlight filtering through the windows seemed to hang in the air without moving. Money bought you quiet like this.

The sound of a chair scraping broke the stillness. It came from behind a door just in front of them. Albert gestured to

Minnie and Edie to follow him, and slowly pushed open the door.

For a moment, Minnie struggled to comprehend what she was seeing. And then, as realisation dawned, she started to shake.

There were two tables positioned side by side. On one lay what Minnie guessed was the Anatomical Venus. The lid had been removed from the stomach to expose the inner workings of the mannequin. Some of the organs had been removed and placed neatly alongside the figure.

On the second table lay the remains of Daisy Mountford. She had been positioned to mimic the Venus, her left arm raised above her head, her cheek turned to rest gently on the arm. Her other hand cradled her hair. A string of pearls lay round her neck.

She had been cut from her throat to her stomach, the skin peeled back. Lying next to her was a pile of fleshy remains, blood spilling from them and dripping slowly onto the floor. Some part of Minnie's brain that was able to detach itself from the horror of the scene guessed that these were the same organs as had been removed from the Venus.

Standing behind the two bodies was Linton. From the tips of his fingers, all the way up the sleeves of his shirt, almost up to his armpits, he was dark with blood.

Minnie turned to Edie, who was standing behind her, and instinctively raised her hand to Edie's eyes. 'Don't look,' Minnie murmured. 'Don't look.'

Albert was motionless, his hands held out in front of him as if to ward off an invisible assailant.

Linton raised his eyes and smiled gently at them, blinking vigorously all the while. 'Why, Minnie!' he said with genuine affection, but his voice low and broken, as if he had not spoken for some time. 'How lovely to see you again. I trust you've forgiven me for the little fracas in the ice house? Although I have to say, you did give me quite the bruise with that lamp.' And he chuckled to himself, rubbing the back of his head with a bloodied hand.

'And Albert!' he continued. 'What a pleasant surprise. If you've come about the Godwin membership, just try again, dear boy. I'm sure we'll find a place for you sometime. Right now, as you can see, I have my hands a little full.' He held them out in front of him and frowned. 'In fact,' he said, 'this is all rather unfortunate timing.'

Edie pushed past Albert and Minnie. With one quick glance, she seemed to take in the atrocity that Linton had created, then sharply turned her head away. Minnie noticed the ribbons on Edie's dress trembling as her whole body started to shake. She reached towards Linton, stopping just short of touching him. Quietly she spoke his name.

'Teddy? What's happened, my dear?' she said, her voice gentle and high-pitched, as if speaking to a child. 'What have you done to Daisy?'

Linton flinched at her words, then shook his head vigorously. 'Not me, Edie. I found her like this. Both of them. Daisy and Venus. Just like this.'

He withdrew his watch from his pocket, blood smearing across his waistcoat as he did so. He stared at the watch face as if it were a puzzle he had no knowledge of. 'Very strange,' he said. 'I thought I'd been home maybe five minutes, but my watch seems to suggest otherwise. I found her. Just like this,' and he gestured again towards the table. 'Daisy.'

It was as if this mention of her name awoke him, as if

he saw her for the first time. He reached towards the dead woman, and then his face crumpled and he started to cry. So hard, his whole body convulsed and he was coughing, gasping for breath. He stumbled towards a chair and sat, his weeping slowly subsiding.

Edie turned towards Albert and Minnie. There were tears in her eyes, and she shook her head in disbelief.

Albert murmured something and then broke off, as if unable to find the words.

Although Minnie had her head turned steadfastly away from what lay on the table, the smell of Daisy's blood seemed to fill the air, permeating Minnie's skin, inching its way under her fingernails, into her hair. Bile rose in her throat, and she struggled not to vomit.

'Teddy,' Edie said, taking a step closer to Linton, her voice still lowered, 'it's over, my dear. They've got too much evidence. There's no escape.'

Linton looked at her, all colour drained from his face. He stammered her name and blinked rapidly, sending his whole face into the familiar convulsions.

'I … don't understand,' he said haltingly.

Anger flared inside Minnie. 'What is it you don't understand?' she said, her voice so high and panicky it sounded like someone else speaking. 'That Edie finally plucked up the courage to tell us what's been going on? Is that what you don't *understand*?'

'Edie?' Linton said, ignoring Minnie, and reaching a bloodied hand towards his wife. She pulled back, and Minnie took a step closer to her.

'They know, Teddy,' Edie said. 'They worked it all out. Agnes. The ice house. How you needed to keep Rose and Lionel quiet.'

'But … that wasn't me. You know it wasn't me,' he said, his voice rising with panic.

'Not the normal you, no,' Edie said. 'But something comes over you, don't it, Teddy? Something that makes you kill. Agnes and Rose, Lionel, and now poor Daisy. And we'll say that. In court. We'll get you the best barrister in the land. I'll give evidence. Explain about the Venus. I'll tell them everything.'

Minnie flushed with anger. Even now, after all he had done to her, Edie was still caring for him. Trying to protect him. Making excuses.

Edie again took a step towards Linton, but Albert moved forward, taking her by the arm and pulling her back closer to the door to stand by Minnie.

'We need to fetch the police,' Minnie murmured.

Albert nodded his agreement, and Minnie turned to leave. Just as she placed her hand on the doorknob, a gentle scraping echoed in the quiet of the room. They all turned towards the noise. The drawer of the side table positioned by Linton's chair was open, and Linton had a gun in his hand. His finger was on the trigger, the gun cocked and ready to fire.

The room felt even stiller, as if the presence of the gun had sucked up all the air.

'You need to start telling the truth, Edie,' Linton murmured, his gaze fixed on her. 'Stop telling lies about me.'

'She ain't lying,' Minnie said, never taking her eyes off the gun, and moving closer to Edie so the two women were almost touching.

Linton blinked rapidly and turned to Minnie. 'What did she tell you?' he said quietly. 'That I've made her life a misery? Is that what she told you?' He sounded desperate.

Minnie glanced at Albert. He was slowly moving closer to Linton, and he nodded at her almost imperceptibly, urging her to carry on speaking.

'Yeah, that's what she told me,' Minnie said, trying hard to keep the fear out of her voice.

'No, no, no,' Linton said, shaking his head and waving the gun around alarmingly. 'Quite the reverse. Although we were happy. At first. Weren't we, Edie?'

Edie nodded her head slowly in response.

'And then it just went wrong, didn't it?' Linton continued. 'Too many … differences, is that what we'll call it? Your world. My world. We thought we could make them overlap, didn't we? But, in the end, you just can't fight upbringing. My mistake.' And he laughed to himself, as if everything he had said was one enormous joke, before raising the gun in one swift movement and aiming it straight at Edie.

Edie screamed. Without thinking, Minnie pushed her. Edie stumbled and fell against the table with the Anatomical Venus, knocking it over and sending both her and the mannequin crashing to the ground. Minnie turned back. Linton was still holding the gun. And now she was directly in the line of fire. She took a step backwards, and there was a blur of movement to the side of her. Albert. He shouted her name as he hurled himself across the room, knocking her to the ground and winding her. At the same time, a deafening bang rang out.

Minnie lay on the floor for a moment, her ears ringing from the noise of the gun, a wave of nausea sweeping through her. She forced herself to move, and turned towards Albert. He lay on the floor, gripping his shoulder. He lifted his hand and it came away red. He gazed at his hand, a look of puzzlement on his face that terrified Minnie almost more than anything else she had seen that day. She reached out to touch him, and Linton leapt to his feet and made for the door. Albert lunged for him, but he was too far away. As Linton passed her, Minnie turned and grabbed him by the ankle with both hands. He kicked back at her, his foot making contact with her cheekbone. But she held tight, yanking at his leg, and he lost his balance. As he fell, his head cracked against the door frame, and the gun fell from his hand, skittering across the floor.

Minnie heaved herself up and stumbled towards the gun. She grabbed it, and then looked up. George, the red-headed footman, was staring at her, his eyes glazed with panic.

'Fetch the police,' she gasped, her ears still ringing from the gunshot. 'And a doctor.' Then she staggered across the room to Albert, and held him in her arms, trying desperately to staunch the flow of blood.

THIRTY-THREE

Albert winced as he laid the newspaper down on the table in Tansie's office. Teddy's bullet had merely grazed his shoulder, and the doctor had predicted there would be no permanent damage. But his arm was stiff and sore, nonetheless.

Minnie smiled sympathetically and rubbed her face. A spectacular bruise had emerged where Teddy had kicked her, but she had escaped a black eye. She glanced at the newspaper headline: 'Music Hall Murders: Lord Linton to Plead Insanity?'

'Not a great surprise,' Albert said. 'Although, given a choice between a lifetime in an asylum and the noose, I think I might choose the latter. They're still speculating that Linton might be the Hairpin Killer, but there's nothing to connect him to those murders. It would have been very convenient for John if that had proved to be the case.'

'I see both of you get a mention,' Minnie said, skimming through the story. 'Nothing about me, I notice.'

Albert winced again as he moved in his seat. 'It was John's collar,' he reminded her.

'Thanks to us, it was. If we hadn't gone and laid all the evidence at his feet, he'd never have arrived at the house when he did. By which time, might I add, I had the situation fully under control.'

'Well, whatever the reasons, I'm very glad he turned up when he did. Too late for Daisy, of course.'

'It's Tom I can't stop thinking about,' Minnie said, gesturing towards the room below them. 'Kippy's got him doing a few jobs to keep him busy. And I've asked him to accompany me here and there, give him something to do. I'm glad of the company, to tell the truth.'

They were all battle-weary, changed by what they had witnessed over the last few weeks. The Palace was still open, still functioning, but a pall had fallen over the place, and no one seemed able to shift it. Performances were lacklustre, and people spent as little time there as possible, turning up twenty minutes before their turn and then leaving as soon as they were done.

'Any luck with Tansie?' Albert asked. Minnie had visited him in his lodgings, urging him to come back to work.

Minnie shook her head. 'He's always cared so much about his appearance. But he don't look like he's washed in a month of Sundays. And he's lost weight. It's like he's disappearing in front of your eyes.'

'So who's running the Palace?' Albert asked.

Minnie sighed. 'Everyone's pulling together, but we need someone at the helm. It's funny, I always thought this place ran by itself and Tansie just made a lot of noise, but we're lost without him. Until he gets back, it's me who's making most of the decisions.'

'And how do you feel about that?'

'About as happy as a monkey in a pair of modesty bloomers. But I ain't got a choice. I can't see this place shut down.'

She folded the newspaper with unnecessary deliberation, and glanced nervously at Albert.

'What?' he asked.

'Come for a walk with me? We could go to St James's Park. Feed the ducks.'

Albert frowned. 'It's freezing out there, Minnie. And why the sudden interest in ornithology?'

'There's something I need to talk to you about. I can't do it here.'

'Cake?'

She shook her head. 'I need somewhere private, Albert. Really private.'

He nodded, picked up his coat and followed her out of the Palace.

They arrived at the park, realised they had nothing to feed the ducks with, but continued their stroll regardless. The talk was of trivial matters, both of them studiously avoiding any mention of the case. As they began their second circuit of the park, Albert wondered why Minnie had brought him here, but he knew better than to press. Whatever it was, Minnie would tell him in her own good time. And just being with her like this, in the quiet intimacy that had grown between them in recent weeks, was enough.

Eventually, she inhaled deeply, stopped and turned to him.

'Tea, Albert. What I've got to tell you, I ain't sure how it's gonna come out. So you'll have to bear with me. But first, tea. We passed somewhere quiet a few minutes ago.'

Albert hooked his arm through hers and they found a table at a tea stall sheltering under a grove of trees, their branches bare now in early November. They placed their order and the tea arrived a few minutes later.

'I was a performer, as you know,' Minnie said, stirring the customary alarming quantity of sugar into her tea. 'Minerva the Mimic. Very successful. Full house pretty much guaranteed wherever I performed. And I loved it.' She smiled at the memory, but there was a sadness in her eyes. 'I attracted a lot of attention, on and off stage. Men.' She stirred her tea again, unnecessarily.

'Most of them I weren't interested in. Too young, too old. Usually just too stupid. But there was one.' She paused again, picked a few specks of lint from her dress and took another deep breath.

'James Beresford. Voice you could cut glass with. A proper toff, he was. His uncle was a bishop, brother in the House of Lords. You know the sort.'

Albert nodded.

'Lovely hands, he had. Smooth and pale. Like he'd never had to use them for nothing his whole life. Which was probably true, 'cos he threw money around like it was going out of fashion. Told me he loved me. And I, like a fool, believed him.'

She broke off again, gave Albert a brief sideways glance.

Albert said nothing.

'I loved him too. Thought it was the romance of the century. Music hall girl and Lord Nob. He said we'd get married, he just needed a little time to talk his parents round.'

'I take it they didn't agree to the idea?'

Minnie stood abruptly. 'Walk with me,' she said. 'This is the difficult bit.'

They abandoned their tea and started on the same route they had covered previously, circling the lake, passing matrons with perambulators, a few elderly couples braving the cold, children playing.

'There was a baby,' Minnie said at last.

'A baby?' Albert asked. 'You've never mentioned you have a child.'

'There *was* a baby. Or what you might call the beginnings of a baby.'

With all his heart, Albert wished she didn't have to tell him what she was about to say. That he could go back to when she was Miss Ward, insisting on calling him Albert, and the most difficult thing they had to deal with was what cake to choose from Brown's.

'He told me he would marry me,' she said flatly. 'He *swore* he'd marry me. Only his parents wouldn't take too kindly to a christening taking place before a wedding. So he arranged an appointment with his friend. A doctor, he said.' She stopped and looked up at Albert. 'I was fifteen, Albert. I didn't have no mother to tell me what a fool I was being. I believed everything he told me. So I went to see his *friend*.'

Albert found he was holding her hand. He wanted to tell her there was no need to say any more. He knew how this story ended. But it was her story. Only hers to tell.

They started walking again. Ahead of them, a young man was struggling to keep his dog under control as it edged ever closer to the water's edge.

'There was so much blood,' Minnie said quietly. 'I wouldn't have thought anyone could bleed that much and still live. The so-called doctor bundled me into the back of a cab and told me to get myself home. I couldn't go back to my lodgings. Not like that. They'd have shown me the door. So I went to Rose and Ida's.'

She paused, her gaze resting, unseeing, on the dog, who had won the battle with his master and was now fully immersed in the lake.

'I remember, when I got out of the cab, the blood had gone right through my clothes and stained the seat. The whole cab reeked of it, and the cabbie swore at me, said I'd have to pay more. I had no money. The doctor fella had given the cabbie enough to get me to Ida's and that was all there was. Ida came out of the house like a terrier after a rat.' Minnie gave a half-hearted smile as she recalled the memory. 'Told him to sling his hook or she'd have the coppers on to him. And then she took me in. Her and Rose. Found money they didn't have for another doctor. A real one.'

She stopped, her head drooping lower onto her chest as if all the air had gone out of her, as if she was no longer his fearless, unstoppable Minnie, but closer to one of the mannequins Linton might keep in his collection. She held his hand in her own, squeezed it tight.

'No children. That's what he told me. I won't be able to have children.'

Her tears fell onto Albert's hand. In the distance, a child shrieked in play. Minnie dropped his hand and continued walking.

'That's why it's mattered so much,' she said. 'Finding Rose's killer. Without her and Ida, I don't know where I'd be. And last week, in Linton's house? The way you saved me, without even thinking about yourself?' She smiled softly. 'What a good man you are, Albert. When I first met you, that day when Ida hired you, and you sat on that stupid chair that barely held your weight, and charged Ida almost nothing. You opened your mouth and I thought, here we go again. And I've been fighting you ever since. Or fighting myself. Telling myself you were just like the others. Just like him. But you ain't, Albert. So you need to know the truth. I don't want you to go on thinking if you give it time I'm gonna come round.'

'But I don't understand,' Albert said. 'If you're worried that I'll disapprove of your having had a relationship, that's nonsense. I'm no saint myself.'

She smiled ruefully. 'Well, you didn't take too kindly to that photograph of me, did you? But it ain't that. What James did to me? It made me feel like nothing. Worse than nothing. I felt so *stupid*. I couldn't bear to set foot on the stage again, all those eyes looking at me, weighing me up like something in a butcher's window. I needed money fast. I knew how to play the piano, had learned a few tunes. So I thought I'd try my hand at writing a song. The rest you know. But it's taken so much hard work to get to where I am now. I'm safe. I earn my own money. I've got a decent set of rooms, friends I can trust at the Palace.' She turned to him. 'I'm not sure I can get you to understand what all that means, Albert. How difficult it is for a young woman like me to get to a place like that in her life. I ain't prepared to give it up.'

'I'm not asking you to,' he said.

'I know you ain't. But it's like I've built a wall to protect myself. And I can't knock it down. For a while I thought – maybe – we could have a future together. But what we've seen these past few weeks? There's so much darkness out there, Albert. And it's made me afraid all over again. I just want to hide away.'

'Then hide with me.'

She shook her head and said nothing for a moment. A child wandered near them, kicking a ball listlessly along the pathway.

'Besides,' she said, nodding at the child, 'a fella like you should have children.'

'Overrated,' Albert said.

A half-smile struggled to her lips, and she raised a hand to his face, wiping away the tears he hadn't even realised were there. 'Don't be daft,' she murmured. 'You'll make a lovely dad.'

They turned and continued walking.

'This James Beresford. What did he have to say for himself when you caught up with him?' Albert said, although he already knew the answer.

'Never did, did I? As soon as he dropped me off with his doctor friend, that was the last I saw of him.'

'Did you try to find him?'

''Course I did. I was quite the detective, even in those days. Turned out James Beresford weren't his name. His uncle weren't a bishop neither. I went everywhere I thought he might be. But it was like he'd vanished into thin air. Would have made a great act at the Palace. The Amazing Disappearing Toff.' She paused for a moment, then said decisively, 'So, that's my story, Albert, and I'd be grateful if we never talk of it again.'

They passed a man selling stale bread. Albert handed over a coin, and they fed the ducks.

Minnie walked with Albert back to his house. At the front door, he drew her towards him.

'However long you need, Minnie,' he said, his chin resting on the top of her head. 'I'm not going anywhere.'

She said nothing, then pulled herself free of his grasp and walked away.

Albert entered the house and was wearily ascending the stairs when Mrs Byrne materialised from the drawing room. She eyed him carefully.

'If you let that girl slip through your fingers, Albert, you are a bigger fool than I ever gave you credit for.'

Albert paused, and then slowly continued his ascent. 'She won't have me, Mrs B.'

'She'll have you. Just give it time.'

THIRTY-FOUR

Although it was four months since they had first met, Minnie's friendship with Edie was still new enough for her to feel overawed at being invited to the woman's home. Teddy's trial had resulted in a verdict of guilty but insane, much as the newspapers had predicted, and he would be seeing out the remainder of his days in Broadmoor. The house on Holland Park Road was up for sale and Edie had moved to more modest lodgings near Regent Street, one of a terrace of thirty or so newly built houses. Those either side still looked unoccupied but Edie's had a neat frontage, with a few flowers decorating the window boxes.

Minnie mounted the steps and knocked, surprised when Edie opened the door herself.

'One's finding it rather difficult to get staff, don't you know,' Edie said, adopting a languidly aristocratic accent. 'When your husband's a lunatic murderer, people worry it might have rubbed off, apparently.'

She embraced Minnie and showed her into the morning room at the rear of the house. Sunshine flooded in, and two comfortable-looking armchairs were positioned by the French doors looking out over the garden. A fire was burning in the grate; the day was bright, but still chilly, and Minnie was glad of the warmth.

She looked round the room as she removed her hat and coat, placing her bag beside one of the armchairs. There were legacies of Edie's days on the stage: posters from various theatres and music halls, all of them with her topping the bill; programmes from benefit nights; a large china figurine of Edie in the working woman's outfit she was most famous for. The room itself was comfortable but modest. Given Edie's taste in jewellery, Minnie had expected something more flamboyant.

As if reading her thoughts, Edie appeared at her side and said, 'Did you think I'd have more? Murder trials have a way of draining the resources. Wait here, my dear, and I'll get the tea.'

She exited by a door in the corner of the room and Minnie heard her descending the stairs and preparing the tea things. Not even a scullery maid, then. Things must be bad.

Minnie moved over to the fire to warm herself. On the mantelpiece, amongst the memorabilia of Edie's days as a performer, was an item that looked as if it might have come straight from Teddy's collection. A piece of card with the image of a woman, tears frozen on her cheeks like fat beads, her gaze fixed on the viewer. Her heart was visible in her chest, pierced with what looked like a number of swords.

Edie resurfaced from the kitchen and placed a tray on the table by the French doors. She saw the card in Minnie's hand.

'Something of Teddy's?' Minnie asked, unsure of how much Edie was willing to share about her husband's peculiar appetites.

Edie laughed. 'You ain't a dolly worshipper, are you?'

Minnie looked blank.

'Catholic,' Edie said. 'That's Mary, Mother of Sorrows.

Each of them swords in her heart represents one of the hardships she underwent.'

'I didn't take you for a believer,' Minnie said.

'Oh, I'm not. Not any more. It was an image my ma used to have, hanging right where I could see it first thing in the morning and last thing at night.' She gave a bitter laugh. 'Ma liked to remind me that it was me what brought all the sorrow into her life. The Virgin Mary had nothing on her, apparently.'

'Sounds awful. Why would you want to remind yourself of it?' Minnie asked, placing the card back on the mantelpiece, and moving to sit on the empty chair.

'To always keep in mind how much better things are now,' Edie said grimly. 'How everything I've ever done has been worth it, to get away from that life.'

She poured the tea and passed Minnie a cup. 'Tansie back at the Palace yet?' she asked.

Minnie shook her head. 'It's taking a while.'

'Perhaps we need something to coax him back. A benefit night for Cora's family, maybe?'

'He started organising one, but he ran out of steam. I don't think he's got the heart for it.'

'I'd offer to headline, but I ain't sure that would help.'

'It'd bring in the punters.'

'For all the wrong reasons. No, best I stay away. Besides—' She broke off, raising her hand to her hair. Her fingers were still adorned with rings, and you'd need a keen eye to know they were paste. 'I might be able to call in a few favours,' she continued. 'And Tansie's been working the halls for years. If my name don't get us anywhere, Tansie's will. See if you can persuade him, Min.'

Minnie nodded. Edie refilled her teacup as Minnie glanced out of the French doors, admiring the pots of daffodils on the terrace. She remembered the man who had attacked her in the Cremorne, the single red rose he had worn in his lapel, and how unlikely it had seemed in the middle of October.

She realised Edie was talking, and she hadn't been listening. Her lack of understanding was clearly evident on her face. Edie smiled. 'I was asking if you ever played that game as a kid.' She had an apple in her hand, which she was expertly peeling with a small knife. 'You know, peel it all in one go. Throw the peel over your shoulder and it lands as the initial of the man you're gonna marry.'

She held out the peel, all in one smooth length, the edges puckered and curved. 'Go on,' she said, 'see if it lands as an A.'

'It ain't like that,' Minnie said.

Edie tilted her head to one side. 'Oh, I rather think it is, don't you?'

Minnie held the peel in her hand for a moment, then placed it carefully on the table in front of her. She found herself wanting to confide in this woman, to tell her of her past and the obstacles it was placing in the way of a future with Albert. 'You and Teddy,' she said. 'Did it ever really work? You know, the class difference?'

Edie looked thoughtful. 'It didn't matter at the start. But, later, it was one of the ways he controlled me, put me down. I'd never marry again, that's for certain. But your Albert? He ain't like Teddy, is he?'

Minnie smiled gently. 'He is a lovely chap,' she conceded.

'And you two make a bang-up couple.'

Edie peeled another apple, the knife with its weathered handle sitting snugly in her hand.

'Nice knife,' Minnie said.

'Another legacy from my childhood. You know I made artificial flowers as a kid?'

Minnie nodded. 'Like my friend Ida. Rose's ma.'

Edie briefly closed her eyes at the mention of Rose's name. She leaned forward and took Minnie's hand. Neither woman needed to mention the pain they felt at the thought of Rose, and Ida's loss.

'The flower-making,' Edie said, 'that was the story my agent spread around when I started on the stage. There's something a bit genteel about it, ain't there? But me and my ma, we couldn't make enough from the flowers, so we used to skin rabbits as well.' She paused, turning the knife in her hand, her thumb rubbing a well-worn groove in the handle. 'You cannot imagine the stink. It gets under your skin, in your hair. It was years before I felt the smell was truly gone.' Absent-mindedly, she lifted a strand of hair, sniffed it, smiled to herself and continued. 'My agent didn't think the idea of me gutting little furry animals was quite so beguiling a tale, so he left it out of my biography. That, and a few other things.'

'Like what?'

Edie gave her a long look, as if she was appraising her carefully. Then it seemed as if Minnie had passed the test, whatever it was. 'When I turned nine,' Edie said, 'Ma figured out she could make a lot more money out of me than she'd ever get from the rabbits.'

She paused, her eyes turning to the mantelpiece and the card depicting Mary, Mother of Sorrows. 'Nine years old and no shortage of gentleman callers. I put up with it for three years. Didn't have a choice, really. Then Ma died. One of my regulars, he worked in the halls. Liked me to sing to him while he was doing the business. It was him I went to after Ma died. He found me work, and the rest you know.'

Silence filled the room. Anything Minnie could think of to say seemed inadequate in the face of what Edie had just shared with her. Edie rose stiffly, taking the empty teapot downstairs. She returned a few minutes later and refilled Minnie's cup.

'I'm going away for a while, Min.'

'Where?'

'Somewhere in Europe. It's cheaper there. And full of people with scandalous stories like mine. Well, not exactly like mine, but you get my drift. You can break a few rules there and no one seems to mind.'

'For how long?' Minnie asked.

Edie shrugged. 'Long enough for the scandal to die down here. Probably a year. Maybe two.'

Two years. It seemed a lifetime. Rose. Cora. And now Edie.

'Or you could stay,' Minnie said. 'Weather the storm. Take up your old act. There'd be no shortage of punters who'd pay good money to see you.' She registered the scepticism on Edie's face. 'People forget. What Teddy did, it's a sensation now, but there'll be something new next week and everyone will move on.'

'Except me,' Edie said calmly, as if measuring every word. 'I can't move on. You told me you suffered from stage fright, it's what stopped your career—'

'And you told me I could do anything I set my mind to. Well, so can you.'

Edie shook her head. 'Just the thought of getting up on a stage, all those eyes turned on me, weighing me up, whispering behind their hands about what my husband did to those poor girls, and how much of it I must have known about.'

'But you didn't know anything. Teddy made that crystal clear during the trial. It was him and that three-fingered fella I met in the Cremorne. Freddie Forrester, weren't it? And Benny something, his sidekick.'

'It don't matter what Teddy said. People think what they wanna think, Min. And I know a lot of people reckon I was in on it all.'

'So, prove them wrong. If you go running off to the Continent, they'll think they were right to distrust you.'

'Maybe they'd be right.'

Minnie said nothing, waiting out the silence, unsure of what Edie was about to say.

'I should have noticed,' Edie said eventually. 'How could all of that have been going on and I never knew?'

'That's just Teddy inside your head. Telling you you're worthless all over again.'

Edie reached out a hand for Minnie's. 'My mind's made up, Min. A year. Maybe two. The time'll fly by.'

Minnie knew that wasn't the case. But she knew that her job as Edie's friend was to support the woman in any decision she made. So she gently nodded her head, and the conversation turned to other, more trivial things.

THE SIXTH STANHOPE

IN WHICH LORD LINTON
ENJOYS A QUIET HOUR

Teddy watched the sunlight move slowly across the cell. For one hour in every day, it came through the window, travelled across the floor and up the far wall before the room was plunged back into gloom. He looked forward to that hour. Much of the time his thoughts were consumed with Edie, Daisy, Agnes. And Minnie, of course. Of the things he would do when he was released.

But that single sunlit hour belonged to Rose.

She'd been a pretty thing. Too tall for his tastes, but pretty nonetheless. Fair-haired, trim. He'd watched her from the bedroom window as she'd changed into those foolish shoes, believing that the house in Holland Park Road was Winter's. Maybe she'd been sweet on Winter after all.

There'd been an energy about her Teddy had found appealing. And she'd been strong, too. Stronger than they'd anticipated when Freddie went to tie her down. He'd thought then that maybe he might keep her after all. Find a use for her. But in the end she proved to be a disappointment, giving it all up far too easily. She told them she'd only spoken to Winter and Billy about finding Agnes's body in the Godwin bedroom. If she'd been a smart girl, more like Minnie, she'd have lied and said she'd told half the world. But with only her and Winter to deal with, and him owning Billy as it was, it was easy to keep a lid on it all.

They stuffed a rag down her throat and tied a bag over her head. She'd fought even harder then, fought like a cat, lashing out and clawing at the bag. It had taken a long time for her to die. Longer than he'd imagined, at least. Then Freddie and his chum had strung her up under the Arches as a warning to Billy. And that was that.

Or so he'd thought.

When she first came to him, he'd been afraid. Who wouldn't be? He knew her, of course, knew she couldn't be real. And yet there she was. He wondered if she'd come to exact some sort of revenge, and in a way she had, sitting each day on the solitary chair and holding his gaze. Every day, the sunlight caught the colours in her hair: the blondes and light browns, and one or two surprising golds. Blue eyes, with the tiniest flecks of green around the pupil. He'd had time to study her. The curve of her lip, the tilt of her chin. And then, with the movement of the sun, she left him.

He wondered sometimes if it would be Daisy who came to him instead. A question on her lips he had no answer for. A man should at least remember killing someone, even if he didn't have a reason for doing it, but for the life of him Teddy had no memory of killing Daisy. The doctors at Broadmoor said the mind had a trick of wiping out distressing memories. Teddy wasn't so sure.

But it was never Daisy who visited him in the sunlit hour. Only Rose. It would be Rose tomorrow. And the day after. It was the nature of this place; time caught in amber, life lived in one continuous present.

And it wasn't so bad, for now at least. He had a few luxuries, necessities in his opinion. Decent food, books. He'd have liked more visitors, Edie in particular. Gillespie told him she was in Italy now, which surely was going to make it harder to secure his release. Her promise to him the last time he'd spoken to her, just before the trial started. A little patience, Teddy, she'd said, and his counsel had urged the same. He must be seen to have paid some sort of price for what he did. A year or two, Edie reckoned. They'd find a team of mad-doctors willing to say anything for a handsome bribe and then he would be free. Europe, perhaps, until the scandal died down. He and Edie could spend a few pleasant months there. And then back to England. There were scores to settle.

He'd grown used to Rose. Welcomed her, truth be told. When he was free, he would find a place for her; a quiet pocket in his life, where she could visit and say nothing.

The light crept up the wall. Only moments left.

THIRTY-FIVE

It was a crisp spring morning. Weak sunshine was breaking through the clouds, but the wind was sharp and it felt closer to winter than spring. The group of people at the graveside huddled closer together, as if for protection against the elements.

Ida reached down and patted her hand on the mound of fresh earth, whispering something under her breath meant for only her child to hear. She rose stiffly and turned towards Minnie and Albert.

'She's got a nice spot,' she said, gesturing towards the apple trees that sheltered this corner of the cemetery, and whose blossom was layering a gentle blanket of the palest pink over Rose's grave. 'She'll be happy here, I reckon. At peace, anyways.'

Minnie turned away, scrabbling in her bag for a handkerchief. Albert reached into his top pocket and handed her his. She took it, throwing him a grateful glance.

'I can't thank you enough, Mr—Albert,' Ida said, correcting herself at a glance from Albert. 'You too, Min, of course. Being able to have her here, inside the cemetery proper. It means the world to me. I don't know how you managed it all so fast, though.'

Albert looked down. 'It was the least I could do, Ida.'

He never liked to ask a favour of his brother-in-law, but having Rose's body moved to consecrated ground once her death had been declared a murder had warranted humbling himself. And it had made Monty feel important, which had, in turn, made life a little easier for Adelaide. She and Albert had reached an uneasy truce, but he was not sure their relationship would ever return to its former state.

'You'll come back to the Palace?' Minnie said, taking Ida's roughened hand in her own and brushing away a few crumbs of soil. 'Tansie's laid on a feast. We'll be feeding the Strand with leftovers for the next fortnight, I reckon.'

'Well, just for a little while,' Ida said. 'As he's gone to all that trouble.'

She glanced over at Tansie, who broke away from his conversation with Tom, Kippy and Mrs Byrne. He walked towards Ida slowly, fiddling with the buttons on his sober black suit which dwarfed his frame now. He glanced nervously at her, as if fearful she might erupt in a display of womanly tears, but she smiled at him and the relief was palpable on his face. He turned to Albert.

'That young lad of yours,' he said. 'Tom, is it? Kippy says he's in need of an assistant, now Billy's gone. Likes the cut of Tom's jib.'

'He's not my young lad,' Albert said. 'If he wants to work with Kippy, that's up to him.'

'He's keen, I reckon. Maybe the three of you can have a chat about it back at the Palace.'

'You're still not ready to take the reins, Tansie?' Albert asked.

Tansie shook his head slowly. 'Not yet. I've been popping

in, mind, showing my face. But … no. Thank God for Minnie, eh?'

The two men looked at Minnie, who had taken Ida's hand and was slowly walking with her to the waiting carriages.

'So how do you pass your time?' Albert asked.

'Well, the monkey's become very attached to me.'

'Not literally, I trust.'

Tansie smiled, his gold tooth flashing. 'I've been thinking about taking him on a little trip to London Zoo. See if we can't find him an outlet for his … needs.'

'Dandy Bob's dummy has had enough, then?'

'All his joints have seized up, and I swear he's got a weird look on his face these days. Dandy Bob's had to get a replacement.'

Albert stopped and turned to face Tansie. 'I think you need to get back to running the Palace, Tansie,' he said. 'Minnie's doing an excellent job, but they need you. She says the heart's gone out of the place.'

Tansie dropped his head, scraping at the soil with the toe of his shoe, dulling the polish. 'Maybe,' he said unconvincingly, and turned, calling out to Kippy to wait for him.

Albert walked towards the waiting carriages. Mrs Byrne was sitting next to Ida, and the two women were deep in conversation, Mrs Byrne holding Ida's hand tightly. Minnie looked up at Albert, and he gestured towards a carriage at the rear. She nodded, and he helped her in.

The journey from the cemetery to the Palace was not long, but Albert and Minnie were silent for most of it. As they turned onto Long Acre, Albert reached into his pocket and removed a business card which he handed to Minnie. 'I couldn't quite stretch to vellum, I'm afraid.'

'Ward and Easterbrook,' the card said. 'Consulting Detectives.'

Minnie smiled as she read it, then shook her head and handed it back to Albert. 'It won't do,' she said.

His smile faded. 'Why not?'

'Well, I know you told me once – in a fit of romance after a very nice fruit sponge, as I recall – that you'd always put me first. But "Easterbrook and Ward" just sounds better. Don't you think?'

He looked down at the card in his hand, afraid to let her see the emotion on his face. 'It can easily be changed,' he said. 'Just so long as you're agreeing.'

'Well, I've got a music hall to run and Tansie to put back together somehow. But … yes. Although maybe something more gentle next time? Fewer bodies? Less weird stuff?'

'I'll do my best.'

She looked out of the window, as they drove down Pall Mall. 'Any news on Freddie Forrester?' she asked. 'Or Benny something?'

Albert shook his head. 'John's on the case, but they've both disappeared. For now, at least.'

The carriage pulled to a stop outside the Palace. Albert leapt out and helped Minnie out. A small crowd had gathered, gazing at the posters advertising Katrina the Human Cannonball, a troop of dancing dogs and Ricardo the man-serpent.

'A man-serpent?' Albert asked, pointing at this last act on the bill.

'Don't ask,' Minnie said.

Just before they entered the Palace, she placed a hand on his arm. Albert turned towards her questioningly and was surprised to see how nervous she looked.

'What?' he asked.

She took a deep breath. 'Ursula,' she said.

'Sorry?'

'My real name. It's Ursula.'

'Good Lord.'

'And that reaction is *precisely* why I don't tell anyone.'

'No, it's – lovely. Just a little unexpected.'

'Well, it's a long story involving a Welsh father and a whimsical mother.'

'Ursula,' Albert said, rolling the name on his tongue. 'Bear-like?'

She nodded. 'It means "little she-bear" apparently.'

'Not entirely inaccurate, then.'

She punched him on the arm. He winced and made an elaborate pantomime of rubbing the spot.

'So,' she said. 'Now you know. And if you tell anyone – anyone, mind – I'll set the monkey on you. And he won't be wearing no bloomers.'

She brushed down her skirts, took his arm, and led the way into the Palace.

THE SEVENTH STANHOPE

IN WHICH EDIE BENNETT
CONSIDERS THE FUTURE

The late-spring sunshine in Rome is surprisingly warm and
Edie Bennett pulls her chair a little into the shade, before
gesturing for another coffee. The waitress, who yesterday
introduced herself as Carlotta, is a pretty thing. Small, with
delicate features. Like one of Teddy's toys.

On the table in front of Edie lies Teddy's latest letter, not
yet opened. She can predict its contents: gentle complaints
about his treatment, questions about her progress in securing
his release, the tone occasionally nudging into belligerence.
Poor Teddy, rotting in Broadmoor. She used to think he was
such a clever chap, but she knows now that was just his accent
and the air of assurance that money bestows.

Carlotta brings her coffee, placing it on the table with a
gentle smile. The girl knows only a handful of English words
and Edie has no Italian, but they're managing to get by with
smiles and nods and elaborate hand gestures.

Always, in Teddy's letters, the insistence that he didn't kill
Daisy. He's got that much right, at least. Albert and Minnie
were getting close and they just needed one more nudge.
Freddie Forrester, whose loyalty swayed like a tree in a high

wind provided the price was right, helped her get the body into the Venus room and she did the rest. A visit to the Palace and a flawless performance as the wronged wife finally willing to give up her secrets. Then the discovery of Daisy's body, laid out like a Venus. It had been an unexpected bonus that Teddy was up to his armpits in the girl's blood. Right through the trial he insisted he hadn't killed her, but it hadn't helped him. If anything, it turned people more against him, his refusal to take full responsibility for all his wicked deeds.

And Teddy had been wicked. From the very moment he met Agnes at the Godwin and took in her tiny frame, he wanted to see inside her. That's what he told Edie. Couldn't bring himself to kill her, though. No stomach for it, which was strange, given what he was able to do to her afterwards. In the end, Edie had agreed to it just to keep him quiet. She'd wanted to do it her usual way, but Teddy said that would leave a mark, spoil the body. Chloroform, then. Except that girl Rose had found the body before they had a chance to move it to the ice house. So, Rose to dispose of. And her fancy piece, Lionel. It had been easy before. All those girls swallowed up by the darkness and no one seemed to care enough to bring it to an end. She should have stuck to what she knew.

She finishes the second coffee and rises to leave. The English newspapers have forgotten Teddy completely, moved on to some other ghoulish murder. She may be able to return home sooner than she thought. It was pleasant, the first few weeks, to wander the streets unrecognised. But she misses it now. Her public need her. And she needs them.

Home to poor, hapless Teddy. And Minnie, of course. What plans she has for Minnie.

She leaves a very generous tip for Carlotta. She wants to

be remembered by the girl so she gets a good table when she comes back tomorrow.

As she walks away, the sunlight bounces off something buried deep within her hair. A star-shaped hairpin. Seven points to the star: one for each of the sorrows of the Virgin Mary. A large green gem at the centre, encircled by clear stones. At first glance they could be diamonds, an emerald. But close up, it's easy to see they're paste.

ACKNOWLEDGEMENTS

I'm one of those people who loves reading the acknowledgements page in a novel. I never thought I'd get to write one myself, but here goes. Apologies to anyone I've left out.

This journey started in 2016 when I undertook the Six-Month Novel online programme with www.urbanwritersretreat. co.uk, partly to convince myself that maybe writing wasn't for me after all, and I could put this whole nonsense to bed. Charlie Haynes and Amie McCracken persuaded me otherwise. Their enthusiasm and positivity gave me the courage to enrol on the MA Creative Writing (Crime Fiction) at UEA. My thanks go to Tom Benn, Julia Crouch, Laura Joyce, William Ryan and Henry Sutton for their guidance and invaluable feedback, nudging me gently towards the kind of novel I should be writing (as opposed to the deadly serious, writerly tome I originally had in mind). My fellow students made the MA an absolute joy from start to finish; they taught me to be brave, to push myself, and never to settle. Laura Ashton, Judi Daykin, Lucy Dixon, Antony Dunford, Jayne

Farnworth, Natasha Hutcheson, Louise Mangos, Elizabeth Saccente, Matthew Smith, Karen Taylor, Wendy Turbin — there are no words but, thankfully, there is still Prosecco.

I have been blessed with other fabulous beta-readers who have provided both encouragement and a critical eye: Bex Barrow, Emily Coutts, Liz Hullin, Jane Still and Helen Walsh, thank you so much for taking the time.

Caroline Birks, Maria Butcher, Mary Scott and Jack Thompson: you'll always be the Daughters of Darkness to me.

Isobel Dixon and Sian Ellis-Martin of Blake Friedmann Agency have keep me going throughout this entire process. I can officially confirm Isobel is the best agent in the world, and I can never thank her enough for believing in this book and sticking with it.

Gallic have been the loveliest people to go on this journey with: cheerful, helpful, enthusiastic and understanding of a debut author's lack of knowledge. My thanks also go to Jaime Witcomb for helping me navigate this new terrain.

Further thanks to: Jemima Forrester at David Higham; Ed Wood and his fellow judges at Little, Brown; Professor Mark Wilkinson, who gave me valuable information on hanging, prussic acid and the freezing of bodies; and George Wakely who kindly showed me around Hoxton Hall and helped provide the inspiration for the Variety Palace.

Teddy and Edie, my two dogs, not only offered me two crucial character names but also forced me out of the house every day to walk them. Accompanying me on all those walks was my husband, Micky, who willingly —joyfully, even — hammered out plot points with me and never once seemed bored. Micky, I hope you know what you do and how much it means to me. You are indeed 'quite the canary'. And, although I wanted to kill you at the time, that 'what if...' moment with the Hairpin Killer made this a much better book. Never dim the lightbulb, even if my face tells you otherwise.

This book is dedicated to my parents, Bridget and Jim, who came to England with nothing and forged a life here. I still have the small suitcase my Dad travelled with and it's difficult to believe you could start a life in a new country with so little. I just wish I could tell them now, how much I value everything they did for me.